CHASE
the
Dark

Steel & Stone: Book 1

ANNETTE MARIE

Cover Design Copyright © 2014 by Annette Ahner
Cover, Book Interior, and Website Design by
Midnight Whimsy Designs
www.midnightwhimsydesigns.com

Cover Photographs (female model) Copyright © 2014 by Miranda Hedman
Model: Miranda Hedman
www.mirish.deviantart.com

Editing by Elizabeth Darkley
arrowheadediting.wordpress.com

ISBN 978-0-9939102-1-0

STEEL & STONE

Chase the Dark
Bind the Soul
Yield the Night
Feed the Flames
Reap the Shadows
Unleash the Storm

CHAPTER

- 1 -

ATTEMPTED MURDER was not how Piper liked to start her afternoon.

As an Apprentice Consul, she had a lot of responsibilities. Unfortunately, one of them was breaking up fights between over-sized, over-muscled idiots. Murderous idiots.

The shouts were the first thing she heard when she walked in the front door after school. Wonderful. She was only ten minutes late. How could the shit hit the fan in only ten minutes? Speed walking and projecting unfazed confidence at the same time—she hoped—she homed in on the sound. Other guests of the Consulate beelined in the opposite direction, varying degrees of irritation on their faces as they cleared the scene. If only she could have left the two asses to duke it out on their own, but she would get in trouble if someone died—even if it were the victim's own stupid fault.

At the bottom of the stairs, she assessed the scene. The two combatants stood in the center of the media room. The bone-rumbling voice of the one had warned her to expect a big guy, but the six and a half feet of tattooed muscle, shaved head, and mean little eyes that filled half the room outdid her imagination.

His opponent, however, was a total surprise: if he was taller than Piper's five foot five, she'd eat her boots. And that would suck, because she loved her boots. They had steel toes and steel-plated shins, all the better to kick ass with.

"Where," the little guy demanded, voice scooping into higher notes of distress, "*is he?*"

Piper launched into a sprint across the room. Shrimpy didn't exactly look like the fighting type, with clean-cut good looks and a modest sweater vest over his polo shirt. Who wore sweater vests? He was going to get shmooshed.

Gigantor guffawed like a baboon—a scary baboon—and gave Shrimpy a shit-eating grin. "Don't know what you're talking about, Ether. Where's who?"

Ether's hands balled into fists.

"Hey!" Piper shouted.

Ether's eyes snapped toward her. Irises black as pitch glared at her. She met his glower and her heart jumped in her chest. She threw on the brakes. Skidding gracelessly, she altered her trajectory to crash into Gigantor's side. Better she piss off Gigantor than Ether. Gigantor had no idea what he was messing with.

She bounced off a wall of muscle, barely eliciting a grunt from Gigantor, and caught her balance. Tugging her shirt back down for a semblance of dignity, she stepped sideways to put a slightly less suicidal distance between her and combatants.

"Gentlemen," she said, going for firm yet calm and hoping her galloping heartbeat didn't give her away. "Let's be civil now. What's the problem here?"

Ether's expression didn't shift from stony anger but Gigantor's lip curled in a sneer as he looked her up and down. So maybe her tight, dark-wash jeans with the knees torn out and her black halter top with a lace-up front weren't professional enough for an Apprentice Consul. Or maybe her shoulder-length hair, streaked black and red, wasn't sleek and blond enough for him. Too bad for him Consuls didn't have a dress code. She could boot his ass to the curb no matter what she was wearing—theoretically, anyway.

She turned to Ether. "Can you tell me what the problem is? Let's get this sorted out, okay?"

He flexed his clenched hands. "I can't find Shishu. *He* knows where Shishu is."

She held back a relieved sigh. If they talked to her, maybe she could sort this out without anyone dying. She glanced at Gigantor. "Who is Shishu?"

The man-mountain grinned again. "Frog."

Her mouth fell open. She closed it. "I beg your pardon?"

"Ether's pet froggy. Cute little frog."

Piper turned to Ether, barely managing to keep her expression neutral. "You have … a pet frog?"

Ether gave a jerky nod, his ebony glare locked on Gigantor. Piper quietly cleared her throat. If Ether was what she thought he was, he could tear Gigantor to shreds with the equivalent effort of peeling an orange. He was pure badassery hidden behind a sweater vest and he was losing his shit over a *pet frog*? She cleared her throat again and turned back to the idiot troublemaker of the two.

"And do you know where Shishu the frog is?"

Gigantor nodded, flashing his teeth at Ether.

She waited a moment. "Where?"

Another grin. He patted his stomach.

Piper blinked. She glanced at Ether, who stared back at her with an equally blank expression. They both looked at Gigantor.

"I'm sorry?" she asked tentatively.

"The frog was annoying. *Ribbit ribbit.* Wouldn't stop. So I had a snack before dinner."

"You … you *ate* his frog?"

"I didn't break any rules. No bloodshed." He grinned. "I swallowed it whole. Wriggled all the way down."

"You—Ether, no!"

Ether sprang for Gigantor. Piper whipped a leg up, slamming her shin into his belly. He grunted as he went over backward. His back hit the floor—and he was lunging up again. An animal snarl tore from his throat as he dropped into a predatory crouch, his stare fixed on her.

She froze in place. "Ether, let's stay—"

Ether jumped her. She grabbed his wrists as his weight drove her down. Somewhere above her, Gigantor roared with laughter. She tucked into a ball, got her feet under Ether as they hit the floor, and catapulted him over her head. She rolled to her feet but somehow he was already up. His fist closed around a handful of her hair and the next thing she knew, she was flying through the air. She hit the coffee table and the legs snapped, dumping her onto the floor.

She rolled over as Ether turned back to Gigantor, murder written in every line of his body. Gigantor's laughter abruptly cut off and his muscles bulged as he prepared to defend himself.

"Stop!" Piper shrieked.

Both combatants went rigid. She paused halfway to her feet, wary at their reaction. Bloodthirsty berserkers didn't normally freeze at her command. Ether and Gigantor straightened from their aggressive poses and focused on the other end of the room. Piper followed their gazes and felt her blood chill.

A newcomer stood in the doorway, cloaked in shadows. Menace clung to him, speaking more clearly than the dark clothing and leather accents to his outfit. She couldn't make out his face but she felt the touch of his gaze as he took in the scene.

"What are you doing, Ether?"

Piper shivered as his voice slid through her like hot silk, rubbing against her bones.

Ether cleared his throat. His eyes were no longer black, but pale blue and wide. "Ash," he mumbled. "Ozar *ate* Shishu and I—"

"And it's your own damn fault. Don't break the rules because you didn't protect your own. No bloodshed."

Ether cringed, not daring to argue. Ash's attention shifted to Ozar. "You're leaving the Consulate tonight."

Ozar blinked vacantly. "What? No, I—"

"You're leaving. Tonight."

Ozar hunched his shoulders. "Yes … right away."

Ash stood in the doorway for another moment. Piper kept her gaze on the floor as his stare swept over her again. If she looked up, he would see her fury and that would be bad. Damn him. This was *her* job, not his. He'd prevented murder with nothing more than his *presence* when she hadn't been useful in the slightest.

It wasn't until Ozar heaved a giant sigh that Piper dared to look. Ash was gone. Ozar and Ether exchanged a dagger-filled look and stalked away in opposite directions. Alone in the room, Piper stepped over the flattened coffee table and surveyed the damage. As an Apprentice Consul, it was her job to enforce the rules of the Consulate. One of those rules was no bloodshed. No fighting. No killing other guests. She was supposed to prevent fights and mediate disputes before they got out of hand.

Dropping onto the nearby sofa, she turned away from the evidence of her failure. The room was decked out with every luxury and priceless technology available, all for the comfort and convenience of the Consulate's guests: flat screen televisions and leather furniture and gaming systems that hadn't been manufactured in decades. What did they do with it? Smashed it apart in stupid fights.

She lifted her arm and touched two fingers to her elbow. They came away smeared with blood where the edge of the coffee table had scraped her. No bloodshed.

Her father was going to be pissed.

◦   ◦   ◦

Piper leaned back in her chair and folded her arms—anything to keep from cowering. On the other side of the wide mahogany desk, her father didn't alter his expression—meaning his scowl. He was always scowling, especially when she was in his office. Probably because she was always in trouble whenever she was there.

The desk lamp lit half his face with yellow light and glinted off his shaved scalp, leaving the other half of his head obscured by shadows. He tented his fingers over the desk.

"Tell me what we do here, Piperel."

She flinched. Only strangers called her Piperel. "At the Consulate, you mean?"

He nodded.

She hesitated. She knew the answer but the simplicity of the query suggested a trick question. "Our primary function is as an embassy for the visiting and emigrated daemon community. Our secondary functions include acting as a hostel and sanctuary for daemons in troubled circumstances or in need of protection—"

"Protection from what?" he interrupted.

"Humans. Other daemons. Anything, really."

"Other daemons," he repeated. She shrank a little in her seat. "And that would include being attacked by other guests while *inside* the Consulate?"

"Yes," she mumbled, unable to maintain eye contact.

Someday she would love to have an actual personal conversation with her father. But he didn't do personal. He only did business. Quinn Maddox Griffiths might be the Head Consul, the ultimate authority in charge of three hundred Consulates across the continent, and an accomplished warrior with weapons mundane and magical, but "parenting" came in on his skill sets somewhere below unarmed lethal combat and above flower arrangement. Not that far above.

He tapped one finger on the desk. "As Consuls, what do *we* do, Piperel?"

"We … keep the peace between daemons and humans, and between daemons and other daemons." It was a simple way to sum up a complicated role. Consuls were not only peacekeepers; they were also negotiators, mediators, judges, and enforcers.

"Tell me how you kept the peace today, Piperel."

She pushed her shoulders back and lifted her chin. "When I became aware of an escalating verbal altercation, I approached the involved guests—"

"How did the situation escalate in the first place? Why didn't you intervene immediately?"

"I was a little late getting home from school and …" She trailed off under the weight of his disapproval. It wasn't her fault class had run late. Marcelo, the dayshift Consul, never waited one minute past four o'clock. She cleared her throat. "I approached the involved guests and initiated a discussion of the issues at hand."

"Did your assessment of the situation note Ether's lack of emotional stability?"

She fought the urge to shrink again. "Yes."

"And you still decided a friendly discussion was the best course of action instead of separating the aggressive parties before it became physical?"

She couldn't help it. She wilted in her chair. "I didn't think it would be something so sensitive."

"That is why you should have fetched a Consul. Apprentices are permitted to intervene in verbal altercations only."

"It *was* verbal-only when I got there."

A long moment of silence passed, more accusatory than shouted words. She bit her tongue. Way to point out her own failure to diffuse the shouting match.

Her father leaned back. "Our primary purpose as an embassy isn't to protect daemons from one another. Our purpose is to protect *the human community* by regulating and controlling daemons. If we can't control daemons, we cease to be useful and we will lose the backing —and funding—of the government. Without their support, we have no power."

She said nothing because she knew that already.

"Who stopped the fight you failed to prevent?"

She chewed her lip. "Another daemon, but they often police themselves. It's one of the reasons—"

"A daemon took control. And not any daemon, but one of the daemons we exist to protect the community from. Do you see the problem here, Piperel?"

She nodded. The whole Consulate system was pretty much useless if dangerous daemons were controlling other daemons.

Quinn surveyed her for a long minute. "We can't afford any mistakes right now. The daemon ambassadors will be arriving this evening." He pulled a file folder in front of him and flipped it open. "Don't you have a class with your uncle?"

She gritted her teeth. Her class wasn't for another fifteen minutes, which he knew perfectly well. She stood, recognizing her dismissal. "Yeah, I'm going."

"No more mistakes, Piperel. More so than any other Apprentice, you cannot fight daemons. You must *prevent* physical confrontations —every single time. Either learn how or give up your apprenticeship."

Her whole body went cold. "But—"

He looked up. "If you can't prevent these kinds of incidents, you can't be a Consul. It's simple fact."

She clutched the back of the chair until her hands ached but no words formed on her tongue.

Quinn turned back to his papers. "Go before you're late for your lesson."

She walked stiffly to the door and let herself out. In the hallway, she pressed both hands to the wall and bowed her head, battling the wave of panic rising in her chest. Lose her apprenticeship? It couldn't happen. She wouldn't let it.

She marched toward the back end of the manor through halls paneled in dark walnut and decorated with oil paintings. The Consulate, because it was the Consulate, had to set the standard for luxury, especially since there wasn't much culture left anywhere else. All three floors, including the basement, were lavishly decorated. There were eighteen rooms on the two upper floors with another dozen hotel-style rooms for guests in the basement. The main level alone had two living rooms, a gourmet kitchen, offices, parlors, meeting rooms, a library, a sparring gym, an infirmary, and more. A lavish sitting area and reception desk filled the marble foyer at the front of the house, a spot she was all too familiar with. As an Apprentice, she spent far too much time manning the front desk.

The upper floor was her favorite. As the living quarters of the Consul's employees, it was a sanctuary for the live-in Consuls and their families—no daemons allowed. Her Consulate housed only her, her father, and her uncle. The other half dozen Consuls who worked there lived close enough to commute.

A warm glow from the recessed lights under the cupboards illuminated the kitchen as she entered. Shadows drifted around the long dining table and a huge square island. Somewhere in the cavernous walk-in pantry, a gooey chocolate cure for her anxiety waited—except the pantry door already hung half open, gaping like an open maw.

She paused, squinting into the shadows. Last thing she wanted right then was company. Grimacing, she circled the island and reached to pull the door all the way open.

Warm hands landed on her waist and she choked on a shriek of surprise.

The hands slid downward to curl over her hips as they pulled her back into a hard body. Hot breath bathed her ear.

"Hello beautiful," a male voice purred.

Piper flung an elbow back with enough force to crack a rib. Chuckling, her assailant slid away as though she were moving in slow motion, his fingers trailing across the small of her back as he retreated. She whirled around with her fists ready to strike.

The young man with wandering hands casually put himself out of easy reach and propped an elbow on the counter. If sex appeal were an artist, he was its masterpiece. Golden brown skin sheathed lean muscle and flowed over the sharp planes of his cheekbones. His hair was an impossible platinum blond much lighter than his skin, his eyebrows dark, and his eyelashes thicker than any man should have. They framed eyes of an exotic amber shade like a dark patina brushed over ancient gold.

Piper gave him her most disgusted glare. "Lyre, can't you ever keep your hands to yourself?"

"No," he replied in his deliciously deep voice. There was no apology in his expression, only grinning amusement at her discomfort. "You're just so easy." His eyelids lowered. "So am I."

She straightened from her aggressive stance and gave him an insulting once-over, taking in his impossible style of metrosexual crossed with a hint of Goth. He pulled it off and did it well. The wide leather cuffs with metal studs shouldn't have looked good next to his sleek gray shirt with its sleeves rolled up to his elbows. The chain running from hip to pocket really didn't match his designer jeans, but it did. Damn, the guy knew what he was doing. Clean, safe, and charming but with that oh-so-sexy hint of bad boy—exactly the kind of guy who would appeal to almost any girl. And that body packaged with that face? Very few women said no to Lyre.

Surprisingly, he didn't seem offended she was one of those few. Then again, he never missed a chance to flaunt his availability.

"Would you mind finding someone else to harass?" she growled. "I'm not in the mood right now."

His mouth quirked up. "I'm always in the mood."

Before she could come up with a retort, the second half of the dream team drifted out of the pantry, a box of crackers in his hand. Piper's back stiffened.

Ash barely spared her a glance as he crossed the kitchen to the fridge. Since he wasn't aiming to terrify two bloodthirsty daemons, the aura of intimidation he carried was muted but still undeniable. Unlike Lyre, he didn't have that cultivated appeal of "I'm a little bad, but you can trust me." Ash was *all* bad. Dressed in black from head to toe, some of it leather. His hair was even more impossible than Lyre's —a wine-red so dark it was almost black. It was long enough to hang in his eyes and the left side was braided alongside his head with a blood-red strip of silk woven in. The loose end hung to his shoulder, the only color in his whole ensemble. Even his eyes were a cool, storm-cloud gray.

She exhaled with a little too much force. "Ash," she greeted him. She'd been aiming for polite but it came out flat and angry.

His slow, sharp gaze turned. She froze, hardly daring to breathe, as he seemed to look right into her, taking her apart piece by piece as though he knew her every secret. She shivered, feeling more violated by his look than Lyre's touch.

Then he popped a cracker in his mouth and the dangerous moment shattered. She sucked in a breath as he nodded an oh-so-casual return greeting as if he hadn't butted into her business and made her look like an incompetent idiot less than an hour before.

Lyre's arm slid around her waist as he took advantage of her distraction. His fingers trailed suggestively up her side.

"Would you get off?" She twisted away, glaring as he laughed and leaned against the counter again. "I just got in serious trouble and I'd like an excuse to punch something soft and bruisable."

His eyebrows rose. "The frog thing didn't go down well with the Head, did it?"

Her shoulders slumped. "You know?"

"Everyone knows." He shrugged. "It's not that big a deal. Ether is an emotional dipshit. Powerful, but a dipshit."

"My father thinks it's a big deal." She scrunched her face and tried not to whine. "Why did Ether even *have* a pet frog?"

"He's pretty amphibious himself, you know. He'll get over it. That frog was damn annoying." He slid a little closer. "But if you need comforting, let me know."

She slapped his hand away before it could reach her. "Quit screwing around, Lyre. I'm in serious trouble, don't you get it?"

"I haven't had a chance to screw around yet," he complained. "What's the big deal about a frog?"

She shot a cold look at Ash in answer. Still munching on crackers, he opened the fridge to ponder its contents. She scowled at his back then ducked past Lyre into the pantry. She grabbed a chocolate bar from the massive stack on the top shelf and returned to the island.

"So?" Lyre pressed. "What's the big deal?"

"It's just such a bad time," she mumbled as she tore open the wrapper. "It would be seriously bad for the Consuls to look powerless today." She took a huge bite, almost moaning as the chocolate melted on her tongue.

Lyre watched her eat the chocolate bar with a little more intensity than was normal. "And what's special about today?"

Ash reappeared from the fridge with a can of cream soda in hand. It wasn't fair. Even with a pink soda can and crackers, he was still frightening.

"So it's tonight then?" he asked. "They're moving it out of the Consulate before morning?"

Her head jerked up in surprise. He met her stare, expressionless.

"Move what?" Lyre asked blankly.

She fought not to shrink under Ash's gaze. How did he know? Sure, the guy had a reputation for being in on just about every secret out there, but only a bare handful of people knew the classified object, the very one being discussed in the confidential meeting that night, was hidden in the Consulate itself. The ambassadors who would be arriving in a couple hours didn't even know the object of contention was in the country, let alone in the manor.

She almost said she wasn't at liberty to discuss it. "I don't know," she answered instead, following a vague instinct that he would force it out of her if he knew she knew.

His eyes narrowed for an instant. He suspected she was lying but didn't say anything. Just ate another cracker.

"I … have to get to my lesson." As she walked out of the room, she glanced back. Ash stood at the counter, staring at nothing. Swallowing hard, she wondered what other secrets he had somehow unearthed, because she had a few she didn't want anyone to know.

CHAPTER

- 2 -

PIPER SLOWLY leaned back into the stretch. Tired muscles complained as her thighs went taut. She lay on her back on the mats, legs bent at the knee and feet under her butt.

"And *then*," she huffed, "he threatened to expel me from my apprenticeship."

Uncle Calder leaned back into the same stretch beside her. His eyebrows climbed halfway up his shaved head. It glistened with moisture from their sparring session. "Do you think that was an unfair threat?"

"*Yes.*"

He lifted his eyebrows impossibly higher. She scowled. Her father and uncle might be identical twins but they were easy to tell apart: Quinn always looked cross, while Calder looked perpetually amused.

At the moment, he was uncharacteristically somber. "You're working with a serious disadvantage that other Consuls don't have. That's all the more reason you need to be more careful about getting into physical altercations with daemons. Today, *you* crossed the line to physical."

Piper sat up with a growl. "Ether was charging Ozar! It was going to get physical anyway. I was trying to keep Ozar from getting killed."

"And who do you think stood more of a chance against Ether? A mature daemon with seasoned defensive skills or an Apprentice Consul without a stitch of magic?"

She snapped her mouth shut, seething at the painful truth.

"Of course your father and I are concerned. I don't think it's unfair to remove you from your apprenticeship if your life is in danger." His look was sympathetic. "We know how much it means to you, Piper. We won't make that decision lightly."

Flexing her jaw, she began another stretch. Because it took magic to counter magic, all Consuls had to be haemons. The word was a slang-turned-official term, short for half-human, half-daemon: haemon. Although they looked entirely human, haemons inherited magic from their daemon parent, giving them a powerful edge. But though she was a haemon, she had no magic.

She leaned into her stretch, glaring at the mats. "I barely got a scratch," she mumbled. "I could have handled it even if Ash hadn't shown up."

Calder gave her a long look. She pretended not to notice.

"Are you sure you can't talk Father into letting me attend the meeting?" she asked. The ambassadors would be arriving in an hour. It was her last chance to get in on the biggest political event of the decade.

"I don't plan to try." Calder angled his legs into a split. "It's no place for an Apprentice. You're lucky you even know about it."

She scowled and almost told him that Ash—impossibly—knew as well but she didn't want to divert the topic. "You don't think I can keep a secret? I haven't let slip a single detail. You two could at least—"

"Drop it, Piper. Not happening."

Exhaling forcefully, she started stretching her arms. It wasn't fair. The biggest deal of the year, happening right in her Consulate, and she didn't get to attend. Everyone right up to the damn president wanted in on the meeting, which was why only a select handful of special ambassadors knew when and where it was taking place. A fake location had been leaked two days ago to send everyone else running in the wrong direction.

If her father hadn't decided to be paranoid, she might have gotten to *see* it when they moved it out of the Consulate.

They finished their stretches in silence. Piper stared gloomily at the wall of weapons across from her, everything from Japanese swords to throwing knives to guns. She was proficient with them all. She didn't need a weapon to put a full-grown man on the ground. If combat ability were the most important part of being a Consul, she'd have her apprenticeship in the bag. If knowledge and experience were key, she'd be in the clear. All that diplomacy and negotiation and de-escalation might trip her up now and then but she was getting the hang of that too—sort of.

However, there was a skill she was missing, one she could never learn, that made her future as a Consul unstable at best. Without magic, her ability to defend herself was severely limited—not that she planned to give up. A full day of regular school plus four hours of lessons every evening was a small price to pay for a career that would never, ever get boring.

After a quick shower, she headed for her father's office for a second time. Maybe if she casually positioned herself nearby, Quinn would spontaneously change his mind and invite her to the meeting.

The office door opened as she was coming up the hall. Quinn stepped out, a briefcase under one arm and a file folder between his teeth. He locked the office door and waved her over. Her nerves twanged with anticipation.

He took the folder out of his mouth and tucked it under his arm. "I was about to look for you."

Her heart leaped with excitement. She tried to look mildly intrigued. "Oh?"

"Nearly all our guests have departed for the night. Danica was scheduled as the on-duty Consul tonight but she's ill. That leaves you and two daemons. I don't want them wandering around while the meeting is ongoing so I sent them upstairs for the night."

She tensed. "*Upstairs?* As in the Consul floor? But they—"

"Just for one night, Piperel. It's only the two of them. I want you to keep them upstairs and out of the way—no exceptions, you included. No one goes downstairs under any circumstances. They are your responsibility to supervise. Understood?"

Her hopes shriveled to nothing. Fantastic. Babysitting duty.

"While I'm in the meeting, I'll leave command of the Consulate to you."

Under normal circumstances, being put in temporary command would have been the perfect opportunity to prove her skills. Today, she'd rather be in on the top-secret, dangerously controversial meeting.

Quinn started to step away and paused. Dipping a hand into his pocket, he pulled out a small black cube. "Would you mind holding on to this for me? I forgot to put it in my room earlier."

He dropped the cube into her palm; it was a tiny velvet ring box. She stared at it curiously. Since he was still watching, she tried to force it into the pocket of her jeans but they were too tight. With a shrug and a smile, she stuck it down the front of her shirt and wedged it between her breasts. Quinn looked vaguely appalled.

"I'll see you in a few hours. Remember—keep your wards upstairs until I say otherwise."

She nodded and he walked away, leaving her alone in the hallway. With no witnesses, she let a scowl take over her face. Top-secret meeting? Nope, she got to babysit instead.

⁂

Piper turned the gemstone over in her hands, watching the dim light from her bedside lamp gather inside its bluish silver depths. It was the size of the end of her thumb and heavier than it looked. Other than that, it wasn't anything special—merely a pretty stone.

Curiosity nagged at her. Her dad wasn't a trinkets person. Why would he care about a gemstone? She bit her bottom lip. Had it belonged to her mother? She stroked her fingers across the smooth surface. Her parents had split up when she was eight. Piper remembered her mother departing in a storm of tears and screamed insults. Her father had slammed the door behind his wife, turned to Piper, who was hiding around the corner, and said, "That was goodbye." Piper had never seen her mother again. One year later, her father had brought home the news that her mother had died in a car accident. He'd told her this the day *after* the funeral and cremation. Piper had never gotten to say a final goodbye.

Black resentment spread through her but she stuffed it down. Unclenching her hand with effort, she stuck the gem back into the ring box and dropped it on her dresser beside her alarm clock. Ugh, one in the morning. Good thing she didn't have school tomorrow. Stepping backward until her legs bumped her bed, she let herself fall over the covers and yawned until her jaw popped.

The evening had passed without incident. The meeting had gone on for hours and finished twenty minutes ago when the ambassadors left. She hadn't seen them but she'd heard assorted voices as the group left the building. She might have indulged in self-pity over missing all the fun but she was too worried about her nearby roommates. Of all the guests to stay behind … She would've preferred Ether and Gigantor-what's-his-name but both of them had taken off after the confrontation downstairs. Instead she'd gotten stuck with the dream team: Lyre and Ash.

They'd behaved perfectly so far. She probably didn't need to lose sleep over them. Lyre was annoying as always but she could handle him. Mostly.

Then again, she didn't really know him. He spent a night or two at the Consulate every month or so but she'd hardly spent enough time with him to judge his integrity and trustworthiness. He only stopped in for their free room and board while travelling from whatever point A to point B he fancied that month. Unlike a lot of their other visitors, he never needed the Consulate's secondary services as a safe house — a place protected against any outside threat. Whatever he did with his time, at least he stayed out of trouble — probably. Their guests didn't always admit their real reasons for "visiting."

Ash, on the other hand, was the kind of trouble others came to the Consulate to escape. She knew even less about him than Lyre. She'd only met him a few times and only once when he was travelling without Lyre. Every time he did stop in, she made sure to avoid him. Unlike Lyre, Ash had a reputation—the kind that stopped a raging fight mid-strike by walking into the room. He was real trouble, not like the silly flirting Lyre indulged in. Lyre couldn't help himself. After all, that's just what incubi were like.

The Consulate served a lot of purposes but everything they did revolved around daemons. Not demons. *Daemons*. Big difference.

There were three "worlds," for lack of a better term: Earth, where humans lived, the Underworld, and the Overworld. Daemons came from the latter two and Earth was stuck inter-dimensionally between them.

The Underworld wasn't Hell any more than the Overworld was Heaven. They were simply opposites. Lyre and Ash were Underworld daemons but they weren't evil demons come to steal human souls—even if Ash's morality was dubious at best. They were merely nocturnal, liked black, and could be nasty if you got on their bad side. Overworld daemons liked white and gold, harps, and sunlight and could be equally nasty if you got on their bad side. There were Overworlders as scary as Ash—or even scarier.

In fact, Piper was of the opinion that Overworlders only liked white and harps because generations of angel mythology had gone to their heads.

Underworlders had the bad reputations, a lot of it unearned. Incubi were pretty harmless most of the time; they got a high and an energy boost off sex. They *did* siphon energy off their partners but they didn't hurt the humans they slept with. In fact, incubi were so damn good in bed they were practically addictive.

Of course, no daemon was *safe*. They were all dangerous in their own way, even the incubi. Some variations, castes as they called them, were worse than others—like Ash's. He was a draconian: the daemon equivalent of a VP in a billion-dollar company. He had the power to do anything he wanted and almost everyone was too afraid to argue—hence his bad reputation. That he and Lyre were buddies was kind of strange. Most daemons were only too happy to get out of Ash's way, as Ether and Gigantor had demonstrated. Piper was smart enough to follow suit.

She frowned at the ceiling. The quiet noise of the TV was gone. Had they finally gone to bed? As acting Consul for the night, she couldn't sleep until she was certain they'd settled in. Shoving herself up and swallowing another yawn, she turned toward the dresser and froze.

For a second, she thought there was a cat crouched on her dresser, the ring box between its front paws. Then small wings unfurled and a long neck stretched out. The creature cocked its head, large golden eyes blinking slowly.

Piper stared at it. It was a vaguely cat-shaped lizard with wings. Its scales were dark and mottled like shadows in a forest, with a black mane starting midway along its forehead and running down its long, sinuous back to end in a soft tuft at the tip of its tail. It stretched its wings and half folded them, shifting its weight as it watched her.

"What are you doing in here?" she asked in a whisper, caught between annoyance and awe. The little creature was a dragonet and it belonged to Ash. All draconians had a dragonet companion. They were a cross between pets and familiars, bonded in a way Piper didn't understand. She'd only seen Ash's dragonet twice. They were shy and avoided strangers.

So why was it in her room?

Moving slowly, Piper slid from her bed and straightened. "Hello, little one," she murmured, inching closer. "Why are you in here, hmmm?" The dragonet scrutinized her, tilting its head from side to side like a puzzled dog. Its wings quivered.

"Shh," she soothed. "Don't be afraid. Aren't you a cute thing?"

The dragonet made a little chirping sound. It opened its mouth, flashing rows of sharp, predatory teeth, and snatched the ring box in its mouth.

Piper stared. Then she panicked. "Hey, put that down!"

The dragonet leaped off the dresser, grabbed onto the wall, and ran along it like a huge bug.

"Hey!" she yelled again. "Get back here with that!" She dove for the creature but it was way ahead of her. It jumped off the wall and landed with liquid grace in front of her door, now open a few inches. The tufted end of its tail vanished through the gap.

She almost ran into the door but caught herself on the wall and flung the door open. She leaped into the hallway and saw the dragonet streaking toward the other end of the house where the second set of bedrooms was located. With a furious growl, she charged into the living room that separated the two wings, way too slow to catch the little bugger. An old paperback book sat on the end table right beside her. Piper grabbed it, took aim, and hurled it across the room without breaking stride.

It smacked the dragonet in the back. The creature did a dragon-style face-plant, tumbling head over heels with wings and tail flailing. It yelped loudly as it sprawled to a stop. Piper immediately felt guilty but she needed that ring box.

The dragonet hopped to its feet as Piper reached it. Spotting the ring box two feet beyond the dragonet, she lunged for it and almost did her own face-plant when the dragonet sprang at her. She fell against the wall and the dragonet's little feet thumped her head as it launched off her. It landed lightly on the floor, caught the ring box in its mouth again, and dove into the air vent, which for some stupid reason was missing its cover.

Piper dropped to her knees beside the vent and listened to the sound of claws on metal. A soft thump came from the other side of the wall. Apparently there was no vent cover on the other side either. She looked up and swallowed hard. She was sitting right outside Ash's room. The dragonet had run straight to daddy for protection.

She frowned at the door. Ash was in there, probably asleep. She didn't want to wake him. She didn't even want to talk to him. What were the chances she could sneak in there and steal the ring box back without waking him?

She considered it for about half a second. Yeah, zero.

Before she could come up with a better plan, the door—a foot in front of her nose—popped open. Shadows spilled out, framing Ash in the threshold as he looked across the living room toward her room. Then he looked down, saw her sitting at his feet, and blinked.

Piper scrambled up, trying not to blush—or stare. Ash wore nothing but loose, black cotton pants. He really should have tied the drawstring a little tighter, because the way the waistband clung to his lean hips, one sharp movement would make them slip. Piper jerked her eyes up and the next level view was even better: lean, sculpted muscles made from hard work and inherent athleticism instead of weight lifting, all beneath warm, honey-toned skin that looked absolutely velvety in the shadows of the doorway—

A soft chirp made her jump and she belatedly noticed the dragonet sitting on his shoulder. The end of the silk strip braided into his hair hung from the creature's mouth, and it tugged on the silk like a cat toy, all the while keeping those gold eyes trained on Piper.

Ash absently pulled the red silk out of the dragonet's teeth with a soft rasp. "What are you doing?" he asked, breaking the oh-so-awkward silence.

She shivered as his voice slid through her again, too intimate as the shadows pressed close. Her brain kicked back in, along with a heady dose of adrenaline; she'd never been alone in Ash's company before.

Fear tickled her stomach, making her want to shrink away. She drew herself up and glared instead. "Your dragonet snuck into my room and stole something from me."

He glanced at the creature on his shoulder. It tilted its head and somehow managed to project total innocence. He looked back at Piper. "Why would she do that?"

She redoubled her efforts not to cower. "You tell me."

His attention slid back to the dragonet. "Zwi, were you stealing again?" he murmured.

The dragonet trilled, its head weaving from side to side as it squirmed in a distinctly guilty way. Ash frowned. "Go get it."

Piper blinked. Were they communicating like people? For real?

With an unhappy grumble, Zwi slid off his shoulder and disappeared into the dark room. Piper stared, not quite able to believe it. Seconds later, Zwi landed on his shoulder, the ring box in her mouth. She gave Piper a resentful look as Ash held out his hand. The dragonet grudgingly dropped it.

Ash just looked at the ring box. Looked at it long enough that panic sparked. She jumped forward and snatched it out of his palm.

His shoulders stiffened. Piper's heartbeat stuttered. It suddenly seemed much darker in the narrow hallway. She inched back a step, fighting to project nonchalant confidence. Predators attacked the weak. He tracked her unsubtle retreat without expression but there was a taste of aggression in the air—a taste of power and blood.

With a sudden huff, he rolled his shoulders and shifted his weight, nearly unbalancing Zwi. As the cloak of impending violence slid away, Piper exhaled sharply. Furtively monitoring his body language, she stuck the ring box back in her shirt. She really needed jeans with functional pockets.

He raised his eyebrows at her storage choice. She shot him a mutinous look. The silence stretched.

Fingers whispered down her sides. Hands caught her hips and pulled them backward. Lyre rubbed against her, purring in her ear. Piper threw herself forward with such force that she almost crashed into Ash. Whirling around, she let her fist fly. It smacked solidly into Lyre's palm and he grinned. Damn supernaturally fast daemons.

"Feisty tonight, my love," he approved, stroking his fingers across the back of her hand. He too wore nothing but sleep pants and was as yummy as Ash—even more so because he didn't make the hair on the back of her neck stand on end.

Lyre's gaze flicked to Ash. "Is this what it looks like? A moonlight tryst?" He pouted. "Why wasn't I invited?"

Recovering her wits, Piper tried to pull her fist out of his grip. "Let go," she demanded. "What are you doing up? Go back to bed."

"Only if you come with me," he breathed, shifting closer. Piper stepped back, her breath catching as Lyre's eyes went dark. Warmth spilled through her in a rising blush as his gaze slowly slid down her and back up again, lingering in obvious places before coming to rest on her mouth. He slid closer still and Piper stepped back only to thump into Ash, still standing in the doorway to his room. She lurched forward but Lyre had closed the gap. She stood between them with nowhere to go, caught in the heat of their bodies, her heart pounding.

Oh no. This was not going to happen.

Baring her teeth, she balled up her other hand and drove her fist into Lyre's stomach. He gasped and took a step back. With no room to get in a good swing, the punch hadn't had much force but it had been enough. Ripping her other hand free, she fell into a fighting stance and drew her other fist back.

A hand closed on her wrist, firm but gentle. Another touched her shoulder and the next thing she knew, Ash had turned her and pushed her out from between them. She sprang away and whipped around again, ready to attack, but it was Ash in front of her, not Lyre. He stood sideways between them, an impenetrable barrier.

"Lyre," he said quietly. "Apologize. You frightened her."

"I'm not scared of him," she snapped, not relaxing her stance.

Lyre's eyes were gold again, the dark heat gone. He frowned and raked a hand through his white-blond hair. "Damn it, Piper. You know I wouldn't do anything. You're the damn Head Consul's daughter, for Taroth's sake."

She gave him a killing look and he huffed in frustration. "Look, I'm sorry, okay? You were never this touchy before."

She folded her arms over her chest and looked away from his questioning gaze. "Things are different now, okay? I don't want you touching me. At all. Got it?"

Lyre watched her silently, his stare intent and oddly calculating. He glanced at Ash, who shrugged and tilted his head in a way that made Piper instantly suspicious. It looked too much like an "I'll tell you later" tilt. Were Ash's secret-digging skills that good?

A sudden crash shook the whole house. She jumped, grabbing the wall as the floor rumbled. Lyre staggered backward and Ash dropped into a half crouch, Zwi clinging to his shoulder. Dust sifted down as everything went still and silent.

CHAPTER
-3-

"WHAT ... WAS THAT?" Piper whispered.

Lyre slowly crouched, matching Ash's ready stance. "That was an explosion," he growled.

"Magic?" she demanded in a hiss.

"Think so."

"It has a haemon signature," Ash said, his voice clinical. "Not daemon."

She snapped straight. Her father?

Ash flowed to his full height, his movements shifting into something sleeker, more predatory, as he moved across the living room toward the stairs. Zwi slid from his shoulder and darted down the hall ahead of him.

"Wait!" Piper cried.

Ash glanced back at her. His normally gray eyes were dark, almost black.

She swallowed hard. "You're not allowed downstairs," she whispered. "I can't let you go down. He said no exceptions." Panic twisted in her stomach. Something had gone wrong with the meeting. Really wrong.

"You plan to wait here, doing nothing?" Ash asked flatly. "What if your father is hurt?"

She clenched her hands to hide their tremble. "No exceptions," she repeated, choking the words out. Responsibility. It hung on her like the weight of chains. If she let the two daemons go downstairs when she'd been told explicitly to keep them upstairs, her father would never overlook it. He expected her to make sure they stayed put no matter what.

Ash looked at her for a moment more, then turned and started toward the stairs again.

"Ash!" He didn't even hesitate. "I said stop," she yelled, her voice high with panic. If he went downstairs, she would lose her apprenticeship for sure. She launched after him.

"Hold up!" Lyre grabbed her arm.

She spun, contorting her arm until she had his wrist in her grip. A yank, a twist, a shove, and Lyre went down with a yelp, his arm bent painfully behind his back. She sprang off him and charged for Ash, who hadn't so much as paused when his friend had fallen.

The daemon turned as she reached him and her roundhouse kick slammed into his open hands. He stepped back with the force of her kick, pulling her off balance. Hopping and flailing, she bared her teeth. Flinging her arms out to create more momentum, she flipped her whole body, her other foot leaving the floor as she rolled in the air, breaking his grip on her foot. She landed hard on her stomach and kicked out with the other foot, slamming her boot into Ash's unprotected ankle. His foot went out from under him but he pivoted on the other with impossible grace, recovering with barely a bobble.

"You're not allowed down there," she yelled. Oh God, she was attacking a draconian. She was so dead. She flung out her foot again anyway, trying to hook his ankle and pull him off his feet. He kicked back and her foot hit his heel with a jarring impact.

"Stop it!" Lyre jumped right over Piper and slammed into Ash, shoving the other daemon into the wall. "Hurt her and you'll never set foot in a Consulate again, you idiot."

Ash snarled, the sound deep and menacing. Piper blanched but Lyre's face hardened with grim determination. "Cool it, Ash."

Slowly, Ash relaxed. He cast a menacing look at Piper, still on the floor, before crossing his arms over his bare chest. Lyre let out a long breath and stepped back. He looked at Piper but she jumped up before he could offer her a hand. Tugging her clothes straight, she glowered and hoped neither of them noticed how much she was shaking.

"Just—wait here. For two seconds. Okay?" With a warning look at Ash, Lyre trotted back across the living room and vanished into his room. He came out almost immediately, a bundle of clothing in one hand. Piper watched him, her heart pounding. The house was silent —too quiet. Why hadn't someone come to tell her everything was okay?

Lyre untangled two hoodies and tossed the red one to Ash. The daemon pulled it on and zipped it halfway, his motions jerky and somehow dangerous. If she hadn't had other things to worry about, she'd have been shocked to be alive after attacking Ash.

Lyre pulled his hoodie over his head before turning to her. "I think we need to go down, Piper," he said gently.

Shaking her head mutely, she slid closer to Ash to better grab him if he tried to make a break for the stairs. He hissed at her, his eyes darkening again. Fear stabbed her. He wasn't even bothering to act human anymore. He was shading—dropping the veneer of civilized human behavior and going all-out daemon. Dangerous or not, she'd thought he had way better control. Daemons usually only shaded when they were exceptionally angry or afraid.

Lyre looked shocked at Ash's behavior too. He shifted in until the three of them were crowded in a tight little knot in the hallway.

"Piper," he began again.

"No," she said shrilly. "You can't. He said no exceptions. If I let you go down there, I'll be—"

"Possibly saving your father's life," Ash growled. "There's a time and place for blind obedience. This is not it."

She met Ash's eyes, still dark with his gathering power—the air was starting to crackle—and felt a flash of dread in her chest. Her father was down there. The house was too quiet. He'd been way closer to the explosion than her. The image of him lying in a bloody puddle made her knees go weak. She spun and lunged for the stairs, forgetting the two daemons entirely.

Hands grabbed her waist and yanked her back. Someone shoved her to the floor before she knew what was happening and weight came down on her back. Her breath whooshed out in a furious yell and she slammed an elbow into her attacker's kidney.

A grunt of pain. "Hold still," Ash snapped above her, his voice no louder than a whisper. "Can't you hear that?"

She realized, belatedly, that Ash was crouched over her, defending rather than attacking. Lyre hovered beside them, fear on his face but his body tense and ready.

"Hear what?" she whispered furiously.

A soft thump came from somewhere below them, followed by a muted crash like a door being thrown open into a wall.

"Father?" she gasped. She squirmed and Ash shoved her shoulders into the floor. "Let me go! What if he's hurt?"

"Be quiet," he hissed, then muttered, "Wasn't that my argument?"

"What is it?" Lyre whispered. "I don't like this."

"Like what?" Piper snapped. "Let me go."

"Quit panicking and use your senses," Ash said. "Whatever that is, it's not your father."

"Huh?" She blinked at the carpet right in front of her nose and tried to slow her racing heart. Her skin tingled and her stomach twisted like she could smell something rancid, but all she smelled was dusty carpet.

"What is it?" she demanded.

"I don't know," Lyre answered tersely. "Be quiet."

The three of them made like statues as they listened to the thumps and crashes from the main floor. It sounded like someone— something—was tearing the house apart. A sudden skitter of fast steps on the stairs made Piper gasp. Ash's dragonet whipped around the corner where the stairs waited out of sight. The little creature tore up to her master and threw herself into him, grabbing his shoulder and burrowing into the back of his neck. She chittered with unmistakable terror.

Then Ash was off Piper and hauling her to her feet. He lifted her right off the floor, spun her around, and dropped her facing in the opposite direction.

"You need to *get out of here*," he said, his tone unexpectedly fierce. His eyes had gone completely black. He slashed a glance at Lyre. "You too."

"What is it?" Lyre asked, taking a tight hold on Piper's arm while she gaped at Ash's black, black eyes. It looked like the entire night sky had been condensed into his face. He'd fully shaded. Bad bad bad.

"It's a choronzon."

The blood drained from her face. Choronzons were a type of Underworld creature. They were bestial, simpleminded, and irrevocably, mercilessly violent. They never left the Underworld.

So what was one doing in the manor?

"Ash," Lyre hissed. "What do we do? It's too strong to fight."

Piper flicked a stare at Ash. Was he even considering a fight? Choronzons were practically invincible.

The draconian hesitated, power sizzling the air around him. Something thumped downstairs and they all went still at the wet-sounding grunt that echoed up the stairs. The choronzon was at the bottom.

Sucking in a breath, she grabbed Lyre's arm and reached for Ash —but changed her mind when his gaze sliced her way.

"Come on," she hissed, tugging at the incubus. "I know a way out. Come on!"

Lyre grabbed the hood of Ash's sweatshirt and yanked the draconian after them as Piper raced to her bedroom door, taking them even closer to the stairway and the choronzon. They piled into her room and she locked the door. She doubted it would slow the beast. She didn't know exactly what a choronzon looked like— something about tentacles. None of her textbooks had pictures, but either way, she knew it was big.

She threw open her closet doors and started flinging clothes out. Four shoe boxes followed, then an armload of old stuffed animals.

"What are you doing?" Lyre asked. The irritation in his whisper made her look up right as he pulled a pink bra off his shoulder and tossed it onto her bed. Ash edged behind Lyre to get out of the path of flying clothes, his attention on the door.

Piper threw another handful of laundry out of her way and found the tiny panel where the floor joined the wall at the back of the closet. She pressed it. A loud click echoed through the closet and a section of wall popped inward. She shoved it open to reveal a narrow, dark tunnel.

"Flashlight," she muttered, backing out of the closet. "Need a flashlight and—"

Wood groaned as weight pressed against the bedroom door.

Ash backed into Lyre to get away. He scooped his dragonet off his shoulder and tossed her toward the closet. "Lead the way, Zwi. Piper, follow her."

The dragonet landed lightly and its scales turned white. The long line of its mane stayed black but its body was now bright as snow. It darted into the closet. Piper slid in after the creature. The passageway was so narrow she had to turn sideways to fit. Zwi almost glowed in the dark. Piper followed, shuffling as fast as possible. Lyre swore when his clothes caught on something and tore. The soft click of the panel closing again told her Ash had made it in.

Wood splintered loudly, the sound muffled by the walls. The choronzon was in her room.

She followed the beacon of Zwi's scales until the dragonet vanished. Piper stopped dead, her foot finding the edge of a drop-off in the dark. Lyre was right behind her, his breathing quick.

She reached out, feeling blindly for the first rung. "Damn it," she whispered. "The ladder is gone." She hadn't been in the passage in a few years because her father had taken out the ladder to keep her from sneaking around the Consulate at night. She wished she'd remembered that five minutes ago.

A huge bang made Lyre jump into her, almost knocking her in headfirst. The hideous sound of tearing wood echoed down the tunnel and a dim light filled the cramped space.

"It's in the passageway," Ash growled. "Just jump!"

She hesitated on the edge. Wood shrieked as it was torn from its nails, gunshot snaps as the studs broke. The choronzon was bulldozing its way into the narrow passage.

"Go!" Lyre didn't wait for her response. He shoved her.

She plummeted, knees bent for the impact. Pain shot up her legs when she landed. She tried to roll to absorb the impact but slammed into a wall. A whoosh of air was her only warning and she pressed into the side of the chute as Lyre landed beside her. There was no room for a third person.

"Go!" Lyre yelled.

She squeezed into the last stretch of the passageway. A flash of dim white ahead—Zwi, waiting for them at the exit. The crashing and snapping from above was as deafening as a landslide.

Piper reached the panel. Panic gripped her as she felt around wildly for the release latch. Lyre crowded in behind her. Ash joined them, breathing heavily. Piper thought she smelled blood. Where was the latch? Her hands slid all around the edges, picking up slivers from the rough wood. *Where was it?*

The floor shook as something impossibly heavy hit it. The choronzon was on their level. Bile jumped into Piper's throat as the horrible stench of carrion filled her head and her nose.

A rough hand grabbed her shoulder and flattened her into the wall. Ash slapped his other hand to the panel and all the hair on Piper's body stood on end as electricity filled the air. With a flash and a boom, the door was blasted right out of the wall. Lyre somehow squeezed out ahead of her and into the front foyer. He spun and snatched Piper's arm, hauling her out. They both turned back as Ash appeared in the opening. Half out of the opening, his eyes went wide.

His feet went out from under him as something grabbed him from behind. A blood-red tentacle as thick as an arm spun around his neck and he was yanked back into the dark passageway with a strangled shout.

"Ash!" Lyre roared. He lunged to his feet, then spun to shove Piper toward the hallway. "Get help," he yelled. "Get your dad. Quick!" Without a backward glance, he dove in after Ash. There was a soundless concussion from inside that made dust sift from the ceiling. A low, bestial howl tore through the air.

Piper spun and charged down the hall. Ash might freak her out but she wouldn't stand there while a choronzon tore him apart. She reached the meeting room and flung the door open. It was empty. She'd known it would be. The meeting had ended half an hour ago when the ambassadors left. That meant they'd gone to get the secret object. Throwing herself back out of the room, she ran down the hall, through the kitchen, and plowed into the back door. With shaking hands, she undid the bolt and burst out into the cool night air.

Across the dark yard, before trees swallowed the grass and the forest took over, a small toolshed stood alone beside a huge oak tree. Piper sprinted to the shed. The entrance to the Consulate's top security vault was outside because the spells protecting it were too dangerous to be in the house. Only the Head Consul could open it and he visited it only once or twice a year. She threw the flimsy doors open and stopped dead.

The six-inch-thick metal door of the vault set into the concrete floor of the shed hung wide open, but that wasn't why she'd stopped. If there were people inside, of course the door would be open.

What she hadn't expected was the dead man sprawled across the floor, his slit throat gaping like a bloody, toothless grin.

After one terrified heartbeat, she noticed his black eyes. The man was a daemon—one of the ambassadors? Breathing too fast, she stepped over him and started down the stairs. Her hands trembled and she wished she'd grabbed a weapon. Barehanded, she wasn't much use.

The stairs went far deeper than a single story and at the bottom was another steel door. It too was wide open and there was another bloody body beside it; the daemon was slumped against the wall, staring blindly. Skirting around his legs, she walked into the main vault. Steel shelves lined the walls on both sides to create one wide corridor down the center. Metal boxes, each neatly labeled, sat in rows on the shelves. Close to the entrance, the shelves were untouched. At the opposite end of the vault, boxes were tumbled across the floor and the shelves were bent and twisted like a massive force had blasted them backward.

Dead ahead the last door waited, open and beckoning.

Piper darted through the obstacle course of deformed metal and scattered debris. She reached the threshold and grabbed the frame to stop. Her gaze flashed across the cement cube and what she saw didn't immediately register.

Bodies. Blood. Dead people.

This was where the explosion had detonated. The walls were stained black. Burnt blood made fantastic patterns over every surface. She couldn't tell how many people were in the room, only that all of them had been thrown with killing force into the unyielding cement walls, their bodies burned and broken.

Her father was one of them.

A choking sound scraped her throat as she fell to her knees beside the nearest body and turned it over. Blackened skin flaked at her touch. The face was burned away but the clothes were wrong. She staggered to the next. These mangled corpses were all that was left of the ambassadors. But where was her father?

She stumbled to the other side of the room. Heedlessly grabbing the legs of the top body on a pile of four, she dragged it out of the way. She couldn't see properly. Tears flooded her eyes and she couldn't breathe right.

"Father?" she choked. "Where are you?" She kicked an arm out of her way and shoved another burnt corpse into the wall. Under the last body in the pile, the edge of a familiar white shirt peeked out, splattered with blood.

"No," Piper gasped. Grabbing the burnt thing on top—not even recognizable as a body—she heaved it away to reveal the last one. Her knees hit the floor. Shielded behind the other three, this one hadn't been burned as badly. Ghostly white, slack and lifeless, the face was turned away but she recognized the clothes, the build, and the shape of that so-familiar person.

"Uncle Calder?" she whispered. Of course her uncle had accompanied the Head Consul. Of course.

Hands unexpectedly gripped her upper arms, pulling her away. She couldn't stop staring, couldn't think, couldn't breathe. Arms crushed her against a chest that smelled like spices and cherries.

"Shh," Lyre crooned to her, his voice trembling. He rocked her, his arms too tight. "Don't cry, Piper. Shh."

She was barely aware of the sobs tearing out of her chest. She clung to him, eyes squeezed shut against the sight of her uncle's burned face.

"Damn," another voice whispered. Ash's dark presence slid past her left side. "Is this … ? Damn, it's Quinn."

"N-no," Piper gasped. "It's Uncle C-Calder." Lyre squeezed her even tighter. Her father and uncle were identical twins but Quinn had been wearing a suit with a dark shirt. Calder had been wearing a white dress shirt.

"It is?" Ash repeated, startled. "But he—wait. He's alive."

Piper jerked back so hard Lyre staggered. "What?" she shrieked. She tore away and spun to find Ash kneeling beside her uncle, his hands flashing over Calder's bloody chest. She dropped down beside him and grabbed Calder's limp hand. "Will he make it?"

Ash didn't immediately answer, his mouth tense with concentration. "He's right on the edge. Curse the Moirai. I'm not a healer."

"You have to try!"

"I *am*. We need—"

Boots clomped in the doorway. She and Ash looked up at the same time.

"You need to step away from the man and cross your arms on your chests in an X," ordered the uniformed man in the door. A large black rifle rested in his hands, identical to the guns held by the three men behind him. "Slowly now," he added.

Lyre, his face white, crossed his arms as instructed, pressing his palms against his opposite shoulders in a position that made it impossible to quickly cast magic without hitting himself. Piper rose carefully to her feet and followed suit, her hands shaking. Ash copied her, his eyes glittering like obsidian.

"Help him, please," she whispered to the man, jerking her chin at Calder. "He's going to die."

The man, his black uniform marked with the symbols of a prefect —the police force of the daemon community—gave Calder a brief glance. Without changing expression, he gestured to the men behind him.

"Arrest them."

CHAPTER

-4-

PIPER SLUMPED on the bottom stair in the front foyer and tried to pretend she was calm. She stared at the silver bands of metal around her wrists.

Lyre fidgeted beside her, standing with his back against the wall and his cuffed hands trapped behind him. Apparently, he was more dangerous than her, so his wrists were behind his back. His eyes darted around the empty space, returning every few seconds to Ash.

The draconian was leaning against the same wall as Lyre but was slouched in semiconsciousness. If the prefects thought Lyre was dangerous, then they thought Ash was a walking atomic bomb. Not only was he cuffed, but he'd also been collared with a magic-depressor and gagged. The former made him so drowsy he couldn't focus. Shimmers kept rippling over him in random patterns as his dampened magic weakened the glamour that made him look human.

All daemons were a little—or a lot—paranormal in appearance, but most of them could use magic to disguise themselves. Completely changing their appearance took a huge amount of magic, but they could fool the eyes and the senses with touches of power. The more human-looking they were to start with, the less magic they needed in order to walk around in public. Lyre, for example, didn't bother changing the color of his unnatural-looking hair and eyes because it wasn't worth the effort.

Ash, on the other hand, probably needed quite a bit of glamour to pass as human. It must take a lot of magic to keep his appearance as semi-human as it currently was, since he didn't change his hair even though dark wine-red would be almost impossible to replicate with dye. He probably relied more on a *don't-see* projection when he was around humans—a mental aura that made him blend into the background. Humans would simply fail to notice him as long as he didn't do anything to draw their attention.

At the moment, Ash was barely managing to keep up his glamour. Piper squinted, trying to make out his real face through the sporadic shimmers. He was human enough in shape that his face was about the same without glamour, but she kind of thought he might have a tail. Daemons were aggressively secretive about their real appearances so she only had a general idea what he might look like underneath the magic. Volunteers to model for textbook illustrations were a little hard to find.

She couldn't blame the prefects for taking precautions with Ash— he wasn't the kind of daemon you wanted ticked off at you—but the prefects were treating *all* of them like criminals.

The front door swung open and the sergeant in charge of the prefect team walked in. He was a big man with bigger muscles and an expressionless face that was the result of a missing sense of humor. His flat stare slid over Piper and Lyre to stop on Ash.

"How's my uncle?" she demanded, her voice too shrill. "Is he alive?"

The sergeant shot her an impatient look. "Yes, he's alive. He was moved to a medical center."

"Will he be okay?"

The man shrugged uncaringly, his gaze moving back to Ash. The door opened again and another prefect came in. He stopped beside the sergeant, looking scrawny and weak-chinned in comparison.

"Sir, the magic signature is definitely haemon, not daemon." He jerked a thumb at Ash. "The explosion wasn't him."

Piper's eyes narrowed to furious slits. "Excuse me, but we already told you the explosion went off while me, Ash, and Lyre were upstairs. Ash wasn't anywhere near the vault."

The sergeant ignored her but the other one looked over with what might have been pity. "He could have set it up in advance," he told her, "but we know for sure now he didn't."

"I've barely been five feet from him for two days," Lyre said angrily. "*None* of us did a damn thing wrong. Why are you arresting us?"

"I've heard your version of events," the sergeant said dismissively. "Until we have some cold, hard facts, none of you are going anywhere." He looked at the prefect. "Anything else?"

"The expert is sure the magic signature belongs to …" The man glanced at Piper. "To the one you suspected."

The sergeant nodded slowly. Piper ground her teeth. "What are you arresting us for, then?" she snapped. "What are the charges?"

Taking a clipboard from the prefect and flipping idly through it, the sergeant didn't bother to look at Piper. "We can't charge you with the deaths of nine daemons or the attempted murder of a Consul since the magic isn't yours, but I imagine 'accessory to murder' and 'grand larceny' will stick just fine. Maybe even 'conspiracy to commit crimes against the peace,'" he added thoughtfully.

The blood drained from her face and she was glad she was already sitting. "What?"

"Piperel Griffiths," the sergeant said, his voice going hard and flat as he finally looked at her, "would you like to tell me where the Sahar is?"

She froze in place, unable to breathe. How did he know about the secret object that her father was supposed to have given to the ambassadors in the vault?

"It would be in your best interests to come clean now," he continued, stepping closer to loom over her. "I'm sure we could bring the charges down to something less … treasonous." His expression softened slightly. "Did Quinn force you, Piperel?"

She stared, not understanding.

"Or was it these two?" the man asked, jerking his chin at Lyre and Ash. Lyre's mouth hung open, his face a mask of horror. "You don't have to protect them, Piperel. They can't hurt you now."

"What … what are you talking about?" she whispered.

The sergeant's expression hardened again in a flash. "One of two things happened here tonight, girl. One: Quinn betrayed his position and stole the Sahar with your help. Or two: *You* betrayed your father and stole the Sahar with the help of these two animals."

"It's stolen?" she repeated blankly. The special artifact was gone? The man's words slowly sank in and Piper felt hot blood surge through her.

"*My father did not steal it!*" she yelled, leaping to her feet. "Why would he? Even if he wanted to, it's been here for months. Why would he steal it in front of a bunch of people?"

"Then tell me this, girl," the sergeant growled. "Where is your father now? Why wasn't he in that room with everyone else? And why," his voice slowed, "does the magic signature of that explosion belong to the Head Consul?"

Piper couldn't breathe. Her knees gave out and she sat on the step again with a thump. "It's not," she whispered.

"It is," the man said coldly. "The Sahar couldn't be removed from its spot in the vault without the combined efforts of three skilled magicians. Perhaps that's why he waited … although why he didn't find some excuse to get his brother out of that vault first is beyond me."

No. Impossible. Quinn wouldn't have almost killed his brother. It wasn't even conceivable.

"You're wrong," she choked. "You're wrong."

"Quinn created the blast. That is fact." He leveled Piperel with a stare that held no mercy. "Now we must determine your role in this heinous crime. You say you heard the explosion from inside the house. Why didn't you immediately investigate? You surely could have reached the vault before Quinn exited it."

Piper was shaking so much she could barely talk. "We couldn't because of the choronzon."

"What choronzon, Piperel? Anyone could have smashed the furniture."

"I saw it," Lyre said loudly, anger finally giving him a voice. "It tried to kill Ash. We fought it off."

"*You* fought it off? A choronzon?" The man snorted. "Try something more believable."

"We did! It wasn't very strong. Its power was limited and it was acting strange, but—"

"I'm not questioning *you*, rake. Speak again and we'll gag you too."

Lyre paled at the same time his eyes flashed to near black. He flexed his jaw but said nothing more. Ash's head came up, his eyes briefly focusing as they cut across the sergeant like a knife on flesh.

"Now, Piperel," the man went on, "quit with the games. Quinn is gone. So is the Sahar. You and these two daemons are the only ones still alive on the property—with the exception of Calder Griffiths, who was left for dead. Do you really expect me to believe you had nothing to do with this?"

"You should believe it, because it's true." She glared, tears threatening to spill over. "And my father didn't steal it. Something else must have happened, and you can't figure out what."

"You're a liar, Piperel Griffiths," the sergeant said. "If I were your father, I would have shipped you off to a human boarding school years ago. You don't belong here."

Piper gasped and hunched like she'd been punched in the gut. "I'm a haemon," she retorted weakly. The man snorted again as four prefects stumped down the stairs and joined their sergeant in the foyer.

"Sir," the first one said. "The entire house has been searched. The Sahar isn't here, and we found no clues as to where Quinn may have gone to ground with it."

The sergeant nodded like this didn't surprise him. Piper stared dully at the floor between her feet, aching inside and shaking on the outside. This was so wrong. Everything about this was wrong. The police, even the daemon police, were supposed to be the good guys. Why did she feel like she was in enemy hands?

The cold voice of the sergeant spoke the next order with no emotion. "Search them."

She looked up as a prefect descended on her. It was the scrawny-looking one who'd watched the entire interrogation with a nervous, uncomfortable tic to his eyebrow. He gave Piper a subdued smile as he asked her to stand. She pushed to her feet, wobbling on weak knees, and tried to stare at nothing as the man patted her down. Beside her, Lyre glared straight ahead while another prefect turned his pockets out and checked inside his mouth.

Two more heaved Ash to his feet. The draconian leaned heavily on one while the other checked him over.

"I think the collar is too strong for him," the man acting as a prop told the sergeant. "I would have figured he could handle it, but he's gone almost comatose."

"It's not the collar," the sergeant replied dismissively. "Well—yes, it's the collar, but only because he's lost so much blood. Keep it on him. Dragon-boy can handle it."

Piper jerked her head around and stared at Ash. Blood loss? Where was he bleeding? One of the sleeves of his borrowed red hoodie was torn off, but—

His glamour shimmered again and, focusing this time, she saw the red stain running all the way down his left arm. It looked like he wore a wet, crimson glove from his bicep to his fingertips. She gasped, half reaching toward him before the cuffs cut into her wrists.

"What … ? When … ?"

"The choronzon," Lyre muttered out of the corner of his mouth. "He hid it because you were already hysterical when we found you. Didn't think you needed to see any more blood."

She clenched her hands. "Is he … ?"

"He'll be fine. Bleeding's already stopped. He's tough, don't worry."

The man checking Piper finally got her boots off to check the soles. She made no effort to help as he tugged on her socks then worked his way back up, patting every inch of her. She went rigid when he checked the back pockets of her jeans. Making semi-apologetic noises, he slid his fingers along the waist of her jeans. She fought the urge to knee him in the face.

The sergeant watched impassively as his prefects thoroughly frisked them. It wasn't until the man gingerly patted the top of her chest above her bra that Piper remembered. She unintentionally sucked in a huge, panicked gasp. The sergeant turned and the prefect checking her paused. Trying not to hyperventilate, she let the tears she'd been holding back spill over and twisted her face into a mask of fear. "D-don't," she cried, hunching to shift her breasts away from the man's hands even though he hadn't made a move to check under her shirt. "Don't touch me!"

The prefect snatched his hands back like he'd been burned. The sergeant made a disgusted noise. "Hurry it up, Jaeneson. Check her head and be done with it."

"Sorry," the prefect muttered under his breath as he ran his fingers through her hair and checked inside her mouth. "Okay," he announced loudly, "she's clean."

"So are these two," another prefect said.

The sergeant scowled. "Fine. Move them to the van while we tape this place up. I don't want a single thing disturbed before we get the sniffers in here."

Piper tried to look scared instead of guilty as the prefect who'd patted her down helped her get her boots back on before leading her toward the door. Lyre followed, practically stepping on her heels, and two more prefects managed to get Ash walking. She didn't relax until they'd been loaded into the back of an unmarked black van parked outside the doors. The last prefect slammed the door shut, submerging the van in darkness.

"You okay, Piper?" Lyre asked softly.

"Yeah," she whispered. Nine people were dead, her uncle was barely alive, and her father was missing and suspected of stealing one of the most important daemon artifacts of the last five hundred years. But she was okay—for the moment.

"Lyre," she breathed as quietly as she could. "Do you know what the Sahar looks like?"

"I know what the legends say," he whispered back. "The Sahar Stone is small, like a robin's egg, and supposedly made of quicksilver."

Piper struggled to breathe normally. Carefully, she pressed her upper arms against her breasts to squeeze them together and felt the uncomfortable press of the black ring box still lodged in her bra—the ring box Quinn had told her to keep safe—with the mysterious silver stone inside it.

"Lyre," she croaked weakly. "We need get the hell out of here before they realize I have the stolen Sahar."

⚬ ⚬ ⚬

"Hurry," Piper hissed.

"I'm *trying*," Lyre hissed back.

In the barely-there light coming through the tiny window that separated the driver's compartment of the van from the back, she watched Lyre tinker with the buckle at the back of the gag in Ash's mouth. The gag was made of heavy leather and fit between the draconian's teeth like the bit in a horse bridle. A plate inside depressed his tongue, preventing him from making any intelligible sounds. On the off chance he managed to cast magic with the dampening collar around his neck—unlikely—and his hands cuffed behind his back—almost impossible when he couldn't aim the spell— the gag prevented him from using an incantation to control his magic.

Lyre had wrestled his arms around in front of him in spite of his handcuffs and was now trying his damnedest to get the gag off Ash.

"There!" he exclaimed in a whisper. With a loud click, the straps of the gag fell away. Piper reached over and plucked the nasty contraption out of Ash's mouth. The draconian slit his eyes open and licked his lips with a relieved sigh.

"How you doing, buddy?" Lyre asked. "Were you following along?"

Ash slowly nodded. "We're in deep shit," he summarized. The end of his statement slurred badly and his eyelids fluttered. "Goddamn collar."

"I can't get that off," Lyre said. "It needs a key."

"How's your arm?" Piper whispered, inching closer. She and Lyre knelt on either side of Ash, who was stretched out on his stomach, his cheek pressed against the dirty floor of the van.

"Been better," he muttered. "What's the plan?"

"Uh." Lyre blinked at Piper. "We were hoping you'd tell us."

"Me? Why me?"

"Because Piper and I are fresh out of ideas on how to get these cuffs off and get out of the van."

"And then we have to find my father so we can prove he didn't steal the Sahar or kill those people," Piper added.

Ash blinked rapidly. "All right. Umm." He took a long, deep breath. With focused precision, he flexed his shoulders and bent his elbows until the chain between his handcuffs was pulled taut. He grunted softly and the muscles in his arms bunched. His hands clenched tight into fists as he strained against the chain.

With a pop, the chain snapped.

"Holy crap." Piper picked up a bent link. "How did you do that?"

"With effort," Ash grunted as Lyre helped him sit up. Blood dribbled from under the cuffs. The draconian took a deep breath. Placing both hands over the collar around his neck, he began to mumble under his breath—an incantation. Piper slid back, unable to believe it. Ash was going to magic off the magic-dampening collar? Exactly how powerful was he?

Lyre backed away too, putting his back against the van doors. The air grew hot and dense around Ash, and with a hissing crackle, the collar crumbled to dust. Ash dropped his hands, a tired but satisfied look on his face for a brief moment.

Then his eyes rolled up and he fell backward.

Lyre jumped forward but Ash snapped back to consciousness when he hit the van floor. Swearing softly, he allowed Lyre to help him back up. Piper jerked her hands in their cuffs, wishing she could help.

After a few minutes of deep breathing, Ash used a touch of magic to break Lyre's handcuffs and then Piper's. Rubbing her wrists in relief, she watched Ash face the back door of the van. How would he get the door open without the prefects noticing?

"Wait," Lyre whispered. He tugged nervously at his hoodie. "Are we sure we want to do this?"

"What do you mean?" Piper hissed.

Lyre met her glare without flinching. "If we take off now, everyone will think we helped Quinn kill those people and steal the Sahar, especially since we actually *have* it."

"My father did *not*—"

"I know, Piper," he interrupted quickly. "But that's what they'll think."

"We have to," she said fiercely. "If we stay, they will eventually find the Sahar on me. We can't hide it and we can't throw it away; it's the only proof I have that my father didn't steal it. He gave it to me to keep safe. He must have known something would go wrong."

"She's right," Ash murmured. "We have to get it away from the prefects or it will vanish without a trace while we burn for the crime."

"All the more reason to get it away from here." After Lyre nodded in reluctant agreement, she looked hopelessly around the steel-lined interior of the van. "How do we get out?"

Ash, moving like every muscle hurt, shifted toward the double doors at the back of the van. He tilted one ear toward the door and held perfectly still as he listened. Then his teeth flashed in a brief, unexpected grin. He clucked his tongue softly.

The doors clicked loudly and one of them cracked open.

Ash pushed the door a little more and a large pair of golden eyes appeared in the gap—Zwi, the dragonet. She made a soft trill and Ash crooned something to her. With a quick glance at Piper and Lyre, he slid through the gap and out into the night. Scrambling onto her feet under the low roof, Piper slid through the gap. She almost collided with Ash, who was hovering in the shadow of the van with Zwi curled around the back of his neck like a cat. A set of keys hung from her mouth with the bulkiest key, obviously for a vehicle, between her teeth. Her mane was ruffled with self-importance.

Lyre squeezed out of the van and nearly pressed against Piper in his anxiety. A dozen yards away, the Consulate was lit up like a party house. Dark figures moved in and out. A group of handlers were leading several dog-like creatures around the perimeter of the house. Prefect cruisers, their purple and orange lights flashing, were scattered over the manicured lawn.

Ash slid around the corner of the van into the deeper shadows on its far side. Piper took one last longing look at the Consulate and followed him, Lyre on her heels. The draconian crept to the passenger door, peeked in the window, then took the keychain from Zwi. He fit the largest key into the door and quietly unlocked it. Opening it just as carefully, he gestured for Piper to get in. Breathing fast, she crawled onto the wide seat, keeping below the windows. Lyre climbed in after her, kneeling on the floor and hunching his torso over the seat.

Ash scooped Zwi off his shoulder and put her on Lyre's shoulder. "Wait here," he whispered to the three of them. He shut the door with barely a sound and vanished from the window.

"Where's he going?" Piper whispered shrilly.

"There are two prefects guarding the van," Lyre whispered back. "On the other side."

As the seconds crawled by, Piper's legs twitched from adrenaline. Then the driver's door popped open and Ash jumped in. The key was in the ignition the next second and the engine started with a cough of protest. He shifted the vehicle into gear and, with more self-control than Piper could have managed, let the van roll into motion. His knuckles were white from his grip on the steering wheel, one hand and arm still coated in dried blood, but he didn't accelerate as he wove between parked squad cars and waiting prefects. No one looked twice.

They were half a mile along the long drive of the Consulate when Ash finally put his foot down. The van's engine roared and he turned off the vehicle's lights. The road and bordering trees vanished in the darkness. Only the pale blue light low on the eastern horizon offered any point of reference.

Piper sat up on the seat, staring at her trembling hands so she didn't have to look at the invisible road whipping beneath the van. She was sure Ash could see fine but that didn't make it any easier to endure. Lyre shifted from the floor to the seat and slumped against the door, pale and shaky.

She swallowed hard and didn't ask Ash where they were going because she didn't want him to say he didn't know. They were fugitives. Not only were they wanted by the prefects for conspiracy and nine counts of murder, but everyone thought they'd stolen the Sahar. Once it leaked they were the top suspects, every power-hungry daemon out there—and they were *all* power hungry—would start hunting them. Every haemon with more ambition than morals would be after them. Every human who wanted to compete in the dangerous daemon community would be on watch for any hint of them. There was nowhere safe to go.

And the fact that they *had* the Sahar only made it worse.

She closed her eyes. The only two people in the world she could trust right now were sitting on either side of her and she couldn't trust them at all. They were daemons. Her only flimsy insurance was the accusation against them. Whoever possessed the Sahar would be hunted for the rest of his life, as the three of them would now be hunted. Everyone wanted the Sahar, but no one wanted anyone else to know they had it.

She cracked an eyelid open to peek at Ash's profile. She hoped he knew where he was going because she didn't have a single idea. She didn't know what to do at all. All she knew was she had to find her father—and she didn't have a clue where to start there either.

CHAPTER
- 5 -

PIPER HAD NEVER been so tired in her life but she couldn't sleep. Lyre snored quietly, curled up in the passenger seat of the car Ash had stolen after they'd ditched the prefect van. She was stretched out in the relative comfort of the backseat, trying to enjoy the cessation of movement. Even though the sky was heavily overcast, the afternoon sun stabbed her aching eyes. There was no shade at their current stopover.

She had never spent much time in the city; the Consulate was located just outside the city, near a decent neighborhood where Piper went to school. She'd only ever seen the slums from its outer edges.

After escaping the prefects, Ash had taken them straight into the city, driven until the van ran out of gas, found a vehicle with a full tank, then driven for hours more. Daemons had ways of tracking people that had nothing to do with physical clues or scent and Ash hadn't taken any chances. He'd circled, backtracked, crisscrossed, and otherwise created a tangled mess of trails through the whole city. The prefects would know they were somewhere in the city but wouldn't be able to pinpoint their location without a systematic grid search.

Piper sat up slowly, stretching aching muscles. Curling up beside the window, she stared at the depressing scenery. Their junker of a car was parked between two vehicle skeletons. The lot was a wrecking yard for old cars, the dead machinery scattered randomly or stacked in flattened piles. Their car blended right in, though it did have more intact windows than most.

She looked past the car graveyard to the dilapidated streets. Seventy years ago, the area had probably been full of trendy shops and restaurants. Now, the bones of a few cars slowly dissolved into rust in front of boarded-up buildings, nasty-looking bars, and nastier-looking apartments. Most cities were pretty much the same. Bombs and biological warfare and weapons of mass destruction had left civilization in ruins. The war had lasted only three years and killed more people than anyone had bothered to count.

Before humanity could finish destroying itself and Earth, daemons had sacrificed their anonymity to preserve their favorite playground. In one swift move, they butchered military leaders across the planet, destroyed the remaining weapons of mass destruction, and left the surviving humans to sort through the rubble. Not exactly diplomatic, but it had worked.

It took people a long time to get over the sudden revelation that "demons" and "angels" existed and weren't anything like the myths. It was taking society even longer to get over the war.

Piper rubbed her face. So tired. She'd been up for almost thirty hours. She hadn't eaten in half that time. But her mind wouldn't shut up and let her rest. Everything was shit. How was she supposed to sleep when her whole life was in pieces around her feet?

As much as fear crawled through her over her own fate, it was fear for her family that had her wide awake. Her Uncle Calder, burned and broken. "On the edge," Ash had said. The prefects had transferred Calder to a medical facility, but what if treatment had come too late?

Then there was her father. What had happened in that vault? She knew beyond any doubt that Quinn hadn't betrayed the Consulate by trying to steal the Sahar. If there was a Consul with unshakable honor and integrity, it was her father. But the prefects had been convinced her father had caused the explosion. Even Ash had said the magic signature was haemon, and there'd been only two haemons in that vault.

Lyre had tentatively suggested that Calder wasn't as innocent as he seemed but Piper had shot that one down instantly. Calder was the most loyal man she knew.

The most puzzling part of it all was that her father had given her the Sahar before the meeting. That meant, in spite of what the sergeant had said about needing three magicians—meaning Quinn, Calder, and one of the ambassadors—to remove the Sahar, her father had somehow gotten it out of the vault in advance. He'd expected something to go wrong.

She stared at the torn fabric ceiling of the car. Was that why her father had found a reason to send her upstairs? But where was Quinn now? Why had he vanished?

Why had he abandoned her when she needed him most?

She swallowed again before the prick of tears overwhelmed her. Giving up on sleep, she quietly pushed open the car door and stepped into the cool afternoon. Beyond the front bumper of their car, a haphazard pile of crushed cars was stacked fifteen feet high. Halfway up, in a shaded nook created by a car bent nearly in half, Ash sat on a crumpled hood, nearly invisible in the shadows. He'd volunteered to keep watch while she and Lyre slept, but since she wasn't sleeping anyway, he might as well get some rest.

She knew he was watching her as she climbed wearily to his perch. With a wary peek at his face, she gingerly sat beside him and scooted back into the welcome shade.

"Hey," she mumbled, feeling awkward.

He slid an appraising glance at her and didn't answer. She shivered under his cool look, wishing he would drop the creepy aura for once.

Dark smudges created half-circle bruises under his eyes and his arm was covered in dried blood that he'd made a half-hearted effort to rub off. Even in a torn hoodie and black PJ bottoms, he managed to look badass. Maybe it was the bloodstains. He ignored her after his initial assessment, staring across the parking lot, his focus shifting ceaselessly as he watched for signs of life.

Piper was too tired to worry about his unfriendly silence, but soft trills made her look over again. Zwi hopped off the crumpled car behind them and dropped onto Ash's head. With her little lizard hands gripping fistfuls of his bangs, she trilled a sort of greeting at Piper, then curled her neck to look upside down into Ash's face. He irritably waved her out of his line of vision.

Piper waited for Ash to move his pet. He looked ridiculous with his dragonet hat and his hair sticking everywhere. Ash kept on staring across the lot, oblivious. Maybe he didn't deliberately cultivate a persona of intimidation; he simply was that way. She didn't find the thought comforting at all.

Zwi made another cheerful little sound and jumped into Ash's lap. He absently stroked her head and she closed her eyes blissfully. Piper tried not to stare, befuddled by the sight of the draconian cuddling his pet.

"You can take a break now, if you want," she said finally, forcing her gaze across the lot. "I can't sleep."

"It's fine," he murmured. His usually silky voice was as gray as the clouds with fatigue. "You should keep trying. You need rest."

"You need it more," she said stubbornly. "You fought a choronzon," she continued, ticking it off on a finger. "You lost a gallon of blood, broke your handcuffs, blasted off that nasty collar, knocked out two prefects, stole a car, and drove for hours. I think you need sleep more than me."

He finally really looked at her, his expression bemused. "Do you still have it?"

She patted the top of her shirt. "Yep."

His gaze dropped to her chest but she couldn't get offended; he wasn't sizing her up like Lyre would. He sighed and leaned back. "What a mess."

With a glum nod, she propped her chin in one hand. "I don't have a clue what to do."

"I've been thinking it over," he said, his words coming slow and heavy with thought. He stared at the lot, but this time his gaze was distant. "The prefects assume this was all engineered by Quinn, but we know his involvement was of a different nature; he already had the Stone and he gave it to you." He brooded for a few seconds. "There must have been a third party at the Consulate last night."

Piper straightened. "What do you mean?"

"Someone set that choronzon loose, didn't they? Not only that, but it was being magically controlled; it came after us like a bloodhound on a scent. And who killed the guards outside the vault? If Quinn did it, as the prefects think, would the ambassadors have casually accompanied him into the vault? Unless one of the group joined late, killing the guards secretly on his way in …" Ash's voice dropped into a thoughtful murmur, more to himself than Piper. "It would have been someone unexpected … perhaps Calder, but if he was involved, why was he attacked along with the ambassadors? No." He slowly shook his head. "The choronzon is the giveaway. Neither Calder nor Quinn would have loosed that beast in the house with you in it."

Piper leaned back slightly, silent as she watched Ash think. She'd never had an actual conversation with him before. It was weird.

"A third party makes sense," he said. "Someone had to smuggle the choronzon out of the Underworld and transport it to the Consulate. Maybe they thought they needed to keep us too busy to interfere; maybe they didn't know it was just the three of us in there." His jaw flexed. "Or maybe they did. Anything less than a choronzon wouldn't have been enough to distract *me*."

She raised her eyebrows but he was still talking.

"While the choronzon was tearing the manor apart, someone, more likely a group, snuck into the vault after Quinn and the team, killing the guards on their way in. Quinn and the ambassadors would have been cornered. The new group probably tried to time it right as Quinn removed the Sahar from its protections. Did they immediately realize the Stone was a fake? It wouldn't have been hard to tell if they'd opened the box."

Ash rubbed a hand over his face. "It must have been a desperate situation. Why did Quinn attack like that? Unless …" He frowned.

"Unless what?"

He met her frightened stare. "Unless he was attacking the intruders and not the ambassadors. Maybe it was already too late for them. I saw bullet casings on the floor."

"You think the intruders had already shot the ambassadors and … and Uncle Calder?" She hadn't noticed casings or gunshot wounds, but the explosion had mangled the bodies.

"Think about it," Ash said in a low voice. "No one is expecting them. Three men with guns could have taken out everyone in that vault in seconds. There was nowhere to hide and the element of surprise would have delayed their retaliation long enough for three attackers to shoot multiple people. The would-be thieves would have spared Quinn so he could give them the Sahar in case there was some sort of additional protection on it. Instead of surrendering and likely being killed as well, Quinn tried to kill them instead."

"But he must have failed," she said, her voice quavering. "There weren't any extra bodies and why else would he have vanished?"

Ash nodded. "I agree. I think the intruders kidnapped Quinn instead. After that explosion, they had to leave quickly but still needed to question him on the whereabouts of the real Stone."

Panic flared through her. She jerked straight. "We have to find him! If they think he knows where the Sahar is, they'll torture him until he tells them. We have to save him."

Ash looked at her without emotion. "And you know where they've taken him?"

She wilted. "What do we do?"

"Quinn is a highly intelligent, magically gifted haemon; he'll have to take care of himself for now. We have our own lives to save first."

"But—"

"Our enemies are twofold." He spoke right over her protest. "The daemon and haemon communities will be a threat once it gets around that we have the Sahar. Then there's the threat of the prefects; it will take something significant to clear our names." He scowled. "If it weren't for the prefects, we could solve our problems easily enough. We'd just have to arrange for the Sahar be stolen from us in a public scene. Once everyone knew we didn't have it, we'd be safe."

She wondered how you could "arrange" to be publicly robbed. "But we can't do that because it will look like we stole the Sahar first."

He nodded. "I know."

"So … what do we do?"

Ash was silent for a long minute. His gaze was distant, his expression tired, but there was a tightness to his face, a flex of the muscles in his jaw that spoke of anger—fury even. The cast of the shadows sharpened his cheekbones and hid his eyes, heightening the clinging sense of menace. He seemed calm enough, yet Piper's instincts thought he wasn't calm at all … more like he was murderously angry.

But when he spoke, his voice was so weary and somber that she doubted her assessment.

"We got screwed. I think they initially intended to take the Sahar and frame Quinn, but we ended up looking guilty instead."

Piper twisted her hands together. "If we *didn't* have the Sahar, we'd only have to prove they stole it. What are we supposed to do?"

He inhaled slowly and let it out in a sigh. "I'm still working on that. We can't decide anything until we know who is responsible. We have no idea what type of power we're up against."

"They're probably Underworld daemons." She folded her arms and looked across the lot. "Who else would be able to find and control a choronzon?"

Ash shrugged. "It's a possibility, but the right Underworld allies could have arranged that for them."

She sighed. What they needed was a witness or something, someone who could provide more clues … someone who'd seen these people. But all the witnesses to the crime were dead or missing.

Well, all except for one.

"Uncle Calder," she said.

"What?"

She turned toward him, excited and anxious at the same time. "Uncle Calder. We need to ask Uncle Calder what happened. He's the only survivor aside from my father and we won't find my father until we find the attackers."

Ash opened his mouth, probably to argue, but closed it again. "I think you're right," he finally said. "We need more information and he's the only source."

"Excellent! So we find out which medical center he's at and sneak in to talk to him …" She trailed off, her excitement draining away as the enormity of the challenge sunk in.

"We should wait until tomorrow night," Ash said, "to increase the chances that Calder will have recovered enough to talk. We can't wait too long or they could move him."

"Right," Piper agreed faintly. Medical facilities, as a rule, had tough security. Plus Calder was the only person of interest who wasn't missing or escaped and would probably have prefect guards day and night. They also had to figure out which facility he was at. They couldn't start phoning at random; no one would give that kind of information to unidentified callers.

"We can work out the details after we've all slept," Ash said.

She nodded vaguely. The more she thought about it, the more impossible it seemed. "I'll wake Lyre and send him up so you can sleep too," she said as she shuffled to the edge of the car pile and began to climb down. She was almost to the ground when Ash spoke again.

"Piper," he said, his voice low. "Keep the Stone close."

She swallowed, staring upward. Maybe it was her imagination, but she was sure if she could have seen his face, there would have been a terrible, violent fury written across his features.

◦ ◦ ◦

With the beginnings of a plan in place, Piper was finally able to sleep. At some point before she woke, Ash and Zwi had stolen them some snacks and bottled water from a store a few blocks away. Fed and refreshed, the three of them went over their plan, playing out every scenario they could imagine.

Throughout their discussions, she kept an eye on Ash, but he showed no flashes of rage or any other emotion. He looked as inscrutable as ever and slightly creepy with that soul-searing stare.

His freaky factor had improved once he'd gotten rid of the blood on his arm. He'd even braided the red silk ribbon along the side of his head again to look slightly less disreputable. She hadn't forgotten his violent reputation, though.

Aside from surreptitiously monitoring Ash, Piper obsessively checked that the ring box was still tightly lodged in her bra. At this rate, she would have a permanent dent in her flesh, but after waking with the box worked halfway out, she wasn't taking any chances.

They slept through the following day, taking turns to watch for signs of prefects. Ash's convoluted trail was working; there was no sign of a search. Maybe the prefects had given up, though Piper didn't put a lot of hope into the thought. She wasn't that lucky.

Shortly after nine o'clock the following evening, Piper crouched behind a dumpster with Ash and Lyre on either side of her, staring across the street at the brightly lit medical center.

Ash had decided they should start with the medical center closest to the Consulate. Piper's heart pounded. Aside from the lights, the place looked deserted.

"Ready?" Ash whispered.

Piper nodded, glancing at her comrades. Both were unrecognizable in stolen jeans, black t-shirts, and runners. Both daemons had adopted new glamours, opting to look like normal humans with nondescript brown hair and eyes. Apparently, changing eye color required a lot of effort. Ash looked unremarkable, and hopefully forgettable, but Lyre was the same level of mouthwatering gorgeous as usual, only in a different color scheme—all part of the plan.

She glanced at her own unflattering jeans and blah gray t-shirt. If Ash was keeping his end of the deal, her hair was now tacky bleach blond and her eyes would be blue instead of green. She'd had no idea daemons could apply glamour to other people, but Ash was no regular daemon. Even for him, it was tricky and took a lot of concentration; it also required him to be touching her, which was why they were holding hands. Awkward.

Lyre took a deep breath, rose to his feet, and strode boldly out into the street. She and Ash watched him vanish through the double doors and into the medical center. They waited. After three minutes, Ash tugged her up and, trying to look like holding his hand didn't bother her at all, she let him lead her to the doors. Her heart felt like it was beating against the back of her throat.

Inside, the bright lights made her squint. A long counter shielded by thick, scratched plastic overlooked a large waiting room full of mismatched chairs. On either side of the counter, barred doors like jail cells offered glimpses of long halls. Patients being admitted were buzzed through the right side door. Patients on their way out used the left side door. A bored security guard sat on a chair inside the right-hand door, reading a tattered book.

Lyre leaned against the plastic barrier, talking to the middle-aged nurse on the other side of the desk. She was the only other person in the room besides the security guard. Her attention was fixed on the incubus's face and a bright blush stained her cheeks. Every couple of seconds, her gaze would sweep as much of his torso as was visible before locking on his face again.

Ash steered Piper to two chairs near the security guard's door and plunked down, managing to look irritated, bored, and anxious at the same time. Piper perched on the edge of her seat, breathing too quickly and knowing she looked anxious, bordering on panicky. Ash cast an impatient look at the desk as though he were waiting his turn to talk to the nurse. Piper bit her lip and tried not to stare at Lyre. When an incubus really turned on the charm, it was risky to even look at him.

Lyre leaned against the barrier as if it were the only thing stopping him from swooping down on the woman right where she sat. His eyes smoldered like muted fire, roving across her face as though he couldn't stop himself, and that sexy half-smile tugged at one corner of his mouth. He murmured through the circle of holes in the plastic that enabled conversations, his words soft and intimate. The woman giggled, pressing one hand to the base of her throat.

Piper looked away, teeth clenched as she suppressed an uncalled-for urge to drape herself over the incubus. That poor woman didn't stand a chance. A human might have wondered why the nurse was buying it; not only was she twice Lyre's age, but even in her youth, she'd probably never had such a good-looking young man look twice at her. It was all part of the incubus magic; women always fell for it, no matter how unlikely his attention, how exaggerated his compliments, how farfetched his promises. No girl was immune.

The nurse drank in every one of Lyre's hot looks and velvet words, blushing even more brightly. Barely two minutes later, she stood and sauntered toward the gate, her wide hips swaying. The light overhead blinked green and a low buzzer sounded. Smiling without breaking eye contact, Lyre pushed the barred door open. The security guard barely glanced up from his book. The incubus stopped inside the door, one hand resting on a steel bar as he let his worshipful stare travel slowly over the nurse as if she were Aphrodite's reincarnation. Even Piper was impressed by his acting skills; incubi generally went for the young and gorgeous.

Ash slid from his seat, pulling her by the hand while she shook off the haze of inappropriate fantasies parading through her mind. Damn horny incubus thoughts.

Lyre moved away from the door as Ash took his place. He lured the nurse down the hall so smoothly she never even noticed Ash and Piper coming through the still-open door. The security guard looked up and saw them. His mouth opened furiously. Ash stood in the threshold, staring like he'd forgotten where he was. Panic flashed through Piper. Before the guard could speak, she plastered on a vacant smile and plopped down on his lap. His jaw dropped, his protest forgotten.

"Hi," she said breathily, batting her eyelashes. Unfortunately, she wasn't a succubus, so the man stared at her for only a second before he looked at the oblivious Ash with an "is she effing crazy?" look.

Ash was still holding her hand. She slung her other arm around the man's neck and cuddled in. "I missed you, daddy," she cooed in a little girl voice. "Where have you *been*?" She giggled brainlessly.

The guard looked outraged at being mistaken for dad-aged. With a sudden shake of his head, Ash finally snapped out of it. He mumbled an apology as he leaned over her as if he were going to pick her up. Instead, he caught the guard's wrist. The air sizzled with magic and the man's eyes rolled back. His head lolled as he went limp and started snoring.

Piper lurched to her feet and shoved Ash with both hands, forcing him out of the way. As he stepped back, her hair blinked from blond back to red and black. "What the hell was that, Ash?" she spat. "You almost ruined everything."

He again looked down the hall, his nostrils flaring. Without a single word of explanation or defense, he shook his head and turned toward the nurse's desk. Piper almost burst with fury but before she could say anything else, Zwi sprang onto the desk, a file folder already clamped between her teeth. Ash scooped her off the desk and passed Piper the folder. She swallowed her anger, saving it for later, and snapped the file open. It was her uncle's. Could Zwi read?

"He's in room 344," she read. "Damn. I was hoping he'd be on the main level." She skimmed the page. "Thank God. It says he's expected to recover … anticipate scarring … damage to left eye … broken ribs on right side … oh no."

"What?" Ash demanded.

"It says his throat was damaged from …" She squinted at the page. "From inhaling superheated air during the explosion. What if he can't talk?"

"Only one way to find out," Ash muttered, grabbing her hand. Her hair turned blond again. "Let's find the stairs."

Lyre had vanished with the middle-aged nurse. Lucky for him, he didn't have to do anything with the woman—an incubus talking dirty could keep a girl distracted for quite a while. The idea was to get in and out without anyone in the medical center realizing something shifty had happened. Ash couldn't put everyone to sleep.

They passed two cranky-looking nurses on their way down the hall. Piper had to work hard to act natural, but Ash, like all daemons, was a flawless actor. The nurses barely glanced at him. She hoped Ash hadn't noticed how sweaty her palm was getting. What she wouldn't give to have a weapon hidden on her somewhere; they could run into gun-toting prefects at any moment.

They found the stairs without incident. As they began climbing, Piper's nerves ratcheted higher. Ash glanced at her and she knew her anxiety was triggering instincts he normally kept suppressed—those pesky hunter instincts that made him want to pounce on fearful prey.

Reaching the third floor, he peeked through the heavy metal fire door and immediately ducked back inside. Zwi changed color to match the whitewashed brick walls and slipped through the crack. Piper clutched Ash's hand and leaned closer.

"Prefects?" she mouthed.

He shook his head. "Doctor," he whispered.

She squinted at him. "Uh, so what's the problem?"

"He's a daemon," he explained, peering through the crack. "He'll recognize me as daemon straight off."

The minutes ticked by, their precious time trickling away. Sooner or later, someone would find the sleeping guard and shake him out of his magic-induced nap. The guard would then wonder where those two kids had gone. And Lyre couldn't keep the nurse busy forever.

As she waited, a flicker of motion caught her attention. A big, black spider clung to the wall near the landing a few feet away. She sucked in a breath and inched back. It crawled a little farther up the wall. She stared, barely breathing.

"What are you doing?" Ash hissed.

She blinked, realizing she was pushing him into the door in her unconscious attempt to get away from the spider. "Uh—"

"Where are my keys?" someone male demanded right on the other side of the door. A female voice muttered a reply, then the guy growled, "They were in my pocket a minute ago." Another female mutter. "I didn't *drop them.*"

Ash smirked into the line of light leaking between the door and jam. Piper smiled nervously. Zwi was brilliant.

"Let's go," Ash said as the thumping footsteps retreated. He straightened and stepped boldly through the threshold. Piper leaped to follow, delighted to leave the spider behind. The hallway smelled strongly of chemicals and was quiet with a sleepy sort of stillness. Closed doors lined the hall, each with a number. The nearest was 302.

"Which way?" she whispered.

A trilling sound made them both look up. Zwi clung to the ceiling, a ring of keys in her mouth and her wings flared for balance. She scuttled off toward the east end of the building. Together, she and Ash strode after her. The hall seemed to go on forever but the room numbers weren't increasing fast enough. Shouldn't there be more security guards or something? The entire floor was totally silent.

The hall took a sharp left. Ash and Piper crept to the corner and peered around it. Halfway down the hall, just as they'd feared, two prefects stood guard on either side of a closed door. They looked bored out of their minds but both had holstered handguns. This was where things got dicey.

Ash pulled her back and let go of her hand.

"Change of plan," he whispered. "I have a better idea."

He stepped back and closed his eyes. Concentration tightened his features. His whole body shimmered like he was standing on the hottest pavement ever. He grew taller and his clothes brightened into pale blue doctor's scrubs. A goatee formed on his face and he aged fifteen years. The shimmers faded and a total stranger stood in front of her, holding a clipboard under his arm. She was betting he was an identical replica of the doctor with the missing keys.

"That's ... wow," she breathed. "I didn't know you could take glamour that far."

"It's not glamour. It's an illusion."

Piper frowned. Wasn't glamour a type of illusion? Ash told her to wait there and stepped confidently around the corner.

Zwi appeared beside her, poking her pale nose around the corner to watch her master. Piper followed suit. Ash had reached the prefects. He looked down at his clipboard and said something.

It happened so fast Piper would have missed it if she'd blinked. The illusion vanished as Ash slammed a fist into each prefect's throat. They collapsed in unison, unable to make a sound. The draconian hit one then the other with his sleep spell. Piper rushed around the corner and ran to meet him.

Well, so much for the no-suspicious-behavior strategy. Maybe the prefects would assume the doctor was crazy. Together, they dragged the prefects into an empty room across the hall. Then, shaking slightly with nerves, Piper reached for the doorknob to room 344.

The door swung open before she touched the handle.

CHAPTER

- 6 -

AT THE SAME TIME the door handle disappeared from under her hand, Ash yanked her back. He backed up so swiftly Piper tripped on her own feet.

Two men stood in the doorway grinning—no, leering. They were daemons. Even though their glamours made them essentially indistinguishable from humans, Piper had years of training in recognizing daemons; it was more a gut instinct than any sort of telltale sign. Daemons just had this *feeling* to them.

These two looked like leather-clad bounty hunters, heavily muscled and tattooed, no less than six and half feet of nasty bully mixed with powerful arrogance. One of them massaged his knuckles as if he couldn't wait to use them. The second, sporting a blond Mohawk, folded his arms with difficulty—too much bulging muscle —and kept on leering.

Knuckles gave Piper a dismissive sneer and focused on Ash.

"So," he rumbled like that one word said everything.

Mohawk licked his lips. "Figured you'd show up here, dragon-boy. Come to finish the shmuck off? You shoulda killed him right the first time."

"What are you doing in that room?" Piper demanded.

They ignored her. "You've blown it," Mohawk went on in his gravelly voice. "Were you actually stupid enough to steal it and get caught? Damn, that's amateur. Tempted, were you?" He shook his head in mock sadness. "The boss ain't happy, dragon-boy. He wants it. And he especially didn't want the damn prefect-patrol involved."

"You're on our hit list now, buddy," Knuckles added with another leer.

"Maybe if you give it to us, *we* won't kill you," Mohawk said. "But unlikely. Either way, you're dead."

Piper swallowed hard. As she'd known would happen, rumors had leaked into the daemon community that they had the Sahar. Ash was well known; of course would-be thieves of the Stone would track him down first.

"I didn't steal it." Ash raised his eyebrows. "Do I look like I possess infinite power?"

"That don't mean a thing," Knuckles said. "We hear it's hard to use. Still figuring it out, ain't ya?"

"Besides," Mohawk said, rolling his shoulders to loosen the muscles, "even if you didn't steal it, everyone still thinks you did. Just as bad, wouldn't you say? You screwed up. Boss doesn't tolerate anyone who screws up his business. You know that."

Piper looked back and forth between Ash and Mohawk. The conversation wasn't quite making sense anymore. Had she missed something?

"But I think you did steal it. Couldn't resist a bit more power, could you? Hand it over now and I'll kill you quick and clean—better than what the rest of the boss's beasts have planned for you."

Ash exhaled. He angled closer to Piper and brought his mouth to her ear. "I'll take care of these two," he whispered. "You get in there and talk to your uncle. I'll meet you outside."

"Can you handle them?" she whispered back, eyeing the two goons. They oozed cruelty, but more than that, the air around them was already crackling with magic. They weren't minor daemons.

"I'll be fine," he said, sounding grouchy.

"What will it be, dragon-boy?"

Ash turned to the goons, looked at them for a long moment—and then walked away.

"If you give us the—hey!" Mohawk yelled. "I'm talking here!"

Ash kept on walking. Both goons started after him with angry snarls, striding right past Piper as though she didn't exist. She stared after them. Wasn't it customary to *taunt* your enemies to make them follow you? Remembering what she was supposed to be doing, she rushed through the open door and snapped it shut behind her. She then turned to the lone bed in the room and her heart squeezed in her chest.

The man on the bed was wrapped in so many bandages he was unrecognizable. Beeping equipment, made up of chunks of mismatched machinery patched together, surrounded him. New hospital equipment was scarce so repairs were made with whatever was available. The overhead lights were dimmed, leaving everything layered in shadows.

Piper crept to the side of the bed. Bandages were wrapped around his head and over his left eye. In typical Uncle Calder fashion, he seemed to sense her presence and his right eye cracked open. The green orb, exactly like hers, gazed at the ceiling before drifting over to her. It widened in shocked recognition.

"Uncle Calder," she gasped, and to her horror, she burst into tears.

With shaking fingers, she found his hand under the blankets and clutched it, weeping like a little kid. It took her several deep breaths to get under control. Sniffling, she tried to smile.

"Sorry," she gasped, swallowing repeatedly against the lump in her throat. "I was so afraid you'd died …"

He managed a bit of a smile, impressive with tape all over his face and a tube in his nose. She squeezed his hand and sniffled again. Okay, focus.

"Can you talk?" she asked.

He twisted his lips into something like a grimace. No, apparently.

"Okay," she muttered, thinking fast. "Okay, just listen then." As succinctly as she could, she outlined everything that had happened since the explosion in the vault. "And we can't clear our names unless we find out who did this first," she finished.

Calder's mouth hung open, whether with shock or horror she couldn't tell. Piper paused, then swallowed hard. "Did—did Father kill everyone in the vault?" she whispered.

He blinked rapidly and his lips formed a silent "no."

She slumped in relief. "I knew it," she breathed, then quickly straightened. "So do you know who attacked you?" She twisted her hands together. "Did you recognize them or … or something?"

Calder didn't respond, staring at her with the strangest look, almost like he was afraid to answer. Finally, after what felt like a full minute, he gave the tiniest nod.

She squeezed his hand and leaned forward, her heart pounding. "Who?" she demanded. "Who was it?"

He stared back at her helplessly, his lips forming silent words. She'd always sucked at lip-reading. She swore under her breath and looked around the barren room. Leaping to her feet, she grabbed the clipboard off the foot of his bed, tore off a sheet, and flipped it to the blank back.

"Okay," she said breathlessly. "I'll recite the alphabet. Close your eye and when I hit the first letter, open it. We'll spell out a name."

He smiled his agreement. She began, making it all the way to S before his eye opened. She wrote it on her paper and started again. The next letter was A. Then F. The letter E followed, but Calder wouldn't close his eye after that.

"Safe?" she read. She held up the paper. "'Safe' is the name? That's not a name!"

He stared at her, frowning. Apparently she wasn't getting the message.

"Are you telling me to be safe? Or go somewhere safe instead of trying to find these people?" Fury launched her to her feet. "Don't you get it? There is nowhere safe for me anymore. I'm a fugitive. If the prefects catch me, they'll lock me up forever. And if they don't get me, some daemon or haemon is going to skewer me and steal the Stone."

Calder closed his eye again and Piper almost screamed at him she was so mad, but then he opened it and gave her a "get on with it" look. She realized he wanted to spell something else. Forcing herself to sit again, she started the alphabet. O-F-F-I-C-E.

"Office?" she repeated blankly. "Safe and office? Your office is not safe!"

His brow furrowed. Safe. Office. How did those two words equal the attackers? Then it clicked.

"The safe in Father's office," she said triumphantly. Calder smiled. "You have information in there? I don't know the combination."

Calder closed his eye and they started the spelling game again, this time with numbers. 14-25-9. The combination.

"Thank you, Uncle Calder," she whispered, leaning down to give him a gentle hug. "We'll find out who these people are and we'll get Father back. I promise."

He slowly mouthed two words: Be careful.

"I will, don't worry. Ash and Lyre are helping me."

Instead of appearing comforted, Calder's face scrunched with worry. He looked at her chest, then back to her face. His mouth moved again, forming a single word—oh! Sahar. He was asking about the Sahar.

She patted her chest. "It's right here. I still have it."

He squinted at her hand over the hidden box and gave her an imploring look.

"You want to see it?" She huffed and muttered about him not believing her but she still stuck a hand in the front of her t-shirt and pulled out the little black ring box. She flipped it open, glanced at the little gray stone, and held it out for her uncle to see.

He looked at the Sahar and paled so fast she could almost see the blood draining from his face. His expression was unmistakably horrified.

"Uncle Calder?" she yelped, jumping up. "What's wrong? Are you in pain?"

His mouth opened—and the hospital exploded.

Piper hit the floor, clutching the ring box to her chest as the floor quaked. Equipment fell off stands and crashed to the floor. A wave of low-level electricity rippled through the air in the wake of the explosion—magic. She lifted her head, realizing the building hadn't exploded. But something had.

She launched to her feet, stuffing the box back into her shirt, and dashed to Calder's side. Seeing he was okay, she grabbed him in a brief, intense hug.

"I have to go. I love you."

When she burst out the door of the room, she found a medical center in chaos. Nurses were running everywhere. Patients had come out of their rooms and all the missing security guards had finally materialized. With people screaming and running around like idiots, no one noticed Piper. She looked around wildly, trying to remember which way the stairwell was.

A piercing scream cut through all the noise and a woman came tearing down the hall at full pelt.

"Monsters!" she shrieked hysterically. "Monsters in the lounge!"

Another boom shook the building so hard half the people crowding the hall fell over. Piper grabbed a wall for balance, breathing fast. "Monsters" meant daemons without glamour. She knew of only five daemons in the building—Ash, Lyre, Mohawk, Knuckles, and Doctor Daemon. Piper was pretty sure she knew which three were having an all-out battle in the lounge.

She ran in the direction the screaming lady had come from. Come to think of it, why was that daemon impersonating a human doctor? No matter how good at healing magic they might be, daemons weren't allowed in medical centers that treated humans; some castes liked to feed off pain and suffering.

At the end of the hall was a large open room full of chairs, sofas, and tables with magazines—a lounge for visiting family members to wait. As she barreled up to the opening, a sofa came flying out. Piper ducked and it crashed into a medical cart behind her.

Something roared inside the lounge—something big, mean, and completely inhuman. Before she could decide if she dared enter, ten feet of hairy minotaur stalked out. It had hooves like cinder blocks and massive bull horns. Its black eyes scoured the hall, mad with fury and, judging by the blood gushing from the deep wound across its belly, pain. Piper gaped. How had that *thing* been disguised in glamour? It wasn't possible.

After a moment of dead silence, the hall behind Piper erupted in a cacophony of terrified screams. The minotaur flinched at the sound then roared. The force of the sound knocked her back and she clamped her hands over her ears. The people behind her stampeded down the hall, trampling the slow and weak in their panic.

Maybe she should've been running away too.

The minotaur looked down and spotted Piper standing there like a dimwit. Even armed to the teeth she wouldn't have been a match for this beast. Maybe a haemon with magic would have had a chance, but she had nothing but her own strength and brains—not enough against a ten-foot mutant bull.

Another massive crash sounded from somewhere behind the minotaur. He flicked one cow ear backward. The fight was still going on in the lounge. Was Ash battling the second daemon? She snapped a glance past the beast's legs, trying to see into the room beyond.

The minotaur charged. Piper leaped forward and the beast's fist smashed into the floor where she'd been standing. Tiles shattered and the cement beneath split. She landed between its massive hooves. Collapsing into a compact ball, she rolled out from under it and sprang up. It took all her willpower not to look into the lounge for Ash. The minotaur was already turning. She grabbed a nearby metal chair and swung it into the back of the minotaur's knee.

It grunted angrily and spun around. She dove between its legs again, landing in another roll that carried her farther away from it. She came out on her feet and ran. She made it three steps before she realized she wasn't going anywhere. A wall of a dozen armed prefects, rifles raised, blocked the hallway.

"Fire!" someone yelled.

Piper threw herself onto the floor. The minotaur howled as twelve bullets tore into its flesh. Not enough to kill it, but as she craned her neck to look over her shoulder, it staggered backward into the lounge.

"Is that the Griffiths girl?" a prefect exclaimed.

Piper shoved herself up in a panic. Twelve guns turned to point at her. She slapped her arms in an X across her chest: the universal sign of surrender.

"Hayes, Coffey, arrest her."

Two guys in the front passed their rifles to their neighbors and unhooked handcuffs from their belts. Not being a daemon, she supposed she wasn't scary enough to warrant firearms. They were average-sized guys but prefects were never average fighters, meaning Piper had about a ten percent chance. Lucky for her, she was tough too.

She tried to look meek and defeated as they approached. When they were a step away, the closest one reached for her wrist.

Magic exploded from the lounge like a bomb going off, the shockwave blasting past them and making everyone stagger. Something inside the lounge shrieked in pain. The minotaur roared. Piper's fist snapped out and hit the nearest prefect in the diaphragm. He dropped his cuffs and doubled over. She whirled around, foot flying, and slammed her boot into the thigh of the second guy. He stumbled but didn't fall. He lunged for her. She pivoted to the side, caught his arm, and twisted it. With a yelp, he went down, yielding to the pressure she was putting on his arm before the bone snapped. She stomped her foot on his belly. He rolled over, spewing his supper.

Three more prefects circled her, looking pissed. She dropped to the floor and swung out one foot, sweeping the feet out from under the first guy. The second tried to jump on her. She rolled onto her back and slammed a double-footed kick right into his groin. His face went bloodless and he sank to his knees, unable to breathe for the pain. Pulling her legs down hard, she flipped her body off the floor and landed on her feet. Prefect number three came at her and she went to jump backward, but something grabbed her ankle.

She staggered and had to deflect the charging prefect's punch with her forearm. Feeling like her arm must have snapped in half, she ripped her foot out of the grip of the first prefect she'd downed. The third prefect swung another fist toward her face. She stepped inside his swing—no one ever expected that—and ducked to shove her forearm into his hip. She grabbed his ankle with her other hand and shoved the two-hundred-pound man right off his feet. Amazing what a little leverage in the right spot could do.

Dancing back from the prefect already rolling to his feet, she realized prefect number one was getting up too. Then she looked past them and froze.

"Steady," a prefect at the back of the group called.

Every gun was pointed at her. This time she knew they meant business. The prefects she hadn't permanently downed took a few steps back, getting out of the potential crossfire.

"Hit one more of my men and we'll open fire," the man at the back called. "Lie on the floor with your hands on the back of your head. Now!"

Before she could obey and get arrested, or disobey and get shot, the air rippled. Electricity filled the atmosphere, crackling like lightning about to strike. She heard a weird rushing sound, then there was harsh breathing right behind her; someone stood at her back.

"Are you going to shoot *me*?" The voice that asked the question was deep and guttural, sepulchral and alien in a way that froze everyone in the vicinity.

Every gun was now aimed at a point just over Piper's right shoulder. She tried to keep her breathing steady as fear tightened every prefect's face. Men who had faced the ten-foot minotaur without batting an eyelid, trained and seasoned fighters, were staring over her shoulder with shaking hands and pale faces.

She slowly licked her lips. "Ash?" she whispered.

He shifted closer until he brushed against her back. "Do you have what we need?" he breathed. The heat of his body made her shiver.

"Yes," she breathed back.

He huffed in relief, sounding almost normal for a second. Then he slid one arm around her waist, delicately as though he were afraid of accidentally crushing her.

"Don't move or we'll shoot," the prefect leader yelled.

"That," Ash said as he extended one hand in front of Piper, "would only make me angry."

Piper stared at his hand, too shocked to move or to think. His outspread fingers were black with a dull gleam like leather, the tips smoothly forming long claws. Large black scales covered the back of his hand and ran up the top of his arm like an armguard. The scales gave way to human skin, leaving the underside of his arm disconcertingly normal. Somehow, that was even freakier.

The air grew hot around them. It sizzled. The lead prefect jerked like he was about to yell the word that would riddle Piper and Ash with bullets, then light flashed in Ash's palm and everything exploded for a second time.

The concussive explosion of air blasted the prefects off their feet and sent them flying backward. Guns fired wildly, bullets ricocheting off the ceiling. Ash scooped Piper against his chest, then the world spun as he launched forward so fast it was like being shot out of a cannon. Wind tore at her face as they shot across the entire length of the hall in two seconds flat. Solid brick wall waited for them but Ash wasn't slowing.

His hand snapped outward, another flash of light, a massive boom. They burst out the brand new hole in the wall in a rush of cool night air and flying debris. They soared out over the road, three stories up, but they didn't fall. Somehow, they glided easily in a wide curve toward the ground. As they touched down, Piper looked over her shoulder and saw giant, graceful, leathery black wings folding neatly as they pulled in toward Ash's back. She blinked and they were gone.

She wrenched away from him and spun around but he was already shimmering back into glamour.

A small shape flew out of the darkness and Zwi landed on Ash's shoulder, chittering frantically. Piper watched the little dragonet's wings fold up until they lay flat on the creature's back, miniature versions of her master's hidden appendages.

Zwi made another chattering sound and turned to glare at Piper. She blinked. Then Ash slowly sank to his knees, shoulders slumping. Zwi flapped her wings and chirped wildly, clutching his shoulder. Piper jumped forward and dropped to a crouch in front of him, grabbing his shoulders and almost knocking Zwi off him.

"Ash? Ash, are you okay?"

CHASE THE DARK | 73

He looked up, unfocused and listing to one side. "Ummm," he breathed. "Probably not. Didn't go so well."

Piper pulled his arm over her shoulder and looked him over. His damn black t-shirt disguised the fact he was bleeding—a lot. Again. Couldn't this guy go three days without nearly dying?

"Come on, get up," she coaxed. "We have to get off the street. Lyre is waiting for us."

"Mmm," he mumbled incoherently, but with her help he managed to get to his feet again. He leaned on her as they staggered toward the alley. Zwi jumped off his shoulder and flew ahead, her black scales making her invisible in seconds. Ash breathed heavily and limped with each step. His blood was soaking her shirt. Another deadly fight like the one with the choronzon. Once again, he'd made it out barely walking. She glared up the alley, nursing her fury as more of Ash's blood ran down her side. If she didn't stay angry, she would panic. He was hurt. Really hurt.

"Piper," a voice hissed. Lyre appeared from the gloom, Zwi hanging off his shoulder. "Shit! Ash!"

He ducked under Ash's other arm and together they hauled him down the alley, down a few more, and ducked into an abandoned garage. Piper pushed the rotting door closed and shoved a shelving unit in front of it, then hurried to where Lyre was helping Ash sit against a wall. Zwi keened in a tiny, panicky voice, shivering against her owner's side. The incubus cupped his hands and a small blue light appeared. He pushed it into the air and let it go. It hung there like a tiny moon.

Ash was breathing hard, staring at nothing. "Ow ..." he whispered.

Piper and Lyre exchanged frightened looks. He grabbed Ash's cheap t-shirt and ripped it up the side. Piper gasped.

Ash had been gored. His stomach was a bloody mess like he'd been raked across the belly with a gardening claw. Blood was all over him. Neither she nor Lyre could do a damn thing for a wound like that. He needed surgery to put his insides back inside him.

"What ... what ... " Lyre's hands fluttered over the wreckage of Ash's stomach, not daring to touch.

"Two daemons were waiting for us," Piper whimpered. With nothing else to do, she balled up the torn shirt and pressed it against the wound—as if that would help. He'd merely die a little less quickly. "One was a minotaur."

"Stupid animal," Ash muttered. His eyes rolled toward Lyre, feverishly bright and dull at the same time. "Ripped his filthy head off."

Piper blinked, wondering if he was remembering the fight right.

"What about the second one?" Lyre whispered.

"Cottus, the bastard," Ash mumbled. "Got me when I killed Henoces before he could … go after Piper again …"

Lyre swallowed hard. "Why would Cottus attack you? Unless—"

Ash's eyes darted toward Piper.

Lyre bit off his sentence, then pressed both hands to his face. "This is bad."

"'S not so bad," Ash breathed, almost smiling. "Piper got … stuff … you know." His breathing was getting faster, harsher.

"Ash, you're dying," Lyre snapped. "I don't care about the Stone right now."

"Oh," Ash muttered. "Yeah, guess … not." He frowned. "Dying, huh … Sucks."

Her lips trembled. "You can't die," she told him angrily. "You told me you'd be fine. I thought you were tougher than this! Isn't half the Underworld afraid of you?"

"Nah," he said breathily. His head thumped back into the wall behind him. "They're scared of … boss."

"What boss?"

"Fucking boss," he mumbled. "Hate him."

"What are you talking about?"

"Piper, leave him be." Lyre's voice shook.

She looked at the t-shirt. It was soaked through, blood dribbling over her hands and down her arms. Her hands shook as she kept on pressing it against his wound. Tears spilled over her cheeks.

"Stupid daemon," she choked. "Stupid. Getting killed. Look what you've done."

"Don't cry," he whispered, sounding vaguely surprised.

"I'm not crying!"

"I was going to … die anyway … You heard. I screwed up … big time …"

"Huh?"

"Stole." He was gasping now. "Cursed … Stone." He slid a little sideways as he looked at Piper. "Sorry …"

"Sorry for what?" she demanded, angrily wiping tears from her face. "You saved my life. Twice."

"Three … times …"

"Shut up!" Furious and beside herself with helplessness, she tried hard to hold on to some composure. How could she just sit there while he died right in front of her? What was she supposed to do?

The door to the garage burst open, knocking the shelves over. Piper's jaw fell open, fear spinning through her.

Doctor Daemon stood in the doorway, staring at them.

CHAPTER
-7-

"You!" Piper yelled. She tried to make her glare as threatening as possible. "Get the hell out."

Not surprisingly, he didn't listen. He stepped inside and closed the door. The air crackled with magic as he did something to it, probably sealing them in. Lyre stood and put himself between them and the daemon. The doctor, still in his scrubs, stepped farther into the room.

"The prefects are searching for you," the doctor said. "I've hidden your trail, but the mask will only last until sunrise. We shouldn't waste time."

"Waste time how?" Lyre spat. "Like resisting you killing us?"

"I'm not here to kill you."

"Like we'd believe—"

"I am Vejovis."

Lyre's mouth opened but no sound came out. Piper stared, not quite sure what to think. If the daemon truly was Vejovis …

Depending on their magic and race, daemons could live a human lifespan or they could live as long as forever. Some of them were very, very old and Vejovis was one of the oldest. He was an

Overworld daemon, and though Overworlders liked to pretend they were the good guys, in reality they were just as bad as Underworld daemons. Vejovis, however, had truly renounced the typical violence of his kin and dedicated himself to the healing arts—so the legends said. He was the best healer in any of the worlds but rarely seen or heard from.

There was no way to prove this daemon was Vejovis, but it was a risky claim to make. If the real Vejovis heard about it, vow of nonviolence or not, there'd be hell to pay.

"You—you—" Lyre took an urgent step forward. "Please heal him. I beg you."

Vejovis smiled coolly. "That's why I'm here."

"Get lost," Ash rasped unexpectedly.

"Now, now," Vejovis said calmly to Ash. "I estimate you have ten minutes left. If you want to live to hate me for the rest of your life, I must begin immediately."

Piper immediately leaped away from Ash and gestured for Vejovis to approach. "Heal him, please. Ash, keep your mouth shut and let him or I'll kill you myself."

Ash grunted. His face twisted with what could have been pain or loathing. What was his problem with Vejovis?

"I'd like you two to please leave the room," Vejovis said over his shoulder as he kneeled beside his patient. To Ash, he said, "Release your glamour. I need to see what I'm doing."

Piper paused, looking curiously over her shoulder in spite of the gravity of the situation, but Lyre grabbed her arm and hauled her up the flight of stairs at the back of the garage. The second floor had a small, musty apartment that hadn't seen human habitation in a long time. It was well populated with small, four-legged inhabitants though. She wrinkled her nose at the mouse crap everywhere and found what looked like a relatively clean kitchen chair. She thumped down and went to press her hands to her face before realizing they were covered in Ash's blood. Her fingers trembled.

"Will he be okay?" she whispered.

Lyre sat in the chair beside hers. "I hope so. Vejovis is a legend."

"Why does Ash hate him?"

"No idea."

She bit her lip and looked at the incubus. "Is it bad that we left them alone?"

Lyre sighed. "Ash wouldn't have dropped his glamour if we were there, and then he would have died. The worst Vejovis could do is kill him … but why bother when he was minutes from death anyway?"

"Why wouldn't Ash drop his glamour in front of us?"

"Well … in front of you," Lyre corrected. He stared at the filthy tabletop with bloodshot eyes. "He wouldn't want to frighten you."

"Ash would die just to not *frighten* me?"

He exhaled sharply. "No. But he would have argued and resisted like the stubborn idiot he is and by then it would've been too late."

"Why does it matter so much to him?"

"You don't get it, Piper. You think you know all about us but you're still just a child. How many daemons have you seen without glamour? Some don't look pretty or cool or interesting. Their real forms are alien, or ugly, or frightening. We don't show humans what we look like, because after you see, you *never* forget. You'll never believe we're human again."

"You're *not* human."

"And your human head knows that but your gut doesn't. Once you see us without this mask, this disguise," he gestured to his body, "your gut will know it too. Some daemons you can't help but fear. You will *always* be afraid. It's human nature."

"I'm a haemon," she said flatly.

"You're human where it counts."

Piper folded her arms and glared at nothing, but she couldn't stop picturing Ash's black-scaled hand, the deadly claws, that glimpse of a wing. Maybe she didn't want to know what he actually looked like.

Leaning back in her chair, she tried to relax, but she couldn't stand to sit still with nothing to do but wonder if Ash was dying below them with no one but a daemon he hated for company.

"I don't understand," she said, mainly to fill the silence, "about those daemons that attacked Ash. The minotaur and that Cottus guy …" A memory of a textbook page floated into her mind's eye and fear trickled through her. "Uh, when Ash said 'Cottus,' he didn't mean *the* Cottus, as in Cottus of the Hecatonchires brothers, did he?"

"Cottus the Striker," Lyre agreed tiredly. "One of the nastiest, most expensive mercenaries in the Underworld."

"And Ash *fought him*?"

"Unsuccessfully, considering the end result," Lyre muttered darkly.

She chewed on a fingernail. Compared to Cottus, Ash's reputation was like a summer thunderstorm to a volcanic eruption. Cottus was an ancient daemon with several millennia of accumulated nastiness.

"Who's this 'big boss' that sent Cottus after Ash?"

Lyre stared at the table as if he was concentrating hard … or thinking fast.

"You know about the main families in the Underworld. The 'big boss' would be the head of one of those families."

She frowned. The loose authority structure in both the Underworld and Overworld revolved around a handful of extremely powerful and ancient families; their names were familiar to everyone, most having been ascribed long ago to gods and goddesses of mythology. Acting in the role of regional dictators, they were always competing against one another for power and breaking into minor wars. Though the daemons had put an end to human war, they were hardly a peace-loving people.

Laying a hand over her chest where the Sahar was hidden, she frowned at Lyre. The Sahar's history was long and convoluted, but the tale generally went that a member of the most powerful Overworld family, the Ra family, created the Sahar five hundred years ago. Unfortunately for them, the Underworld families heard about it. It was stolen shortly after its creation, rumored to be in the possession of the Hades family. After that, the Sahar's travels got murky. Only in recent years was it leaked that the Hades family had it again. When the Ras found out, they demanded the Sahar be returned to them.

With the Sahar between them, the two families were on the verge of all-out war. The Ras insisted the Stone was rightfully theirs. The

Hades family denied they'd ever stolen it, and besides, after five centuries, it was finders keepers.

After years of Consul-mediated negotiations and pressure from other families, the Hades family surrendered the Sahar to the Consuls for safekeeping. While the Sahar was secretly transported to the Head Consulate, negotiations had continued until an agreement was reached: the Hades family would allow the Sahar to be returned to the Ras on the condition it was sealed away forever. The meeting three nights ago had been to hammer out the details before the Stone was secretly transported to a neutral meeting place. There, both families would witness its permanent sealing beneath the earth, buried beneath their most powerful spells.

Cottus's "big boss" could be the head of any of the Underworld families, up to and including the Hades family. That one of these families was directly involved was terrifying. Piper had hoped it would take them longer to get organized.

She wrapped her arms around herself and pulled her feet onto the chair. "What does it do?" she asked softly. "Why does everyone want the Sahar so badly?"

Lyre gave her a considering look. "Do you know how lodestones work?"

She nodded. The magic that daemons and haemons used was fueled by their body's energy. Without recovery time, they needed an outside source. There was a way to make hard metals and gemstones store energy. With a lodestone in hand, a daemon could draw energy from the stone to fuel his magic. The harder the material, the more energy it could hold and the longer it could hold it. Daemons were the main reason diamonds were so expensive.

Lyre looked at his hands, slowly flexing his fingers. "The Sahar is an unlimited lodestone, the only one in existence. It can hold an infinite amount of energy. Whoever holds it has infinite power at their disposal. What daemon wouldn't kill for that?"

Piper swallowed hard. An unlimited lodestone? That would explain the fervor it inspired in daemons and haemons.

"They say it's nearly impossible to use. No one's had it long enough to figure it out." Lyre smiled wryly. "Apparently the Sahar is picky about who gets to access its power. All lodestones take a bit of breaking in; they attune themselves to whoever uses them the most, and then they're as easy to use as any tool. But breaking them in is tough. It's almost more work to drag the energy out than it is to cast the spell."

She nodded again, lost in thought. Lodestones were expensive but most daemons who could afford them had only a few. Haemons had a lot more trouble with lodestones. Breaking them in, as Lyre had put it, could take months or even years depending on the stone. A daemon couldn't simply pick one up and use it. They were easy to charge but difficult to use. Charging lodestones was big business for the daemons and the main reason they visited Earth.

Daemons couldn't put their own energy into lodestones—something about magic and energy being intertwined. They could put spells on things but they couldn't put magic *in* things. However, they *could* put human energy into the stones. So daemons came to Earth and harvested the easiest form of energy to capture: emotional energy. They didn't need a lodestone; the lodestone was like carrying a storage battery around for emergencies. Daemons could draw energy straight into their bodies if they wanted.

But they couldn't just walk up to a random human and start siphoning. The human had to be giving off pretty significant emotional energy first. Over thousands of years of stealing human energy, some daemons had developed specialized skills for that very purpose.

Incubi were a good example. Through their appearance, skills, inherent charm, and magic, they could inspire lust in humans—forget-your-own-name kind of lust. Lust did in fact count as an emotion and incubi were adept at capturing that energy. It didn't hurt the human and face it: most women weren't going to complain about getting the undivided attention of an impossibly hot man. Succubi, the female equivalent of incubi, were equally talented. The Overworld daemons had their own version: the cupid. They didn't incite lust in humans; they created temporary, obsessive infatuation that tended to ruin relationships. Either way, it made for good emotional energy.

There were other daemon emotional specialists who homed in on one particular emotion like fear or hate or jealousy. Some daemons went for positive emotions. Piper's favorites were the seraphim: a widely varied group of Overworld daemons who loved love. The daemons with the best, most effective emotion-inciting skills were the ones who did good business charging lodestones for other daemons. Although she'd never asked him, Piper was pretty sure that's what Lyre did for a living. She was certain he was very good at it too.

The daemons' dependency on humans for energy was the driving force behind the creation of the Consulates. Before the war and the public revelation of daemon existence, daemons had to sneak around to collect energy. Human mobs and other daemons were a constant threat, so the Consulates evolved as safe houses; Consuls kept humans away, provided safe room and board for visiting daemons, and made trips to Earth productive instead of life-threatening.

The Consuls' roles grew with time. Now, Consuls also held a court of sorts for daemons who wanted a fair decision in a dispute. Consuls acted as negotiators and record keepers for deals and agreements. They hosted diplomatic meetings between the Overworld and Underworld to keep the peace.

After daemons had come out to the public, the Consuls had taken on another role: arbitrators between human society and daemons. The government trusted the Consulates to keep the majority of daemons in check and the daemons in turn trusted the Consulates to keep humans from turning on them.

Piper bit down on her lower lip. That's what she wanted, what she'd always wanted: to be a Consul—a judge, guardian, diplomat, and arbitrator all wrapped into one.

Dealing with daemons wasn't easy, whether they respected the power of the Consulate or not. It took quick wits, a strong personality, and the ability to back up authority with force when necessary. To match daemons who could and did respond aggressively with magic, a Consul needed magic of her own. Piper could be the smartest, strongest, toughest candidate ever, but without magic her chances of being inducted as a Consul were nonexistent.

She'd never had a drop of magic. She didn't even know what having magic was supposed to feel like. Haemons, born to a human and daemon, inherited physical traits from their human parent; they always looked fully human. But they could also inherit a significant portion of the magic capabilities of their daemon parent. The ability to wield magic was built into a dominant gene carried on the X chromosome inherited from the daemon parent.

Piper didn't have a daemon parent. Her father was haemon and so was her mother. Instead of being half-and-half, she was one-quarter daemon times two. Her parentage wasn't unheard of, but around eighty percent of haemons were as sterile as mules; that didn't make for a lot of fertile haemon couples.

Of those couples that could have children, most refused to reproduce because of a horrifying trend: every female child born to two haemon parents died before reaching puberty.

Male offspring didn't suffer any kind of unusual mortality rate. They grew up normally, developing magic just like a regular haemon child. But the girls *all* died.

There were a lot of theories, some dating back hundreds of years. It most likely had something to do with that gene on the X chromosome, especially since the daemon/haemon birthrate suffered the same mortality rate for girls. Boys only inherited one X chromosome—one magic gene. But girls inherited two X chromosomes—two magic genes. And that, apparently, was a death sentence.

Except for Piper. Despite having two haemon parents and, theoretically, two magic genes, she hadn't died.

It was a miracle. She had beaten the odds. However, unlike the male offspring, she hadn't inherited a drop of magic. Maybe the two magic genes had cancelled each other out. Maybe she hadn't inherited any and that's why she was alive. Either way, most Consuls thought Piper's father should have sent her off to a human boarding school a long time ago.

Brooding in silence, she sat curled in her chair as the minutes dragged by. Lyre stared at nothing, his brow furrowed. Every few minutes, he glanced toward the stairs. There were no sounds from the lower level, only the occasional tickle of magic in the air.

Two agonizing hours later, quiet footsteps announced Vejovis's approach. The Overworld daemon tiredly rubbed one blood-splattered thumb against his goatee as he sat across the table from them.

"He'll live," he said. "The scars won't be too bad as long as he takes it easy for the next forty-eight hours."

"Thank you," Lyre said. "How can we—"

Vejovis waved a dismissive hand. "You owe me nothing. I follow my calling, nothing more."

"Ash recognized you in the hospital, didn't he?" Piper asked. "The moment we got into the main building," she added, remembering Ash's sudden, distant distraction once they'd gone through the security gate.

Vejovis shrugged. "I wouldn't be surprised. He's unlikely to forget me."

"Why does he, uh … ?"

"Loathe me?" Vejovis suggested with a dry smile. "He does indeed despise me. You see, I saved his life once before."

"He hates you for saving him?"

"Yes," Vejovis replied, his gaze losing focus and his voice going slightly dreamy. "I saved the wrong life, you see."

"Um," she said, sharing a confused glance with Lyre.

"I didn't realize, of course," the daemon went on vaguely. "His survival was the least important of everything at stake that night. Saving his life cost him everything. He will never forgive me."

"What are you talking about?" Lyre asked in a hushed voice.

Vejovis refocused on them. "It is his story to tell, not mine. But I will warn you now. If the three of you survive this …" He sighed slowly. "He will need your forgiveness. If you can."

Piper's brow wrinkled. "Huh?"

The daemon stood. "My dear child, do not forget. Daemons are not humans. We live lives you cannot comprehend, ruled by a world you know nothing of. If you cannot forgive him when the time comes, then you are not strong enough to stand among us."

"Forgive him for what?" she demanded angrily. "What the hell are you going on about?"

He tugged his bloodstained scrubs straight, ignoring her. "I have a car parked outside. You can have it. If you will accompany me," he said to Lyre, "we can lay him out in the backseat. It will be twelve hours at least before he wakes from the healing sleep and he will be hungry …"

Vejovis's voice trailed away as he and Lyre descended the stairs. Piper sat alone at the table, staring at nothing. What was Vejovis talking about? What would she have to forgive Ash for?

But then, he had already apologized to her, hadn't he? For what? Something he'd done or something he'd planned to do? He'd been dying and half delirious. It probably didn't mean anything. He'd saved her life and Lyre's. Without him, they never would have gotten free from the prefects, let alone avoided immediate recapture. They never would have been able to break into the medical center, although she half wished they hadn't.

She swallowed hard and pulled the scrap of paper out of her pocket.

SAFE

OFFICE

14-25-9

Cryptic warnings and nagging suspicions aside, at least she knew where they had to go next.

CHAPTER

- 8 -

"I DON'T KNOW, PIPER," Lyre said slowly.

She gave him a stern stare from the passenger seat of the beat-up old four-door. They'd driven in winding circles for hours after leaving the abandoned garage where Ash had almost died. Just like the draconian had done on their first escape, they'd made their trail so convoluted no supernatural tracker would be able to find the end of the tangle. Finally, with the morning sun cresting the horizon, they'd parked in an overgrown park where they had both fallen into an exhausted sleep.

"We can't wait for Ash to wake up," she explained for the third time. "We have to move quickly. It won't be like the medical center. They won't be expecting us to go back to the scene of the crime."

"Isn't it the other way around?" Lyre asked skeptically. "I thought criminals *did* go back to the scene of the crime."

"Well, *we* are, but only because we need the information in that safe."

"But without Ash to help …"

Together, they looked over their shoulders. Ash lay comatose over the backseat, his dark red hair clashing terrifically with the puke-yellow fabric and the scratchy gray blanket they'd found in the trunk and draped over him. He hadn't so much as stirred in the last ten hours. Zwi was curled in a miserable ball on his chest, watching them with unfriendly golden eyes. She'd gotten so overprotective of her unconscious owner that Piper and Lyre couldn't so much as touch him without the dragonet hissing and baring her teeth.

Piper took a deep breath and turned back to Lyre. "Look. The information in the safe aside, we're starving and thirsty. We haven't showered in days. We need clothes and supplies. The Consulate is the easiest way to get everything we need." When Lyre opened his mouth to argue, she rushed on. "All we have to do is check the place out. If there's any sign of people, we can come back here and wait until Ash wakes up."

Lyre frowned at her as he thought it over. "I don't get why we can't wait. You know I don't have a lot of magic, Piper. I'm okay in a fight but I've got nothing on Ash. Of the three of us, he's the powerhouse. It doesn't make any sense to go when he's unconscious."

"We can't wait, Lyre. Every day brings the prefects closer to finding us—not to mention all the daemons after the Sahar. And then there's my father too. He needs our help. Even if Ash woke this minute, it'll be another day before he'll be in any shape to do anything physical and days more before he'll have any magic to use! I bet he used all his stores in that fight."

At her last words, Lyre's face froze in an "oh!" expression of epiphany. He lunged over the back of his seat and, ignoring Zwi's warning hiss, grabbed Ash's wrist. Fumbling with Ash's wide leather wristband, he pulled it off and thumped back into his seat. He flipped the wristband over to reveal the inner lining.

Three huge, flat, wine-colored stones sparkled in the sharp light of the sunset. They were embedded into the leather, polished but irregular in shape, and laid out so that two would rest against his inner wrist and one would sit against the top. They were big, all three the size of the end of her thumb.

"Those aren't rubies," Piper said, swallowing hard.

"Conundrum," Lyre said absently, studying the gems. "Damn. Two are empty, and the third has only a little left."

"Conundrum," Piper repeated, staring at the twinkling jewels. "But the only stone better than conundrum is diamond. Where did Ash get *three* huge conundrum lodestones?"

Lyre shrugged, still absorbed in the stones. "These are excellent quality. They could hold a lot." He looked up, meeting Piper's gaze. "If these stones were charged, then Ash could help right away. Even if he wasn't up to a physical fight, he would be all set in the magic department."

She looked at the lodestones, frowning. "But how will we charge them?" She gestured out the car window. "We're in the worst neighborhood in the worst district of the worst part of the city slums. What people there are around here won't be helpful. They'll probably try to rob us, kill us, and stuff our bodies in the trunk of our own car, unless they stole that too."

Lyre gazed at her, saying nothing, a wrinkle between his brows as though he was considering something he was afraid to suggest.

Piper stared back for a minute before she figured it out. "No way! No freaking way! *Me?* You want *me* to donate? Forget it!"

Lyre gave Piper an up-and-down look with one eyebrow raised. "Don't overreact or anything, Piper."

She swallowed a nasty retort. "Sorry, but—*really?* You can't be serious."

He shrugged, leaning back against his seat, way too nonchalant. "Why can't I be serious? Daemons and haemons with magic don't throw off energy the way humans do—our energy feeds back into our own magic—but since you don't, you know, have magic …"

She gritted her teeth. "I wasn't arguing about the mechanics of it."

"Then what's the problem?"

"I am not having sex with you!"

He threw his head back and laughed. God help her, he was sexy. "Really, Piper, are you that naïve? I don't have to have sex with you to charge these lodestones." He swung the wristband back and forth like a pendulum, then rolled his eyes. "Besides, you're the Head

Consul's *daughter*. And besides *that*, I don't sleep with virgins anyway."

Her expression blanked and she hitched an unconvincing scowl on her face to hide anything else that might show up on it. "If you're not suggesting sex, then what?" Lyre was an incubus; there was only one kind of energy he collected.

Shadows were starting to gather in his eyes. The air seemed warmer, heavier. "Sex is the entrée, Piper," he said, his voice going softer, deeper. "There're still all kinds of appetizers."

She swallowed hard, not quite able to look away. "I don't think that's a good idea."

Something that had nothing to do with lust or passion flickered across his face—something angry and resentful. "Don't take this the wrong way, but … you owe Ash, Piper."

"I—what?"

"He almost died protecting you. He's been unconscious all night, used all his magic, and made himself completely helpless to save you from that minotaur. You heard what he said: Cottus got him when he killed the minotaur to keep it away from you."

"But—"

"Do you know how many enemies he has? Half the Underworld would kill him given a good chance."

"But—but why?"

"Because of who he is. Daemons he's never met want to kill him. He's done nothing but keep us safe and this is a chance for *both* of us to help him." His intense expression softened. "I can't charge these by myself, Piper."

She bit her lower lip. "No sex."

"No sex," he promised solemnly.

Her nerves twanged like guitar strings. This was a bad idea. *Bad* idea. Incubi were unbelievably good at twisting any and every situation around until it seemed like intimacy made perfect sense. But even if Lyre's real motive was to fool around with her, she wanted to help charge Ash's lodestones. What else could she do for him? Giving him back an immediate source of power, the ability to protect himself, was the only gift she could give him to make up for his sacrifices. Come to think of it, she didn't even understand *why* he kept taking these risks for her.

Lyre propped an elbow against the steering wheel as tension melted from his body. Piper swallowed against the blush rising in her cheeks. The incubus smiled slowly, that half-grin that always made him look playful and seductive. The gold faded from his eyes as shadows gathered in his irises. He was shading fast and if he decided to ignore her no-sex stipulation, she probably wouldn't be able to stop him. She probably wouldn't want to.

Her breathing picked up as his stare slid slowly down her body and back up again, leisurely and caressing. A slow-building heat washed through her but her anxiety was climbing almost as quickly. Lyre licked his lips as his gaze settled on her mouth. Damn, he was good. He hadn't done anything yet except *look* at her.

"Um," she choked. "I changed my mind."

"*Piper*," he complained. In another minute, he would be too far-gone to take no for an answer. Lyre was about as respectful and morally sound as incubi came but he was still a daemon with powerful instincts. One did not play hard to get with an incubus.

"Look," he said, taking deep breaths as if he was trying to stay calm and clearheaded. There was a soft, purring undertone to his voice that made her blood heat. She felt feverish. "Let's just start small. A kiss? If you're too uncomfortable, then I'll go take a walk."

"A kiss," she repeated breathlessly. Holy crap, she was burning with the urge to melt into his arms. Incubus magic was powerful stuff. She slowly licked her lips.

He nodded encouragingly, one hand wrapped around the steering wheel in a death grip. His eyes were totally black now, bottomless magnets that drew her stare with irresistible force.

"Okay," she whispered.

Carefully, as though he didn't want to make any sudden movements, he let go of the steering wheel. She fought not to recoil as he slid cautiously from his seat to hers until their hips were pressed together and she was squashed against the door. The seat wasn't quite big enough for two.

They stared at each other, her trying to stay calm, him trying to gauge her mood.

She could feel his heat and smell his musky, masculine scent—spicy and alluring with that odd but yummy cherry undertone. He slowly lifted one hand. His fingertips brushed her cheek and she jumped. His touch trailed over her cheek and down the side of her neck, leaving shivery tingles in its wake. He curled his fingers gently around the back of her neck, his palm hot against her skin. His stare held her prisoner and she couldn't find her voice to tell him to stop. She didn't know if she wanted to. He leaned closer and she closed her eyes.

His lips brushed hers, soft, almost questioning. She held perfectly still, trying to pretend that one little touch hadn't sent her heart racing. Then he pressed his mouth to hers. Heat swooped through her belly and spread like fire through her blood. Her hands sank into his hair, pulling him closer. Her mouth opened and he kissed her more deeply. Wild need rushed through her. She was on fire and he was everything she needed, everything she craved so desperately. Without thinking, she hooked her leg over his thigh, pulling him on top of her as she fell back into the car door. She arched her back to press against him and he grabbed her thigh to help pull her other leg around him.

"Lyre," she panted, tearing her mouth away from his to gasp for air. "I—I changed my mind."

"What?" he growled against the corner of her mouth. "You are *not* going to tell me—"

"I want you."

He froze, not breathing. Then, with a frustrated snarl, he shook his head. "No, you can't change your mind now. You're not thinking clearly anymore. You—"

She grabbed his face and jerked his mouth down on hers. He crushed their lips together with another growl, then pulled back.

"Piper, you—"

"*Lyre*," she moaned. She grabbed at the hem of his shirt, trying to pull it up. She was on fire. Only he could quench it. "*Please*."

He hesitated, his face hovering over hers, hands curled tightly over her hips, his eyes black as pitch. His resolve was weakening.

"I think I overdid the aphrodisia," he whispered.

She grabbed the neck of his shirt and pulled down so hard a seam tore. "Now," she demanded, tightening her legs around him. His hands slid up her bare sides, pushing her shirt up with their motion. She arched her back invitingly as his touch lit her skin on fire and made her ache for him, desperate for more.

As she arched back and he pressed against her, the car door behind her made a snapping sound and popped open.

Piper shrieked as she fell backward. Pain shot through her spine as her torso fell out of the car but her legs stayed tangled around Lyre. She hung for a second before her legs came free and she landed on her head. The rest of her slid out of the car and she crumpled in a heap.

"Piper? Piper, are you okay?"

She panted, blinking like she'd just woken up. Her body ached like she had a terrible fever but the pain wasn't from the fall. She swallowed hard as she carefully sat up.

Lyre hung out of the car, one hand stretched toward her. His eyes were visibly lightening back to gold and he looked freaked out. He stared at her like he'd never seen her before. "Holy *shit*," he breathed.

"Y-yeah," she stuttered. She was starting to shiver as the fire in her blood died, taking all her body heat with it. "What—what did you *do*?"

She was sure she would be furious with him in a minute for turning her into a puddle of crazed lust, but right then she felt more shell-shocked than anything else.

"I—I was trying to calm you down. You were nervous and …" He trailed off, his brow furrowing. He licked his lips. "You're not a virgin, are you."

It wasn't a question. Her cheeks flushed and she dropped her gaze.

"I'm sorry, Piper," he said, sounding so miserable she had to look up. "I just assumed … aphrodisia magic has only half the potency on virgins, so I didn't think it would do much more than …" He trailed off, shaking his head and looking almost as embarrassed as Piper felt.

She stood and brushed the leaves off her jeans. "Let's pretend that never happened, okay?" she said, glancing at him and hoping her face wasn't as red as it felt.

He tilted his head, mischief sparking in his safely gold eyes. "Pretend you never attacked me in a fit of passion, demanding my—"

"Yes," she snapped. "It. Did. Not. Happen."

"What about that *kiss*? You went open-mouth first, so—"

"Did *not* happen."

He grinned at her. She threw her arms in the air. Incubi. There was no reasoning with them. She grabbed the back door. "I'm going to sit back here for a bit," she muttered grouchily. Lyre would never let her live this down. He should be begging for her forgiveness for overdosing her on his seduction magic, but at least he'd painted her embarrassment in a layer of humor that made it easier to deal with. So she'd begged him to sleep with her. She hadn't been in her right mind. He'd even tried to resist, which was pretty impressive for an incubus.

Ignoring Lyre's snickers, she crawled into the back of the car. With Ash sleeping across the seat, there was nowhere for her to sit except the floor. She curled up by his feet, ignoring Zwi's suspicious stare. She licked her lips, shivering a little when she found they still tasted like Lyre—honey-sweet and a little spicy. The taste of incubi.

"Lyre?" she murmured, closing her eyes.

"Mm?"

"Don't tell anyone, okay? That I'm … I'm not …" She trailed off dejectedly.

He was quiet for a moment. "I promise."

She exhaled slowly. "Thanks," she whispered.

No one knew her secret. Not that losing her virginity was such a terrible thing, but she knew her father and uncle would think it was way too soon. It wasn't *that* she had lost it; it was *how* she had. She'd made the biggest, stupidest mistake of her life, and if Quinn found out, he would never let her become a Consul. He would see her mistake as proof that she wasn't right for the job, because Consuls always had to approach and deal with daemons with complete neutrality.

Piper had blown that lesson so badly she would never be able to make up for it.

o   o   o

Piper had never met a daemon quite like Micah. It was obvious at first glance he was an incubus—beautiful golden-brown skin, pale hair, black-dusted gold eyes. The physique of a god, a smile that could charm anything alive. At sixteen with her birthday coming up in a few weeks, she'd met enough incubi to know what they were like. They *always* flirted with her. Secretly, she liked their attention. Most daemons ignored her like she was a total nobody but the incubi never did. They couldn't resist her.

When Micah first talked to her, it was all she could do not to swoon. He was gorgeous even for an incubus and his voice was unbelievable—deep but smooth and a little husky with a subtle, throbbing suggestion of heat—but she knew all incubi wanted only one thing. So while she enjoyed every second of his attention, she still made it clear he wasn't getting anywhere with her.

Unlike the other incubi, Micah didn't tease and flirt for an evening then move on. He hung around the Consulate for three days, charming and polite but always with that hungry, appreciative gleam in his eyes that said he thought Piper was beautiful. He wanted her and she liked that he did. How could she not? Micah was unrivaled. He could have any girl in the world and he wanted *her*.

But incubi were always after one thing and she knew better. He went on his way and she missed his attention, but mostly she was relieved.

Then he came back. He stayed for a week, following Piper around, sweet and helpful. He told her things about daemons no one else had. He told her she was beautiful, and smart, and funny and he was so earnest and sincere, she believed him. When he left, he kissed her cheek goodbye. She blushed so hotly it felt like her face was on fire.

She secretly counted the days until he came back. Only two weeks passed before he returned to see her. Together they snuck out of the Consulate and he took her on a midnight walk through the countryside. He asked if he could hold her hand. He barely took his gaze off her face the entire night.

For three months he courted her, staying at the Consulate for days on end or tapping her bedroom window in the middle of the night for a few stolen hours where they'd walk all across the night-draped property, fingers intertwined while they talked. The first time he kissed her, she almost died. He made her crazy with wanting him but always asked before every little step, his expression questioning and somehow a little vulnerable, never quite sure if she would say yes. But she always did. She couldn't deny him anything. Not when he looked at her as though she was the only woman on the planet. Not when he whispered, with an embarrassed little smile, that he'd never felt this way about any girl. That he wanted to just be with her, not in bed with her.

After three months of secret meetings and sweet kisses—and some not-so-innocent kisses—he asked her to stay the night with him. She'd never been with a man before and she knew it wasn't a good idea to lose her virginity to an incubus. Firstly, under normal circumstances, incubi were users—they used girls for sex, plain and simple. Secondly, incubi could and did set a standard that no normal man could meet. It wasn't smart to start out with undiluted whiskey when you'd never had a sip of wine before. And thirdly, she knew she was already breaking the rules. Consuls had to always remain impartial and objective toward the daemons visiting their Consulate. It was their job to treat all daemons equally; favoritism would undermine the very foundation of the Consulates.

But Piper was in love. Micah was in love with her. She wanted him so badly she could hardly sleep at night. So she said yes.

He was everything she'd ever imagined. He made her feel things she'd had no idea she could feel, more intense than anything she'd ever experienced. He was brilliant, skilled, and attentive to her every desire—a god of passion. He drank her in, enjoying every inch of her as she enjoyed every inch of him. Every night that week, she snuck out of the Consulate to spend it with him. She was deliriously happy, unable to believe this gorgeous, amazing daemon was hers. On the seventh night, as they lay together in sleepy, harmonious silence, she leaned close and whispered that she loved him.

She'd always remember the way his face turned toward her, his shadowy eyes glinting oddly as he smiled.

"Do you?" he whispered back.

Confused by his expression, she nodded mutely.

Slowly, he rolled out of the bed and stretched, naked and devastating in his perfection. Then he turned back to the bed, towering over her with a smile on his perfect lips that held not the slightest hint of warmth.

"That's too bad, babe," he said, callous and dismissive, "because you were a pretty good lay for a virgin, but I don't love you. Never did."

Each word stabbed her like a knife. He drank her in, but this time it was her shock, her pain and humiliation, and finally her horrified shame that made him lick his lips and smile like a satisfied cat. Then he turned and walked out of the room. It was the last time she ever saw him.

Micah had played his game carefully. Even if his every word and touch had been a lie, Piper had been perfectly willing right until he walked out. He'd requested her explicit permission at each step and he'd never used aphrodisia on her. He hadn't broken the rules of the Consulate. No one, not even Piper, could cry foul.

She could cry, though, and she did for days. Even worse than falling in love, than being used, was her feeling of shamed stupidity. Micah was an *incubus*. How could she have fallen for his act? How could she have believed he loved her?

That's when she finally and completely lost her innocent fascination with daemons. It was so easy to be intrigued by them—they were exotic, mysterious, attractive. Not to mention intelligent, witty, and often worldly and wise in ways humans weren't. Her father and uncle had warned her over and over during her training that daemons weren't gods. They weren't any better than humans, even if they thought they were. That aristocratic attitude meant they often treated humans poorly and the biggest mistake a human or haemon could make was to believe daemons truly were superior.

Thanks to Micah, Piper would never make that mistake again. Micah was impossibly gorgeous, but that didn't make him better than a human boy. Even his looks were fake, enhanced by glamour. His charm was a lie, his sweet compliments utter falsehoods, and his affection nonexistent.

She may have learned her lesson, but far too late. If a rumor ever reached her father's ears—and she was sure there were rumors; Micah would have crowed about his success to his peers—Quinn would decide once and for all that his magic-less, not-really-a-haemon daughter didn't have what it took. He would send her off to a human boarding school—to a boring, daemon-free life that would never and could never include him or Uncle Calder.

She couldn't let that happen. She would rather jump off a bridge than live the rest of her life as a human. She would rather rot in a prefect prison for stealing the Sahar.

Sighing, she rested her head against Ash's knee and denied the tears trying to escape. She wouldn't cry over Micah or her mistakes again. She would do whatever it took to prove to her father that she could be a Consul. If he ever found out the truth, she hoped he would have enough faith in her to let it go.

Thinking of the stern, distant face of her father, who wouldn't call her by anything but Piperel, she couldn't make herself believe he would.

CHAPTER

-9-

"THIS IS A BAD IDEA," Lyre muttered.

"Shush," Piper hissed.

They knelt in the bushes thirty feet from the Consulate, trying to decide if the building was deserted or not. The doors had been blocked off with "DO NOT CROSS" tape that undoubtedly had some kind of spell on it. All the windows were dark, everything silent. It looked void of life, which, while good, made Piper feel hollow inside. The Consulate wasn't supposed to look like that.

"Are we really going to climb that tree?" Lyre whispered, staring across the back lawn at the towering maple.

"How else would we get inside? We can't use the doors."

"There are plenty of windows on the ground level."

"They'll be expecting that. I used to get in and out of my room all the time using that tree."

"But—"

"Let's go." Without waiting for his agreement, she broke into an awkward jog while staying crouched low. The dark windows stared at her as she rushed across the exposed lawn and into the shadows of the old tree. Lyre followed, grumbling something about crazy teenage girls.

After one quick glance for signs of life, she swung onto the lowest branch. She climbed swiftly, reached the right branch twenty feet in the air, and glanced down. Lyre grinned at her from the branch below hers, enjoying her surprise. Right. As much as he whined like a five-year-old about doing anything remotely dangerous, he was a daemon and therefore both athletic and annoyingly coordinated. He was faster than her, stronger, more agile, and had better reflexes. It wasn't fair.

"So," he said conversationally, checking out the bone-breaking drop to the ground, "how will this get us in your window? We're too high."

"My window is over there." She pointed halfway along the outer wall. "We have to jump onto the roof."

"Oooh," he drawled sarcastically. "Of course. That makes perfect sense."

She crouched on her branch, took aim, and leaped across the two-foot gap between the branch and the eaves. She landed on all fours on the roof and crawled out of Lyre's way. He sprang onto the roof with irritating ease. Stupid daemon not appreciating his abilities.

They shuffled down the roof, performed a complicated bit of acrobatics to get onto her windowsill, and pried it open. She'd long ago rigged the screen to pop out and they swung into her dark bedroom barely five minutes after setting out. Piper stopped in the middle of her room. It had been torn apart. Her belongings were scattered all over the floor, her books torn apart, her mattress and pillows slashed open. There was a gaping hole in the back wall of her closet where the choronzon had forced its way into the secret passage.

Lyre touched the back of her hand in sympathy. She grabbed his fingers and squeezed.

"The choronzon didn't do all this," she whispered.

"No," he agreed somberly. "I imagine it was the prefects searching for the Stone."

She nodded slowly. Yes, that would explain it. With a sigh, she gave Lyre a push toward the door. "Go get your and Ash's things. I'll change and pack some stuff."

Once he was safely out of the room, she stripped out of her grimy clothes and hid them under the bed. With a huge sigh, she pulled on some clean underwear. That was *so* much better. Then she dug into the bottom drawer of her dresser and pulled out her gear. She put on a pair of casual-looking jeans that had hidden sheaths built in. The daggers that went with the jeans were gone. After choosing a bra with good support, she tucked the Sahar's ring box into it. Yeah, she could put it somewhere else, but it felt safest right over her heart. She picked several tops, layering them one on top of the other in case she didn't have access to more clothes for a while, and topped it off with a long-sleeved gold shirt. After putting her butt-kicking boots back on, she unearthed two long knives the prefects hadn't found and tucked them into the empty sheaths in the tops of the boots. She was never again leaving her bedroom without at least one weapon.

For the last of her gear, she put on her armguards. The leather covered her arms from the backs of her hands up to her elbows. They had metal plates in them for protection when blocking punches or strikes and the material was imbued with magic-dampening spells that would dilute any spell thrown at her.

Feeling strong and competent for the first time in days, she found a backpack and shoved some more clothes in it. All her full-size weapons were kept in the sparring room on the main level, assuming the prefects hadn't confiscated everything. She was zipping the bag closed when Lyre slipped back into her room, two similar black packs in one hand. He too had changed into fresh clothes: jeans that fit exactly right, a casual black t-shirt that wasn't tight yet left no doubt that he was deliciously toned, and a silver chain around his neck that disappeared under the neck of his shirt. He looked mouthwatering, as usual.

"Hey beautiful," he said with a crooked smile.

She rolled her eyes. "Got everything?"

"Yep."

He passed her his bags and she hauled all three backpacks to the window and shoved them out. They landed in the bushes with a muffled crash. Piper dusted her hands together and joined Lyre at her bedroom door.

"Any sign of people?" she asked him.

"Nope."

"Excellent."

"We should still be careful though."

"Yeah yeah."

"Piper—"

"*Where* is your sense of adventure, Lyre?" She tossed the question over her shoulder as she strode into the hallway toward the stairs.

"This isn't supposed to be an adventure," Lyre muttered as he followed her. "Besides," he added a little more loudly, "we need to hurry. I don't like leaving Ash alone."

Piper bit her lip as she reached the stairs and crouched to peer down them. She didn't like leaving Ash either, not when he was still unconscious, but they'd hidden the car well and Zwi was guarding him. The clever little dragonet would distract anyone who got too close and lead them on a merry little chase away from her vulnerable master. But still, they needed to be quick.

She trotted silently down the stairs and stopped in the foyer, not liking the memories of the space. There was another hole in the wall where Ash had blasted the exit of the secret passage. Blood was smeared on the floor where the draconian had sat while the prefects interrogated them. Anger swept through her at the thought of the supposed protectors of justice.

"Piper," Lyre hissed.

She heard it—voices down the hall, coming closer.

"Quick," she gasped, spinning around. The closet beside the front door, one door hanging open, beckoned. "In here." She shoved Lyre into the half with the door closed and backed in after him. The familiar smell of her father's cologne wafted off the nearest coat.

" … didn't hear a damn thing," a male voice complained as footsteps drew closer.

"I thought I heard voices," a woman replied irritably.

"You imagined it. Probably because it's so freaking boring here."

Their footsteps stopped in the middle of the foyer. Piper held her breath, pressing back into Lyre. His hands gripped her waist, his body rock hard with tension. The man and woman argued over whether they should check upstairs.

"There's no one there," the man exclaimed. "There hasn't been anyone here for days. This is the stupidest assignment ever."

The woman grunted her agreement. "Fine," she conceded. "But we're supposed to be paying attention. I'm going to stand watch for a bit."

"Suit yourself," the man said carelessly.

The woman passed by the open side of the closet. Barely daring to breathe, Piper turned until she could peek through the gap where the door folded. A blurry silhouette of the woman stood in front of the window beside the front door, barely three feet from the closet, while the man sat, perfectly visible, on the bottom step of the staircase. He was thin and plain with brown hair and a scraggy goatee. He yawned obnoxiously as she watched. Not a daemon or a prefect. Who the hell were these two? And why were they "guarding" the Consulate?

She leaned back into Lyre and turned her head toward him. "Not daemons," she breathed. "Not prefects either. The woman is standing by the window right beside us. The man is sitting on the stairs."

His hands tightened on her waist. He put his mouth against her ear. "Do they look like they'll be leaving soon?"

She shook her head.

"Damn."

They couldn't wait in the closet forever. Ash was alone and helpless in the car, and if there were people guarding the house, there might be people patrolling the property. They had to get the information out of Quinn's safe and get out of the house before they got caught.

"What do we do?" she whispered desperately.

Lyre's fingers flexed while he thought as frantically as her. No ideas popped to mind. They should have waited for Ash. He would have known what to do.

Lyre leaned in close again. "I have an idea," he breathed in her ear.

"What is it?"

"Ummm," he whispered. "Well, she's female."

Piper blinked. "So?"

"Aphrodisia will work on her."

She stared at the opposite wall, trying to figure out how that made sense. "You want to seduce her?" she asked incredulously. "How does *that* keep them from discovering us?"

"You don't understand," he murmured. His hands slid up and down her waist in a quick, anxious sort of massage. "If I hit her with the magic, at the very least she won't keep standing there. And with her male companion five feet away …" He grinned against her ear.

"Oh, you're bad," she breathed, stifling a laugh. "Do it."

He settled his hands on the tops of her hips. "You got it. Uh, but Piper? I suggest you think unsexy thoughts."

She gritted her teeth. Great. She was leaning against an incubus who was about to unleash the full potency of his seduction magic. Even though he wasn't aiming at her, she would get caught in the crossfire.

At first, it wasn't too bad. She started to feel hot like her whole body was blushing and her extremities tingled. Warmth flared in her center. She clenched her jaw and peeked through the crack in the closet door. The silhouette of the woman was having trouble standing still. She fanned herself with one hand, then pressed it against the top of her chest. Her weight shifted from foot to foot and she inhaled sharply.

Lyre laughed silently. The suppressed sound vibrated against Piper's back and she arched back without thinking. He slid one hand around her hip to press against her lower belly but she could tell his attention wasn't on her. Damn damn damn. Her thoughts were starting to get foggy and Lyre's warmth behind her felt so good. Focus. Unsexy thoughts. What was an unsexy thought?

"There she goes," Lyre said, his whisper bubbling with laughter.

Piper looked through the crack as the woman strode past. Her hands were clenching and unclenching as she beelined straight for the guy sitting on the stairs.

He looked up. "What's wr—"

She grabbed his face and kissed him—fully open mouth, tongue and everything. The guy was so surprised he fell into the stairs. The woman straddled him as she kissed him. It took exactly two seconds for the guy to get over his surprise and grab her around the waist. He rolled over and pinned her under him, equally enthusiastic. Their clothes would start flying soon.

Lyre leaned against Piper's back as he peeked through the crack too. "You call that kissing?" he whispered. "I can kiss better drunk with both hands tied behind my back."

Piper wasn't watching them anymore. Lyre's warm breath tickling her ear as he spoke emptied her brain of thought. His laugh made heat swoop through her belly. Her hands found his hair. She tangled her fingers in the soft locks and arched her back, pressing into him.

Lyre sucked in a sharp breath. "Uh, Piper ..."

"Shut up," she breathed. She shifted her hips backward, eyes closing. "You're a mean, mean incubus, you know that?"

"Yeah," he agreed huskily. He slid one hand over her stomach. The other caressed her jaw, tilting her head back. "But as much as I'd like to make it up to you, all my terrible shortcomings and everything, we can't waste our chance to get out of the closet."

"I like the closet," she mumbled, turning her head in the hopes of finding his mouth.

"Uh-huh." He nudged her forward. She tightened her grip on his hair. "Piper," he said firmly, "let me go. We have to get out of here before they finish, which, considering that guy's enthusiasm, won't take long."

She blinked a couple times. "Right," she whispered. "Let's go."

He waited a few seconds. "You haven't moved."

She searched for the willpower to let go. His warmth against her back felt so good, as did his hands touching her. He hadn't let her go either, but then, incubi had even worse self-control than humans. Her knees quivered and she desperately wanted to turn around and kiss him until she couldn't breathe.

No. She needed the information from the safe. They needed to get back to Ash before someone found him.

She unclenched her hands and let her arms fall to her sides. Lyre let out a relieved sigh, although she thought there might have been a note of disappointment in there too. "See if the coast is clear," he murmured.

Feeling cold all over, she stepped to the edge of their hiding spot and looked around the edge of the door. Ewww. Yeah, those two weren't about to notice her and Lyre. They probably wouldn't notice the roof falling on their heads. She gestured for Lyre to follow and they crept out of the closet and across the foyer. The distracted couple didn't so much as glance their way.

Once they were in the hallway, they moved fast. Where two mysterious interlopers lurked, more might be found. Piper led the way to her father's office without spotting anyone else. As she opened the door, Lyre touched her elbow.

"I'll go to the kitchen and get some food," he whispered. "Meet me there."

He continued on as she stepped into the office and closed the door.

The familiar, wonderful smell of home engulfed her, but the sight of the room cut her. It too had been searched with no care for anything. The desk had been broken in half, probably in a search for hidden compartments. The leather chair had been cut open and the stuffing scattered everywhere. Papers covered the floor like a white carpet.

Lips pressed tight, she strode across the debris-littered floor to the floor-to-ceiling bookshelves, the contents of which were piled at its base. The painting that used to hang beside them was three feet away with a great slash through the canvas. She knelt and pressed the tiny catch in the corner above the baseboard.

A soft pop told her it had worked. She swung an entire panel of wall open like a door. Behind it, a huge steel safe was embedded in the wall. The metal gleamed, the lock lined up perfectly at 0. She took a deep breath and began to turn it. When she spun the dial back to finish at 9, she lifted her fingers from the cool metal and said a silent prayer. Grabbing the handle, she pulled.

The door swung silently open.

The safe had two shelves inside full of file folders. Which one did she need? She didn't have time to search them. She looked around wildly and spotted her father's favorite briefcase half buried under the remains of the desk. She grabbed it and pulled. It came free all at once and the desk hit the floor with a loud thump. Piper swore under her breath and rushed back to the safe. She grabbed handfuls of folders and stacked them in the briefcase. When the safe was empty, she forced the case shut and picked it up.

The ceiling creaked over her head.

She looked up sharply—there was someone there. It wouldn't be Lyre; he was in the kitchen. Had the amorous couple heard the desk hit the floor? Knowing she had less than a minute, she rushed to the window and slid it open. When she couldn't get the screen off, she pulled a knife and cut it. Watching the door out of the corner of her eye, she forced the briefcase through the gap in the screen, letting it fall into the shadows at the side of the building. Then she lurched away from the window, shut the safe door, and swung the panel closed to hide the compartment just as the office door flew open.

Piper spun around, her back pressed to the panel.

"Oho," exclaimed a man she'd never seen before. He grinned. "She was right. The girl did come back."

"Of course," said his companion. "That's what scared kids do. They go home."

Both strangers were middle-aged men. One was tall and wiry, the other tall and beefy. They were dressed casually in jeans and jackets with stubble on their jaws that said they hadn't been home in a while.

"Who the hell are you?" Piper demanded. Not daemons, she was sure of that.

"Good question," the skinny one said. "We know who *you* are, Piperel Griffiths."

Uh-oh. "I know who you are too," she mocked, hiding her consternation. "Trespassers who are going to get their asses kicked."

"Mouthy," the heavy one remarked dispassionately. He gave her a considering look. "This is how it's going to work, Piperel. You will come with us quietly or we will use force."

"Come with you?" Piper repeated, taken aback. If these guys were after the Sahar, they didn't need to take her anywhere. "*Where?*"

Beefy smiled a slow, shark's smile. "To your father, of course," he said.

Whatever Piper had been expecting, that wasn't it. Her brain short-circuited. "To … my father?"

"Yes. You do want to see him, don't you? He's not in great shape. He could use a loving daughter's care."

Her shock shattered into fury. "Where is he?"

"Now, now, Piperel." He wagged a fat finger. "Let's keep things polite. Your dad is alive and really not even injured, all things considered. We'll take you to him. Just promise to cooperate." He spread his hands. "Maybe you can even save your dad some suffering. He doesn't want to tell us where the Sahar is. We're starting to think he doesn't even know and that would be very bad for him."

"I don't know where it is."

"You could convince him to tell us."

She snorted. "That's a great idea. Then you wouldn't need either of us alive."

His hands dropped to his sides as he lost patience. "Come with us. Now." He forced a smile. "You belong with us, Piperel."

She clenched her hands. Her creepy meter was off the scale. She *belonged* with them? What the hell?

"I don't think she's going to come," Skinny said, grinning.

"Doesn't look like it," Beefy seconded. "Shall we?"

"Hell yes."

From across the room, Skinny flung a hand in the air. For a second, Piper was confused. Was she supposed to be scared of his dirty fingernails? Then the air crackled with electricity.

The spell smacked her in the face and snapped her head back into the wall. Agony exploded in her skull and her vision went black. She didn't realize she was on the floor until someone rolled her over.

"You fool," the fat one barked. "We weren't supposed to hurt her."

"She'll be okay," the skinny one grumbled. "She's not bleeding that much."

"She's unconscious."

"That's a good thing."

Piper struggled for coherent thought through a groggy haze. Haemons. Stupid haemons with stupid magic attacking her. Jerks. Her eyelids fluttered as the room steadied. The haemons came into focus, leaning over her warily. She wiggled her fingers to make sure they were working—then punched Skinny right in the nose.

He jerked back with a howl. Before Beefy could react, Piper's boot hit him square in the groin. He sank to the floor without a sound, his eyes bulging and his face purple. With her head throbbing, she rolled to her feet and promptly staggered into the wall.

Skinny pulled a hand away from his bleeding nose and made a punching gesture. Piper threw up her arms. The spell collided with her, pushing her back into the wall, but her magic-blocking armguards softened it. He stuck his hand out for another spell but she jumped forward and grabbed his wrist. A twist, a shove, and down he went, roaring in pain as his elbow popped out of joint.

She jumped over him but staggered again. Her balance was shot and every beat of her heart made her head throb mercilessly. Blood was trickling down the back of her neck. She stumbled to the door and stepped into the hall.

"Ugh," she said when she saw who was waiting for her: the passion duo. Their clothes were back on. The woman had a stunned, slightly appalled look lingering on her face.

"It's her!" bad-kisser dude exclaimed. "Shauna, look!"

"I'm not blind," the woman muttered. They were four paces away. Piper wasn't sure she was coordinated enough to run away. They were too far to attack easily.

Before she could decide, Shauna made a sudden circular motion with her hand. The air buzzed with power and invisible bonds snapped around Piper's arms, binding them against her sides. She wrenched at the spell but it was too far above her armguards for them to help.

"Okay, girlie," the wannabe-Casanova said, his tone patronizing, "we got you now. You—"

"Got me?" she hissed. "You think?"

His mouth hung open stupidly. Piper strode forward. So her hands were tied with magic. Not for long.

She bore down on him like a bull, then at the last second swung into a full roundhouse kick that slammed right into Shauna's side. The woman crashed into the wall. Piper's arms came free. She whirled around and grabbed Romeo's arm as he tried a spell of his own. Before he could finish it, she yanked him forward, ducked, and threw him over her shoulder. He landed on his head behind her.

Piper straightened. Haemons. Jeez. Just because they had magic, most of them never learned proper physical defense. They spelled their way out of everything. Well, Piper had no magic to rely on and she could kick a haemon's ass nine times out of ten. It was the daemons who gave her trouble.

She jumped over the moaning loser and trotted into the kitchen. It was empty. "Lyre?" she called.

Fingers whispered up her sides and a voice cooed in her ear, "Hey there, pretty thing."

"Lyre," she growled, spinning around. He grinned and managed to slide his fingers down her hips before she slapped his hands away. "Where have you been? I was almost kidnapped."

"Yeah, I heard, but I was outside stashing the food. You seemed to have things under control." His smile faded and he cupped the back of her head. His hand came away bloody. "You're hurt."

She shrugged it off. "We should—"

Across the kitchen, the back door swung open and hit the wall with a boom. Three more people fell over the threshold.

"Look," a guy yelled. "There they are!"

"Shoot them," bellowed another.

Someone raised a gun. Lyre grabbed her and they both dove behind the island. Something whizzed over their heads and hit a cupboard.

"Was that a tranq dart?" Lyre asked, looking puzzled.

"I did say they tried to kidnap me."

"Why?"

"Beats me."

"Come out now," a newcomer shouted. "Or we'll come back there!"

"What's the plan?" Lyre whispered.

"Ummm." She looked over her shoulder. The pantry door hung open behind her. "In here."

They both ducked into the pantry and slammed the door. Lyre put a hand on the knob and the air went hot for a second. "Sealed it. Won't hold for long though." He glanced around and lifted his eyebrows. "I hope there's a step two to this plan."

"Of course. I don't like closets *that* much."

He snickered. She ducked and pushed a huge box of snacks out of the way. Under one of the shelves was a sliding panel, and beyond it, another secret passageway. She crawled in. Lyre closed the panel after him and they wiggled down the passageway. It opened into a vertical shaft. Unlike the last secret passage, this one had a metal ladder. On the second floor, the passageway came out in the linen closet. Piper pressed against the shelves and waited for Lyre to squeeze his way out, which then left about zero space to stand.

"Another one," he mused, looking around. The light from the hall cast a stripe of yellow across his face that glinted on one golden eye. He smiled crookedly and his gaze wandered across her face.

She cleared her throat. "Escaping, remember?"

"Yeah," he replied in a tone of voice that said he wasn't even listening. He lifted a hand and touched her chin lightly. Then he pressed into her, pushing her back against the wall. She squeaked in surprise—then froze when his mouth brushed the side of her neck.

"Aha," he breathed against her neck. "I knew it wasn't only aphrodisia."

"W-what?" she croaked.

He stepped back as abruptly as he'd pounced. "Just checking," he said cryptically. His fingers were still under her chin. He let his hand fall, his touch trailing from her throat down to her navel.

"Lyre—"

"Shh." He touched her lips with his fingertips. Then he leaned in, and his fingers were gone, and it was his lips brushing across hers. "You can yell at me later. We're escaping, remember?"

"You—you—" She couldn't put a coherent thought together.

"Yeah," he agreed with a satisfied smile. Then he cracked the door open, peeked out, and stepped into the upstairs hall. Piper stalked out after him, seething. Sneaky, manipulative, hormone-stupid incubus. Of all the inappropriate times to try seducing her.

They tiptoed down the hall toward Piper's bedroom. Angry, confused voices echoed from the main floor. With a little luck, they could sneak out the window, grab their things, and get the hell out without any more fun little encounters. Piper's head throbbed like it was going to burst and she was starting to feel sick to her stomach.

A *pfft* noise broke the silence of the upper level. Piper spun around as Lyre jerked to a stop and his hand clamped to the side of his neck. He pulled a dart out of his skin, the feathered pink end looking silly in his hand. His gaze met Piper's in a look of shared fear. He swayed. Piper lunged forward, catching him long enough to ease him to the floor.

"Well, well, well," purred a soft, sweet female voice. "Isn't that adorable?"

Piper jerked upright. Standing at the other end of the hall, a tranquilizer gun held casually in one hand, was a beautiful young woman. This time, Piper had no doubts at all: the woman was a daemon.

CHAPTER

-10-

THE LADY DAEMON was blond, buxom, and had a vicious predatory glint in her big blue eyes. She looked ridiculously out of place in a pencil skirt and silk blouse.

"The Head's daughter." She smiled, flashing perfect dimples. "My my, it seems you *do* have quite the weakness for incubi, don't you?"

Piper bit her bottom lip against the denial trying to escape. It would only make her look stupid.

"Micah told me all about you. But that's not why I'm here. I want the Sahar."

"Doesn't everyone?"

"Where is it?"

"No idea. Go find a mirror to admire and leave me alone."

She smirked. "No, I don't think so. You see, I've been waiting here for quite a while, without the knowledge of those imbecile haemons, of course. While my kin have been hunting you, I chose to lie in wait instead. Much more my style."

"Uh-huh. Admit you're a lazy ass."

Her mouth flattened. "Give it to me and I promise to kill you quickly."

Piper snorted, trying to hide her panic. Her chances of winning against the daemon weren't good, especially not when her head hurt so badly she was about to toss her dinner. She nudged Lyre with the toe of her boot but he didn't so much as twitch.

The daemon curled her fingers and claws glinted at the tips. Time was up. What did she do? She stepped back from Lyre, out cold and helpless. She had to get the daemon away from him.

"All right, I do have it," she said loudly. "But you can take it over my dead body."

She turned and ran. The daemon yowled like an angry cat and charged after Piper. How was she running in that skirt? Piper bolted to the stairs and jumped them two at a time, leaping the last five at once. She hit the floor and went into a roll. She came up on her feet and darted down the hall opposite the one where she'd beaten up the haemons. The daemon came tearing after her.

Piper whipped around a corner, down a smaller hall, and saw the door she wanted. She ran right into it, managed to turn the handle, and fell onto the mats on the other side. She rolled as the daemon pounced, landing right where Piper had been. She scrambled up.

The sparring room was the size of a swimming pool, two stories tall, and covered in mats. The far end had punching bags, a climbing rope, a rock wall, human-shaped dummies, and a pulley system with moving bull's-eyes. The opposite wall was lined with various weapons and sparring tools. The rest was wide-open space.

Piper lunged for the wall of weapons. She reached for a bladed staff but the daemon pounced again. Piper dove, rolling away, and came to her feet right beside a row of practice swords. She grabbed a bokken and whirled to face the daemon.

The woman stopped a few feet away, eyebrows shooting up at Piper's choice. "A wooden sword?"

"A wooden katana," Piper corrected. She hefted the polished, narrow weapon. It might not cut but it was solid, heavy wood. Better than nothing.

"Hmph. Foolishness." The daemon raised her hand and flicked her fingers casually.

Piper threw an arm in front of her. The diluted spell knocked her several steps back but she kept her footing. Hoping for the element of surprise, she charged. The daemon smirked and lifted one hand to catch the bokken. Piper changed direction and swung low, slamming the wooden blade into the top of the daemon's thigh. The woman yelped and staggered back. Piper swung again, aiming for the woman's head.

Unfortunately, daemons have impossibly fast reflexes. The woman ducked and snapped out an arm. Her fist hit Piper in the shoulder, knocking her sideways. Before Piper could recover, the daemon kicked the back of her knee. Piper fell into a roll and came up again facing the daemon. Blondie smirked.

"Not good enough." She slowly advanced.

Piper silently agreed but twisted her mouth in a sneer. "What would you know? Probably never had a real fight in your life." She made her voice go high-pitched. "What if you broke a nail, oh no!"

Blondie stopped and smiled slowly. "You don't know much about us, do you? Well, let me show you something before you die. What we *truly* are." She spread her arms out wide.

It would have been the perfect opportunity to attack but Piper was frozen with shock as the woman's body shimmered. And then her glamour was gone and it wasn't a woman standing in front of Piper.

It was a really big cat. Sort of.

Her face was almost the same except her icy blue eyes were huge and had slit pupils. Her hair was coarser, exactly like the yellow fur that had sprouted over her entire body. Her clothes were gone. Her legs had warped at the joints into something hideously feline, yet her furry arms were mostly human but with huge nasty claws. A tufted tail flicked back and forth behind her.

"Umm," Piper breathed, licking her lips. "Sphinx?"

"Good girl." The daemon ran her hands down her front, smoothing the fur. "Do you think now that I cannot fight?"

Uh, no. Definitely not. Sphinxes were notoriously vicious. "You haven't told any riddles."

"What?" the creature spat.

"Riddles," Piper said, blinking away her shock. Lyre hadn't been kidding that some daemons did not look good without glamour. Blondie wasn't so pretty anymore. "Sphinxes and riddles, you know. Aren't they kind of your thing?"

"Ugh," the sphinx snarled. "No! I hate riddles. Whatever stupid human came up with that nonsense needs their spinal column removed."

"Right," Piper said. "You're too dumb and blond to come up with any, aren't you?"

The sphinx hissed like an angry cat and dropped into a crouch. "Here's a riddle for you then, idiot girl. What has no magic, is an incubus slut, and is about to die? Hmm?"

Piper tightened her grip on her sword, trying frantically to think of a plan—any plan. "That was just lame," she told the sphinx.

The creature sprang. Piper swung her sword, slamming it into the sphinx's shoulder, but the cat-woman's momentum sent Piper flying anyway. She landed hard on the mats and rolled to her feet. She scoured the room for an idea, because if she didn't get one soon, she would be shredded to ribbons. Blondie was toying with her, probably hoping Piper would give up the Sahar after a few bruises.

The sphinx stood between Piper and the real weapons, leaving her with access to nothing but practice weapons. As she backed away from the sphinx's slow prowl, her gaze darted from the punching bag to the climbing rope.

"I have a riddle for you," Piper said, skittering backward. "Want to hear it?"

The sphinx's lip curled. "No."

"You sure? Bet mine's better than yours."

The creature hissed and leaped six feet to crash into Piper. She managed to deflect the claws with her bokken but her aching head smacked the mat when she landed on her back. Shadows crowded her vision. She kneed Blondie in the gut and flipped the woman off her, then staggered to her feet. Oooh, woozy. Not good.

"What's your riddle then, clever little slut?" the sphinx hissed. She flexed her furry, clawed fingers.

Piper backed toward the far side of the room, nerves twisting in her belly. Her plan had better work or she was kitty meat. "It's definitely better. It goes like this …" She stepped behind a punching bag and poked her head around the other side. "Three parts. First part: What's made from a living thing but was never alive?"

The sphinx blinked stupidly, then lunged at the punching bag. Piper danced away and ducked behind a foam man on a pole. "Second part: What binds, burns, and chokes all at once?"

The sphinx leaped on the foam man and ripped his head off. Piper jumped out of the way and grabbed the climbing rope. The sphinx growled, slowly approaching, her eyes darkening to black. She was about to start using magic again. Piper sucked in a sharp, nervous breath.

"Third part," she said slowly. "What triumphs and defeats in the same instant?"

The sphinx went still. Piper could practically see her brain straining. "That's not a riddle. It's nothing but nonsense."

"No, it's—"

With a furious yowl, the sphinx sprang.

Piper threw herself into the rope. She swung away as the sphinx skidded on the mats. Piper swung back. She jabbed with her sword on the way by before landing behind the sphinx. She dropped her sword. With the end of the rope still in one hand, she jumped on the sphinx's back. The creature spun wildly. Piper rolled off the sphinx's other side, passed her end of the rope over the main length, and threw all her weight against it.

The loop of rope around the sphinx's neck snapped tight. When it jerked taut, it momentarily lifted the sphinx right off her feet. Her eyes bulged. Piper strained against the rope until her legs gave out and she collapsed to her knees, aching and exhausted. Her right arm was bleeding with shallow scratches she didn't remember getting. The sphinx crumpled to the mats, clutching her neck.

Piper dragged herself to her feet. "It *was* a real riddle," she panted, one hand against the stitch in her side. "The answer was the rope. It's silk, comes from bugs … rope burn and whatever … and it helped me win and you lose." Sphinxes might not be obsessed with riddles, exactly, but they were fatally curious. Stupid cat had to hear the whole riddle. Thank God the bimbo had been so easy to distract.

The sphinx slowly rolled over on her stomach, holding her throat with one hand. She was down but she wouldn't be staying that way. Time to go.

Piper ran for the door. Right as she was wondering desperately how to singlehandedly carry Lyre out of the house, the incubus opened the door and casually leaned one shoulder against the frame. He looked over at the stunned sphinx.

"Personally," he said, "I prefer a little less hair."

She stumbled right into him, shaking her head wordlessly. "Can we go now? Please?"

"Sure thing, gorgeous."

He wrapped an arm around her waist and hurried her back down the hall.

"How'd you wake up so fast?" Piper asked as they came to the T-shaped intersection of halls.

"It was the wrong dose for a dae—shit."

"There they are," the skinny haemon from the office yelled. Casanova was right behind him at the end of the hall, along with the haemons Piper had already roughed up.

"This way," Lyre said, yanking Piper in the opposite direction. She tried to run but her legs had turned to Jell-O in the aftermath of too much adrenaline. The haemons barreled down the hall toward them, closing fast.

As they reached the hallway intersection, the sphinx appeared from the third branch of the hallway, spitting with fury and still clutching her throat. The whole group of haemons squealed as they plowed into her. A horrible cat screech filled the hall and magic blasted.

"Um," Lyre said. "Shall we continue on then?"

"Sure," Piper said faintly. A wall exploded as someone's spell missed. "Quickly?"

They jogged to the front door and let themselves out. Piper waited in the trees while Lyre collected their packs of clothes, the briefcase, and his tote of food. Together they hauled their bounty into the dark trees. Ten minutes of walking and Piper recognized the little clearing where they'd hidden the car. She eagerly strode forward, shoving past a thorny bush.

The car was no longer covered in branches. All four doors hung open like the vehicle had been ransacked. The seats were empty.

Ash was gone.

CHAPTER

-11-

PIPER WOULD'VE LIKED to say they didn't panic, but she and Lyre both flipped out for a solid five minutes—searching the obviously empty car, running around the nearby woods, swearing a lot. Then Zwi showed up and led them three dozen yards into the trees where Ash was camped out on a branch.

Apparently, the three haemon goons who'd burst into the kitchen at the worst possible moment for Piper and Lyre had been returning from searching their car. Luckily, Ash had been awake—wondering why the hell he was alone in an unfamiliar car in the middle of a forest—and had been able to ditch the car before the goons found him.

Reunited, they rushed back to the car, threw their things into the backseat, and drove for the next two hours. While Piper filled him in on what he'd missed, Ash alternated between yawning and eating, devouring half the food Lyre had packed before falling asleep again.

As they drove, she held the briefcase on her lap and resisted the urge to open it. She would mix up the files trying to read them in the car and she couldn't risk sabotaging her only chance to find out who'd kidnapped her father. Well, her second chance, because she'd already blown her first chance.

Now that she was away from the Consulate and its "guests," she couldn't believe how much of an idiot she was. She hadn't thought about it at the time, more concerned with staying un-kidnapped and alive, but those haemons had to be part of the plot that had resulted in her uncle being terribly injured, Piper being blamed for stealing the Sahar, and for her father being kidnapped. They knew where her father was.

Why hadn't she made them tell her? Why hadn't she at least tried to get some clues out of them as to their identities? Failing that, she could have gone with them. That would have been the fastest way to find Quinn—but then she would have been delivering the Sahar right into their hands and putting herself at their mercy. Maybe not a good idea.

Either way, she hadn't done any of that. She hadn't found out a single useful bit of information about her attackers. When they'd first mentioned her father, she'd been determined to find out the truth, but then the head-to-wall collision had happened. Nothing like a concussion to make you lose your train of thought.

Why had they tried to capture her? Who cared about her? Her only importance in this whole mess was being the true possessor of the Sahar but only Quinn knew that for sure. Somehow he had kept that secret, though she couldn't imagine how if they'd drugged him. Drugs, magic, and a little time could make anyone spill any secret.

Her hands clenched. She needed to find Quinn. Quickly. Not only because he was in danger and being held prisoner, but also because she had to get to him before they made him reveal she had the Sahar. No one could know the truth. They didn't even have a plan yet. If it got out they had the Stone, they were screwed.

Lyre eventually drove them to a block of rundown apartments where a daemon friend of his rented a flat. Said friend was currently in the Underworld, which meant the place was empty. As the sky began to lighten with dawn, they crept into the apartment building and Lyre used a touch of magic to pop the lock. Once inside, they barricaded the door just in case.

Stumbling with fatigue, Lyre headed straight for the shower. Piper hadn't found out until after the fact, but the sphinx hadn't been the only daemon spying on the Consulate. Lyre had been ambushed outside the building and barely managed to win a fight for his life. Incubi were lovers, not fighters, but it seemed Lyre could deal some punishment if properly motivated.

Piper could have used a shower too but she headed straight for the dusty kitchen table. Ash sat in a rickety chair as she carefully unclasped the briefcase and lifted the lid. The pile of files looked even bigger crammed in the tiny square.

"What the hell?" Ash muttered. It was probably the fifth time he'd spoken since waking. The normally quiet daemon had gone emo-worthy reticent since his near-death injury. If she hadn't had bigger problems, she might have been concerned.

"There was a lot of stuff in the safe," she said defensively as she eased the first three folders off the top. "I didn't have time to go through it."

He grunted and accepted the first stack of folders. She took three and sat beside him.

"I think we should skim through the folders to get an idea of what each is about," she told him. "Then we can shortlist the ones most likely to have answers and read those in detail."

Ash nodded and opened the first folder. He glanced down the first page, flipped through a couple more, then closed it again. "Financial records for the Consulate," he explained as he pushed that one to the left side of the table.

She opened her first folder. It was a list of suppliers for the Consulate: persons and businesses that could be relied on to supply all the necessities the Consulate needed to function. She closed the folder and dropped it on top of the financial folder. Her next folder was huge and contained a list of daemons banned from Consulates across the continent, with a short description of them and what they'd done to get banned. She hesitated over it, then pushed it to the other side of the table. Revenge could make people—and daemons—do crazy things.

By the time Lyre joined them again, she and Ash were two-thirds of the way through the briefcase. Most of the folders were obvious non-candidates. With Lyre's help, they made it through the last ten files in a quarter hour. Twenty-four were in the unlikely pile. Six were in the short list.

One was the list of banned daemons. One was a list of current and former Consuls from across the continent. The Head Consul was the top authority and managed three hundred other Consulates, so that was a huge folder too. Another one contained profile pages of daemons considered "high risk" that were known to frequent the Consulate's district: daemons branded as aggressive, violent, and unconcerned with law.

The last three files were case studies of groups the Consulate needed to keep an eye on. One was a group of Overworld daemons who wanted to rule the world, or, as their recruitment speech went, "engender a new Earth where peace, tolerance, and high quality of life are enjoyed by human and daemon alike as guided by the generous and fair hands of a central ruling council of Overworld leaders." They called themselves the Saviors, which Piper thought was likely to get them shot. For the most part, the Saviors were harmless, mainly because their "peace for all" mantra hadn't attracted any powerful daemons to their cause. Therefore, no one paid them any attention.

Another was about a human establishment that offered free services to daemons—services of a personal nature. All the daemons had to do was "forget" any kind of protection and never bother coming back to check if any little haemons had resulted. It was essentially a haemon breeding service. Seriously messed up. Even more messed up because, according to the file, it was pretty popular with daemons *and* human parents-to-be. There were certain concerns that the facility might be trying to create a haemon army.

The last file was about a sect of haemons who opposed daemon interference on Earth. Called the Gaians, they wanted to eject all daemons from Earth and allow them to visit only under extremely controlled circumstances. Publicly, they claimed to be fighting for human rights; they protected humans from daemon "milkers" who "stole human energy without consent," and vehemently protested against daemon trickery, bullying, attacks, blah blah blah.

Behind closed doors, their real agenda was more nefarious; by removing daemons from the picture, haemons would become the most powerful beings on Earth—the perfect opportunity to take control. The Gaian haemons were almost as arrogant as most daemons, thinking their magic made them superior to humans and therefore humanity's logical rulers. Their group was dangerously popular among haemons. They easily attracted followers because being a haemon wasn't fun most of the time; humans who knew what they were didn't want anything to do with them, but daemons didn't like haemons either. A lot of haemons would see the chance to not only boot out the daemons but also make a place for themselves in the world as a well-worthy cause.

She finished reading the file and set it on the table. Lyre tapped his fingers on the back of the file about the Saviors while Ash watched her.

"What do you think?" she asked.

"These Saviors." Disgust lined Lyre's voice. "They haven't gotten anywhere because they have no power to back them up. The Sahar would solve that problem."

"The breeding facility," Ash put in with the same tone of aversion, "if it is in fact aiming to generate a fighting force, would likely seek the Sahar as well."

She looked at the file lying innocently in front of her. The Gaians —the name was painfully familiar.

"I think it's the Gaians," she whispered.

Lyre frowned. Ash stared like he was trying to see her thoughts through her skull.

"They have the resources," she explained. "They're the largest group with chapters all over the continent. And they have a history of violent stunts, like burning down that Consulate two years ago."

Lyre nodded slowly. Ash's expression was indecipherable.

"Plus," she added, "as the largest group, they'd have enough people to station those haemons at the Consulate to wait for us."

"For you," Ash corrected softly.

She pressed her lips together; she'd already told them everything her haemon attackers had said, but they were stumped too as to why the haemons had been after her specifically.

"I think we can discount the Saviors," Ash mused. "The presence of the haemons in the Consulate makes them the least likely."

"Maybe either the breeders or the Gaians were trying to recruit Piper," Lyre suggested.

"Why?" she asked bitterly. "I don't have any power to add to their ranks."

"Not magic," Ash murmured, "but you have knowledge."

"Knowledge?"

"About us. Daemons."

She blinked. "I do?"

"So modest." Lyre's expression morphed into a wicked grin. "Well, modest about some things. Not modest when it comes to—"

"*Lyre,*" she hissed.

"What? I'm just saying you're no blushing—"

"Lyre!"

He laughed. Ash looked between them, his eyebrows inching upward.

She cleared her throat loudly. "As I was saying, the Gaians are our best bet."

"Is that what you said?" Lyre asked. "I thought we were still discussing it."

"I ..." She scowled at the folder. "This is the kind of thing the Gaians would do."

Ash leaned forward. "You know about them?"

"Only a little."

"How?"

She scowled deeper, refusing to look up. "My mother had ... Gaian sympathies. She talked to me about them sometimes. Before she left." And then died.

Lyre winced. "That must not have gone over well with your dad."

She'd suspected for years her mother's attitude toward the Gaians had probably been at the root of the argument that had driven her mom out of her life forever.

Ash tapped the Gaian folder. "The breeders are localized and self-focused. The Gaians are more widespread and aggressive in their ambitions."

Lyre nodded. "Sounds like the Gaians are our best bet. What next?"

No one spoke.

"We need proof they were the ones who attacked the Consulate," Piper said. "And if they did do it, then they have my father too."

"So we need to find them," Lyre said. "Once we find your dad, he'll know what to do next."

She nodded. "The file doesn't say where they are. I think they operate like a—like a club, almost. Or a military reserve. They live normal lives except for certain meeting times."

"I don't imagine they meet in any kind of pattern that could be tracked," Ash said. "They probably change the time and location of each meeting."

"Then how do we find them?"

"We could go back to the Consulate and kidnap one of them," Lyre suggested.

"I doubt they'll still be there," Ash said. "Now that Piper knows to expect them, she wouldn't go back."

Lyre sighed. "Yeah, and once the rumors about us being there get out, all our Stone-stealing pals will head straight for the Consulate. Not my thing. I like small, intimate get-togethers, not huge, bloodbath parties."

Ash shrugged like either worked for him.

"So what then?" she asked. She turned to Ash. "Do you know anyone we could ask?" When he didn't answer, she made an impatient sound. "I know your reputation, Ash. Don't pretend."

He frowned and leaned back in his chair. "There is one person I could ask," he admitted. "It would be a risk. Anyone who knows me will know I supposedly have the Sahar."

Lyre's brow pinched with worry. "Who are you thinking?"

"Lilith."

"No way," the incubus groaned. "You want to take Piper to the Styx?"

"Why not?" she interjected dryly. "A visit to the mythical river of the Underworld sounds like a great vacation from all this fleeing for our lives."

"It's a nightclub," Ash explained shortly. He tipped his head back and closed his eyes. "Lilith is the only daemon I know with no interest in the Sahar."

Piper tapped her lips with one finger. "Why is Lilith different?"

"Because she has everything she wants already." He looked ready to go back to sleep as he added, "Lilith is a succubus."

"Yeah," Lyre grumped. "The happiest succubus on the planet."

"Why?"

"Because she owns a dance club full of sex-crazy humans."

Okaaay. Someone was a little jealous. Incubi and succubi had something of a rivalry going over who was better at seduction.

"What makes you think Lilith will know about the Gaians?"

When she spoke, Ash started slightly like he'd drifted off. "She knows something about everything. I'll go tonight and see what she can tell me."

"*We'll* go tonight," she corrected firmly.

"No."

"Bad idea, Piper," Lyre said. "Ash will work better alone."

"Forget it," she snapped. "This is my father's life hanging on what we find out, not to mention *my* life. Besides," she said to Ash, "are you going to leave me alone with the Sahar? What if I'm attacked again?"

Lyre pouted. "What am I? A piece of furniture?"

Ash frowned at her. She met his steely stare and didn't flinch. There was no way he was going without her. No. Freaking. Way.

He read the determination in her face. With a sigh, he leaned back again. "Fine. Come. If you don't like what you see, that's your fault."

"Fine," she snapped. Did he think she didn't know what nightclubs were like? Not that she'd ever been to one … and a nightclub run by a succubus was bound to be … but still. She could handle it.

Ash and Lyre decided to share the double bed in the bedroom, leaving Piper with the sofa. Her head was buzzing with the information from the file and anger burned in her gut. She couldn't wait to find the Gaians and teach them what it meant to mess with her family. She had no idea how she would sleep with the next phase of their plan to come at nightfall, but the moment she lay down, sleep crashed over her.

❂   ❂   ❂

Piper sat at the kitchen table and listened to the silence.

She imagined cities had been noisy places before the world went all to hell. Now, they were too quiet. Even though the apartment building was on a main street, she heard almost no signs of life. Towns were much better places to live in than the wrecks of once-great cities. It didn't help that the neighborhood was on the edge of the slums.

She'd woken a couple of hours ago. After a long shower and a good meal, she was feeling refreshed and ready to get a move on. Urgency made her skin twitch. They'd lost so much time already. As of sunset that night, four days had passed since the attack on the Consulate. Four days that Quinn had been missing. Four days for the prefects to get closer to finding them. Four days for more power-hungry daemons to join the hunt. She wasn't sure how they hadn't been found yet. It was only a matter of time before their luck ran out.

Impatience chewed at her but she'd wait another hour before she woke Ash and Lyre. They both needed sleep. If Lilith the succubus came through, the three of them could be heading to the Gaian headquarters that very night. There had to be a meeting place of some kind nearby if she remembered her mother's comments correctly.

Trying not to think about it, she straightened the file folders still covering the table, aligning them all at right angles to the table edge. When that was done, she stared around the barren apartment for a minute then flipped open the nearest folder. It was the one with the profile pages of high-risk daemons. She began to idly flip through the profiles, reading a little off each page and studying the occasional accompanying photo. Most of the daemons were very nasty indeed. Some were deliberate killers. Others were predators who couldn't control their instincts well enough around humans. A handful of them were dangerous in other ways: breaking laws, abusing their power, or luring innocents into trouble. The more infamous daemons she'd already learned about during her training.

Not all daemons had good self-control. A lot of Piper's training involved a proactive approach to daemon nature—avoid triggering their instincts and causing them to shade. She knew some humans who didn't even know what shading was. The thought made her shudder.

The most important knowledge a person could bring to any interaction with a daemon was that the daemon's mind wasn't built like a human's. They had two modes: logic-driven and instinct-driven. Ash and Lyre were both exceptionally good at staying in logic mode, which was close enough to human behavior that they could pass as human and interact smoothly with the general public. But when that switch got flipped into instinct mode, a mental state called shading, that's when things got dicey.

A daemon in instinct mode was not logical. He wasn't necessarily out of control, but he wasn't seeing the world through rational eyes; he was seeing the world through the eyes of a predator. His reactions were reflexive, instinctive, and often violent. You couldn't reason with him, couldn't talk your way out of a confrontation. Shaded daemons didn't listen to words; they read your body language, scented your fear or anger, and gauged your strength as compared to their own. If you made a wrong move, they reacted. Whether it was right or wrong didn't matter. Whether it was illogical, illegal, immoral, or uncalled-for didn't register. They obeyed instinct, whether that instinct was to defend or, most often, to attack.

A shaded daemon was equivalent to a wild animal. All you could do was try not to provoke an attack, back away slowly, and get the hell out of their way as soon as possible.

She'd come close to seeing Lyre fully shaded in the car when they'd attempted to charge Ash's lodestones. He'd been right on the edge. If he'd gone completely into instinct mode, he wouldn't have stopped. His instincts would've overridden all thought or reason and he would have pumped aphrodisia into her until she was just as willing as any other girl—at least until the magic wore off.

Shivering at the thought, she focused again on the profile pages. She perused them from last to first. Only a few sheets from the top of the stack, she flipped to a page that made her heart stop in her chest.

A photo of a familiar daemon was centered at the top of the page. It was Ash.

There was no doubt it was him. He was partly in profile, concentrating on something distant. He obviously wasn't aware of the photographer. His dark hair was exactly the same as she knew it, braided with that strip of red silk. His gaze was colder than she'd ever seen—his expression hard and unyielding. He looked as dangerous as the other daemons in the folder and far more deadly.

She turned to the identification information.

Name: Ashtaroth
Origin: Underworld (region unknown)
Caste: Draconian
Age: 18-21
Risk Level: 5

She took a deep, shaky breath. Ashtaroth. Did Lyre know Ash's full name? The –taroth ending wasn't meaningless. It was extremely bad news. Underworld daemons swore by Taroth.

Nearly everyone familiar with Underworld history knew the story. For thousands of years, six families—not five—had ruled the Underworld, with the Hades family as the most powerful. They were constantly at odds with their closest rivals, the Taroth family, until about five hundred years ago.

A daemon named Nyrtaroth had been the head of the family then. Nyrtaroth had done something—killed someone or maybe a lot of someones—and the Hades family had lost it. They'd turned on the Taroth family in a bloodbath coup, wiping out everyone except a few younger kids, whom they enslaved and eventually killed. Maybe a handful had escaped but the family itself was broken forever, never to reunite. The bloodline had died out generations ago.

A few daemons claiming to be Taroths had surfaced in the intervening centuries and all of them had been nasty pieces of work. Being outcasts had turned them vicious and most of them died young and violently. There was no record at all of a living Taroth in the last hundred and fifty years.

She'd never before encountered a demon with –*taroth* as part of his name. Was it a coincidence? Could Ash possibly be a distant Taroth descendent? The bloodline was supposed to have died out. Her eyes dropped to the page again.

It was jerked out of her hand.

Zwi backed up the length of the table with the paper clamped in her mouth. Her body had turned a threatening shade of red.

"Give that back," Piper ordered.

Zwi hissed around her mouthful of paper.

"Give it back!"

The dragonet jumped off the table. Piper leaped up but it was already too late. Zwi dashed across the room, her head held awkwardly high to keep from tripping on the paper, and squeezed through the gap where the bedroom door wasn't quite closed.

Piper sank back into her chair. She wasn't about to burst into that room demanding to see a profile of Ash's crimes. Her gaze slid down to the page beneath Ash's in the folder; that daemon liked to hunt humans for sport and was known to have killed at least fifteen innocent people. She knew Ash had a bad reputation and she knew he was dangerous, but was he really like these monsters? He was rated the highest risk level, reserved for known killers.

Ash wasn't shy about using his power to get what he wanted— whatever that was. But she'd been starting to think he was a decent guy beneath that cold stare and menacing reputation. He'd saved her life three times. He'd almost died protecting her. That made it easy to forget his real nature. If he was a Taroth descendant … Every supposed Taroth for the past five hundred years had been a vicious killer.

She closed her eyes and saw his black-scaled hand stretched in front of her, each finger curving into a deadly talon. She saw again how swiftly and effortlessly he'd incapacitated the prefect guards in front of her uncle's hospital room. She relived the terror of that blast of magic he'd used to take down twelve armed prefects at once.

He was dangerous. But she trusted him anyway.

She had no choice.

CHAPTER
-12-

WHEN THE BOYS finally ventured out of the room at nine that evening, it was obvious they'd prepared well for the night's outing.

For possibly the first time, Ash captured Piper's attention before Lyre did. He was back in black, looking once again like the mysterious, intimidating Underworld daemon she'd avoided at the Consulate. Black jeans, heavy boots, and a black shirt with a skull design in silver splashed across the chest. The sleeves had been torn off to bare the mouthwatering curves of his biceps, and his forearms were wrapped in studded leather bracers. A silver chain was wrapped several times around the bracer on his right wrist and another chain hung over his lean left hip. A little extra glamour had darkened his hair to ebony and hidden the red silk tie braided in it.

With effort, she closed her mouth. Damn. Ash was … was *badass*. Dark, sexy, and oh-so-yummy badass. Lyre oozed so much sensuality she'd never really noticed Ash that way before.

Well, she was noticing it now. His mien was still tinted with danger, still intimidating without any apparent effort on his part, but … it was seriously hot.

The memory of the profile page reared in her mind's eye like a bucket of cold water in the face. She swallowed hard and turned her gaze resolutely to Lyre—but he was no safer to look at.

Gone was the respectable charmer with a hint of naughty. He was clad in black and red to Ash's black and silver. His hair was now bleached to dramatic white, a sharp contrast against his warm skin. Dark gray jeans, tighter than Ash's, a bit more chain, a bit less leather. Black t-shirt with a red dragon coiling up one side. Interestingly, his jeans had been ripped down the side of one leg, then sewn boldly together again with a narrow strip of black leather.

She looked back and forth between them, trying to keep her breathing rate normal. Lyre noted the direction of her stare. With a sly smile, he sidled over to Ash and slid an arm over the draconian's shoulders. He leaned into Ash and gave Piper a slow, distinctly wicked smile.

"Two for one is always an option," he purred.

Piper clenched her jaw as her cheeks flushed. Ash gave Lyre a withering look and shrugged away from his arm. She closed her eyes and counted to ten in an attempt to get the image of the two of them out of her head. It burned into her retinas instead. Great, now how would she suppress dirty thoughts for the rest of the night? Lyre's libido was rubbing off on her.

"I guess I'd better change too. Is this, uh, the dress code?" she added, gesturing to Lyre's outfit.

He gave her his impish half-smile. "We're on the conservative side. Feel free to test the boundaries of obscenity laws."

"Oh, why," she drawled, "didn't I think to bring my studded leather corset?"

After retreating into the bedroom, she opened her backpack of clothes and sighed. Not having expected a racy nightclub to pop up on their sightseeing list, she hadn't brought much in the way of club wear. In the end, she selected tight, low-rider jeans and her usual butt-kicking boots. For a top, she cut four inches off the hem of a tight black halter top and pulled it on. Her midriff was totally bare. There. Lyre would be happy. For finishing touches, she put on her spelled armguards, added a long chain from Lyre's bag around her waist, and hid daggers in her boots.

She slipped into the bathroom adjoining the bedroom and tried to work a little life into her black- and red-streaked hair but gave it up as a bad job. With a sigh, she headed back to the main room. As she reached the half-open door, a thump from the main room made her freeze. Imagining killer daemons bursting into the apartment, she crouched at the opening and peered into the room.

A lamp had fallen over, somehow landing without shattering. Zwi was sitting on top of the shade, wings flared and something dark in her mouth. She lowered her head and growled at someone across the room.

Ash appeared, half crouching and grinning like she'd never seen him.

"Give that back, you little monster." The rough words were laced with amusement.

Zwi chattered in a haughty fashion, tossing her head. Piper realized the dragonet had Ash's lodestone wristband in her mouth. Zwi stuck her rear end in the air and swished her tail like a cat about to pounce. Ash lunged for her but she leaped away. He dove after her and she mock-snarled as she ran across the back of the sofa and ducked under the coffee table. Ash stuck an arm under the table and tried to grab her.

Piper blinked and glanced around the main room for Lyre, but the incubus had stepped out. Hidden behind the door, she watched Ash chase his dragonet in another circle around the room before he finally pinned her on the sofa and scooped her into his arms. Unaware of his audience, he slid down to sit on the floor beside the window and pried his wristband out of Zwi's mouth. She gave it up reluctantly, still growling and trying to wrap her little clawed feet around his hand.

He tucked the band in his pocket, then tilted Zwi onto her back and tickled his fingers across her belly. She squirmed and trilled, grabbing his hand with all four feet and trying to gnaw on his knuckles. He pulled his hand free and scratched under her chin. She went limp with bliss and started to purr like a cat—a cat with gray scales, a black mane, and big wings.

Ash idly petted her as his gaze turned toward the window. The softening touch of humor and affection was already fading. The ugly orange light of a streetlamp shone through the barred glass, casting harsh stripes of light and shadow over his face. The room seemed bigger and emptier, too quiet and lonely, as he sat in the far corner beneath the jail-like window, staring off into the night. He bowed his head over Zwi and lightly touched her scaled cheek like she was the only friend he had in the world.

Piper backed silently into the bedroom and straightened. She bit her bottom lip, feeling vaguely uncomfortable—like a voyeur. At the same time, her opinion of Ash softened a little. It was nice to know he could grin like a normal person, play around with his pet, and even show affection. He wasn't as cold as he appeared. Maybe that meant he wasn't as dangerous either ... but she doubted it. She'd already seen him in action.

Ruthlessly burying the mental image of that profile page and its condemning number five, she shook her head to clear her expression and banged the door loudly as she strode out of the bedroom.

For some reason, she was expecting a change in Ash when she appeared—an embarrassed flinch or an accusing glare. Instead, he glanced over casually, still sitting on the floor with Zwi in his lap, and gave Piper's appearance an assessing onceover. Apparently she passed, because he nodded and returned to staring out the window.

She stood there stupidly, not sure how to react. Most of her wanted to throw her hands up and stalk away, screw him and his stone-faced reticence. But then she thought of his grin when he'd faced off with Zwi. There was a nice guy behind those walls. Somewhere.

So she crossed the room and sank to the floor beside him.

"How's your stomach?" she asked. "I never thought to ask if you'd healed all right."

"It's fine," he said. His expression darkened slightly. "Thanks to Vejovis, of course." *The bastard.* He didn't say it, but she could hear the words in his tone.

"He was weird," she commented. "Is he immortal?"

Ash shrugged. "Who knows? Either way, he's ancient with unrivaled healing skills. I was knocking on death's door by the time he showed up but he still managed to bring me back."

"Same as the last time, huh?" she said softly.

His jaw tightened. He didn't look at her. "He told you about that?"

"He said he saved your life once before but you hated him for it because … because he saved the wrong life."

Ash said nothing.

She could tell he didn't want to talk about it but curiosity got the better of her. "Whose life didn't he save?"

His jaw flexed again and he looked away as Zwi chirped in a concerned way and head-butted his stomach.

"My sister," he whispered.

Piper sucked in a sharp breath. "I'm sorry."

Ash stared at nothing, seeing memories. "If that bastard had left me and taken her instead, she wouldn't …" He shook his head sharply. "It was a long time ago."

"That doesn't make it hurt less," she murmured. "How long ago?"

He shrugged. After a moment he realized she was waiting for an answer. "A couple years," he muttered. "Maybe a few more than a couple, I guess. I was fifteen."

Fifteen. So young to have been prepared to die so his sister could live.

"How old was she?"

An even longer pause this time before he answered. "Thirteen."

She nodded sadly and looked down, studying the bruises on her knuckles from punching ugly haemon faces. She touched one of her brutally short fingernails and heard a long-ago voice chiding her for chewing them. Knowing he didn't want to talk about it, she offered a painful memory of her own in return. Yay for sharing.

"My mom left when I was eight," she said. "She walked out and never came back after a big fight with my father. She died a year later. I never got to say goodbye."

A bit of the stiffness receded from his posture at the change of subject. "You didn't see her at all after she left?"

"No. She didn't come back and I had no way to contact her. She never called or anything."

"That must have been some argument."

She nodded. They sat in silence, lost in dark thoughts. Then with a crash and yelp, Lyre careened through the doorway, his sexy outfit spoiled by his obvious fear.

"Uh, guys?" he panted. "We've got company. Squad of prefects just broke down the main door."

o   o   o

By the time they dumped all the file folders except the one about the Gaians in the oven for burning, grabbed all their stuff and hid it under a bed, and snuck out the door, the prefects had searched the entire main floor. They were ejecting all the non-fugitive residents into the street as they went along.

Piper, Ash, and Lyre rushed silently down the hall toward the far staircase—but not fast enough.

"Stop," Ash hissed. "I hear them in the stairwell."

A rumble of voices at the other end of the building warned them another group of prefects had reached the second level.

"Do we fight?" Piper whispered, remembering Ash blasting a dozen prefects out of his way.

Lyre shook his head. "When I was scouting, I saw two more prefect cruisers and a SWAT van on this block alone. If we put up a fight, we'll have all of them on us."

They turned and rushed back down the hall but now they were caught between two groups. Jumping out a window wasn't an option if there were prefects in the street. What were they supposed to do?

Half in a panic, Piper grabbed the nearest door. It was locked. "Damn it," she hissed.

Ash grabbed the handle. Magic sizzled in the air. He yanked the door open and Piper swore again. It was a utility room. A big furnace type thing and a bunch of pipes filled almost the entire space except for a spot right in front of the door.

Voices echoed up the hall and they heard the prefects banging at the first apartment.

Lyre threw a frantic look over his shoulder then dropped to the floor and crawled underneath the boiler thing. It was barely large enough for him to squeeze his shoulders through.

"Hide," he barked over his shoulder. "And lock the door again!"

With a wild look at Ash, she backed into the tiny square of floor space. Ash squeezed in with her and pulled the door shut. It locked with a loud click and they were submerged in almost complete darkness. Only the flicker of a pilot flame deep in the furnace offered any light.

"Ouch," Piper hissed when Ash stepped on her foot. "Where now? We can't just stand here. They open the door and we're caught."

"There's an open space at the back of the room," Ash whispered. "Can you get to it?"

She turned awkwardly and almost fell over. Ash grabbed her shoulders, his elbow hitting something metal with a loud clunk. He would have a bruise from that. His body was warm against her back and already she was starting to sweat from the airless heat in the room. At the far end, beyond a tangle of pipes and equipment, she could in fact see a dark blob that might have been a shadowy square.

"You first," she whispered. Voices outside the room were drawing closer.

"Hurry up," Lyre rasped from his hidden spot under the boiler. "Curse Moirai's luck, this is uncomfortable. And hot."

She and Ash did a sort of slow dance turn until she was pressed against the door and he was able to squeeze between a set of pipes and climb over some other metal junk as he worked toward the back of the room. Piper gingerly followed. Her heart pounded in her throat and it was so dark she could hardly see what she was climbing over. When she reached the "open space," she almost cried from frustration.

It was a tiny box of an opening with piping running everywhere and only enough space for Ash to cram into the corner. Where was she supposed to go?

A male voice yelled something, so close the prefect could have been standing outside the door. The boiler hummed too loudly for her to make out the words but the authoritative tone was unmistakable. With no other option, she squeezed into the space and folded up pretty much on Ash's lap. There was nowhere for her legs, so she stuck them under a jam-packed cluster of pipes that were only six inches above the floor. Her boots hit something hidden underneath that made a crispy crunchy noise like dry straw. Terror swept through her as she waited for a horde of rats to swarm her legs but nothing happened.

"Well," she muttered, "this is awkward."

"Don't complain," came Lyre's voice from off to her right, slightly breathless. "I think I'm getting heat stroke under here."

"Quiet," Ash hissed.

Piper bit her lip and listened. There were voices right outside the room. The door handle jiggled as someone tried it. Another jumble of dialogue then the voices moved away. Ash relaxed—and Piper blushed as every one of those muscles she knew he had flexed under her.

She licked her lips and tried to think unsexy thoughts. Since when did she have this problem with Ash? She'd thought Lyre was her kryptonite.

In spite of the massive discomfort of being scrunched in a stuffy room full of hot metal pipes with spider webs everywhere, she couldn't ignore Ash behind her. Like, *right* behind her. As in, her back was pressed against his chest, his breath hot on the side of her neck, his thigh flexing under her like he was uncomfortable—which he probably was. And somehow, in spite of the icky, musty room, she could smell him: a delicious, warm, fresh scent like sun-heated mountain air. How could he smell so damn good at a time like this?

For a solid five minutes, they sat in silence, listening to the distant sounds of the prefects dismantling the apartment level. She wondered what they'd make of the oven full of magic-roasted papers.

Maybe that kind of thing was normal around here. At least the prefects didn't have any magical trackers or they would have walked straight to the correct door instead of searching each suite.

Her train of thought was interrupted when Ash abruptly jammed his hands under her butt and heaved her a couple inches off his lap so he could straighten out his leg. He settled her back down again with a sigh of relief. She took several deep breaths and tried to pretend her heartbeat hadn't kicked up to a gallop—or that she was inappropriately aware of his hands now resting casually on her waist.

"So," Lyre whispered conversationally, "you do like your closets, don't you, Piper?"

"Oh yeah," she hissed back, heavy on the sarcasm. "This is my favorite one yet. Machinery is so totally my thing."

Lyre snorted. "I think my favorite closet was the first one. Remember?"

"Remember what?" Ash asked. His breath on her neck made her shiver. She didn't want to be thinking about past closets right then.

"I zapped a haemon with aphrodisia," Lyre explained. "Sort of riled up Piper a bit by accident."

"Lyre!"

"What? It's the truth."

"You don't have to tell everyone."

"Ash isn't everyone."

"If that was the first closet," Ash interrupted, "what was the second one?"

"Ah, well." Lyre paused. "Not as interesting."

"Lyre was riled up too," Piper mocked.

"Was not!"

"Then why did you kiss me?"

"I—well—um."

Piper bit her lip. Thinking about kissing was not a good idea. Maybe Ash thought so too, because he shifted a little under her. She bit her lip harder.

"So is this the third closet then?" he muttered. "Or were there more?"

"Uh, no, this is the third."

"No kissing happening in this hellhole," Lyre grumped. "If I stop answering, I've passed out from the heat. Just FYI."

They fell silent as the voices came closer again. These prefects were awfully chatty considering what they were doing. Piper strained her ears. Her leg was starting to itch annoyingly. She twitched it ineffectually; she couldn't reach it to scratch when everything from her knees down was under those damn pipes.

The prefects were now having their discussion right outside the door. The handle jiggled again. Now that they'd searched the whole floor without any luck, they were checking the less likely places.

Ash had gone rock-hard with tension but Piper was having trouble focusing because it felt like something was tapping her leg above the top of her boot and she was about ready to scream from the itchy, tickling feeling. She jerked her leg but the tapping merely moved to her knee. Momentarily forgetting about the prefects, she shoved backward until she'd squashed Ash flat into the wall, creating just enough extra space to get her one knee out to scratch it.

Her knee came out from the under the pipes—and she screamed.

Ash clapped a hand over her mouth at the last second. Her muffled squeal was covered by the crunch of metal as the prefects broke the lock on the door. Ash clamped his other arm around her middle like a vice.

"Hold still," he hissed in her ear.

The door to the utility room flew open.

An electric charge of magic rushed through her, coming from Ash. He whispered something in another language. The shadows around them thickened and darkened—but not enough to hide what was sitting on her leg.

The hugest, freakiest spider she had ever seen was lounging on her knee, tapping its two front legs against her jeans like it couldn't quite decide if they were edible or not. It was a dirty white color with yellow joints, skinny long legs, and two huge fangs that wiggled around like it was chewing something. Huge fangs less than an inch from her skin. She didn't think her jeans would stop them.

She probably should have been concerned about the prefects shining flashlights all around the room or Ash nearly crushing the air out of her to keep her still, his hand tight over her mouth. Instead she was frozen, staring at the spider, petrified. The urge to leap up screaming was almost too much.

"Clear," one of the prefects announced.

"Yeah, no one is going to fit in there," the other agreed. He started to turn, his light skimming along the floor. "Wait, what's that?"

Ash's hand twitched. The spider inched along her leg.

"Oh, it's only a gauge. The glass reflected the flashlight," the guy mumbled. "Let's go."

They backed away and swung the door shut with a bang. All of them jumped at the sudden sound—including the spider. It leaped like it had been launched off a springboard, right at Piper's chest.

She lost it. She screamed into Ash's hand and flailed like a mad thing. He held her down, straining to keep her in place as she hit her elbows and knees against the pipes. He turned, dumping her onto the floor and pinning her.

"Hold still," he growled. "Where is it?"

"Where's what?" Lyre squawked. "What's wrong?"

Piper went stiff as a board. Ash crouched over her, a knee on either side of her as he craned to try and spot the insect. She bit her lip so hard she tasted blood, tears streaming from her eyes. Her muscles quivered. Give her minotaurs, sphinxes, anything but *spiders*.

"I don't see it," Ash whispered.

Something tippy-tapped against her stomach.

She made a muffled screech of horror and pushed off the floor with so much force she shoved Ash into the pipes above them. His head hit one with a clang.

"On my stomach," she gasped, fighting back the scream writhing in the back of her throat.

Ash flipped her over. A lump quivered under the hem of her shirt. He yanked her shirt up so fast it made a ripping noise and he snatched the spider off her with his bare hand. His fist clenched and orange spider guts squirted from between his fingers.

Piper gasped for breath as her panic started to cool. Ash shook his hand, sending spider bits flying, then wiped it on the bottom edge of his jeans. He peered at his palm again.

"The little bastard got me," he muttered.

"It bit you?" she gasped.

She lurched halfway up—and belatedly realized there was no room for her to sit up. In fact, there was no room to move. In their spider-spawned wrestling match, they'd somehow gotten turned around so Piper was on her back, her legs bent, knees sticking up, shins jammed against the same pipes she'd had her legs under before. Ash was kneeling on top of her, the backs of his legs pressed against the tops of her thighs. He was bent double under the pipes with one hand on the floor by her head to brace his upper half.

"Would somebody tell me what the hell is going on?" Lyre snarled.

"Spider," Ash replied, examining his palm.

"A spider?" Lyre repeated mutinously.

"A freaking huge spider," Piper corrected, half angry, half humiliated. "Crawling up my leg. It got in my shirt!"

"Can you blame it? I'd want to get in your shirt too."

"Lyre, this is not the time."

"According to you, it's never the time."

"Would you shut up? We have enough problems already." She reached for Ash's wrist. "Let me see your hand. Did it get you bad?"

He allowed her to turn his hand around. Two red-rimmed marks pierced the side of his hand, but it wasn't turning funny colors. Yet.

"There are no spiders in this region dangerous to people," he said. "Besides, I'm immune to most poisons."

She blinked. "You are?"

"Yeah." His eyebrows rose. "Bugs don't really … bug me."

Piper pulled a face. Lyre snorted. "Very witty, Ash."

Ash's mouth twitched in a hint of a smile. The horrible corny pun was to cheer her up. She took another deep breath. "Sorry for losing it. Spiders just … yeah."

"Everyone has their weak spots," he murmured.

"Except you," she grumped.

"Even me."

"Really? Like what?"

He hesitated, then glanced upward at the pipes two inches above his head. "I don't like ... confined spaces."

Piper blinked, then glanced around. "Uh, confined as in *this closet* sort of confined?"

He winced slightly. "Underground confined spaces, mostly, but I can't say I like closets."

She smiled, feeling a little better, although Ash hadn't had a meltdown over being in the closet. Then again, the closet hadn't attacked him.

With a sigh, she looked over their awkward positioning but couldn't see an easy way to fix it. Ash shifted his shoulders uncomfortably.

"How much longer should we wait?" she asked in a whisper.

"Five more minutes," Lyre mumbled, "and I'll be unconscious." His voice sounded distinctly woozy.

"I can't hear anything," Ash said. "Let's get out of here."

He managed to crawl back through the gap in the pipes without stepping on her. She followed, and after checking the coast was clear, they pulled Lyre out by his feet. His face was beet red and shiny with perspiration. He half hung off Ash's shoulder as they stumbled away from the utility room.

As they snuck downstairs and out into the blessedly cool night air, Piper couldn't stop glancing at Ash every minute or two. He'd been nicer about her freak-out than she'd had any right to expect. She'd almost gotten them caught. His casual forgiveness made her wonder how badly he might panic when confronted with *his* phobia. She really didn't want to see a panicking draconian with enough magic to blast them all into next week.

She followed behind the two daemons, her eyes and her thoughts lingering on Ash.

CHAPTER
-13-

WHEN IT CAME to disreputable streets, McIntyre Boulevard was the most disgraceful area Piper had ever seen. The streetlights were broken and the windows of every building were shattered or boarded up. Trash littered the streets and the rusted-out skeletons of cars sat along the crumbling curb. It stank of old urine.

The only spot of life on the whole boulevard was a warehouse-sized building lit up like a runway. Bone-deep bass thumped down the block. The front doors appeared deserted as she warily followed Ash toward the entrance. Lyre walked beside her, uncharacteristically quiet with suppressed excitement. He absently twisted Ash's leather brace around his wrist as he walked.

On their way over, Ash had grumbled about his lodestones being drained. Lyre had responded with his usual respect for privacy.

"Piper and I tried to charge them for you," he said baldly. "It didn't go so well."

Ash flicked a startled glance at Piper, but whether he was surprised that she'd tried or that it had gone badly, she couldn't tell.

"Your fault," she told the incubus, her voice sharp with a *shut-up-now* warning.

"My fault?" Lyre repeated incredulously. "You're the one who jumped me—"

She punched his shoulder so fast he didn't have a chance to dodge. He yelped and stepped away from her. "Jeez, Piper. Fine, it wasn't your fault." He scowled at her. "But it wasn't my fault either that it didn't work. I couldn't siphon your energy."

"Why not?"

"I guess you're more haemon than we thought. It wouldn't work, same as with a normal haemon or daemon."

She looked between the two, confused. "But I don't have any magic."

Lyre shrugged. Ash looked thoughtful. Piper didn't get it. How could she have magic-positive energy but no magic? It wasn't fair.

After that, Lyre had boasted he could have all three stones charged by the time they left the club, so Ash had passed his wristband over. Even though none of them had spoken a word about it since, Lyre seemed excited about the challenge. Piper didn't want to know if Lyre planned to charge the stones by soaking up the lustful atmosphere from the sidelines or by getting down and dirty for energy.

The three of them walked to the heavy metal doors at the front of the building. She could almost make out the music now. Lyre reached for the door handle but Ash touched his shoulder.

"Wait," he said. He turned to Piper and frowned thoughtfully for a second. Then he reached out and combed his fingers through her hair. Air that felt scorching hot then icy cold coated her head before the sensations vanished.

"Nice," Lyre complimented Ash.

She pulled a lock of hair in front of her face. It was shining, coppery auburn—her natural hair color. "You used glamour?" she asked. "But I thought you had to be touching me for that?"

"Um." He rolled his eyes upward, avoiding her stare. "It's not glamour."

"Huh?"

"I burned the dye out of your hair."

"You—you did *what?*"

"It's your natural hair," he muttered defensively. "The streaks were too recognizable." He glanced over, saw her still gaping at him, and turned quickly toward the door. "Let's go."

He pulled the door open and walked in. Still fingering her hair and not sure how ticked off she was, Piper followed. It was almost pitch black inside. The music, no longer muffled, was a dance beat twisted into something pulsing and frenzied. She followed the glint of Ash's chains down the long hall, the music growing louder with every step. Ahead, dim, red-tinted light was mostly blocked by a massive, man-shaped shadow.

Ash clasped forearms in a friendly way with the bouncer and said something Piper couldn't catch over the noise. The huge man's teeth flashed as he grinned and he waved them on. Ash didn't wait. Piper rushed after him and swung around the corner to find a room she definitely hadn't expected in an underground club.

The hallway had doubled in width. On either side, long tables stood like sentries, draped in red velvet. Covering almost every inch of the tabletops were masks: stylized, jeweled, feathered, and beaded masks with long ribbons. Half of them were recognizable as animal countenances; the rest were fantasy creations. All of them had a sinister cast to them.

Curved glass cases protected the masks and a masked attendant stood behind each display. The male attendant, with a grinning snake mask, wore no shirt and had scales painted over one shoulder. He spread his hands invitingly across his display. The woman on the other side, wearing a feathered peacock mask, was already reaching under her table. She produced a black mask and handed it wordlessly to Ash. He accepted it with a nod.

"Choose one," he said over his shoulder to Piper. He turned away to affix his mask to his face.

"But … why?" she asked. On closer inspection, the man's display had smaller, more feminine masks than the opposite side.

"Because the Styx is an anonymous sort of place," Lyre replied absently, perusing the woman's masks. "I'll take that one," he decided, pointing to a ruby-studded fantasy countenance with long red and black ribbons.

Piper turned to the man's display and swallowed. They were all beautiful but vaguely creepy. How was she supposed to pick one? The silent attendant recognized her confusion. He reached under the glass and lifted a silvery mask with a delicate, pointed snout and large, silky ears. He passed the stylized fox face to her.

"This one?" she questioned. He nodded. She shrugged and put it on, fumbling the trailing ribbons as she tied the mask in place. Whatever.

"Come on," Lyre said, his red and black mask in place. It looked doubly sinister with his golden eyes peering out, the strange angles pulling her gaze irresistibly to his. Ash was already walking down the hall, his steps quick with impatience. The hall curved again and he vanished around the bend. Piper trotted after him, rounded the corner, and stopped to stare.

There were only two colors of light in the massive room that opened in front of her: red and blue. The red came from everywhere, radiating dimly from under the bars, out of the cracks in the walls, and from hidden pot lights. Blue flickered and flashed from strobe lights and spotlights. Everything else was black that reflected the colored lights. The effect was eerie beyond words. The red light suffused the smoky air as it subtly pulsed, while the blue lights flashed all over the room in time to the eardrum-bursting bass.

The club was packed. Bodies swayed and writhed to the music and crowds formed dense spots of black around the bars and what looked like some sort of stage at the far end. Small tables with stools surrounded a dance floor that took up the entire center of the space.

Everyone in sight wore a mask and most wore costumes to match. Piper gaped at the sight of a hundred bodies moving to the beat until Lyre took her elbow and steered her straight into the mass of dancers in the wake of Ash's retreating back. They made their way toward the main bar at the back of the huge room. The flashing, flickering lights made it hard to see, but it would have required pitch blackness for her to stop staring.

The club was in the middle of the worst neighborhood in the city. Its patrons were clearly not local. The costumes were sophisticated, expensive, and, for the most part, barely there. The most common theme ran along the same lines as Ash's and Lyre's new outfits, but way less conservative. Piper swallowed hard as her gaze flicked from skimpy leather to heavy chains to corsets, ribbons, lace, and fishnet. Hair in every unnatural shade was styled in every extreme. A couple dressed in matching costumes that looked like slightly menacing koi fish swayed together. The masked faces of the dancers swam through the pulsating light, anonymous and mysterious.

Maybe it was the masks or maybe it was the club, but lack of inhibition was as much a theme as the red and blue lights. There was everything short of intercourse going on around her. When she passed a woman in tight red strips of material and a cat mask sandwiched suggestively between two men, Piper forced her gaze to Ash's back and kept it there, thankful for the mask hiding her expression.

Ash led them straight to the bar, stopping beside a girl wearing a black and purple corset, purple panties, thigh-high fishnets, and a dragonfly mask. Piper resisted the urge to cover her ears with her hands; her head was going to split from the blaring music.

She looked toward the stage for distraction. It was a long raised strip draped in black and red velvet, highlighted by circling spotlights. There were three silver poles and three gyrating dancers. The dancers were wearing almost nothing except their masks. Lyre watched with interest. She rolled her eyes.

As her gaze travelled away, a man sauntered past her and her jaw dropped.

His mask was superb, stylized like a white lynx face, but the furred ears that poked through his hair were swiveling to follow sounds and the long, swishing white tail behind him was as real as his legs, which ended in paws. He was unmistakably a daemon.

She stared openmouthed, then jerked her gaze across the faces of the nearest dancers. They didn't look shocked or fearful. They were staring, yes, but with keen interest and obvious attraction. Without the slightest sign of self-consciousness, the daemon insinuated himself onto the dance floor and was immediately surrounded by a group of hip-swaying girls. One stroked his ear suggestively. Piper swallowed hard. He was either a daemon who'd gotten real creative with his glamour, or he was a neko daemon and wasn't bothering with glamour at all. He was a lot less mutant-looking than the sphinx, but his alienness was unmistakable.

Breathing a little too fast, she surveyed the club again more carefully. Neko-boy wasn't the only daemon there; most of them were in varying stages of un-glamour. One, no doubt an Overworld daemon like the neko, had done herself up like some sort of gold and blue fairy, wings included. Others were more subtle, scattered at random throughout the crowds of humans, but all of them were receiving triple the attention of the opposite sex.

What the hell was going on with this place? Daemons did not walk around without glamour. They just *didn't*.

Someone tapped her shoulder. Piper turned and her heart skipped. The man's glossy black mask was gorgeously done but frighteningly realistic. It seemed to be a part of his face, the planes of it curving over his forehead and cheekbones to form a countenance that was both feline and reptilian. The mask cut in at the hollows of his cheeks to reveal tantalizing strips of his defined jaw line. Elegant, curved horns swept back from the sides to cover his ears.

She blinked and realized the dragon-masked man was Ash.

Heat rushed into her face and she was doubly glad of her own mask. He gestured for her to follow him. Hoping he hadn't noticed her shocked staring, she fell into step behind him. How could she not have recognized him?

Giving Lyre a whack in the back of the head to get his attention off the pole dancers, Ash led the way to a partially hidden door in the far corner of the club, guarded by two masked bouncers who nodded amiably at Ash as he went through.

Stairs spiraled down, lit by recessed red lights. Ash pushed open a door at the bottom and the sudden change took Piper by surprise. A brightly lit, business-like hall stretched in front of them, leading to a posh, professional sitting room that would have looked right at home in a Consulate.

Ash stopped in the center of the room and pushed his mask on top of his head. "They're letting Lilith know we're here. She should join us in a minute."

Pushing his mask up as well, Lyre wandered over to a chair and sat. He had a vague, punch-drunk sort of expression on his face. Probably reliving his walk across the lust-crazed dance floor.

Piper exhaled slowly. "So what's with the daemons here?" she asked.

Ash shrugged. "Sometimes it's liberating to be who you are."

"Plus the female attention," Lyre said dreamily. "Some humans love that sort of stuff."

"But …" She frowned at him. "Didn't you say daemons don't show off their true shapes because we'll never believe they're human again?"

"The daemons here don't want people thinking they're humans," he told her. "They want attention, not anonymity."

She raised her eyebrows. "Have you ever gone around this club with no glamour?"

He flashed her a grin. "No. I can get all the attention I want without cheating."

"How is *not* using glamour cheating?"

"Lyre is less attractive with his glamour," Ash said unexpectedly. "By our standards, I should say."

Piper blinked in surprise.

Lyre looked amazed too. "Do mine ears deceive me, Ash? Did you just say you're attracted to me?"

"Your ears deceive you."

Piper snorted. "You must be pretty lust-drunk, Lyre. You're flirting with the wrong gender now."

He blinked, then looked a little embarrassed. "Uh … yeah, maybe." He gave his head a little shake and stood again. With a languid stretch, he minced over to Piper's side and slid a hand across her stomach, curving it over her opposite hip. He leaned against her side and grinned as he put his lips to her ear.

"They say dancing is like sex with clothes on," he purred. "I think we should try it."

With an exasperated huff, Piper yanked out of his grip, stumbling in her haste. Ash caught her arm and pulled her up, and somehow she ended up leaning against him. She blinked at him, caught off guard. He looked a little surprised too.

Lyre let out a sudden growl. "Back off, Ash."

Insulted at his possessive tone, Piper turned toward the incubus—and took a shocked step back into Ash. Lyre's eyes had gone *black*. Totally black. He'd shaded in five seconds flat!

"Um, Lyre?" she whispered.

He bared his teeth, his attention on Ash. "Back off," he snarled.

Ash slowly raised his hands and deliberately settled them on Piper's waist. A low rumble, a growl almost below the level of hearing, vibrated through his chest. With her heart pounding in her throat, she craned her neck for a glimpse of his face. Shit. Ash's eyes had gone black too—even faster than Lyre's.

Breathing deep and fighting for calm, she tried to ease away from Ash, but his hands tightened like vices and pulled her back into him. Lyre's jaw went tight. What the hell was going on? Why had both of them completely lost their heads at the exact same moment?

Lyre's mouth twisted in a snarl. "Let go of her," he said, biting off each word. For a second, Piper thought he was regaining some sense. Then he added, "I claimed her first."

The blood drained out of her head. Oh, this was bad. If it hadn't been *Ash* holding her, she would have put a boot between his legs—but she didn't want to die tonight.

The draconian slid one arm around her waist, trapping her with his iron strength. His other hand cupped her throat, tipping her head back. She resisted the instinct to fight him as he forced the submissive, exposed-throat position on her. Fighting back would only inflame his instinct to dominate her. He put his nose to her hair and inhaled with his eyes closed—before those black eyes snapped open to lock on Lyre in a scorching stare both challenging and mocking.

Lyre snarled at the taunt and stepped aggressively forward until he was pressed against Piper's front and right in Ash's face. Piper gasped, caught between them and fully aware of the danger of her situation. Her two companions, who under normal circumstances would've jumped to her protection, were now the greatest threats to her safety. That's what happened when daemons shaded, when instinct took over. Unpredictable was an understatement. If the violence simmering between them erupted, chances were they would forget entirely about the all-too-breakable girl in their way.

"Um," she tried again, keeping her voice assertive but neutral. "Guys? You're both my friends and everything, but I don't belong to either of you. You *both* need to back off."

Slowly, like spotlights shifting, the two daemons focused on her. Her breath caught as she met Lyre's black stare. It was a wolf's stare, predatory and merciless, lacking in the light of higher consciousness that separated humans from animals. She swallowed hard.

"Lyre," she whispered. "Please."

His empty stare held, unchanging.

Ash was perfectly still, his hand still warm against her throat, a deadly chokehold one flex of his fingers away. His arm around her waist suddenly tightened.

"Bitch," he hissed.

The air sizzled. Ash flicked his hand out, and with a mini-concussion, Lyre was blown backward off his feet. Before Piper could react, Ash released her and whirled around.

"Lilith, you jealous, scheming bitch," he rasped, his voice guttural. "I'm going to rip out your heart."

A silvery laugh rang through the room. Piper spun around.

With a smile playing about her full lips, the young woman leaned casually against the doorframe. She was gorgeous. She put sunsets and the northern lights to shame. Her amber-brown eyes were huge and magnetic, her long, pale blond hair luxurious. Her figure was flawless. She wore jeans and a simple white blouse that showed little skin but enhanced every perfect curve.

Staring at the girl, Piper felt her self-esteem crash and burn.

"I was merely having a little fun, my lovely dragon." Her smile was so radiant and guileless that Piper had the sudden urge to apologize.

"That was no game," Ash growled. "We could have killed her."

Lyre stalked forward to stand shoulder to shoulder with Ash. Piper found herself standing behind them, mentally struggling to catch up.

"Aphrodisia isn't a toy," the incubus snarled.

Lilith tilted her head and her eyes flickered to ebony and back. Ash and Lyre both stiffened and stepped forward in unison before jerking themselves back. Ash made a hideous low-pitched snarl that no human throat could have produced.

"Do that again and you won't like what happens next."

Piper took a deep breath as she finally understood. Lilith had hit Ash and Lyre with her succubus magic, which, as the opposite of incubus aphrodisia, only worked on men. That's why they'd gotten all competitive over Piper out of the blue. Aphrodisia didn't work well on daemons, but when used fast and hard, it spurred a reaction far more dangerous than a lustful human.

"Can't you forgive a girl her curiosity?" Lilith pressed one hand contritely to her chest. "You've never brought a lady friend to my club before. I was merely interested in whose partner she was." Her head tilted again as her gaze drifted to Piper. "But it seems she stands between you, claimed by neither. How … daring."

"I don't belong to anyone," Piper snapped, surging into motion. She strode around the two daemons and planted herself in front of them, arms folded. "And if you mess with them again, you'll regret it."

The succubus threw her head back in another bell-tone laugh.

"A human girl protecting *you*?" She covered her mouth with a hand, stifling another laugh. "How the mighty have fallen. Do you fear me so much, Dragon?"

"I don't make mistakes twice."

"We'll see." Lilith smiled like they were all best friends and gestured to the sofas. "Shall we sit? May I offer you any refreshments?"

Lyre turned without a word and thumped down on the nearest sofa. His jaw flexed back and forth. Piper grudgingly turned her back on Lilith. Ash gave her a ghost of a smile, his gray stare reassuringly normal. He sat beside Lyre and since Piper didn't want to sit on the same sofa as Lilith, she perched on the armrest beside him.

The succubus glided to the sofa and perched primly on the edge. She appraised the three of them with a mysterious little smile.

"I see my charms are not what you came to appreciate," she said with a self-deprecating giggle that had a bit of an edge. Her gaze drifted across Piper and back to Ash.

"So then ..." Her head tilted to one side and she smiled like a cobra about to strike. "What might I do for you?"

CHAPTER
-14-

"WE'RE LOOKING for information," Ash supplied.

Lilith's face brightened with interest. She tapped a finger against her bottom lip. "What sort?"

"A renegade group of haemons."

"Oh? Is that all you can tell me?"

Ash was silent. Piper bit her tongue, determined to let him do what he did best.

"Would this be related to ... a certain notorious lodestone that is presently missing?"

"Maybe."

She pursed her lips and smoothed her blouse over her chest. Piper scowled. Lilith couldn't go twenty seconds without somehow drawing attention to her *assets*.

"Ash, my dearest, you didn't fall to temptation, did you?" For the first time, genuine emotion infected the succubus as her perfect forehead wrinkled. "*No one* can help you if ..."

"I didn't steal it."

"But the rumors—"

"Are wrong."

"That makes no difference." Lilith leaned forward. "Your name even now is being whispered in the darkest corners of the Underworld. Samael himself believes you're guilty."

Piper inhaled sharply. Samael was the head of the Hades family and the very daemon who was supposed to have returned the Sahar to the Ra family.

"That is why I must find this haemon group," Ash said, his voice soft, intense. "*They* are the thieves. I must prove their guilt to clear my name—before it's too late."

Lilith bit her bottom lip. "Even that may not save you."

"I know."

"But you must try," she said with a nod. "This would be the Gaians you're asking of, correct?"

"Yes," Ash said, relaxing slightly.

"How did you know?" Piper blurted.

Lilith smiled coolly. "I know something of everything, little dove. The Gaians have been drooling over the Sahar since it resurfaced. They made a bid to steal it once already, eight years ago." She returned her attention to Ash. "What do you need to know?"

"Where can I find them?"

"In the city? Everywhere."

"Their base of operations in this area," he clarified impatiently.

Lilith straightened, her chin lifting and her hands folded neatly in her lap. A sudden feeling of foreboding trickled through Piper.

"Divulging that kind of information … why, my haemon patrons would be most unhappy with me. They might even refuse to return. If I am to lose customers, I must have something in return."

"I thought you wanted to help Ash," Piper cut in, anger spinning through her at Lilith's selfishness.

The succubus smiled. "I do. But I didn't get where I am by giving things away for free, Piperel."

"You—"

"What do you want?" Ash interrupted.

Lilith let her gaze slowly slide over Ash, the tip of her tongue sliding across her lips at the same pace. "If I asked for you, would I get you?"

Ash flicked a glance at Piper and shrugged.

"Y—"

"No."

When everyone turned to look at her, Ash included, Piper realized the angry denial had come from her. She blinked, then folded her arms and tried not to look astonished at her own response.

"I'll pay your price, whatever it is," she said. "This is my problem more than his and he's done enough already. It's my turn."

"Piper—" Ash began in a low voice.

"No! I can do this." She glared at everyone. Where her sudden determination was coming from, she didn't know. Jealousy of Lilith's impossible beauty was a part of it, but she kept thinking of everything Ash had done and suffered since they'd started this. He shouldn't have to sacrifice anything else for her.

"Piperel," Lilith said in the patient, you-are-an-idiot tone the snobby girls at school had down pat. "Honey, a night with me is hardly costing him anything. I dare say it would be more gift than burden."

"I don't care. I'm doing this."

Lilith leaned back and smiled at Ash. "Well. Isn't that sweet? She's still protecting you. How chivalrous."

Piper clenched her teeth at Lilith's gender-bending word choice.

"Dear Piperel's fiery determination is so admirable," Lilith continued, her smile turning viciously sweet. "I would like to put that fire to good use—in the ring."

"*No!*" Ash and Lyre both exclaimed at the same time.

"What ring?"

Lilith's smile was now utterly serene. "That is my offer. I will give you the exact location of the Gaians' headquarters. In return, Piperel will fight in the ring until a full loss."

"No goddamn way," Lyre shouted. "Forget it!"

"Not happening," Ash growled.

"*What* ring?" Piper asked again.

"The fight ring, of course." Lilith scrutinized her fingernails. "The Styx offers many kinds of entertainment."

"You mean like boxing?" Piper asked. "Or mixed martial arts?" She could do that.

"She means no-holds-barred dog fights, only with daemons instead of animals," Lyre cut in furiously. "They aren't fights to the death, but they don't generally stop until someone is beaten unconscious—that's a full loss."

Piper swallowed hard. Okay, maybe she couldn't do that.

"But you're a Consul-in-training, aren't you, Piperel?" Lilith asked sweetly. "Surely you know how to fight."

"Of course I do."

"Then what's the problem?" The succubus glanced slyly between the two daemons. "Are you two so soft you can't let her fight her own battles?"

"It's not a battle, it's a bloodbath," Ash snapped.

Lilith's head tilted. "You would know, wouldn't you? What's your winning streak in my ring right now, Dragon? Twenty?"

Piper shot a glance at Ash, but his expression was unreadable. "Piper is a haemon," he said tersely. "You can't put her in that ring with daemons."

Lilith sat back and folded her arms. "I've made my offer. It stands."

"Lilith—" Ash began, anger creeping into his voice and sending a shiver down Piper's spine.

"I will have her in my ring, Ash," Lilith said with absolute finality. "Or no deal."

Piper exchanged a look with Lyre. Ash glared. Lilith merely waited, her beautiful face locked in a mixture of stubbornness and triumph. She knew she had them.

What choice did they have? They needed Lilith's information and every minute wasted brought them closer to capture. Nerves tightened in her belly.

"I won't be beaten into unconsciousness," she said. "There's no point if I can't use your information afterward."

"That is true," Lilith said, beaming at this sign of cooperation. "Unfortunately, those are the rules. Every entrant stays in the ring until he—or she—loses a match. The very best fighters fight a dozen or more matches before they tire out and lose. After ten consecutive wins, the option of withdrawing is allowed, but not under any other circumstances. If I changed the rules for you, it would undermine the entire system. I can't do it."

Ten wins? Piper knew that would be impossible.

"Could I fake it?" she asked. "Like, take a few hits and pretend to get knocked out?"

Disdain twisted Lilith's lips. "That bad habit is not tolerated. The referee will call an end to a match if the loser has been dealt a fair amount of punishment but is still conscious, but anyone attempting to get out of completing a match by feigning injuries is ... soundly punished. There is no way your opponent wouldn't know."

"Piper, we'll find another way," Lyre said, leaning forward to meet her gaze. "No one comes out of those matches without a few broken bones *at least*. Sometimes people die."

"He's right," Ash seconded, his voice low. "We'll ask someone else."

Piper took a deep breath and let it out slowly. They didn't have time to go to anyone else and Ash had already admitted Lilith was pretty much his only source of information right now. Anyone else would ambush him for the Sahar.

She slowly shook her head. "We don't have the time or the resources," she told them. "We'll just have to hope for the best."

"You have no idea what you're agreeing to," Lyre exclaimed furiously. He turned to Lilith. "What the hell are you playing at? Why are you trying to get Piper killed?"

"It's business, my dear Lyre." Lilith shrugged delicately. "I haven't had a female in my ring in months. Even if she only lasts a single round, it'll boost attendance for weeks."

"I'll be her opponent then," Ash said, his voice dark and rumbling. "I'll be the one to defeat her—without doing her serious harm."

A truly ugly look flashed across Lilith's perfect face. "You'll have to continue the rounds until you take a full loss."

He nodded shortly.

"But Ash—" Piper began.

"Shut up," he snapped, searing her with sudden, icy anger. "If you hadn't volunteered for this, it wouldn't be a problem."

She sat back, as shocked as if he'd slapped her.

"She has to win some matches first, though," Lilith said, not sounding happy at all. "I won't have you giving her an easy out in her first round."

"She can fight one opponent and then me."

"You can be her fifth opponent."

"She won't last that long."

"Her fourth then. Surely she can win three fights. I will arrange for her opponents to be … reasonably well-matched."

Ash glanced at Piper. She gave a jerk of her head in assent.

"Deal," Ash said.

"Deal," Lilith echoed.

As a cat-like smile of satisfaction bloomed across Lilith's gorgeous face, Piper wished she knew exactly what she'd agreed to do. Surely the ring couldn't be *that* terrible.

Within the hour, she would know exactly how wrong she was.

●　●　●

The daemon howled. His opponent wrenched his arm backward another inch and the shoulder popped out of its socket. Piper couldn't hear the sound of it over the screaming crowd but seeing it was bad enough. The daemon writhed in agony as the other combatant backed away, raising his fists triumphantly. Unbelievably, the downed daemon dragged himself to his feet, awkwardly slanted with his arm hanging limply. He bared his teeth, blood streaming down one side of his face as his opponent turned back to him.

She looked away as the inevitable winner of the match made his final attack. A hideous scream of pain rose above all other sounds before cutting off abruptly. The crowd gasped in unison, then roared in approval. Standing half-hidden in the curtained doorway where fighters entered the arena, she looked across the roughly two thousand humans and three hundred or so daemons packed onto the wide tiers that ran around the half-circle side of the huge basement room. Wild energy stretched every face and a morbid ecstasy radiated from the mob.

At the lowest point in the room, the raised ring drew the eye like an ugly scar on an otherwise unremarkable face. Though a little larger than a typical boxing ring, it had the usual ropes stretched from corner pole to corner pole. An equally high stage ran across the back of the space, where the announcer in his crisp white suit strode back and forth excitedly. The wall behind him had two enormous screens that must have cost Lilith a year's profit each. One showed dramatic close-ups of the fights and slow-motion replays. The other displayed a kind of scoreboard with a profile of each combatant that included his age, history, skill ratings, recent victories, and odds.

Between the two screens was the most frightening thing in the whole room. It was a huge game show wheel, but the outer border wasn't marked with prizes for the spinning arrow to select. Instead, the wheel was divided into four unequal quarters. On the left and right, a symbol like two crossed fists glowed white on a green background. At the bottom of the wheel, a slightly smaller red quadrant showed a sword crossed with a spear. The smallest quarter at the top showed neither fists nor weapons on its solid black background, only a white skull and crossbones.

"*Laaaaadies and gentlemen,*" the announcer called, drawing Piper's attention back to the ring. Two referees were dragging the bloody, unconscious loser out of the ring. They dumped him on a stretcher and marched him out a door on the other side of the ring. It looked like he'd gotten his other arm dislocated too.

The announcer flung a hand out toward the daemon still standing in the ring, waving idly to his fans in an uber-masculine, bulging-muscles way.

"Our victor, Grudge, has won his ninth match. Yes, ladies and gentlemen, he has won *nine* matches! You all know what that means: should he win his next match, he has the option of walking away from the Styx Ring undefeated. Only a tiny handful of our competitors make it this far. You are watching history in the making!"

The crowd screamed. Piper tried to take a deep breath. She glanced over her shoulder as Lyre hurried to her.

"Where's Ash?" she gulped. Fear was starting to make her hands and feet tingle.

"Getting ready," Lyre said tersely. "Have you been watching this guy?"

"His last three fights, yeah," she said.

"Can you take him?"

"I—I think so. Depends on the kind of match."

"He'll be tired by now. Take advantage of it."

She nodded. Lyre gripped her elbow. "You can do this, Piper. You're going to kick ass."

She nodded again. "Kick ass. Yeah." It was hard to feel confident when Lyre looked so pale.

"Remember. Only three matches. You can make it through three, then Ash will help you really convincingly lose." He smiled wanly. "Everyone loses to him, so it won't surprise anyone."

After nodding for a third time, she started to turn toward the curtain again when Lyre grabbed her in a crushing hug. "You'll be fine," he muttered into her hair like he was trying to convince himself more than her. "Ash and I will be watching the whole time. If it looks like you're in big trouble, Ash will get you out, rules be damned."

He finally let go and together they peered through the curtains. The announcer was finishing a summary of Grudge's fighting history to give the daemon a chance to catch his breath.

"But ladies and gentlemen, I imagine you're curious about our champion's next challenger? This individual must be brave indeed to take on the Grudge. But—my goodness—our next challenger is not what I expected."

The crowd quieted as their attention focused on the announcer.

"This challenger—I don't believe it, but this challenger is not a daemon. Ladies and gentlemen, we have a haemon challenger!"

The crowd let out a bloodthirsty roar. The Grudge smirked, foreseeing an easy victory.

"But—but wait. I am quite frankly stunned. Ladies and gentlemen, that is not all. This brave haemon challenger ..." He paused dramatically. "This courageous soul is not even a man!" He spun on his heel and pointed toward Piper's curtained doorway. "Ladies and gentlemen, I give you *Minx!*"

Minx? She could thank Lilith for that demeaning nickname.

Lyre gave her a shove and Piper stepped out from behind the curtain. There was an ominous silence as she stepped out into the full view of over two thousand stares. She scanned a hundred nameless faces, all watching her. The weight of their judgment pinned her in place.

Someone in the front row wolf-whistled. The silence broke as cheers, catcalls, and boos erupted through the whole space. Apparently the crowd was divided on whether they liked her or not. Sucking in a desperate breath, she put her shoulders back and strode toward the ring.

"The mysterious young Minx, ladies and gentlemen, is an amateur fighter from the east end of this great city. She wouldn't tell us much about herself—but," he lowered his voice conspiratorially, "some suspect she's found her way to the wrong side of the law."

That was true enough. At least Lilith hadn't made up some story about Piper fleeing a brothel and learning to fight on the streets while defending herself against lascivious men. She stopped in front of the ring, dismayed to discover the raised floor was chest-high on her. She glanced at the silently watching bouncers. None of them offered her a leg up. Grimacing, she hauled herself up and awkwardly rolled under the lower rope. The floor of the ring was so stained with old blood splatters that its original color had been lost. She clambered gracelessly to her feet as the crowd laughed and booed.

The announcer started blabbing again, talking about Piper's fictitious past wins in some other fight club. She had no attention left for listening, because now that she was face to face with Grudge, her confidence was melting like ice in the desert. He was a lot bigger than he'd looked from a distance. His biceps were as thick as her thighs. He grinned evilly. Overall, he looked like a scruffy sailor, with tattooed arms, a buzz cut, and a crooked nose from being repeatedly broken. Of course, being a daemon, he probably didn't look like that at all. Like all the fighters, he wore a simple black cloth mask that covered the top half of his face.

"And now, ladies and gentlemen, we spin for the match!" The announcer cried. The crowd cheered, then went quickly silent. Dread iced her stomach as everyone in the massive room focused on the big game show wheel. The announcer grabbed the arrow and spun it hard.

It whirled around, spinning past a green section. Past black. The other green. The red. Green again. It spiraled around the wheel, gradually slowing. Piper couldn't breathe. Please please please. Let luck be with her.

The arrow slowed and finally came to a stop on a green quarter with two crossed fists.

"A fist match," the announcer yelled. "Yes, ladies and gentlemen, Minx will fight Grudge with nothing but her wits and skills. A fist match! No weapons, no magic allowed. Combatants, get ready!"

Piper jerked her attention back to Grudge and pressed her back against the corner post behind her. The daemon grinned from his corner.

The bell rang.

Grudge stepped forward. He flexed his arms, leering as he slowly approached. He intended to toy with her first. Piper jumped away from the post before she got cornered and started to scuttle along one side of the square. Grudge turned with her. The announcer was yelling things and the crowd was shouting taunts and encouragement, but Piper focused on her opponent. She had to win.

Grudge stopped. He let his gaze drop and stared pointedly at her breasts. Then he met her eyes and licked his lips. The message was clear. Piper stopped her sneer before it could form, keeping her face slack and fearful. She hadn't had a change of clothes, so she still wore her tight jeans and midriff-baring halter top. The only difference was her hands and wrists were wrapped in white tape so she didn't split her knuckles on anyone's face. Oh, and there was no ring box stuffed in her shirt; Lyre had the Sahar while she was in the ring.

She nervously reached up to adjust her mask. Grudge immediately lunged forward. Ha. Piper's hand, already positioned next to her jaw, was ready to fly. While he was still cocking his arm, Piper flung her fist out with the whole force of her body behind it. Her knuckles smashed into his throat with a satisfying crunch. He staggered backward, clutching his neck and hacking. Piper pivoted on one foot and slammed the other boot into his lower gut in a perfect roundhouse kick. Grudge doubled over. She brought her elbow down on the base of his skull, then kneed him in the face as he started to collapse forward. He went over backward instead.

In a normal fight, Piper would have stopped there, but she had to knock this beast out to win the fight and she couldn't lose momentum now that she'd used up the element of surprise. As Grudge fell backward, she kicked him hard in the kidney. He wheezed. She kicked him again in the gut. He curled over onto his stomach to protect it and Piper jumped onto his back, jabbing her knee hard into his lower back. Then she grabbed his arm, twisted it in a wrestling hold—then twisted a little more. He let out a howl. Piper gritted her teeth and wrenched. His arm popped out. She hoped his last opponent would get to see the replay when he woke up.

Piper grabbed at his other arm for another pain-inducing hold when Grudge heaved over sideways. She fell off him and rolled, but not fast enough. With daemon speed, he rolled on top of her.

"Bitch," he hissed in her face. He drew back his good arm for a punch that would break Piper's jaw.

She gasped and jabbed her fist into his left side. Bone gave way. He reared back with an agonized shriek. She'd seen him get hit there two fights ago and suspected his rib had been cracked—it had—and now it was broken.

As he clutched his chest, on his knees and straddling her, she sat up and punched at the same time, hitting him full force right between the legs.

His face went white and he squeaked like a dog toy. Piper scooted out from under him and rolled to her feet. He bared his teeth, his expression promising pain. She smiled, lifted one foot, and slammed her kick-ass boot into his face. There went his nose again.

Grudge keeled over and was motionless.

The silence was absolute as one of the referee-bouncers started counting. Piper stood where she was, breathing hard and wondering if the crowd should have been cheering or something. The silence was creepy.

The bouncer reached ten and signaled a KO. The announcer cleared his throat.

"Ladies and gentlemen—your victor, Minx!"

CHAPTER

-15-

THE SILENCE STRETCHED for a heartbeat longer, then like a flipped switch, the crowd roared. It wasn't exactly a cheerful sound, almost begrudging as though she'd won but had forgotten to do something in the process.

"Yes," the announcer called excitedly, "our new challenger Minx has become the new champion, defeating nine-time winner Grudge *without taking a single hit.* Our first bloodless fight in months!"

Ah. That was the problem: she hadn't met the proper quota of blood and violence before winning. Well, too damn bad for the crowd. She wanted to get through this in one piece.

The bouncers hauled the mountain of limp muscles that was Grudge out of the ring. Piper backed into her corner and glanced at the scoreboard. Her own photo, taken right before the match, stared across the room. Somehow she looked enigmatic and coy in the black mask, her natural auburn hair windswept and possibly sexy—or maybe just messy. She waited with mounting nerves while the announcer prattled on about drink deals and betting rules. Her odds had increased impressively from 99–1 to 33–1. Nice.

Contrary to her official odds, she knew her next match would be ten times as difficult as that one. Grudge had been in the ring for an hour and a half and she'd been able to analyze his style for weaknesses before having to face him. She'd known he'd attack if she pretended to be distracted and where to hit when he pinned her. Most of all, she'd had the element of surprise because no one had known what she could do.

Her next opponent would be fresh. If he were on top of things, he would have watched her last fight and would now know what to expect. And if he were smart, he would already be planning a strategy, whereas she couldn't plan anything until they began their match.

"Our next challenger, ladies and gentlemen, is also a newcomer to the Styx Ring, but with credits from many of our sister clubs. I give you—Rattler!"

As the crowd cheered and the announcer started listing off the challenger's stats, Piper focused on the daemon coming through the curtains. At first glance, she knew she was in trouble. The man was slight and rangy with a fluid walk and a bounce in his step that said he was light on his feet. She gritted her teeth. Maybe Lilith thought she was doing Piper a favor by giving her an opponent around the same size, but instead, she'd taken away Piper's advantage of speed and agility over heavyweights. A smaller guy was also less likely to underestimate her.

Rattler swung into the ring with a haughty smirk stretching his mouth and Piper amended her last thought. A small *human* guy wouldn't underestimate her, but even an undersized daemon had an ego big enough to crush small towns.

She eyed him, hoping for some clues as to his fighting style. His shaved head, covered with a snake-scale pattern that may or may not have been a tattoo, gleamed in the spotlights. He was shirtless like most male contestants and wore simple black sweats that wouldn't impede his movements; he probably didn't rely on a boxing style. On his chest was a mark like a caduceus with a winged staff and two snakes twined about it.

Piper blinked disbelievingly. Really? He was advertising his caste? How arrogant was he?

Then again, if he were in fact a nāga, he would be excessively arrogant. Snakes were like that.

Rattler studied her as she studied him. He constantly shifted his weight, ceaselessly moving, his gaze roving without slowing. He grinned savagely before turning toward the giant wheel of match types as the announcer spun the arrow. Piper watched apprehensively. Green, red, green, black, green, red, green. It slowed, ticking past the black quarter and down into safe green. It slowed more. Piper held her breath. Stop, she begged silently. Stop now.

The arrow dropped to stop one peg into the red section. The weapons match.

The crowd screamed and roared its support. Piper swallowed hard and glanced toward the curtained doorway. No sign of Lyre or Ash. She hoped they were nearby, because there was every chance she was about to lose a limb.

A referee approached the ring with a box. In it were her three choices: a dagger, a spear, and a sword.

"And now," the announcer shouted, "as you all know, the current champion chooses first. Although we at Styx Ring try to limit rules as much as possible, weapons matches are closely supervised. Deliberate maiming or killing strikes will equal a life ban from the Styx and our sister clubs. After all, we don't want to run out of able fighters."

Piper hesitated over the three weapons. She not only had to consider what weapon would suit her best, but what choices she was leaving her opponent. The dagger suited her style but the spear had a long reach that could potentially keep unfriendly blades away. In the end, she selected the sword, the middle ground, so she wouldn't be left with too extreme a disadvantage against either remaining weapon.

Rattler surveyed the remaining selections and chose the dagger. Piper wasn't sure if that was good or not. She weighed the sword in her hand; it was a well-balanced katana. She had a good amount of experience with the weapon. They faced each other as the announcer called out for them to get ready. The bell rang.

Rattler swayed forward, shifting from foot to foot as he tossed the dagger from hand to hand in the opposite rhythm as his feet, so effortlessly Piper knew she was definitely in trouble. She angled her sword and breathed deeply. She had to take him down before he could get in close.

She lunged in and feinted a high strike. He called her bluff and almost gored her with the dagger before she swept the sword around. He was supernaturally fast and dodged out of the way, dancing back with a grin on his face. She went on the offensive, making short, quick strikes that kept him retreating. He evaded every one, too fast and agile. Damn Lilith. Why had she set Piper an opponent with all the same strengths as her—only stronger?

Frustrated and scared, Piper swung her next thrust a little too hard. Rattler ducked low under the blade and the dagger whipped toward her thigh. She shrieked and flung herself backward, slamming her shin into Rattler's head before hitting the floor on her side. Stinging pain burned across her thigh. She rolled fast and lunged to her feet. He didn't give her time to check her wound. He attacked again and she parried the dagger with her sword. As she pushed his weapon aside, his free arm cocked back. His punch caught her jaw and sent her spinning into the ropes.

She straightened and flung the sword behind her without looking first. A sharp yelp told her it had connected. She whirled around and bounced off the ropes as he was still stumbling back with a shallow graze across his chest. The crowd screamed pointlessly at the blood.

Again, he retreated as she pursued. It shouldn't have been so difficult. She had a three-foot katana against a twelve-inch dagger! She had every advantage, except Rattler's speed turned it into a disadvantage. Her long, bulky sword was too clumsy and slow against his quick knife.

He scored three more scratches on her, shallow but painful, and an agonizing kick to the knee that would leave a massive bruise. She landed nothing more on him, limping backward as he began to press her. She was going to lose—and need about a hundred stitches if this kept up. If she didn't win at least three matches, Lilith wouldn't give them their information and all this fear and stress and pain would be for nothing.

Rattler leaped at her so suddenly she reacted instinctively, jumping back on her bad leg—exactly as he'd intended. Her bruised knee buckled. She went down and saw him coming down with her, the dagger aimed for her shoulder. He was going to run her through! A shoulder wound wouldn't kill her but it would hurt like hell.

Out of pure desperation, she tossed her sword aside and barely managed to grab his hand with both of hers as the point of the dagger sank into the soft spot above her collarbone. She braced against his downward push with all her strength. Fire raged in her shoulder. He leaned a little harder and the blade sank in another inch. He wasn't even trying, the bastard.

She rocked her head back and forth as she fought for enough composure to figure out what to do. He swayed his head back and forth in the same rhythm, his creepy pale blue eyes sliding into a darker shade. Piper gasped, clenched her jaw, and heaved her hips up and to the side, dumping Rattler off her. She rolled on top of him and sat on his chest, still gripping his dagger hand. Anger flashed across his face. She threw all her weight onto his hand, forcing it slowly down. He grabbed her hair with his other hand and yanked until she choked back a scream. She pulled one hand off his dagger and punched him in the solar plexus. He choked too.

As quickly as she could, she flipped backward into a roll and jumped up. Spotting her sword, she grabbed it as he stood. He was ticked now. She held her sword in front of her and, resisting the urge to glance at that telltale caduceus mark on his chest, she began to casually wave the tip side to side like she was indecisive—except she wasn't, not at all.

His eyes immediately began to follow the point of the sword. Back and forth, back and forth. Pale blue irises began to disappear in dark shadows. She started to tip her head side to side in the same motion. He watched, mesmerized. He started to sway in time to her movement. Breathing slowly, keeping every motion smooth so as not to disturb the entrancing rhythm, she began to slide a foot forward with each sway. Painstakingly, she closed the distance between them. He couldn't tear his eyes away.

When there was a cautious four feet between them, she gave her sword one more sinuous wave—then lunged in with silent intent. The sword sliced across his lower ribcage, cutting to the bone. He howled and raised his dagger but she ducked toward his opposite side and dropped into a low, sweeping kick that took his legs out. He slammed down on his back. She was up again instantly and she screamed as she drove the katana into the same fleshy spot in his shoulder that he'd aimed for on her. The blade ran right through him and into the floor beneath. She released the hilt and stomped on his hand to free the dagger. She grabbed it, pounced on his chest, and pressed it to his throat.

"You lose," she hissed.

Hate burned in his face as the announcer shouted that the referee had called her victory.

"Your next opponent will kill you for preying on a caste weakness," he snarled in a soft, tenor voice. "That's worse than cheating to us, bitch."

"Well maybe you shouldn't have stamped your caste on your chest, huh?"

He bared his teeth at her.

"Besides," she said, standing and handing the knife to the nearby bouncer, "I don't think it's unfair when you had every other advantage." She smiled sweetly and none too gently yanked the sword from his shoulder.

He stood, ignoring the blood running down his chest and back. With a contemptuous sneer, he spat on the floor at her feet and swung out of the ring. She watched him go back through the entrance curtains, figuring he planned to whisper poisonous words in her next opponent's ear.

She stepped backward and sagged against the corner post. Her legs trembled. Her arms ached. She checked the slice in her thigh; it was shallow and had mostly stopped bleeding. Her other scratches looked nasty but had clotted well. The one on her upper arm could probably use stitches. The puncture in her shoulder would definitely need stitches. It wasn't bleeding a lot but it wasn't going to stop by itself either.

Breathing deeply to oxygenate her weary muscles, she catalogued her injuries. The cuts didn't worry her as much as the bruises. She would have to be careful with her knee. Her right arm had taken a hit, and her left shoulder. A nasty bruise was forming on her right hip, visible above the hem of her jeans. She had no idea how she'd gotten it.

She let her head fall back and listened with half an ear as the announcer praised Piper's second win. The crowd was excited. Girls didn't normally win twice—they didn't normally win once—and the novelty had the spectators in a tizzy. But some faces were stiff with anger. The daemons in the crowd understood how the second fight had ended much better than the humans. Like Rattler had said, they were not happy. To them, she'd cheated—but him using his preternatural speed and reflexes on her was somehow fair?

She took a deep breath. One more daemon to beat.

The announcer launched into an introduction of her next opponent. He was a handsome daemon of medium build, dubbed Thoth. Piper couldn't help but snort at the name—an ancient Egyptian deity who, among other things, maintained the balance of the universe? Please.

As the announcer began to list off Thoth's credentials, she slowly straightened. Her gaze flicked to the scoreboard. His odds were 2–1 to win. His record was sixteen consecutive wins. This guy was *not* an amateur. He was a bloody professional fighter. What the hell was Lilith playing at?

Thoth jumped into the ring and landed lightly on the balls of his feet. He smiled in a charming sort of way at Piper but his eyes were icy cold. This daemon wouldn't know warm, fuzzy feelings if they curled up in his lap and mewled like a kitten. She didn't have an inkling of what his caste might be and he would make sure she couldn't make a reasonable guess. She ignored the announcer as she stared him down, trying to learn something from that arctic, burgundy stare. He almost made Ash look friendly.

"And now, we spin the match wheel!" the announcer cried excitedly.

Piper reluctantly turned to watch. Whatever it landed on, she would probably get her ass handed to her. Pain was coming.

The arrow whirled around and around, slid past the black quarter and stopped on green—another fist match. Maybe she could get away with broken bones instead of being gored with a blade. The crowd cheered as the announcer called for them to get ready.

The bell rang for the third time.

Being an experienced professional fighter facing a bruised, exhausted girl, Thoth didn't bother with a cautious approach. He skipped forward like a kid at the park, swatted Piper's initial block out of his way, and rammed his fist into her belly. She doubled over and dropped to her knees. Thoth graciously backed up until Piper could breathe again. Still gasping, tears streaming down her face as she sincerely hoped her spleen hadn't ruptured, she dragged herself to her feet.

She was no match for him.

Telling herself to quit whining, she tried to focus through the pain. She had to win. No choice. Everyone had a weakness. What was his?

Thoth came forward again. Piper darted out of her corner and fell into a defensive stance. She had three black belts. She could stand her ground.

Thoth launched at her. She evaded two strikes, blocked another, then he caught her wrist and pulled her into a shoulder-wrenching throw. She slammed into the mat on her back. When she didn't get up fast enough, he gave her an encouraging kick in the ribs. If Piper lived through this, she was going to drag Lilith into the ring and replay every move from this fight with the succubus on the receiving end. That jealous bitch! She'd given Piper an impossible opponent to punish Ash for daring to not adore her.

Piper got up, managed to defend herself for another twenty seconds, then Thoth got a good grip and threw her over his shoulder. She managed to land in a roll but her legs were so tired she flopped out of it instead of coming up on her feet. Gasping, she grabbed the ropes to pull herself up and sagged against them. She heard the crowd as if from a great distance as Thoth strode toward her.

She was going to lose and Lilith, the petty cat of a woman, would refuse to tell them anything. Piper wouldn't be able to find Quinn in time. She wouldn't be able to clear her name or piece together the shards of her life into something livable. No. It wouldn't end like this.

Piper's black belts weren't the only fighting styles she knew. There was one her uncle had hired a man to teach her as a last resort—the *only-if-you're-dying* backup plan. It wasn't a style of fighting a Consul generally needed because Consuls generally didn't kill anyone. It was the kind of style that required absolute perfection in its execution or it would backfire in the worst kind of way. Piper had never used it in an actual fight before. Did she dare attempt it for the first time on an opponent who outmatched her in every way when she was already exhausted?

At this point, did she have a choice?

She screamed as she lunged off the ropes at him. Taken aback, he shifted to a defensive pose for the first time. She struck but he was too fast. Blocked it. She tried again. He blocked and countered with a punch that hit her shoulder and knocked her back. Gritting her teeth, she lunged in again.

They circled on the floor, Piper taking the punishment as she waited for her chance. Twice she went down. Once she landed a hit on him but with no real damage. Then, finally, she saw her chance. He stretched out a hand for another grab. This time, she was quick enough. She caught his arm. And before he recognized her intent, she broke his elbow.

A roar of pain escaped him. She didn't pause. Her elbow snapped a rib. She grabbed his hand and twisted it just the right way, tearing the ligaments until he was screaming. His other fist flew out of nowhere and hit her jaw. She fell into a staggering crouch, then locked his foot and punched the side of his knee three times until something in it tore too and he fell on top of her. She shoved him off, grabbed his other leg, and pulled it into an agonizing hold. She leaned back with his leg, stretching the tendons running down the front of the thigh until he screamed again. She knew how excruciating the pain was. Her teacher had demonstrated the move on her to ensure she would never treat it as a toy.

She pulled a little more. He howled. Pass out, she silently begged, teeth clenched. Pass out, please. She leaned back another inch, pulling those tendons to the breaking point. He slammed his fist into the floor, begging for release. If she tore his thigh, he might never regain full use of the leg. She looked frantically at the referee. He glanced at the announcer and at Thoth, then nodded. He raised his hand, signaling a victory.

Piper dropped her hold and scooted back. Her legs were trembling so badly she couldn't stand.

Thoth lay still, panting, then turned over and slowly sat up. For a moment, she thought he would attack her. Then he saluted her, a mocking tilt to his fingers, before gingerly sliding under the lower rope to the cement floor beyond. Cradling his broken elbow and torn-ligament hand, he limped out.

Piper flopped onto her back. She'd done it.

One more fight to go. And it might end up being the worst of all four.

CHAPTER

-16-

PIPER SLUMPED back against the ropes, eyes closed. Her breath rasped in and out, tearing at her lungs. Her whole body hurt and bruises throbbed everywhere, but she could only feel relief—relief and weary satisfaction. She'd done it. Against all odds, with nothing but her own skill, she'd beaten three bloodthirsty daemon fighters.

The crowd roared, a building crescendo of anticipation. The announcer was praising her last fight, working the spectators into a betting frenzy. She half listened, concentrating on ignoring how much she hurt.

"Now," he called. His voice abruptly dropped to a dramatic whisper in the microphone. "Ladies and gentlemen, we all admit Minx has accomplished three shocking victories. Her last was narrow, we all know it, but she succeeded with a show of guts, determination, and skill we can't help but admire. I—I wish, for her sake, that I had better news for her next match."

The room quieted.

"Ladies … gentlemen … The Styx brings fighters of all ages, skills, and backgrounds to its ring. But every once in a while, we are graced with the presence of a legend. There are fighters—and then there are warriors. Bred to fight, to win … to kill.

"Tonight, one of our legends has reappeared. Yes, after an absence of over a year, one of the great warriors has come to once more test his strength against our fighters.

"Ladies and gentlemen—I give you *Dragon!*"

A heartbeat of silence and the room exploded with screams and cheers. She breathed deeply, waiting. The two thousand voices rose in a building crescendo, then abruptly quieted.

Piper opened her eyes.

Ash stood in the ring across from her.

A simple cloth mask that left only the lower half of his face visible had replaced the elaborate dragon mask. His jaw was tight but he managed a small, approving smile when she looked at him. He'd stripped to a thin, sleeveless black shirt, his black jeans, biker boots, and leather wrist braces. When she'd seen him shirtless before, he'd been all toned muscle sheathed in warm, honey-toned skin. Now, his shoulders were marked with strange designs in dark red, very close to his hair color, that disappeared under his shirt. Was that glamour? Or had he dropped part of his glamour instead?

He flexed his hands, wrapped from knuckles to elbows in black tape. Piper unconsciously balled her hands into fists. She swallowed hard. Even knowing he was on her side, facing him across the blood-splattered ring made her heart pound and a fresh wave of adrenaline rush through her. He was so frighteningly still, possessing that balanced, unfailing readiness of a true fighter.

The crowd howled their approval of this match up. The announcer shouted over them, crowing about Dragon's past winning streak. Then, with an excited shout, he stepped over to the match wheel and spun it as hard as he could.

The entire arena went silent as everyone watched the arrow spin around and around. It started to slow. They needed a fist match. If Ash was going to convince the crowd he was beating her to a pulp without hurting her—much—then they desperately needed a fist match. Anything else would be ten times as hard to fake.

The arrow whirled around, gradually slowing. The whole room held its breath. Tick-tick-tick. It rushed down the right side and slowed as it dropped into the red weapons match. Tick, tick, tick. It clicked into the left-hand fist match, arching upward, almost all its momentum gone. Tick … tick … *tick.*

Silence.

Piper stared, dread sliding through her. The arrow had stopped in the tiny black quarter—the one with the skull and crossbones.

The brawl match. The "anything goes" match where both weapons and magic were allowed. The crowd burst into frenzied cheers. Piper hugged herself against the sudden chill in her blood. Lilith insisted Piper lose in a satisfactory way or the deal was off. The spectators wouldn't be satisfied by anything less than all-out violence for this match. Brawls were the favorite.

With trembling fingers, Piper once again chose the katana from the three offered weapons. When the man turned to Ash, he waved a hand and tilted his head in a mocking, arrogant shrug that clearly said, "I don't need a weapon against *her.*"

The spectators went wild as the announcer called out the Dragon's refusal to take a weapon. They seemed to find it pretty exciting, maybe because it evened the odds a bit, but how the hell was she supposed to use a katana without killing him?

"Fighters, ready!" the announcer bellowed.

The bell shrilled.

Not knowing what else to do, she lunged forward, blade first. Ash flowed forward to meet her. He was barehanded. How was he planning to make this work? She searched his face, hoping for some sign of the plan.

He lunged so fast she reacted without thought—she swung the deadly blade at his face.

He arched backward and the sword swept over his head. Then his arm clamped around her middle and he flung her across the ring. She slammed down hard, the wind knocked out of her, barely holding on to her sword. Holy crap! She gasped for air and rolled to her feet amidst a cacophony of cheers and catcalls. Ash waited for her, looking confident and unconcerned.

Fine. She wouldn't go *that* easy on him then.

She slid forward, then feinted left. As soon as he started to move, she reversed the blade, aiming to nick his side.

He smacked the blunt top of her blade with the back of one arm, knocking it off course. Then he grabbed her wrist. She couldn't stop her shriek as he slammed a leg into her stomach, knocking her flat on her ass. Once again, she couldn't breathe. Damn it. She knew she was supposed to be losing—and he could have kicked her *way* harder— but something in her wouldn't go down without a fight. She sucked in painful breaths on the dirty ring floor. Ash was standing close, waiting—a little too close.

She rolled and kicked at the same time, ramming her booted foot into his ankle. His foot went out from under him but she knew he wouldn't fall. That's why her roll brought her close enough to kick again—this time right into the nerve in his inner thigh.

He went down.

She was vaguely aware of the shrieking crowd as she threw herself on him. He grabbed her wrist before she could bring the katana into play. She sat on him and tried to punch him with her other hand. He caught her fist. They froze like that, staring each other down as Piper bared her teeth and strained against his superior strength. Ash's lips twitched. The crowd bellowed their support, though for whom she couldn't tell.

Before Ash decided on his next move, she yanked up one leg in a feat of female flexibility and hooked her leg on his elbow, wrenching his arm down with her full weight. He almost broke her arm when he didn't let go of her wrist. Then he arched his back with enough force to throw her off and flipped on top of her. She used the same throw-off move on him before he could pin her and they rolled across the floor, wrestling for control of the katana.

Ash finally wrenched the sword out of her hand but he didn't have a good grip on it. It flew out of his grasp, skidded across the floor, and fell off the edge of the ring. The crowd groaned as one. Piper managed to break free and rolled away before jumping to her feet. Ash leaped up in one graceful move. She twisted her mouth and he made a face back. Yeah, he'd lost the sword on purpose.

Breathing hard, she slowly sank into a ready stance. Ash copied, his lips stretching into a tight smile. Piper swallowed. This was the part where she got beat up.

They attacked at the same moment. Piper's legs ached from the strain but she managed to dance away from his first attempt to grab her. She punched. He blocked. She side-kicked, ducked, and tried to jab him in the kidney. He blocked again. She jumped back and let loose a volley of attacks. He blocked every one with impossible swiftness—then his fist flashed out and caught her shoulder, sending her spinning. She turned a full one eighty and let herself fall forward onto her hands. At the same time, she kicked with both feet, doing half a handstand as she tried to plant her boots in his gut.

He somehow twisted to the side and caught her right leg. She kicked his knee with her left foot and he dropped her before she got thrown again.

She scrambled up and spun to face him. He tensed but didn't attack. His smile was gone now and he looked frustrated. She tried to give him a "what the hell?" look through her mask. What was he waiting for? The crowd was getting restless at the lack of blood and pain. He stared at her, trying to communicate a thought, maybe, then gave his head the tiniest shake.

She inhaled sharply and glanced toward the yelling mob. He was right. Nothing they could fake would satisfy the crowd. Ash would have to seriously hurt her—unless there was a way to give them something else to scream about?

She clenched and unclenched her hands. No ideas popped into her head. Damn it! Now what?

Time was up. Ash sprang.

This time he was on the offensive and it was Piper blocking and dodging for all she was worth. She couldn't catch everything and though it burned her pride, she knew he wasn't using the full scope of his skill. The stupid draconian was just that good. When his third strike caught her in the diaphragm, she dropped to her knees at his feet, clutching her belly and unable to breathe. Her legs trembled with exhaustion. Her arms ached, the muscles threatening to seize. Ash started to step back while she recovered.

Before managing a single breath, she leaped up and tackled him right in the stomach. He staggered back but didn't fall. Her strength gave out and she fell back, still holding a handful of his shirt. With a loud ripping sound, the side seam tore.

She dragged herself to her feet. The crowd was screaming again— Ash had pulled his torn shirt off and chucked it out of the ring. Piper could only stare at him. The tattoo-like markings curled over his shoulders and wound down one side of his chest. A curl of the design circled the spot over his heart. She licked her lips nervously as she looked across the ecstatic crowd. The beginnings of a plan began to take form.

Pushing her shoulders back, she lifted her chin and gestured imperiously for Ash to come at her. His lips parted with surprise, then he stepped forward in a slow prowl. When he was barely two steps away, he lunged.

She threw herself at him with everything she had left. She summoned every last drop of energy, every bit of fighting passion she had left. She screamed her frustration as he caught her every attack. She didn't try to hide her anger. Her attacks got wilder and more desperate, but Ash pushed back, driving her into a corner of the ring. The corner post was one step behind her when she flung her foot out in a roundhouse kick with enough power behind it to bruise even if he caught it. Wisely, he slid backward out of range.

Piper planted both feet and mouthed as subtly as she could, "Charge me."

He didn't immediately react, merely shifted casually like he was setting his feet. Then, so fast she almost wasn't ready, he ran at her. She screamed like a wild woman and lunged forward to meet him. At the last second, she leaped at him so she was completely airborne. He crashed into her, grabbing her at the same time she grabbed him with arms and legs both. His momentum was so strong that they both slammed hard into the post behind her.

She might have been brained right then but Ash managed to cup one hand behind her head to cushion the impact. His other hand had a fistful of the back of her jeans, holding the waist so she didn't slide down him. She had both legs wrapped tight around his middle, her hands clutching his shoulders.

Time slowed. The noise of the crowd disappeared. Ash was pressed hard into her, crushing her against the post, his body hot against her front. His bare chest rose and fell as he breathed deep. His hand formed a fist in her hair and pulled her head back until their eyes met in a stare that cut right through her. His irises weren't quite black but close. His strength was all around her, holding her, pinning her helplessly. She met his stare, her teeth bared fiercely.

Then she grabbed his head and yanked his mouth down onto hers.

It wasn't a gentle kiss. Ash's mouth met hers and it was like a flame meeting oil—fire and raging heat. She arched into him as he shoved her into the post, pressing them even tighter together. His mouth moved with hers, against hers, fierce and carnal and demanding. She clamped her fingers over the back of his head and pulled him closer still, demanding even more. His hand tightened in her hair and she tilted her head farther back as their kiss deepened into something even wilder.

Seconds later—minutes later?—Ash pulled back with one last nipping bite to her bottom lip that made heat plunge through her middle. They held there, faces inches apart, both panting for air. Piper wasn't sure she could have unlocked her legs from around him even if she'd wanted to. Which she didn't. She'd never had her legs around such perfect abs in her life.

That's when, belatedly, she noticed the crowd's reaction. They were all on their feet and the noise level was deafening. They were screaming and cheering.

So swiftly Piper squeaked in surprise, Ash pulled her off the post. The next thing she knew, he'd flipped her over his shoulder in a fireman carry. The air whooshed out of her. Ash turned and lifted one hand in a gesture of triumph, his other arm clamped over the backs of her thighs to keep her in place.

"Well," the announcer called jubilantly. "It seems the Dragon has claimed his prize!"

Piper scowled, then forced her expression into something that hopefully looked dazed but still lustful, like a proper fighter girl so passionate she'd fallen for her opponent instead of thrashing him. Ugh. Reduced to a prize for a man. She'd never be able to show her face in the club again—not that it was a big loss.

To the tumultuous applause of the crowd, Ash leaped out of the ring and dropped four feet to the cement floor while hardly jostling Piper. Yeah, he'd definitely been holding back in their fight. With fans screaming their victorious hero on, Ash strode purposefully across the main floor to the exit hall. Piper could hear a minority of boos and swearing from the bloodthirsty sadists amongst the spectators but her idea had worked. This club was all about passion— of multiple kinds—and the top floor of the club showed as much. The crowd had seemed extra excited in the more risqué moments of their match. Turning the fight into a different kind of passion had saved them, even if it hadn't quite played out the way she'd planned.

The noise grew muffled as they moved down the hall, not that Piper could see much of her surroundings while hanging upside down over Ash's shoulder. He found a door and opened it. She glimpsed a small infirmary room as he stepped inside and pushed the door shut. Then he tilted Piper forward and slid her off his shoulder onto her feet, which meant she slid down the front of him on her way to the floor. Cue another swoop of heat in her middle.

She found herself standing right against him, his hands hot against her sides as she cooled from the exertion of the fight. Her hands were somehow resting on the bare skin of his chest and she realized a little late that her legs were quivering so badly she probably couldn't have stood without leaning against him. He helped her limp to the stretcher-like bed and sit on it. His fingers brushed the underside of her chin, tipping her head back. He lightly touched a sore spot on the side of her jaw, then gently pushed her mask off her face and dropped it on the bed beside her.

She stared at him uncertainly, trying to read his expression behind the mask he had yet to remove. His fingertips were still resting against her cheek. The sudden desire to pull his mouth back to hers nearly made her melt inside.

But then his fingers slid away and he glanced around the tiny room.

"That was a clever plan," he murmured. "More than I thought of."

"Y-yeah," she said shakily, thrown off by the manic desire she had to wrap herself around him.

"Good strategizing. You'll make a good Consul."

She stared wordlessly. He flicked a glance at her, then stepped toward the door. "I'll get a nurse for you."

"Ash," she blurted. She jumped to her feet and nearly ended up in a puddle on the floor. She staggered but managed to grab his arm. He turned toward her. She hesitated, then pushed the black mask off his face. His expression was inscrutable.

She touched a red scratch on his cheek, no doubt courtesy of her fingernails. She didn't remember doing it.

"Ash, I …" She swallowed. "I mean, you …'"

The door to the room burst open.

"Holy shit," Lyre exclaimed, grinning ear to ear and looking shell-shocked at the same time. "That was *inspired*. Whose idea was that? That is the hottest kiss I've ever seen—if *kiss* is even the right word. I don't know if kisses count on that scale—and I would know, wouldn't I?" He laughed.

Piper dropped her hand from Ash's face and stepped away, her cheeks heating. She had kissed Ash like a hopped-up succubus in front of two thousand people. Her father and uncle had better never hear about this.

Before Piper or Ash could answer, Lilith stepped through the door. Her beautiful face was tight with fury.

"What," she demanded, "was *that*? That was *not* a brawl match. You didn't even use magic!"

"How were they supposed to have a brawl match without Ash killing Piper?" Lyre demanded.

Lilith ignored him. "That was an embarrassment. And you!" She pointed violently at Ash. "You've ruined Dragon's reputation."

"The crowd was happy," Piper said defensively. "Plus, you know, a little variety besides blood and broken bones might be good for business."

"I had to refund all bets placed on your match," Lilith spat. "I've lost thousands! If you think that stunt will win you any infor—"

Ash stepped forward, swift and silent. He stopped right in Lilith's face, his black, frozen eyes paralyzing her mid-word.

"The conditions were met," he said, and his voice was ice-cold silk that slid under Piper's skin down to her bones. She and Lilith both shuddered. "Piper won three matches. I won the next match in a manner that satisfied the majority of the spectators." The silence hummed with waiting violence. "You will hold to the bargain."

His last statement was an unyielding command. Negotiation or refusal was not an option.

Lilith licked her lips, unable to look away. Finally, grudgingly, she nodded. "I will give you your information. But don't think I'll ever bargain with you again, Dragon."

He smiled. Slowly, he leaned down until their lips were an inch apart and put two fingers under her chin. "Oh, I think you will, Lilith," he crooned. Then he stepped around her and walked out of the room.

Lilith stared straight ahead, breathing fast, fury and hunger written across her features. She drew herself up, gave Piper a look of death, and gestured at Lyre to follow her. "Come. My records are upstairs."

Lyre shot a rebellious glance at Lilith for her lofty command before turning to Piper. He pulled the black ring box out of his pocket and poked it halfway into her shirt before she smacked his hand away. He grinned and winked, then hurried after Lilith.

Piper plucked the box out, checked the Sahar was still inside, then hid it safely out of sight down her shirt. She wobbled over to the bed and sat, exhaling loudly as she wondered where Ash had gone. Holy crap. He was scary. Sexy scary. No—just scary, she corrected. Very, very scary. Not sexy at all. Creepy scary—a Risk Level 5 threat. Lyre was sexy. Ash was dangerous.

Some girls were attracted to danger. Piper was smarter than that. Yeah, she was. Definitely.

She hugged herself and worked to blot out the memory of how his mouth had felt, soft and hard at the same time, fierce, demanding, wild. Dangerous.

Oh man. She was in big, *big* trouble.

CHAPTER
-17-

AFTER A NURSE came in and stitched Piper up, she headed upstairs, hoping to find Lilith's office and her two daemons. Instead, she ended up in the middle of the dark, mazelike club floor, unable to find the right door into the back room. Since she had the opportunity, she found a deserted corner and took a few minutes to collect herself. Not only was she still aching from head to toe, but random tremors kept running through her limbs from too much adrenaline.

She leaned against the wall and glared "come near me and die" daggers at anyone close by. It seemed to work and only one barely coherent drunk guy approached her. She pinched his ear until he started whimpering and he left looking a lot more sober than he'd come.

The whole experience in the ring was starting to blur like a bad dream. Had she really beaten up three daemons and gotten beat up in turn by them? Had she stabbed one through the shoulder and done the third serious damage?

Had she really kissed Ash passionately in front of two thousand witnesses?

It had been a good idea. The crowd had been teetering on the edge, turned on by the male/female fight. Turning it into something besides a fight had set off a thousand various fantasies for the spectators. Working her and Ash's fight into a moment where kissing him would make sense had taken a bit of planning. It had been a logical, calculated move.

Right up until she actually kissed him.

She'd never had a kiss like that. She would never admit it to Ash, but it had been the most exhilarating kiss of her life, hands down. And that was something, considering the majority of her kisses had involved incubi. However, that did not mean she was falling for him. No way. He was disturbing, dangerous, and too powerful. She knew nothing about him except he had a bad reputation. He was keeping secrets. Everything about him was secrets.

Besides, she'd already learned her lesson when it came to daemons: Do. Not. Get. Involved. One, they liked breaking human and haemon hearts; her past with a certain lying incubus aside, she'd seen a lot of that with other daemon seducers. And two, it was against the rules for a Consul. She needed to be neutral and objective, not tangled up in daemon affairs and daemon love lives.

So, note to self: Do not kiss Ash again. Ever.

Piper nodded. Yes, problem solved. She would simply never kiss him again. It would probably be a good idea to apply the same rule to Lyre, but he, unlike Ash, was the one initiating the kisses. That made it a bit harder.

Tickling fingers whispered up her sides. Exasperation rolled through her; speak of the devil. She jerked away and turned.

"Lyre, would you …"

The words died on her tongue and her mouth hung open gormlessly. The exquisite piece of mouth-watering man behind her was not Lyre. Golden skin, pale blond hair, and the body of a god suggested incubus, as did the distinctly daemon aura. A mask covered his entire face, a fantasy countenance of teal and gold, but recognition flooded through her, undeniable. Without thinking, she reached out and pushed his mask up.

That face. It was like a punch in the gut. So perfect it almost hurt to look at him. His mouth curved in that charming smile, so sweet and open it could win over the devil himself.

"Micah," she choked.

"Piper." Oh God, his voice was even better than she remembered —deep and husky with that hint of a throb that made heat flare through her.

"W-what are you doing here?" Damn it, she was stuttering. Emotions boiled inside her and as much as she wanted to meet his innocent smile with icy disdain and cutting wit after the way he'd used her and dumped her, she couldn't think. Her brain was clogged with a hundred memories and feelings.

"I come here a lot," he said, simultaneously sliding closer. She immediately backed away. His eyebrows drew together. "Piper, honey, please listen."

"No."

He bit his bottom lip as hurt brushed subtly across his breath-stopping face. He slowly exhaled. "Pipes, please. I need to explain."

"I don't want to hear it." She looked around wildly, desperate for rescue. This was her worst nightmare. She'd never wanted to look in his beautiful, deceiving eyes again.

He stepped closer, reaching for her hands. She jerked back. He froze, tension lining his shoulders in his sexy sleeveless shirt before he managed to relax.

"I—I can see even begging for your forgiveness won't be enough," he said, somehow sounding like he was talking softly even though they were both nearly shouting to be heard over the music. He rubbed two fingers over his forehead, looking miserable and torn. His gaze came up, hesitantly meeting hers. "If you want me to leave, just … just say so. I won't bother you again. I only wanted …"

She hung there, suspended between the need to run away from the pain his presence caused her and the need to hear what he'd come to tell her. Nothing he said could make what he'd done okay, but could it ease the knife in her heart a little?

"What?" she managed. "Spit it out."

Hope lit his face, almost breaking her heart all over again. He eagerly stepped forward, then checked himself. Watching her reaction carefully, he took one of her hands in both of his.

"Piper." A deep breath. "I—An apology won't be enough, I know that. I can't ask you to forgive me. I could plead at your feet for a year and never make up for my behavior. But I … I have to explain. It won't fix anything, but … it would ease a little of my guilt."

He drew closer and reached out to gently push her silver mask on top of her head. His expression softened as he took in her face. "Piper, sweetheart, I'm so sorry. There's no excuse for how I left you, but please know. I—" His eyes squeezed shut. "That same day, before you joined me for the evening, I received news from—from home." He swallowed. "Terrible news."

Piper's breath caught.

"It's not an excuse," he said, abruptly angry. He looked up sharply at the ceiling. "Not an excuse. I took my own inner turmoil out on you. I was in so much pain that I lashed out, trying to make you hurt too. You—you looked so deliriously happy, so content and peaceful—everything I couldn't feel that day, everything I couldn't even stand to see. And then you said"—his voice cracked—"you said you loved me, and I …"

He bowed his head, his hands squeezing hers painfully. "There was no love in me that day, Piper. None. Only pain."

"I—I—" She didn't know what to say. She couldn't think.

His head came up again and he pulled her closer until the only thing between them was her hand in his. "But that doesn't mean I didn't care for you, Piper—that I didn't feel the same as you the day before. Every word—I meant it. That last night, I acted like the cruel demon so many humans think we are. I can never make amends."

"But you—you never came back—"

He let go of her hand and pulled her into a tight hug. She stood stiffly in his arms, staring over his shoulder. He pressed his face against her hair.

"I was so ashamed, Piper. I knew I'd hurt you terribly. I couldn't stand to face you and see how much pain I'd caused you. I was afraid to see hate in your eyes when you looked at me."

She did hate him. Didn't she? He slowly drew back, his hands on her shoulders as he searched her face. God, he was beautiful. Remorse aged his features.

He slowly slid one hand to her chest and pressed it over her heart. Her heart pounded against his palm. "I can't repair the damage I did, Piper," he said, his expression soft. "I can't apologize enough and I can't ask for your forgiveness. But please tell me that—that you understand? That I never lied to you, that you were everything I said you meant to me?"

She stared. He looked back with such intensity that it was hard to hold his gaze. When she remained silent, his hand closed around the neckline of her shirt and his brow pinched. He leaned closer.

"Piper, I—"

He flew back so fast he seemed to vanish. Then he crashed into the bar and Ash was standing in front of him, a hand fisted in the front of the incubus's shirt, the black dragon mask once again hiding his expression. Piper stood there, gaping, her mind scrambled into incoherency.

"If you touch her again," Ash snarled, pressing his fist into Micah's throat, "if you so much as *look* at her, I will rip off your balls and feed them to you. Do you understand?"

Micah gasped and choked, half-suffocated. He gave a jerky nod.

Ash, the air around him sizzling with power, released the incubus and stepped back. Micah slowly pushed himself up, looking from Ash to Piper to a spot directly beside her. Lyre stepped into her peripheral vision, hovering protectively at her side.

Micah straightened. His chin lifted and that satisfied, cat-like smile claimed his lips, cold and uncaring. He slid a look between Piper and Lyre and cocked his head, his expression scathing.

"He won't be as good as me," he mocked.

Ash lunged for him. Micah barely managed to slide out of range, his derisive laughter ringing behind him as he ducked onto the dance floor and vanished in the writhing crowd.

"Sleazy maggot," Lyre growled. He turned to Piper. "Whatever he said, Piper, ignore it. The guy is a freaking slime ball. A really well-disguised slime ball."

"Is—is he?" she forced out. Her insides burned with everything she was feeling.

"Yeah," Lyre said, glaring at the spot where Micah had vanished. "Sex isn't good enough for the little prick. For a few years now, he's been trolling around looking for the *greatest challenges*." His voice went high with contempt for the last bit. "He's all about the conquest now, trying to find women no other incubus can score and seducing them."

She swallowed hard and wondered what kind of expression was on her face. Ash was watching her. His mask hid his expression but there was a sad, knowing look in his eyes.

"And the sick bastard," Lyre went on obliviously, "he gets off on dumping them as painfully as possible once he makes his score. Micah has a streak of cruelty a mile wide, but of course, being an incubus, humans can't tell."

Well, that explained a lot. Micah had gone after her because, as the sheltered virgin daughter of the Head Consul, she'd been a challenge worthy of his efforts. She stared at nothing, reeling from the emotional blows. So nothing about their three months together had been real. Nothing at all.

"So whatever sweet talk he was making," Lyre told her, finally turning toward her, "forget about it. He's not worth a second of your time, and … Piper, are you okay?"

"I'm fine," she said, her voice too high-pitched.

"You're wound tighter than a—uh, you don't want to hear that analogy," he corrected quickly. "You're really tense. What's wrong?"

"N-nothing."

Lyre looked at Ash then back at Piper. "What did Micah say to you? Whatever it was, he was lying, you know."

Her throat worked. "I know."

"So then what …" He pushed his mask up and gave her a very long look. Horror slowly traced itself across his face. "Piper … no way. Micah was … ?"

She couldn't meet his eyes. Humiliation turned her insides to ash.

Lyre looked at her a moment longer, then turned to Ash. "Let's kill him."

"Planning on it."

"Now?"

"We have to deal with the Sahar first."

Lyre swore. His expression was darker than a thundercloud. His eyes were nearly black. Ash's arms kept flexing like he could barely restrain himself. She wondered dully when he'd put his black skull shirt back on.

"Did Lilith come through for us?" she asked.

"Yes," Lyre said. "We have the address."

"Are we doing it now?"

"That's the plan."

Ash nodded and headed toward the exit. Lyre turned to follow but Piper hesitated. As her roiling emotions began to settle, soothed by Ash and Lyre's fury on her behalf—gratifyingly homicidal fury— she wondered why Micah had sought her out. He'd obviously recognized her even with the mask. Had he seen her fighting in the ring? Why would he come talk to her, pretending heartbroken remorse? To toy with her emotions? To see how much more pain he could wring out of her? Maybe re-seducing a girl he'd already broken was his latest brand of challenge. She pressed a hand against her chest where his had rested, wondering if he'd been imagining breaking her heart again even as he felt it beat.

She pressed her hand a little harder. Then she dipped her fingers into the top of her shirt.

Terror seized her.

"Ash," she screamed. At her cry, he whipped around so fast he was a blur of motion. "He took it! *That lying bastard stole it from me!*"

Ash spun and charged into the crowd before the last word was out of her mouth.

She unlocked her muscles and sprinted after him. Lyre's shocked expression shattered into frightened fury and he ran after her. She followed the path Ash had bulldozed through the mass of people, leaping over fallen dancers without slowing. The draconian moved without hesitation and, in half a minute, the mob was forcing an opening to let him through. Piper and Lyre ran after him, struggling to keep up as the gap in the crowd closed like breaking waves.

Ash led them back into the posh sitting room where they'd first met Lilith but he didn't stop. He ran right through the room and down the hall behind it. Piper sprang over the coffee table, her heart slamming into her ribs. If Micah got away … She couldn't even consider the possibility. She might as well write her life off as totaled. Complete high-speed, head-on collision totaled.

At the other end of a long hall, Ash slammed through a door and charged up a flight of metal stairs. She had no idea how he knew where to go—up? Why would Micah go up? She ran after Ash, too breathless to shout a question. The stairs were followed by another flight and Ash drew ahead, too fast to match. Piper careened upward, Lyre on her heels. Another door slammed open above them.

When she reached the landing, the threshold framed the flat roof of the warehouse, fifty yards from end to end. She ran out into the cool night, terrified and bewildered.

Ash stood at the far edge of the roof, staring upward.

"What are you doing?" Piper gasped as she and Lyre rushed up to him. "Where's Micah? Where next?"

Ash didn't look at her, merely stared upward, face hidden by that damn mask. He slowly raised an arm and pointed to the sky. Piper stared at the velvet black night. Then she saw it, blinking white and red lights in the sky, hundreds of yards away: a helicopter.

"No," she choked. "Micah is—?"

"The trail ends here," Ash said.

Lyre swore, his voice low and intense.

"But—but—" She whirled on Ash and grabbed the front of his shirt, forcing him to face her. "You can fly, can't you? Use your bloody wings and get the Sahar back. *Get it back!*"

"I can't outfly a helicopter."

"Try!"

"I know I can't."

"Do something!" she screamed in his face.

He jerked away with a snarl. He ripped the dragon mask off, giving her a brief glimpse of his eyes, black with rage and desolation, before he smashed the delicate ornament on the cement roof at his feet. He turned away from her, motions jerky with suppressed violence. The air crackled with power. Piper backed away, teeth clenched with desperation even as she gave him room to regain control. The blinking lights of the helicopter shrank in the distance — too far to chase, too fast to catch, impossible to track.

"It's gone," she whispered. She looked at her hands, knuckles bruised from her fights. All for nothing.

The Sahar was gone.

CHAPTER
-18-

THEY STOOD on the roof in silence. There was nothing to say.

She was a fool. An idiot. A stupid girl blinded by a handsome face and charming smile. Micah, that lying bastard, had gotten the better of her twice. If only she hadn't let herself hope. If only she'd walked away as soon as she'd recognized him, told him to take his apology and shove it. Instead, she'd clung to the insecure, naïve hope that maybe he'd cared about her after all.

She swallowed a bitter laugh. Cared about her? Never. He'd just been a wolf hunting the most well-guarded lamb.

"Someone must've hired him," Lyre muttered. Piper started—it had been silent for so long. Ash didn't move, standing a few feet away, his back to them, his shoulders rigid with tension. Every few seconds, he would flex them like a weight was crushing him and he couldn't find a bearable way to hold it.

"What?" she asked dully.

"Someone must've known about your past with him, so they hired him to find you. Who better to track you down than someone who knew you and could get close to you?" He laughed bitterly. "And the last person anyone would expect to be hiring out. Filthy mercenary."

She choked on the tearful apology trying to claw out of her throat. Apologizing wouldn't fix anything, and if she were Lyre, she would never forgive such a stupid mistake. No point in asking.

"Someone with money," Lyre went on, scrubbing a hand through his hair with unnecessary force. "Not just anyone can hire a helicopter. Must be one of the warlords."

Piper grimaced. *Warlord* was another term for the heads of the ruling daemon families.

Lyre was silent for a moment. "We're screwed."

Giving up on composure, Piper sank to a crouch and pressed her face against her knees. The tears finally broke through her self-control, streaming silently down her face. They would be fugitives for the rest of their lives, and those lives would be short. Ambitious daemons had barely had a chance to start hunting them. Soon, they wouldn't be able to walk down a street without being targeted by Stone-hunting daemons. And that wasn't even taking into consideration the prefects. If caught, they would be thrown in prison and left to rot. Without the Sahar, there was no way to clear their names.

An arm settled over her shoulders.

"Shh," Lyre whispered. "Come on, Piper, it's not over yet. We can still track down those Gaian bastards and get your dad back. He'll be able to help us."

She shook her head. Yes, they could save her father—only to condemn him to the same fate as her. The whole world would think he was a mass murderer. She couldn't clear his name either. His whole career, his entire life's work, was nothing but ashes now.

"It's all my fault," she whimpered. "I'm so sorry."

"Shh, no, it's all our faults, Piper," Lyre said gently. "Me and Ash were right there and didn't notice anything. Micah is a slippery bastard."

A tiny sob scraped her throat. She swallowed it convulsively and tried to wipe her tears. They kept falling, as ceaseless as rain. Everything ruined. Everything gone. Ashes to ashes, dust to dust. How could she have screwed it all up so badly?

Black boots appeared in front of her. Knowing her daemon companions could tell she was crying anyway, she looked up. Ash stood in front of her, cloaked in shadows. He was unnaturally still, his expression blank as stone. Her breath caught as she waited for him to move, speak, something.

His hands clenched. Unclenched. Then, to her bewilderment, he began yanking at the braid on the side of his head where the red tie was woven. He pulled at his hair until the silk strip came free. He held it in one fist, hand balled up tight, then extended it toward her. Automatically, she held out her hand, palm up.

With a flick of his wrist, he let the silk fall from his hand, one end still tangled in his fingers. The other end dropped and landed with a solid little thump in her palm. The end of it was rolled around something small and heavy. Ash pulled the tie up and the hidden object slid out with a sibilant whisper.

As soon as it hit her palm, Piper knew what it was.

The Sahar.

The *real* Sahar.

And in that same moment, she realized it had been a long time since she'd held the real Sahar.

It was too heavy for its size, as though something much larger had been compacted down into that tiny silver oval. It shimmered, lit from within, magnetic and entrancing. As she felt its strangeness radiating into her skin, she knew she'd only touched the real Sahar once before, the very first time she'd taken it out of the ring box in her bedroom.

She stared for so long that by the time she looked up, Ash was almost finished braiding the red silk back into his hair. Beneath her numb shock, emotion was beginning to stir. But not happiness. Not relief, not even surprise. She would feel all those things later.

Right now, it was horror building inside her—horror that was slowly crystallizing into fury.

The draconian didn't meet her stare. His face in shadow, he looked above her head, his features stiff and cold. Defensive.

"You gave me a fake." She didn't recognize her own voice, the soft, sliding tones lined in ice. "When did you switch them?" she asked slowly. "The first day," she answered herself. After their narrow escape from the prefects and long morning drive through the city, the ring box hadn't quite been tucked in her shirt when she awoke. Ash had re-braided his hair—after hiding the real Sahar, close and safe where no one could steal it short of scalping him.

She rose to her feet, facing the draconian. He looked back at her, hiding in shadows. She wanted to see his face. She wanted to see guilt.

"You stole the Sahar from me. You stole it the first time I slept." He'd even warned her, hadn't he? His parting words before she'd gone to sleep: *Keep the Stone close.*

"Piper," Lyre interjected quickly, standing as well. "This is a good thing. We have the Sahar. Ash protected it for—"

"For *us*?" she finished sharply. Ash didn't move, didn't flinch under her hateful glare. "Don't be stupid, Lyre. He was protecting it for himself. It was perfect, wasn't it, Ash?" she mocked. "By the time anyone realized mine was a fake, the trail would be so muddled that no one would be able to trace the real Sahar back to you. You'd get it all to yourself—just what every daemon wants."

Lyre glanced between them again, anxiety rolling off him.

"Piper—" he tried again.

"Why are you defending him?" She rounded on the incubus. "He betrayed us!"

"He saved the Sahar," Lyre yelled back. "So what if he was going to keep the real thing? It all would have worked out in the end!"

"What about my father?" she shouted back. "When it was discovered as a fake, he'd be accused of swapping the Sahar before the Gaians stole it. The Hades and Ra families will go to war. He'll be ruined!"

Lyre looked panicked. His gaze jerked from Ash back to her. "Some things are more important than careers," he mumbled.

"Like what?" she asked acidly. She whipped back to the silent draconian. "What's worth ruining my father's life for, Ash?" She shook her head, feeling like she was shattering inside. "You're a selfish coward. A thieving, lying coward. My father knew you were bad news. He knew—"

She froze as the truth slammed into her. A tremor ran through her body. Rage erupted inside her, boiling up, ready to escape.

"It was *you*." Her hands shook and her stomach twisted. "*You were the reason Father took the real Sahar out of the vault before the meeting. When you came to the Consulate, he knew you were after it. He swapped it with his own fake to be safe. You*—God, how could I have been so stupid?" She shrieked a mad laugh. "You told me yourself, the day after! You were able to guess what had happened in the vault because *you'd already been inside it*. You'd already tried to steal the Sahar, but you recognized the fake."

"Piper—" Lyre began, doubt heavy in his voice.

"You already had a fake," Piper went on, right over Lyre. She stared the draconian down, waiting for him to react, to deny it, to confess, to do *something*. "Why else would you have a perfect fake stone ready to go? You broke into the vault early, intending to leave your fake behind while you made off with the real one. Then, when the ambassadors came to get the Sahar and everyone realized it wasn't the real one, they'd blame my father. They'd accuse him." Her rage crested and broke. "*You were going to frame my father!*" she screamed. Tears spilled down her cheeks. "I trusted you!"

She turned away, unable to stand his stillness, his impregnable lack of reaction.

"Father knew," she choked. "He made me promise to keep you upstairs while they moved the Sahar so you couldn't make another try for it." Her lip curled. "It must have made your day when you found out I had the real Sahar all along. I never should have told you. You betrayed the Consulate, you betrayed my family, and you betrayed us."

Silence.

Lyre stared at the cement rooftop between his feet, his face twisted with unhappiness. Disappointment even. Not like he was surprised, but like he'd hoped for better.

Piper turned around again. Ash looked back at her, his face cold, mask-like, exactly like the photo from his profile page.

"Say something," she demanded flatly.

"Like what?" His toneless, silky voice sent a shiver down her spine. "You've said it all, haven't you? You have the whole story already. No need to consider the other side of it."

"Tell me the other side then," she shot back. Hope—weak, blinding hope, like with Micah—rose in her. This time she quashed it. What could possibly excuse Ash's behavior? He was a thief. A lying, cheating, heartless thief.

He went unnaturally still again, a black statue in the shadows as he hung on an answer. Then he made a rasp of disgust in the back of his throat and turned his face away.

"You have two options," he said. "Take the Sahar and do whatever the hell you want with it. Try to save yourself, your father, whatever. Or we follow through with the original plan."

She clenched her teeth against the fury exploding in her. Screaming at him wouldn't force an answer out of him. He probably didn't want to admit there was no other side to the story. He'd wanted the Stone and he'd done whatever it took to get it no matter who he had to betray. It was what any daemon would've done. Daemons weren't human. You couldn't expect them to hold things like integrity and trust at the same level of importance as a real person.

"I don't trust you," she said flatly. "I'm not doing anything that involves you. Just leave now."

"Piper—" Lyre muttered.

"Go with him then!" For some reason, it was easier to unleash her writhing emotions on Lyre instead of Ash. Looking at him hurt. Burned. Made her ache with all the shattered pieces inside where trust had been. "If you can still defend him, even now, then go with him. Let him lie to you and betray you some more."

"Piper," he snapped. "Get a grip!"

"A grip?" she shouted back, incensed.

"Yeah! You're not thinking clearly. So Ash stole the Sahar— exactly what every daemon this side of the universe wants. And yeah, I think he's an asshole right now. I'm pissed off too, but I also want to live to be angry tomorrow—and maybe even next month or next year. The only way that will happen is if we work together to get ourselves out of this." He lowered his voice. "You know we can't do it without Ash."

She ground her teeth, refusing to admit it. The burning pain of betrayal seared her, worse than when Micah had walked out on her after she told him she loved him. She'd trusted Micah with her heart. Ash, she'd trusted with her life.

Opening her fist, she looked at the Sahar. It glimmered in the faint city lights, pulsing with power. She remembered, mere hours ago, Ash telling Lilith with flawless sincerity that he hadn't stolen it. She snorted mirthlessly. What a liar.

"Fine," she snapped. "Fine, we'll do it your way, Ash. But if you so much as *look* at the Sahar—"

"You'll what?" The demand came out in a hiss. Piper jerked back a step, shocked to see his eyes had flashed to black. He smiled, showing his teeth. "You'll do what, exactly, Piper? Hate me more? Do not forget I gave you the Sahar and I can take it back at any moment." His stare was ebony ice, daring her to challenge him.

She was frozen under his glare like a rabbit caught in a hawk's sight. Forcing her spine straight, she bared her teeth right back at him.

"Why don't you then?" she burst out, furious at him all the more for frightening her. "Take it, then." She thrust her fist at him, the Stone clenched painfully tight in her fingers. "Take it and go do whatever it is you want it for. Will unlimited power make you happy, Ash?" she sneered. "Make up for all the friendships you betrayed?"

A deep rumble vibrated from his chest and his arms flexed—a lot like he was fighting the urge to hit her. She took a hasty step back.

"Why did you give it back?" she asked, forcing her voice into a more neutral tone.

His jaw flexed. He glanced at Lyre then back to her. "The Sahar does me no good if everyone thinks I stole it—"

"Which you did," she muttered.

Before he could reply, his head turned. A rush of beating air broke the silence and Zwi swooped out of the darkness. She landed on her owner's shoulder with flared wings, chattering and trilling. He listened attentively.

"Two teams of prefects with trackers are inside the club," Ash said emotionlessly. "If we're going to leave, it has to be now."

"How do you know that?" she asked suspiciously.

"Zwi was keeping watch."

"Zwi is an animal."

"So are humans."

Lyre stepped in before she could retort. "Let's go then. Now."

Ash jerked his head in a nod. "I'll get a car and meet you one block east of here. Don't be long."

"But—" Piper began.

Ash turned toward the edge of the building. In one swift movement, he swung over the edge and dropped silently out of sight. She listened for a second but didn't hear him land three stories below. Breathing deeply, she clenched her hand around the Stone.

"Come on, Piper," Lyre said.

She turned to the incubus, a little taken aback by the hostile stiffness of his profile. He didn't quite look at her as he gestured toward the fire escape a ways down the south side of the roof.

"What's *your* problem?" she snapped.

"What's yours? You know what, Piper?" Anger sharpened the edges of his words. "I think sometimes people get desperate. And they do desperate things—sometimes the wrong thing. Maybe you should think about that for a while before you call the daemon who almost died saving your life a coward again."

He turned and walked away.

Piper blinked the tears back. It figured Lyre would take Ash's side. Daemons always backed one another. She remembered Ash's incoherent apology when he'd been bleeding to death after the fight in the medical center. He'd felt guilt then—he'd known all along he was doing the wrong thing. A desperate thief was still a thief.

And being desperate didn't make the consequences any less real.

CHAPTER
-19-

THE GAIANS' current meeting place was hidden in the last place anyone would expect—an old Consulate.

The very idea offended Piper. This Consulate had serviced the neighboring city until Quinn was appointed Head Consul. Not just any Consulate could accommodate the kind of traffic a Head Consulate got. A new one on the other side of the city had been built and this one had gotten less and less use over the following years. About a year ago, it had been shut down for good. She had visited it a number of times before it closed, but she'd also been to dozens of others and the particular interior layout of this one wasn't springing to mind.

She, Lyre, and Ash crouched in the safety of the bushes right at the edge of the building's overgrown front lawn. Consulates always had a large, treeless expanse around them to prevent people from sneaking too close. The house was a small, two-story mansion, fortified with steel in some places, marred by peeling paint in others. The barred windows glared brightly. It definitely wasn't abandoned anymore.

214 | ANNETTE MARIE

Their plan was simple. They would sneak around back, scope out a likely looking window, and Ash would have Zwi scout the inside of the building. If her father and the Gaians were there, she, Ash, and Lyre would sneak in to rescue Quinn. They didn't have a lot of time. The prefects who'd come into the Styx would be tracking them.

"Well?" Lyre asked in a whisper.

Ash shrugged. He'd barely spoken on the drive over. He was partway shaded and he either didn't care or couldn't control it. Either way, Piper had enough sense not to antagonize him anymore; she no longer trusted him about anything, including whether he would lash out at her. The scary thing was he could kill her so easily. All it would take was one shaded moment when she was standing too close. Considering he seemed at least as angry with her as she was with him, his control would be even more slippery.

She didn't understand why he was so ticked off. Was he angry that she, unlike Lyre, hadn't shrugged off his actions as "what any daemon would've done"? Had he thought she wouldn't care or that she'd understand his ambitions? Did he think she should've forgiven him?

"I'm going to scout around," the draconian said. "Wait here."

She pressed her lips together before she could argue. Without a backward glance, Ash slipped into the trees, vanishing into the dark shadows. It would be hours yet before the sun breached the horizon and there was only a sliver of moon to cast any light. She chewed her tongue as she squinted at the Consulate. There was no telling how many people were in there.

"Piper," Lyre said in a low voice.

She knew that tone. "Don't bother."

"Huh?"

"You're going to defend him again. I don't care what you have to say. I am not forgiving him for—"

"Piper," he growled. "Shut up. Would you *listen* for once in your life?"

"You're one to talk."

"Shut up and listen!" He glared so ferociously she sat back on her heels and crossed her arms. She gave him a pointed spit-it-out look.

He coolly assessed her. "I know what it's like for you, being the daughter of the Head Consul when you can barely compete in this world. I know you study so hard to compensate for your missing magic. I also know you do a lot of dangerous shit that's over your head because you want to feel like you're strong and so your dad will notice you."

She bristled with each observation until she was nearly spitting. "Mind your own damn business, Lyre. You don't know anything about me."

"I know a lot more about you than you know about Ash. So what makes you think you understand anything about him?"

She huffed, disgusted. "I knew this would be about him. Would you—"

"I'm not defending him, Piper. He went behind my back too. *But*" —he put heavy emphasis on the word—"I also know Ash better than you. And I know he wouldn't do something like that unless he had a really good reason."

"That doesn't—"

"Make it okay," he finished. "I know that too. I've known Ash for four years. You know I charge lodestones for other daemons, right? Sometimes it's dangerous. Harmless daemons don't have lodestones. It's the powerful and the ambitious who have more lodestones than they have time to charge. Do you know how many times Ash has saved my life in the last four years? Do you know how much he's risked for me?"

She met Lyre's stare and said nothing.

"You know what else, Piper? If the Sahar had been mine and Ash had asked me to give it to him, I would have."

By human standards, that was like a billionaire handing over every last penny he owned. "Because he's saved your life before?"

"No," Lyre admitted. "I've helped him too. We watch each other's backs." He exhaled sharply. "I'd give it to him because he needs it more than me."

"Needs it for what?"

"He'll never tell you. I don't think it's my place to either."

"Tell me *what*?"

Studying her, he didn't answer.

She stared back, ready to burst with frustration. "You're not being very convincing, Lyre."

"Honestly, Piper," he said, his voice going cold, "I don't think I should have to convince you. Ash isn't going to try either."

"Because there's no argument you can make!"

Anger simmered in his face. Again, the daemons were angry with her. Ash had betrayed her. Why didn't they *get it*?

"Do you remember what Vejovis told you?" he asked abruptly.

"Huh?"

"He said, 'If you three survive this, he'll need your forgiveness. If you can.'" Lyre raised his eyebrows.

Piper's skin prickled. Vejovis had known Ash had stolen the Sahar.

"He also said, 'If you can't forgive him when the time comes, then you are not strong enough to stand among us.'"

Her hands clenched into fists. Lyre appraised her reaction, then shook his head, disgusted. "Humans. You're looking out a window, thinking you can see the whole world instead of one narrow view of it." He rose to his feet, towering over her. "I'll tell you one piece of what Ash will never tell you."

She went still, frozen by the look in Lyre's eyes.

"For giving up the Sahar, Ash will be killed. He'll be hunted down and slaughtered, like those assassins in the medical center tried to kill him—and almost succeeded."

She sucked in a sharp breath. With everything else going on, she'd forgotten about the two daemon assassins and their threats—that Ash was on their mysterious boss's hit list. Did he need the Sahar to protect himself? But he'd already stolen it from her *before* those guys attacked him. It didn't make sense.

"He's throwing away his last chance—to protect us," Lyre said, interrupting her thoughts. "So maybe you can understand why I don't have much patience with your grudge." With a dismissive shrug that made her feel two inches tall, he looked out across the lawn. "He made a desperate decision for a desperate reason." He cast her a sidelong glance. "Who would you betray for the chance to have your own magic?"

"I wouldn't betray anyone," she snapped. Shivering, she wrapped her arms around herself. The denial was still fresh on her tongue even as a terrible longing rose in her. Magic. To have magic. It would solve all her problems. She would have no problem becoming a Consul— one of the best Consuls. Daemons and haemons wouldn't sneer at her anymore. She'd no longer be inferior. Quinn wouldn't be disappointed in her. Wouldn't be too busy to take part in her life now and then.

She shook her head, banishing that line of thought. A few minutes passed in silence while she dwelt instead on Lyre's words. Would Ash be killed without the Sahar? But then he'd almost been killed in the medical center even with the Sahar on him. There was a huge piece—or several pieces—missing from the picture. Why wouldn't Lyre tell her what was really going on? On top of that, she wondered why Lyre and Vejovis thought she should just forgive Ash. Even if she were willing to forgive one aspect of his betrayal, she couldn't forgive it all. Ash had come to the Consulate intending to steal the Sahar from the vault. When that failed, he'd stolen it from her. She'd thought they'd been in it together but he'd had an escape route all along.

She pressed both hands to her face, trying to squeeze some sense into her brain. Of course she cared that Ash might be killed; no matter how angry and hurt she felt, she didn't want him to die. But at the same time, all she could see was his blank, cold expression as he dropped the Sahar in her hand as if he were doing her some big favor —after he'd *stolen it* from her. If Micah hadn't run off with the fake, Piper never would've clued in. Ash would have walked away with the most prized and powerful magical artifact out there. Everything he'd done since he'd arrived at the Consulate had been angled toward him getting away with the grandest larceny of all time.

Thinking about him was making her want to punch something. She put Ash out of her head and instead fretted about how easily their shaky plan could go wrong. She stared at the silent house, wondering if her father was in there and if he was okay. More than anything, she wanted the safety and security of his presence—the chance to hand over all her problems and let an adult take care of it.

Ash returned in eerie silence, sliding out of the darkness like a ghostly wraith. He explained that he'd found a spot at the back of the house where the tree line came a little closer to the building. Piper and Lyre followed him back through the trees in a bizarre, dangerous game of follow-the-leader, where they had to step exactly where he stepped to avoid making any noise. Even copying him exactly, she still rustled leaves and crunched a few stones underfoot.

They stopped in a well-hidden opening a few feet wide and surrounded by concealing bushes. On the other side of a large, thorny bush, the house seemed to watch them from across thirty paces of overgrown lawn. Kneeling beside the two daemons, Piper chewed her bottom lip, adrenaline pumping through her and making her hands shake. This had to work. Had to.

"Ready?" Ash whispered. He glanced upward. Zwi dropped from a tree branch to land on his shoulder, camouflaged with all black scales. Her mane stood on end as she arched her neck and growled softly. Piper took a deep breath, checking for the loose stone in her pocket. It had felt a lot safer down her shirt in the ring box. She looked at Ash, waiting for him to send Zwi in. He stared at the house, expression blank.

"Uh … Ash?"

He twitched his head sideways, like a fly was buzzing around his ear. Zwi whined plaintively, shaking her head. Ash jerked his head again and pressed both hands to his ears for a second.

"What's wrong?" Lyre asked.

Ash shook his head again. "Weird sound," he grunted. He dug the heels of his hands hard into his ears, hunching his shoulders.

"Is this really the time?" Piper muttered.

He tried to focus on her even as he kept twitching his head. His eyes glazed and he clamped both hands over his ears again. He bowed forward, biceps bunching from tension, and swore under his breath.

"I hear someone coming," Lyre said.

Piper tore her stare away from Ash and squinted through the screen of leaves. Coming around the far side of the building were two people, a man and a woman. The man was carrying a black object the size of a small briefcase in one hand. They studied the tree line as they slowly walked the perimeter of the lawn.

"They're coming this way." She rose into a crouch. "We have to get farther back. Ash, come on!"

The draconian didn't move. He was curled forward, hands clamped over his ears, muscles locked down. She grabbed his elbow and tried to guide him deeper into the trees. It was like trying to move a boulder.

"Shit," Lyre swore. He grabbed Ash's other arm. "Come on, man. We can't stay here. Whatever that noise is, let's get you away from it."

Ash unlocked enough to bring his head up. His face was tight with pain. Together, she and Lyre led a stumbling Ash back into the trees. Zwi clung to his shoulder, her head buried against the side of his neck as she whimpered. Piper winced at every snapping twig under their feet.

"Stop," Lyre hissed. "They're too close."

The three of them held still, listening. The two sentries were apparently doing the same, because all was silent.

"We know you're there," a voice called—the man. Piper's heart jumped into her throat. She exchanged a frantic, silent look with Lyre. "Come out now!"

"Do you think it's them?" the woman asked quietly, her voice floating through the quiet night.

"Shall we find out?" the man asked, sounding eager.

Another moment of silence.

Ash went rigid. His head flew back, hands clamped like vises over his ears. He arched onto his toes like he'd been hit with a cattle prod. His eyes rolled back in his head. Then he collapsed.

She and Lyre grabbed him, easing him down as he shuddered and twitched. Zwi convulsed beside him, squeaking with each jerk of her tiny body. Piper pressed on his shoulder, trying to hold him still.

"Lyre," she hissed frantically. "What's happening?"

"I don't know!"

Voices sounded from the Consulate lawn a dozen paces away.

"Is it working?" the woman asked.

"Not sure," the man answered. "Should I turn it up?"

"Go for it."

Ash arched upward, heels digging into the soft earth. His entire body went rigid. Panic erupted in Piper. He was going into a seizure.

"No," she gasped. She grabbed his shoulder and Lyre helped her roll him onto his side as he began to convulse, limbs jerking violently.

"No!" she cried again in a whisper. She looked up, neck craning toward the invisible man and woman. They were the source of whatever was hurting Ash. They had to be. Without stopping to think or plan, she lunged to her feet and charged out of the trees.

The sentries were waiting for her.

The spell hit her the second she burst out of the bushes, blasting her off her feet. She hit the ground and felt the second spell bind her arms behind her back. She rolled to her feet anyway. Damn it, she shouldn't have run straight at them like that.

"Stop it," she yelled. "Whatever you're doing to him, stop it now!"

The man's face lit. He was young, maybe twenty-two or so, with sandy hair and an innocent face. The woman was around thirty, her curves a little too out of control to be flattering, and her brown hair over-styled compared to her simple khaki pants and t-shirt.

"So it's working?" the guy asked. "Awesome." He grinned.

The woman gave Piper a stern look. "Sit there." She pointed to a patch of grass in the middle of the lawn. "Now. Or we'll turn it up and see what happens to your daemon friend then."

They could make it worse? Not understanding enough to know what to do or how to fight back, she obeyed, her motions rough with urgency and fear. What else could she do? Once she was sitting, arms still bound with magic, the woman pulled out a two-way radio and called for reinforcements.

"We knew you'd come," the guy said, bouncing excitedly on the balls of his feet. The black briefcase sat at his feet, conspicuously out of place. At close range, it didn't quite look right. "We'd already found out who you were travelling around with. What took you so long to come?"

Piper blinked, trying to make sense of what he was saying while her brain kept screaming at her to kick his stupid butt.

"I didn't know where to go," she answered tightly. "What are you doing to Ash?"

"Sound," he replied happily, picking up the briefcase and patting it like an obedient dog. "Ultrasound, to be specific. We can't hear it, but this speaker is blasting out ultrasonic pulses at an extremely high frequency. Draconians don't have many weaknesses, but they're especially sensitive to air pressure. The pressure waves from the ultrasound pulses are basically shattering his inner ears." He beamed a smile at her.

For half a second, she was too horrified to react. "Turn it off," she yelled, half rising.

"Stay where you are," the woman commanded. "You too," she shouted into the bushes. "The speaker can go louder. If either of you move, we'll turn it full blast."

Piper froze, imagining Lyre somewhere in the trees doing the same. If the sound at its current level was making Ash seizure, what would a stronger pulse do to him? Before she had a chance to think of how to get her hands on that speaker, half a dozen people came jogging around the corner of the house. Her heart sank. They were screwed.

A middle-aged man in the group of newcomers quickly took control. Minutes later, Lyre was led out of the trees, collared with a magic-depressor and his arms magically bound behind his back too. She said nothing as he was shoved down beside her but she was only too conscious of the tiny bump in her pocket where the Stone was hidden. Five minutes passed before two guys dragged Ash out of the trees and dumped him on the grass. If he was conscious, it was only barely. Piper hoped he'd passed out. In spite of her begging, the Gaians had refused to turn the speaker off until Ash had been collared too. The young guy held the speaker in a bear hug, grinning excitedly at the success of his toy. He kept glancing at Piper like he expected her to be impressed.

The group of haemons surrounded their prisoners. Two heaved Ash up by his arms, which were bound with invisible ties like her and Lyre. She stared at him frantically, hoping the sound hadn't damaged anything in his ears. As their captors led them around to the front of the building, she tried to control her panic. What could she do against so many? They'd never planned to challenge the Gaians head-on, and if they had, Ash would have led the attack. But with their cruel ultrasound attack, they could incapacitate him instantly.

Worst of all, she was taking the Sahar right into their midst. She couldn't allow the Gaians to get it.

The leader threw open the doors to the Consulate and strode into a foyer, once opulent but now dirty and sad. Piper followed silently, Lyre one step behind. They approached a set of double doors. The man opened both and gestured for Piper and Lyre to go first. The two men dragging Ash came in on their heels. Piper stopped in the middle of the huge room. Once a conference room, the remaining furniture had been pushed against the walls and boxes were stacked neatly in one corner. It looked like the Gaians didn't plan to stay much longer. Nice of them to steal what was left of the Consulate's stuff on their way out.

The only furniture in use were two long tables at the far end, covered in stacks of papers and files, with an unbelievable three laptops sitting on top of them. Working laptops were harder to get hold of than a bottle of fifty-year-old wine. A woman stood at one of the tables, her back to the rest of the room as she studied a screen. Five people stood around her, watching the prisoners enter the room.

Piper stared at the woman's back. Her skin prickled.

The two haemons carrying Ash dumped him on the floor at Piper's feet, leaving him sprawled uncomfortably on his stomach with his arms stuck behind his back. She knelt beside him, nudging him hopefully with her knee. He didn't react.

"We have them, ma'am," the middle-aged man announced. "Found them skulking in the woods out back. Exactly like you thought."

"Did the ultrasound work?" the woman asked without turning. The sound of her sweet-toned yet authoritative voice made Piper's blood run cold. Her hands started to tremble.

"Yes, perfectly. The draconian has been collared and we can put him down at any time with the speaker."

"Well done," the woman said. She straightened from the laptop and turned around. Her face was lovely, with high, aristocratic cheekbones and large hazel eyes. Her auburn hair was tied in a simple bun that matched her sensible gray pantsuit. Her gaze went straight to Piper as a smile stretched across her face. She radiated happiness.

"Piperel."

Warm welcome saturated that painfully familiar voice. Piper couldn't breathe. If she hadn't been kneeling, she would have fallen.

"Mom?" she whispered.

CHAPTER

-20-

DEAD SILENCE RANG through the room. Piper gaped at the smiling woman, unable to think. It was impossible.

With a low, pained grunt, Ash pulled his head up and twisted it to one side to peer at Mona Griffiths. Piper's hands clenched, her arms straining against the magical bindings. He turned his head the other way to meet Piper's shocked stare.

"You said your mother was dead." His voice was a low murmur but the room was suffocatingly silent.

"Dead?" Mona repeated, her brow furrowing.

"I—I—" Piper couldn't speak. She just stared.

"Piper?" Lyre muttered, shifting to stand so close his leg brushed her arm. "What's going on?"

Mona stepped forward, cold anger melting from her face as she spread her arms in an unspoken request for a hug.

"Piper, sweetheart," she said. "I'm not dead. I've missed you so much. You've grown so much." Her eyes shimmered with tears. "You're such a beautiful young lady now."

Piper slowly stood. Lyre hovered right behind her, so close they were almost touching. Her foot was pressed against Ash's arm, another connection to keep her calm. She sucked in a deep breath, fighting the barrage of emotions threatening to overwhelm her.

"I ... don't understand," she finally managed.

Mona glanced at the other people in the room, all eyes watching mother and daughter.

"Gregory, take the two daemons downstairs for the time being. Piper and I need to talk."

Panic jumped in Piper's belly. "I want them with me," she blurted.

Mona frowned. "Piper—"

"You can't hurt them. They're my friends."

Her frown deepened. "They're daemons, Piper."

"They've both saved my life more than once," she said stiffly. "That makes them my friends." Now was not the time to mention betrayals. Whatever she felt about Ash, more than anything she wanted him right there with her.

Mona sighed. "Gregory, take them downstairs but be—careful with them. They can wait there until Piper and I are done talking." She gave the middle-aged man who'd brought them in a meaningful look.

Piper swallowed hard, knowing that arguing would be pointless. As two men approached, Ash rolled onto his back and lunged to his feet. He was standing so quickly everyone in the room froze.

In that moment where no one moved, Ash stepped up to Piper, brushing against her as he put his mouth against her ear.

"Don't forget, Piper," he whispered urgently. "We are prisoners in enemy territory. Your mother is leading these Gaians. Remember what they did in that vault. To your family."

Piper went rigid as she realized the obvious. If Mona was alive and leading this sect of Gaians, then she was the one who, at the least, had allowed the attack on the Griffiths Consulate—the attack that had nearly killed Uncle Calder. And—her heart nearly froze in her chest—her mother must be the one holding her father prisoner, trying to force him to reveal the location of the Sahar.

Ash was jerked away by the two haemons. His stare didn't shift from her as they pulled him away. She watched them steer Ash and Lyre back across the room and out the double doors. Cold shivered through her as the doors closed, blocking the two daemons from her sight.

She jumped when Mona touched her arm, and the binding spell vanished with a spark of magic. She looked into her mother's familiar hazel eyes, eyes she hadn't seen in ten years and had never imagined she would see again. She said nothing as Mona led her to a door off the main room, struggling to reconcile the bombardment of violent emotions making her hands shake. Through the door was a barren office with a sitting area. Mona sat on the stained sofa and patted the sagging cushion beside her. Piper sat gingerly, reeling inside.

"Piper." Mona took her hands and squeezed them. "I know this must be a shock. How do you feel?"

Piper stared into her mom's face. "I don't understand," she finally said. "You're not—you didn't die?"

"No, sweetheart." The cold rage hardened her features. "You can thank your father for that lie. He was determined to keep us apart. If I'd known …"

Another axis of her world shattered. Quinn had lied to her? Lied about her mother being *dead* just to keep them apart? It couldn't be. He too must have believed Mona was dead. Someone else must have tricked him. He never would have lied to Piper about something like that.

Mona squeezed Piper's hands again. "I tried to reach you for a year, Piper. I called, I left messages, I sent friends to try to talk to you. Quinn banned me from the Consulate and eventually threatened to have you shipped off to a boarding school where I would never find you." She exhaled slowly. "I stopped trying then. I didn't want to disrupt your life anymore than I already had. I always assumed you would try to find me once you were older. When you didn't … I thought you must hate me for leaving you."

"No," Piper croaked. "I thought you died. I thought you were killed in a car crash."

Mona pulled her into a crushing hug. Piper squeezed her mother just as fiercely, her heart and mind bursting under the weight of unveiled lies. After a long minute, she leaned back. Her eyes travelled around the room.

"Are you part of the Gaians?"

Mona smiled hesitantly. "I lead this chapter, yes. My affiliations with the Gaians are the main reason your father and I separated."

"I—yes, I knew that. But this Consulate … ?"

"We rotate our meetings among a number of locations. One of our members is a Consul and she recommended this spot. We don't normally gather in one place for more than a single night, but the current situation is a little different." She glanced at the boxes in the corner. "Of course, we can't leave any evidence behind. We don't want anyone guessing … details about us."

Not wanting to face the reality of Mona's involvement in the events of the last week, Piper tossed out another question. "Why would Consuls be allied with the Gaians?"

"Consuls know, even more intimately than most, why change needs to occur. Daemons are parasites, Piper. We can no longer allow them free reign here. They are diplomatically immune in almost every sense. They are petty tyrants who take whatever they want from humankind without restraint." Her expression hardened. "You've been sheltered, growing up in the Consulate. You only know daemons who are on their best behavior. You have no idea what goes on in the dark corners of the city. What daemons do to humans—for fun. What they could do if the powerful among them decided to unleash their magic."

Her mother's expression softened. "We know not all daemons are cut from the same cloth. Overworld daemons, on average, aren't quite as … depraved in their tastes. We don't want to eliminate daemons or even hurt them. We merely want to regulate their visits here to protect innocent humans who have no defenses. Our mandate is simple, and—as you may have heard—very popular. Hundreds more join our cause every year. People are beginning to see that the daemons' reign on Earth must come to an end. It is time for humanity to reclaim our world."

"The daemons' reign?" Piper repeated as her brow crinkled. "They don't reign here. They don't—"

"I realize you find it hard to believe. Your father has taught you his philosophy, I know."

"Did Father always know you were a Gaian?"

Mona shook her head. "I became interested when you were still little, after I'd seen so much daemon violence. By the time I was ready to join, Quinn was starting to suspect something. So one night, I told him everything. I was ..." She paused, breathing deeply, then continued. "I was certain he would see what needed to change as I did and join too. He did not. He exploded. That was the night I left." She shrugged off her dark mood and smiled. "But that is behind us now. We can be together now, Piper. You don't have to join the Gaians if you don't want to. I just want us to be together again."

More than anything, Piper wanted to melt into her mother's arms and never move again, but Ash's words kept circling in her head. She saw Uncle Calder's bandaged face and the burned bodies in the vault. With shaking hands, she straightened in her seat and crossed her arms.

"What happened at the Consulate, in the vault? Why did you try to steal the Sahar?"

Mona bit her bottom lip. "I didn't know Calder would be there, Piper. I swear to you, I didn't know."

Piper shook her head. Calder went everywhere Quinn went. Mona had to know that. "You were there?"

"No. But it was essential we take the Sahar before it was returned to daemon hands. It was far more important than any one life." She gripped Piper's hands hard. "You can't imagine what a powerful daemon could do with the Sahar. It would be a return to the dark ages."

"You killed all those people."

"We had to, Piper." Her eyes pleaded for understanding. "Quinn tried to kill my people in retaliation. He caused that explosion."

"Where is my father?"

"He's here," she said quickly. "He's fine, safe and unharmed. We only brought him here to find out where he hid the real Sahar—using harmless drugs, nothing more—but somehow he doesn't know where it is. It's clear he doesn't have any idea."

Piper kept her face blank. How could Quinn not know where the Sahar was? He'd given it to her hours before the attempted theft.

"What about that choronzon? Did you set it loose in the house too? It almost killed me."

Mona's eyes widened. "Oh no. We had it entirely under control. It would never have touched you."

No, it would have just ripped Ash to pieces instead. Piper pressed her lips together. "Where did you get it? Using an Underworld monster to kill people kind of runs counter to your anti-daemon-violence mandate, doesn't it?"

"We borrowed it from an ally."

Piper waited but her mother said nothing more. "You had people waiting at the Consulate for me afterward."

"I couldn't find you," Mona explained. "I needed to make sure you were safe. They were supposed to bring you here, not hurt you. They've been severely reprimanded for what happened. Piper … I never meant for you to become involved."

"Involved?" Her voice rose furiously. "*Involved?* I've been up to my neck in this shit storm! I was arrested. I'm a fugitive. I've lost count of how many times I've been hurt or almost killed since you tried to steal the Stone."

Mona looked down at her hands, knowing better than to offer another empty apology. Silence stretched between them. After a moment, Mona looked up and appeared to notice Piper's clothes for the first time. She was still in her club outfit and it was definitely worse for wear. Apparently deciding not to comment, Mona took a deep breath.

"Piper, your father and I disagreed about many things and a lot of them had to do with you. He's had ten years with you that I was denied; ten years to make his case." She gazed solemnly at Piper. "Now I want to make my case to you. I want you to come live with me."

She froze like a rabbit caught in a trap. "Mom—"

"I know you're upset and it all seems impossible right now. All I'm asking is a chance to show you my world—a different world from the Consulate and the constant threat of daemons. I won't pressure you to join the Gaians or to support our cause. I—All I want is to share my life with you, Piper, sweetheart. Will you give me a chance?"

Her mouth opened, then closed. A sob tried to claw up her throat, born of the tearing of her heart. Father or mother. How was she supposed to choose? Maybe it should've been an easy choice—the parent who'd raised her, who'd been there all along—but if what Mona said was true, her father had told her the most destructive, life-shattering lie of her life. Even without that betrayal in the equation, Quinn had never made time for her. She had never been his first priority.

"I—I want to talk to Father. He's here. Let me see him."

Pain creased Mona's face before she smiled weakly. "Of course, honey. But there's one thing I want to bring to your attention first. I imagine you'll want to ask Quinn about it yourself." She paused to gather her thoughts. "One of the things your father and I disagreed on was your future. I wanted you to have every opportunity, even if it was … a riskier path than others. Your father always preferred you stay safe and sheltered." She raised her eyebrows knowingly. Piper grimaced.

"I'm talking about one thing in particular regarding your future: magic."

Piper stared blankly. "I don't have any magic."

Mona's stare was intent, almost calculating. "Not anymore, no."

Piper's heart seemed to expand in her chest. She sucked in a sharp breath. "What do you mean?"

"You were born with magic like any other haemon." Mona pressed her lips together hard. "But as you know, all female children with two haemon parents die. When you were six, the age when magic starts to develop, you started to die too."

Piper's whole body went cold. "What?"

"You remember, don't you? The headaches?"

She shuddered at the memory, still vibrant even though she'd been so young—pain beyond description condensed inside her skull, burning her mind to ash. Within six months, the migraines had escalated to the point where she would fall into seizures.

"Your developing magic was killing you. We couldn't let you die. Even though we knew it was probably hopeless, we searched relentlessly for a way to save you. We didn't give up. Just as it seemed we would be too late, we tracked down the best daemon healer in the Overworld.

"He confirmed the long-rumored cause: that female children inherit two magical bloodlines, one from each haemon parent. Male children only inherit the mother's bloodline and develop normally. You were dying because two competing kinds of magic were growing inside you, slowly killing you."

Mona tried to smile. "Did you know daemon castes cannot interbreed? They can consort, of course, but they can't reproduce. You will never see a crossbreed daemon. Only haemons can create what was never meant to be: a cross of daemon bloodlines. And they all die—except you. You are the only hybrid in existence."

Piper stared, trying to calm her pounding heart. "Why didn't I die too?"

Mona pulled her into a hug. "The daemon healer had an idea. It was like nothing I'd ever heard before; magic so complex I can't imagine how he conceived such a thing. Even he wasn't sure it would work." She tightened her arms around Piper. "But he did it. He sealed your magic away inside you, stopping its development. He cut you off from it so it wouldn't hurt you. That's why you have no power."

Piper stared at nothing, reeling inside. So she did have magic—magic she could never use. Magic that should have killed her. Instead, she was alive but weaker than the weakest haemon. A powerless hybrid.

"Once we knew you were safe," Mona continued, "your father decided that was the end of it. He had the healer fog your memory of the healing. He announced we would never tell you so you wouldn't mourn what you'd lost."

Piper was silent, thinking her father had had the right idea.

"But I don't believe that's the end of it." Mona sat back and gripped Piper's shoulders with both hands. "I don't think your magic is lost forever. The healer sealed your two lines of magic away from you—and away from each other. There might be a way to reclaim one side of it and keep the other sealed away. Then you'd be safe."

Piper inhaled slowly, not daring to hope yet hoping anyway.

"Maybe it's impossible. I don't know. But I do know we will never know if we don't try. Your father doesn't want to give you the chance to try. He's always wanted to make all our choices for us."

Mona abruptly rose to her feet and gave Piper's arm a comforting squeeze. "I know it's a lot to take in. Go talk to your father. Ask him for his side. You won't feel better until you do."

o   o   o

Piper drifted in a haze of conflicting thoughts and emotions as she followed the young man who'd been manning the ultrasound speaker earlier. Her head was bursting, her heart aching. She felt so much she couldn't feel anything. Ash's betrayal with the Sahar hardly seemed like anything now that she was faced with the enormity of the lies her father had told her.

She'd thought she understood her life pretty well. Turned out she didn't. She didn't have magic? Actually, she had a deadly magic combo she couldn't use. Her mom had died nine years ago? Actually, she'd been alive all along and forbidden from contacting Piper. Of all the people she could trust, her father was one of only two? Actually, he'd been lying to her and hiding things from her for her entire life.

Her Gaian guide interrupted her inner rant.

"It's good you came when you did," he said over his shoulder, grinning cheerfully as though it didn't matter one bit that he'd used that speaker to send Ash into an agony-spawned seizure. "My name is Travis, by the way. It's great to finally meet you. We were hoping you'd show before we had to leave."

She struggled to focus on his words.

"We figured you'd find out where we were," he babbled on, oblivious to her emotional turmoil, "but if we'd moved before you got here, we would've had to start looking for you again. No way you'd find our new location without insider help."

234 | ANNETTE MARIE

"Why are you moving?" she asked without any real interest. Her mind spun through the revelations of the last hour. She felt sick to her stomach.

"With all this stuff with the Stone, it was a good idea no matter what," Travis explained. "But then we caught this daemon snooping around a few days ago. Now we have a whole group of them hiding in the woods. They haven't come too close yet but they will any day now, we expect. They must think we have the Stone, like the one we caught, but these ones don't want to come bursting in. We have greater numbers than them."

She frowned. "How many?"

"Oh, forty or so haemons here, another twenty nearby," he rambled on carelessly. "The daemons in the woods are only, I dunno, fifteen or so."

Forty in this building alone? Piper frowned, calculating. She supposed if they didn't mind cramped quarters, forty people could fit in the Consulate.

"Then, of course, a huge squad of prefects followed you here. They're thirty minutes out last I heard. We need to be gone before then, so you'll, you know, have to keep your conversation short."

Piper worked to keep her expression blank. Well, shit. Everything was falling apart. Captured by the Gaians, who were led by her supposedly deceased mother, and now the prefects were right behind them. She trailed along in a silent frenzy of ineffective on-the-fly planning while Travis blabbed all the way to the basement and down a long hall, through a locked door, and into another hallway. This one was dim and unfinished, more of a tunnel than a hall. There were three doors, all on the left side.

"The middle room is empty," he said. "This near one has the daemon we captured earlier. The far door is your dad."

Piper glanced at the deadbolt on the nearest metal door. "What are you planning to do with him?"

"Well, some people thought we should kill him so he can't tell anyone about us, but Ms. Santo overruled them." Piper started to nod —of course her mother wouldn't kill a daemon in cold blood—then she froze as the guy continued. "She said he's too good an opportunity to pass up. This is our chance to learn about some of the magic daemons have that we don't. Find out if there's a way to duplicate some of their abilities, like glamour and stuff."

She slowly clenched her hands as outrage kindled. "So you keep him prisoner and, what? Force him to give you magic lessons?"

"Nah, he wouldn't do that. I think the idea was more to experiment on him or something. I don't know, that's not my department."

"Experiment on him," she repeated flatly.

"Yeah," he said excitedly, as emotionally observant as a brick wall. He obviously considered her a full-fledged member of the Gaians already. "Imagine what we could learn. Glamour would be so cool."

"Where are the daemons I came in with?" she asked abruptly.

"Them? Oh, they're in the old food cellar at the other end of the basement. We didn't think these rooms were secure enough. We only had one five-class dampening collar and we used it on this daemon here, so your daemon only has a four-class collar. Might not be enough." He shrugged.

She took a deep breath and exhaled slowly. Then she plastered on a vacant smile. "Sounds good. Say, do you think they'll want to experiment on them too?"

Travis shrugged. "Who knows? Probably not, not without a top-level collar to keep the nasty one tame, and the incubus is useless anyway."

"So what'll you do with them?" she pressed, trying to keep her tone casual.

He spread his hands. "No idea. Maybe just kill 'em."

"Oh … right." She worked to keep her smile in place.

"Yeah. Maybe I'll see how well that ultrasound works." His grin faded as he squinted at her. "What? Don't sweat it. It's not like killing people. They're only daemons."

Piper clenched her jaw and gave a noncommittal nod. She remembered what the file had said about the Gaians; their public mandates were a lot different from their private agendas. Her mother had offered Piper the public face only.

"Are these rooms locked?" she asked.

He nodded as he pulled out a ring of keys. "I'll let you in to talk to your dad and wait until you're done."

She smiled politely, stepped up to him, and slammed her fist into his gut so fast he didn't even have a chance to flinch. As he doubled over, she locked her arm around his neck from behind and squeezed. He flailed and slapped at her like a panicking child. It only took a minute before he crumpled into unconsciousness. Breathing hard, she plucked the keys out of his limp hand.

What a group of hypocritical, self-deluding murderers. She would have to figure out what she thought of her mother leading them later, but she knew she would never join them. No. Way. In. Hell.

Shaking out the keychain, she strode to the far door and started trying out keys. There were a dozen large keys and nearly as many small ones. It took her a while to get it unlocked. Taking a deep breath, she pushed the door open and stepped into the room.

It was a barren cube of cement blocks, not even a window. A pallet covered most of the cement floor, several cheap blankets spread over it. A bucket sat in the far corner. Lying across the pallet was her father. At first glance, he looked fine, sleeping peacefully. Then she noticed the pallor of his skin and the hollowness of his cheeks. His clothes, the same dress shirt and pants he'd worn the night he was kidnapped, were stained and dirty. He had several days' growth of unkempt facial hair.

Without thinking, she rushed across the room and dropped down beside him. Before she could find her voice, his eyes cracked open. He stared at her. Then a grin split his face—a very familiar but un-Quinn-like grin.

The floor seemed to drop out from under her.

"Uncle Calder?" she whispered in disbelief.

"Hey Piper," he croaked.

"But—but—you're not Father!" She mentally flailed. Not possible. Yes, they were identical twins, but she'd been positive the Gaians had kidnapped Quinn, not Calder.

"Nope," he rasped, barely able to get any volume. "It was supposed to be a contingency plan in case … Do you know … ?"

"He's alive," she said quickly. "In a medical center last I saw him." She marveled at the thought—that had been her *father* in the medical center? She gasped as another realization hit her. "That's why you couldn't tell the Gaians where the Sahar is!"

"I have no idea. Only Quinn knows. That's why we switched. How did you find me?"

Piper hesitated, then decided not to get into the technicalities of who knew what about the Stone. That could wait. "We broke into the medical center so I could talk to you—I mean Father. Well, he couldn't really *talk*, and I thought he was you, but he gave me the combo to the vault in his office and I found the Gaian file." Her excitement stalled, replaced with suspicion. "Did *you* know Mom was alive?"

Calder's face tightened. He took a deep breath. "Your father made that decision, Piper. It wasn't my place to undermine his choices."

She opened her mouth furiously, betrayal searing her. He held up a hand. "We can hash it out later. We need to get out of here." His eyes narrowed. "When you say 'we broke in,' who is 'we'?"

She reluctantly shelved her fury. "Me, Ash, and Lyre."

"Ash?" he repeated warily.

She looked away. "Yeah. Don't worry, I know I can't trust him." She frowned, remembering what Lyre had said about Ash's days being numbered without the Sahar. She gave her head a shake. "But we can catch up on stuff later. Right now, we have to escape. The prefects are thirty minutes away and there's a party of hostile daemons camped out back."

"Aren't the prefects a good thing?"

"Not when they think I'm a thief and murderer and you're the treacherous Head Consul who engineered the whole thing."

He blinked. "Well. In that case, I'm all for escaping, Pipes, but there's one small problem."

"What?"

"My leg is broken. I can't walk."

"Your leg? How?"

"I didn't, as they say, come quietly."

238 | ANNETTE MARIE

She frowned. "That makes things more complicated. I might have to get Ash and Lyre, then come back for you."

He nodded, instantly wary again at the mention of Ash's name. She started to stand, then reconsidered. "Maybe we'll get you out of this room first. I can scout ahead for the cellar room while you … stand guard or something. Sit guard. Whatever."

She helped him gain his feet. Calder moved with painful stiffness, so slow and awkward that Piper bit her lip. Short of someone carrying him, they wouldn't get far. He was way too heavy for Piper to do more than prop him up. Together they hobbled out the door and into the hallway. Calder could barely shuffle along, grunting and wincing as he dragged his broken leg. He'd made an attempt to wrap it in torn strips of blanket, but without a splint it wasn't doing much good.

As she drew level with the first door in the hallway, her steps slowed, then stopped. An idea took form in her mind. A crazy idea. She would have a hell of a time getting Calder out on her own but maybe there was help right here—or maybe she'd be letting a tiger out of its cage.

Only one way to find out.

CHAPTER
-21-

"WAIT HERE," she told her uncle.

She slipped out from under Calder's arm, helped him lean against the wall, then approached the door. It took another agonizing minute to find the correct key. Their time ticked away, second by second. The lock clicked. She yanked the key out and flung the door open.

The room was almost identical to Calder's cell but the figure sitting on the pallet couldn't have been more different.

Eyes of an impossibly bright, yellowy green locked on her with disquieting intensity. The daemon was a young man, at least a few years older than her in appearance. He had the kind of sculpted face that surpassed handsome and could only be described as arresting—amazing, sharp cheekbones, a perfect jaw, and those bright, mysterious eyes. His golden-blond hair was long enough to have that carefree tousle women loved. For a second, she felt an unreasonable surge of irritation that she was cursed to be surrounded by impossibly good-looking daemons—but then again, it wasn't hard to be impossibly handsome when it was faked with magic.

This particular daemon lounged on his pallet like it was a throne, studying Piper without expression. Heavy manacles bound his wrists, chaining him to the wall. She swallowed hard, strapped some steel to her spine, and smiled smoothly.

"Good evening," she said in her best game-show-host voice. "I have a fantastic offer for you—one night and one night only!" She held up her ring of keys with a dramatic flourish. "One 'get out of jail free' card, just for you."

His eyebrows rose. Amusement touched his expression but his stare was calculating. He didn't blink nearly as much as she thought he should. She wondered what kind of daemon he was.

"What's the catch?" he asked. His voice ranked up there with Ash's and Lyre's on the delicious scale—smooth and melodic like a classically trained singer. Again, good chance it was magically assisted; Ash sounded different without his glamour. Although, in his case, the surreal, bone-shivery undertone of his voice was *suppressed* by glamour, not enhanced.

"The catch is that you have to escape my way and not yours." Time was ticking but she didn't let her urgency show. With daemons, sometimes you had to act in a way they didn't expect to keep the upper hand. Plus, letting this dangerous creature catch the scent of her urgency would be a disaster. Nice daemons didn't need five-class magic-dampening collars.

"And what," he drawled with a teasing tilt of his head, "might I ask, is 'your way'?" He was playing along. Thank goodness.

"Well," she declared, leaning against the doorframe and swinging the keys on one finger. "Were you to, hypothetically, be granted your freedom right about now, would you say you're the 'escape quietly' type? Or the 'bloody killing spree of revenge' type?"

He made a thoughtful sound. "I could be persuaded in either direction. I can always come back for the killing spree later."

She swallowed. He wasn't joking.

"Well, this offer of freedom requires the quiet approach. You see, there's an unknown number of prefects on their way. We don't have much time."

"Prefects?" He canted his head to the other side. "They would free me the same as you, wouldn't they?"

"And you want to answer all their questions about what the hell you're doing here in the first place?"

He smiled, apparently pleased she was smart enough to see that. "No."

"All right then." She waved the keys again. "Here's the deal. I unlock those chains and you help me carry my injured uncle out of here. Then you can do whatever you want."

"Your uncle?"

"Yes, a fellow prisoner. His leg is broken."

He nodded agreeably. She was getting more suspicious by the second. This guy was way too calm and blasé, both about his imprisonment and this opportunity to escape it. Did he *care* he was chained to a wall? Maybe he got off on that kind of thing.

"I also have to free two of my friends who are locked up," she told him.

"Friends?" His gaze slid down Piper and back up again. She resisted the urge to hide her bare, bruised midriff. "Haemon friends?"

"No, daemon friends."

A flicker of interest. "I see. Fair enough. I agree."

Her eyes narrowed. "And how do I know you won't attack me the moment I get those chains off you?"

He leaned back into the wall, spread his manacled arms, and smiled beatifically. "You'll just have to trust me."

She warily approached him. Stupid, stupid. She knelt beside him and lifted the keys. He held out a wrist. She found the right key on the second try and unlocked the first manacle. His wrist was raw and bruised underneath. He offered the other manacle and she unlocked it too.

He sighed, rubbing one wrist. Then he was on his feet. One second he was sitting—the next he was uncoiling like a jaguar from its den and towering over her. She froze for a second. Then she leaped up too, watching him guardedly and resisting the urge to back away. He was taller than her by almost half a foot, probably within an inch of Ash's height, and built the same way—toned and athletic to the nth degree. The collar obviously wasn't impairing his glamour, because his classy white shirt and dark gray jeans were impeccably clean and wrinkle-free despite his days of captivity. Yeah right.

He tapped a finger against the collar around his neck. "What about this?"

She stepped closer and craned her neck for a better look at the back of it. It was solid steel and the same dimensions as a wide dog collar. The keyhole in the back was tiny and elaborate. She fingered her ring of keys.

"These keys are all too big. I'm sorry."

He shrugged. "I'll get it off another way then." With a sudden flash of a smile, he swept one arm out dramatically. "After you, my lady savior."

She suppressed a flicker of fear—why was he so nonchalant? Who exactly was he?—and projected confidence as she swept her hair back over her shoulders and sauntered out the door like she owned the place. She caught a glimpse of his amused smirk. Keep him off balance, she told herself. It was her only protection. Even without magic, this daemon was more than she could handle.

She stepped into the hallway. Calder had sunk down to sit on the floor, pale and sweating. As the daemon stepped out of the room, her uncle's posture stiffened.

"Uncle Calder, this is ..." She looked over her shoulder. "Have a name, hot stuff?"

"Miysis," he offered. "But I like 'hot stuff' too."

He said it like "*my*-sis." The name was familiar. If he was as powerful as she suspected, she'd no doubt heard about him before. Calder must have recognized the name too, because he started shooting her nonstop warning looks. She ignored him, playing it cool while Miysis was watching.

"I'm Piper. Miysis, could you—"

An explosion blasted so loudly from above them that she staggered into the wall.

"What—"

Another blast above them. Dust swirled through the air. Voices upstairs were shouting. The unmistakable sound of gunfire erupted. Someone screamed.

Piper grabbed her uncle and hauled him to his feet. Miysis looked thoughtfully at the ceiling.

"The prefects must be early," she gasped. "Come on, we have to go."

"No," Miysis murmured. He glanced at her and shrugged. "Some of that is daemon magic."

"Daemon?"

"Mmm."

"Shit!"

"This is bad?"

"Yes." Her hands clenched into fists. "It must be the daemons from the woods. They've come for the Sahar."

Miysis's attention sharpened. He smiled slowly. "It is here then?"

She shook her head sharply. "The Gaians never had it."

He sighed. "Too bad."

"Yeah," she agreed distractedly. "Crap, we need to get out of here."

The daemon she'd freed glanced upward as another blast shook the ceiling. "It will take too long if we all go together. I'll take Calder. You find your daemon friends."

Calder stiffened. Piper slowly turned to face Miysis. "You'll take him where?"

"Out of the building and to safety." He appraised her expression then smiled. "Don't worry, Piperel Griffiths. I would not let harm come to a Consul, especially not to the brother of the Head Consul."

"You—you—how do you know who I am?"

"How many haemons named Piper with haemon uncles named Calder can there be? Your father—and your family—are quite well known, you know."

She scowled.

"I will hide us in the woods. Then, once you've saved your friends, you can join us … and we can have a little talk about the Sahar and who might have it if the Gaians never did."

Ice slid through Piper's veins. She shared a panicked look with Calder. Stupid stupid stupid. She never should have freed Miysis. Yes, he would get Calder out, but the daemon was also going to hold her uncle hostage until she told him everything she knew about the Sahar.

Slowly, she nodded. At least Calder would be safe. She'd worry about the rest later.

"If he gets so much as a scratch," she threatened roughly, "I promise you'll never set foot in a Consulate again."

He smiled, calm as ever. "Do not fear. I will take care of him."

Another explosion shook the house. The screams and shouts from upstairs were coming almost constantly now. After a last glance upward, Miysis slung Calder over his shoulder with an astonishing lack of effort.

"I'll see you soon, Piper. Take care." With a smile that didn't touch those bright, unnatural irises, he and Calder vanished into the hovering dust that obscured the long hall.

Piper stared after them, trying not to panic. Calder had gone from one enemy to another and she feared this one would be even more of a challenge to escape.

Another explosion ripped the air and made the ceiling above creak alarmingly. Piper ran.

ɵ   ɵ   ɵ

How hard could it be to find a food cellar in a basement? Piper ran down her third hall, opening every door she passed. It had only been a few minutes but it felt like a dangerously long time. The confrontation upstairs was turning into an all-out battle. Random explosions of power interrupted the sounds of gunfire. She prayed no one started a fire.

Something heavy and alive landed on her head.

She screamed and ducked. An angry chitter erupted above her and sharp claws caught her shoulder. Zwi chattered nonstop in admonishment. Piper gasped through the adrenaline rush.

The dragonet finally quieted, gave Piper a meaningful look, then jumped to the floor and ran a few steps back the way Piper had come. The creature stopped and growled over her shoulder.

"This way?" she asked. "This way to Ash?"

Zwi made a bird-like squawk and dashed away. Piper charged after the dragonet. When she reached an intersection with three halls and a stairway heading up, Zwi ran down the one hallway Piper had yet to try—of course.

"Piper!"

She jerked to a stop at the base of the stairs. Her mother half fell down the stairs. Her hair was falling out of its bun, her eyes wild. A trickle of blood ran down the side of her face.

"Piper!" She grabbed Piper's arm. "There you are. Thank God you're safe. We have to get out." She looked around wildly. "We're under attack. Those daemons in the woods must have caught wind of the approaching prefects and thought this was their last chance to snatch the Sahar." She tugged hard on Piper. "Come on. This way."

She broke her mother's grip and stepped back fast. "No. I have to get Ash and Lyre out first. I won't abandon them."

"Piper, they're daemons," Mona exclaimed. "They can take care of themselves."

"Not with those collars you put on them. Where's the cellar? I'm going to get them out."

"There's no time! We have to go now."

"No, I won't—"

Mona snapped a hand out. Piper gasped as magic slammed into her, locking her arms to her sides. The force lifted her into the air until she was hanging six inches above the floor. She struggled pointlessly, her feet kicking at air.

"I'm sorry, Piper, but I won't let you risk yourself. You don't understand the danger. This morning we rigged the whole building to explode after we leave. I told you we couldn't leave any evidence behind. If the fight triggers the explosives, everyone in here will die."

"Let me go," Piper screamed. "I won't leave them!"

"I don't care about them," Mona snapped. "I care about *you*. This is just the beginning. I need you with me where you'll be safe. We're leaving." She gestured again. The spell wrapped around Piper pulled her forward, hovering her down the hall toward her mother.

A flash of dark wings. Zwi landed on the floor between Piper and Mona, her mane standing on end all the way down her spine. She bared her teeth and snarled like an angry cat. Mona lifted a hand toward the little creature, magic sparking in the air around her. A cry of denial leaped to Piper's lips. Mona started to cast—

Black light exploded around Zwi. The concussion blasted Piper backward, shattering Mona's spell. She hit the floor on her back. Gasping for air, she sat up.

Zwi stood exactly where she'd been, but instead of a cat-sized dragonet, a full-sized dragon crouched in the hallway. She was the size of a pony. Her half-furled wings made her look even larger. She opened her massive jaws wide and roared. The brutal sound made the air quiver and Piper's blood run cold.

Mona staggered back, craning to see Piper around the dragon filling the hall between them. "Piper, please."

She shook her head, aching inside. Zwi snarled.

Mona's face went whiter. She licked her lips. "Baby, don't do this. Come with me. I'm begging you."

"I—I can't," she choked. "I'm sorry, Mom."

Mona cast one last despairing look at Piper, then turned and ran. She vanished around a corner. Piper's heart slammed against her ribs, aching with old wounds and new ones. Once again, her mother had left her.

Zwi turned, her wings scraping the walls. Piper froze where she sat, trying not to hyperventilate. Those teeth were really, really big. A snarling lion would have been less frightening. The dragon arched her back, blinking slowly, and gave her head a sharp shake. Black light swirled out, then withdrew, shrinking the dragon with it. The haze of magic faded and the cat-sized dragonet stood in the dragon's place.

"Wow," Piper breathed. "Did *not* know dragonets could do that."

Zwi fluffed her mane proudly. Piper staggered to her feet, flinching as something upstairs exploded. Shrapnel peppered the floor above. Zwi jumped up and perched on Piper's shoulder. She pointed her nose commandingly down the hall. Piper broke into a fast jog.

The cellar was a brick-walled room with shelves of old food preserves and an ancient, heavy worktable in the middle. Piper stood in the doorway, trying to figure out where Lyre and Ash were supposed to be. The room was small and clearly empty. The black ultrasound speaker sat in the middle of the table. Had Ash and Lyre already escaped?

Zwi sprang off her shoulder and ran across the room. She darted under the table and started scratching frantically at the floor.

"Zwi?" came a muffled voice.

"Lyre?" Piper exclaimed. She ran across the room and crawled under the table. A wooden trapdoor in the floor was bolted shut with a padlock.

"Piper? Piper, turn it off," Lyre yelled, the edge of panic in his voice audible even through the trapdoor. "Turn off the damn speaker!"

She tried to leap to her feet and slammed her head into the tabletop. She rolled out, grabbed the speaker, and hurled it at the floor. It bounced, bits of plastic flying off. Was it still working? She yanked a knife from the sheath in her boot and slashed the cloth front of the speaker, then drove the blade into the middle of it. Electricity shocked her hand, making her whole forearm burn before going numb. She jerked the knife out again.

"Has it stopped?" she yelled. "Is Ash okay?"

"I think he's coming around. Can you get us out?"

She crawled back to the trapdoor. The padlock key was easy to find on her key ring. She heaved the trapdoor open and peered into a dark pit. Zwi appeared out of nowhere and dove into the pitch darkness without hesitation.

"Lyre?"

His face, pale among the shadows, appeared ten feet down. "Piper. Thank the Moirai. What the hell is going on?"

"I ditched the Gaians and came to get you out. A band of daemons is attacking the house. There's a huge fight going on and the prefects will be here any minute."

"Shit. Can you help me get Ash up? He's in rough shape."

"They told me they wouldn't hurt you," she whispered, furious. She backed out from under the table, grabbed the flashlight she'd spotted earlier on a shelf, and returned to the trapdoor. A rickety ladder that looked a hundred years old led into what she assumed was a cold room under the floor. She swung her legs down to feel for the ladder steps. Climbing into the pit of darkness was nerve-racking. She felt for each step carefully before angling down for the next. The ladder creaked and shifted with her weight.

Halfway down, she put her weight on a rung—and it broke. She shrieked as she dropped, her boot slamming into the next rung. The ancient, rotted wood broke in two. She fell feet-first through the darkness, rungs shattering as she hit them, until she slammed into hard-packed dirt. She crumpled, gasping in pain.

"Are you okay?"

Hands grabbed her shoulders, pushing her into a sitting position. Breathing hard, she managed a nod before realizing Lyre probably couldn't see it. With the table above the trapdoor opening, almost no light made it down the shaft.

"Shit," she panted. "How will we get out?"

Light erupted as Lyre flicked on the flashlight she'd dropped. The tiny space had mostly caved in at some point in the distant past. Wet slime covered the ancient stone bricks that made up the far wall. The floor was nothing but gritty dirt piled halfway up the walls, leaving only a dozen square feet of space with a ceiling so low Lyre's head brushed it even in a crouch. The nearer wall was a slanted pile of loose dirt and rubble from the cave-in.

Ash was slumped in the far corner, eyes closed. His chest rose and fell with each fast breath. Moisture glistened on his face and he was frighteningly pale. He didn't react to the sudden bloom of light. Zwi sat in his lap, her eyes shining eerily.

Lyre looked no worse for wear as he aimed the flashlight beam at the broken ladder. "Damn. I can probably get up if I jump for that last rung, assuming it doesn't break too. But …" He glanced at Ash and lowered his voice. "I don't think Ash is up to leaping for ladders."

Piper glanced at him again. The draconian didn't look like he could even stand. Damn the paranoid Gaians for leaving that bloody speaker going. She couldn't even imagine what Ash had endured while she'd been having heart-to-hearts with long-lost parents and chatting up mysterious daemon prisoners.

"Maybe there's a rope or something up there?" she suggested. "We could pull him up."

"Good idea. We don't have much time. I'll look. You stay here and try to keep Ash calm, but don't get too close to him."

"Too close?"

Lyre leaned toward her, harsh shadows from the flashlight making him look dangerous. "You know he doesn't like closed-in spaces. Add that to the pain from that damn ultrasound and the collar blocking his magic—let's just say he's not fit for company right now."

Piper inhaled sharply in understanding. Ash was one breath away from shading in the worst way.

"In fact," he continued, frowning, "maybe you'd better come up with me."

"No time," she told him. "Get a move on!"

He nodded and passed her the flashlight. With a mighty leap, he grabbed the bottom rung of the broken, hanging ladder. Using strength Piper didn't have, he pulled himself up with his arms until he reached the top. Zwi sprang past Piper and ran up the side of the shaft like a big spider to follow Lyre out. It was too bad her larger form was too big to be helpful in the tiny cellar.

Then Piper was sitting alone in the small, dark hole with Ash. Swallowing hard, she faced the prone draconian.

"Ash? Are you awake?"

He grimaced in answer.

"How do you feel?"

His chest rose and fell. Slowly, his eyes opened. Piper sucked in a sharp breath as black irises slid over her. Ash wasn't on the verge of shading. He was already there.

Before his eyes closed again, she recognized the bright sharpness of suppressed panic tightening his gaze. He hated enclosed spaces and this hole in the ground was about the worst scenario possible. Even Piper, who'd never considered herself claustrophobic, felt nervous and twitchy.

She watched Ash's arms, wrapped around his middle, flex as he silently fought to stay in control. She remembered his steady calm in the boiler room when that spider had sent her into a panic. His strength had grounded her, kept her from losing her head completely.

Exhaling slowly, she came up onto her knees.

"Ash? I'm coming over to you, okay?" He didn't react but at least he'd been warned. Surprising a shaded daemon was asking to be attacked.

She crawled the short distance to his side. Watching him carefully, she sat beside him, shifted over until her side was against his, and wiggled her fingers into the crook of his elbow. Feeling her touch, he relaxed his muscles enough that she could slide her arm through his and hold it to her. She laid her head on his shoulder and took a slow, deep breath. What she was doing was incredibly stupid; Ash had shaded. His logic was being ruled by instinct. Combine that with his panic of enclosed spaces and he was as stable as a fault line. One wrong move and he could lash out, wounding or even killing her.

But they needed him calm to get him out. If she could coax him back from the brink, the more likely they'd be able to get the hell out of the building.

"I'll stay with you," she whispered, hugging his arm. "I won't leave you alone."

He didn't say anything but she felt him relax a little. The sounds of the fight upstairs were muffled, almost surreal. She concentrated on keeping her own muscles tension-free, idly rubbing his arm with one hand. Two minutes, then three, then four dragged by. What was taking Lyre so long?

Ash let out a long sigh. His head tipped back to rest on the wall behind him. Piper smiled, hoping she was helping him. She thought about the Stone in her pocket and pictured his blank expression as he'd dropped it into her palm on the Styx's rooftop. Stolen but returned. A betrayal versus … what?

She started violently as the biggest blast yet shook the house. Ash jerked upright as dirt rained on their heads. Piper gripped his arm hard. Shudders ran through the ground beneath them. Jars of food crashed to the floor in the cellar.

As the shockwave passed, there was a moment of utter, deadening silence.

Everything exploded.

She was blasted back against the wall. Pain burst through her body. Her eardrums shattered from the pressure. The sound was beyond comprehension. The world quaked, heaving like ocean waves.

The ceiling above collapsed on them and Piper knew she was dead.

CHAPTER
- 22 -

GRADUALLY, she became aware of Ash's harsh breathing above her. Her ears were ringing. Her body ached. Aside from Ash, the silence was absolute. Nothing. Complete nothing.

She opened her eyes. Impenetrable darkness. She was alive, wasn't she? She remembered the roof coming down, dirt and stone collapsing in on them as their little square of underground space popped like a bubble. The sound had been incredible—and terrifying. The last thing she distinctly recalled was Ash shoving her down in the last instant before certain death.

He was still there, on top of her, shielding her. His face was pressed against the side of her neck, his breath hot against her skin as he panted. The world was still and silent as though the terrible rending of earth and stone had never happened.

She lay for a moment more, feeling spacey and disconnected. She was … alive. That was good. And possibly unhurt, though she ached so badly it was hard to tell. Ash was uncomfortably heavy. He was taking some of his weight but not enough.

It took three swallows to get enough moisture to make a sound. "Ash?" she whispered.

His head shifted a little, pressing his face harder into the side of her neck. He was still breathing too fast.

"Are you hurt?"

He didn't answer. Her foggy brain struggled for focus as she listened to the utter silence. Fear stabbed her.

She flexed her fingers—dirt beneath her nails. She pulled her arms from under Ash and reached out. Her fingers hit walls of rocky dirt on either side. Terror made her heart pound. She flung her hands upward.

Her fingers hit dirt with painful force. She pressed her palms against the solid earth, not even able to extend her arms.

No. God no.

She twisted, reaching over her head. There was loose dirt piled against a tumble of rocks inches above her head. She'd come a hand's width from having her head crushed by falling stone. She almost wished she had.

Ash panted. A tremor ran through him, his arms quivering on either side of her. He already knew.

They were buried alive.

They were buried in a tiny, coffin-sized bubble, surrounded on all sides by collapsed earth. The entire house could have caved in. The magnitude of the detonation was beyond magic; it must have been the explosives her mom had warned her about. Had Mona or another Gaian set off the blast or had the magic triggered it?

Did it matter? Panic pounded through her.

"Ash!" She pressed her hands into the dirt ceiling, gasping as much as him. How much air was in their tiny hole? How long did they have? "Ash, can you get us out? Ash?" His name came out on a sob.

A low growl, rising from deep in his chest, made her freeze. With escalating terror, she brought a hand down to touch his upper arm.

Her fingers didn't meet skin. Instead, they found a cool, leathery texture. With shaking fingers, she traced one of the armor-like scales that plated his arms. She remembered vividly the sight of his arm, those wide black scales and long claws, from her one glimpse of him without glamour. Those claws were now hooked in the bottom hem of her shirt.

Ash had abandoned his glamour—and she knew why. He was frightened of enclosed, underground spaces. They were trapped in his absolute worst nightmare. He had shaded. Fully, uncontrollably shaded. He could crush her with his impossible strength or rip out her throat before he could stop himself if she made a wrong move. But considering her current chances of survival, it didn't make much difference. It might hurt more though.

"Ash," she whispered. Wet tears trickled down the sides of her face into her hair. "Ash, please."

Another tremor shook him. He suddenly pushed up. His back hit the top of the earth coffin with a thud. Dirt peppered her face. Rough sounds on either side confused her until she remembered his wings. They were scraping the sides of the hole. A sound between a snarl and a whimper escaped him.

"Ash," she gasped. Not stopping to think, she hooked her hands around the back of his neck. She yanked him down, pulling his face to her chest. He slumped, shaking and gasping for air. She combed her fingers into his hair, tracing the braid on the side of his head as she fought to control her terror. If she couldn't, there was no way Ash could.

"Shh," she whispered. "Close your eyes and concentrate on breathing." She inhaled and exhaled shakily, demonstrating. "Calm. Please, Ash."

In the back of her mind, part of her tallied the precious oxygen they were consuming with each panicked breath.

She slid her fingers through his hair and discovered he had horns of some kind. Desperate for something to focus on, she traced their shape. Three curved spines on each side, halfway back on his head. She wondered if they would look striking or frightening. She wanted to touch his wings but doubted he would tolerate it. So she kept stroking his hair as he fought for a semblance of calm. He wasn't having much success.

"Ash, you can do it," she encouraged softly, trying not to sound petrified. "Imagine you're somewhere else."

A violent quiver shook him. "I can't," he whispered. She shuddered as his voice slid over her, alien and sensual even roughened with panic. "I can feel it."

"Feel what?" she asked, hoping him talking was a good sign. Shaded daemons tended not to do humany things like engage in conversation.

"No space," he rasped. "No open space. I can sense open spaces for flying in the dark. I can't sense anything around us. *Nothing—*"

"Shh," she whispered quickly, cutting him off as his shaking increased. She wrapped her arms around his head and neck, holding him tight to her, not knowing what else to do. Hysterical laughter tickled her throat, trying to escape. She was hugging a panicking, fully shaded, un-glamoured daemon. On purpose. His teeth were inches from her jugular, his claws one flex away from internal organs. But what did it matter? They didn't have long left anyway. The oxygen dwindled with each minute.

Even if they could dig through the dirt and stone, which she doubted, there was nowhere to go if Ash's senses were to be trusted. No spaces near them. No way to dig straight up.

"So there's no hope then?" she finally asked, barely able to force the words out.

He concentrated on breathing before answering. "There's at least fifteen feet of solidity above us, then some tiny gaps. Part of the house collapsed above us. I can sense another small space, some sort of tunnel, eight feet to the south, about our level." A long pause. "There's no way to reach it. It's solid earth between here and there."

She fought not to cry. What a stupid way to die for both of them. She hoped Lyre hadn't been caught in the explosion. Maybe he and Zwi were safe. At least she got Uncle Calder out first.

Tears pooled in her eyes. It wasn't fair. After everything she'd struggled for, she would die without achieving anything. She'd never get to clear her name. No one would ever find them. The Sahar was buried with them, lost to the world.

The Sahar.

Piper grabbed Ash, digging her fingers into his shoulders. "Ash, the Sahar! Could you use the Sahar to blast our way out?"

He shook his head, killing her hope before it had barely budded. "I can't use the Sahar ... I already tried. It's not attuned to me. And I can't do anything with this damn collar on."

"But ... you destroyed the prefects' magic-depressor."

"It requires a huge amount of concentration ... I don't think I could ..."

She understood. He couldn't do it because he couldn't calm down. Even their short conversation wasn't helping him; she doubted his thoughts were as coherent as his speech. His muscles quivered, his breath came in desperate pants, and his voice shook. He would probably rather die by torture than this fate.

She choked back a sob. That was it then. The air was starting to feel wrong in her lungs, thin and hot. Time was almost up.

"If I thought it could save us," Ash whispered, "I would try. But I can't blast a way to the surface without the whole house falling in on us."

She nodded, touching the back of his neck to let him know she didn't blame him. She tried to slow her breathing but it was difficult to face death calmly. No other option but to accept the inevitable ...

"What about the tunnel on our level?" she asked abruptly. "Could you blast an opening to it with magic?"

"Everything would cave in, and the force would probably kill you."

Her hands trembled. She balled them up. "What about a series of small blasts? What if you punched a bunch of little holes and tunneled over to the opening?"

He sucked in a breath. "It still might cave in."

"We're dead anyway."

He pressed his face against her throat. His fear was so bad he would rather die where he was than chance being even more buried.

"Ash ... please. Let's try."

He nodded silently. He shifted his arms until he was propped on his elbows, both hands gripping the collar around his neck. The air began to heat. He muttered under his breath, using words to control and funnel his magic toward the collar.

He broke off mid-word, breathing fast. "I can't get it out of my head. I can't think," he choked.

"You can do it." She reached up and found his face. She stroked her fingertips across his cheeks, finding a pattern of scales across the tops of his cheekbones. "You're stronger than anyone I know. You're tougher than everyone. I know you can do this."

She gripped his face in her hands, offering strength and steady calm through the surety of her touch. He stilled. After a moment, he started again, whispering the spell in words she couldn't understand. The air heated, sizzled. His muscles bunched with effort, his body tensing.

The collar broke apart with a hiss of dying magic and disintegrating steel.

"You did it." She threw her arms around him, hugging him tight. "I knew you could!"

He sagged on top of her, breathing hard, this time from exertion. He slid his arms around her and his wings curled down too, doubling the hug.

"That made me dizzy," he said weakly. "I hate those damn collars."

Piper let herself go limp, head lolling with relief and hope. Fear pounded beneath both. "I feel dizzy too."

Ash stiffened. "We need to hurry."

Their oxygen was almost gone.

"What first?" she demanded.

He nudged her as far over as possible in the tight space. She pressed into the rough dirt and he curled over her, shielding her with his body. She bit her lip, moved by his courage in the face of his worst fears. In spite of his own terror, he was still protecting her. A tear slipped down her cheek. He'd protected her life at every turn and she'd been determined to hate him for the one selfish thing he'd done? No wonder Lyre had been angrier with her than with Ash.

With a deep breath, Ash stretched one hand toward the south wall of their hole. A shiver ran through him.

"This is it," he whispered.

She found his other hand and squeezed it hard. Her heart pounded in her throat.

The air crackled. The blast hit the wall.

Dirt rushed over them in a wave. Ash hooked an arm under her and scooped her up as he half rose, pulling her out of the loose earth. She choked back a scream as she realized their hole hadn't caved in — entirely. It was a lot smaller now.

Ash took a couple deep breaths. "If we push the loose dirt into the back corner, I can try again."

"Right," she agreed, grateful to disentangle herself. Her head spun. It was getting harder to breathe.

Together, with a lot of awkward collisions, they shoveled the loose dirt out of the way until they had a three-foot-deep burrow leading out of their hole. Escape was only five feet away.

Ash blasted the wall a second time, strictly controlling the power. Again, the loosened earth tumbled down. They had farther to shovel and it took longer. Piper couldn't catch her breath. Her lungs hurt and her head spun. There was no air.

The tunnel was smaller this time. Ash had to lie flat, with Piper crouched behind him, as he stretched his hand toward the end. Neither of them wasted air speaking. The atmosphere crackled as he prepared for the last blast. If this one didn't break through, they wouldn't have enough air to try again.

The air rippled with the concussion. Dirt flew.

A breeze touched her face. Piper gasped it in and crawled desperately after Ash. The air grew cooler and fresher with each desperate breath. The exit to their rough tunnel was tiny, barely large enough for Ash to squeeze through. She shoved forward and the dirt under her hands dropped away. She fell out and landed on top of him. He grunted as her elbow dug into his stomach.

The stale, damp air of the tunnel never tasted sweeter. She breathed like she'd been drowning all her life. Ash lay on his back, chest heaving as he sucked in air. She flopped on him, resting her ear on his chest, and listened to his heart pounding.

"I …" she panted, "am *never* … going … in a cellar … *again*."

He grunted in agreement.

She huffed a laugh of pure relief, glad she wasn't bawling. She really felt like bawling. Instead, she lifted her head and squinted in the general direction of his face. The darkness was absolute.

"Can we go now?"

"Hell yes. I thought you'd never ask."

She rolled her eyes and warily clambered to her feet, one hand stretched upward in expectation of a ceiling. She found it a foot above her head. "What is this place?"

"Probably an old escape tunnel from the Consulate's original construction," he answered. "Old houses like these often had a few tunnels and escape exits."

She glanced blindly in his direction, surprised to hear his usual voice. Sounded like he was back in control and in glamour. "Which way is out?"

"This way," he said without hesitation. Before she could ask, his hand touched hers. She curled her fingers trustingly around his and let him guide her. He walked with unerring confidence, able to sense their path.

The tunnel went on for at least a hundred yards. Time had no meaning in the blackness. She concentrated on each step, trying not to trip on the slimy, uneven stone floor. Ash was a patient guide, even though she knew he was dying to get out into the open air.

She knew they were close when a breeze touched her face. Ash led her to another trapdoor, set in the ceiling above their heads. Piper stared greedily at the dim shape as Ash shoved the door up and hauled himself out before reaching back in to pull her up.

The trapdoor opened into a dirty, cluttered tool shed. Before she could make out any identifiable outlines in the darkness, Ash broke the locked door and rushed out into the night. She dove out after him, surprised to step out into steady rain. Cold water peppered her face, the most refreshing thing she'd ever felt. Trees surrounded them; the tunnel had brought them some distance from the house.

Ash dropped onto the wet grass, sat for a second, then flopped onto his back. He closed his eyes, letting the rain wash his face clean. Piper looked at herself, unsurprised to discover she was covered in dirt that was fast turning to mud. Beyond caring, she slumped beside Ash. He was still shockingly pale.

"You were amazing," she told him. "You saved my life. Again."

"You saved mine," he murmured. "The only way I would've gotten that collar off without you was if I had broken my own jaw trying to tear if off." He was quiet for a second. "I was nearly out of my mind enough to try."

"At least you didn't scream," she offered. "I screamed with the spider."

His mouth quirked in a tired smile.

She sighed and leaned back. "If the asshole Gaians hadn't put that stupid collar on you in the first place, we could've been out of there in no time."

He gave her a strange look, his irises still dangerously dark. "Piper, that collar saved your life."

She blinked. "Huh?"

He sat up and rubbed both hands over his face and into his hair. "Piper … when the cellar first came down, I was so crazy with fear that I would've blown up half the house myself to keep from being buried. I wouldn't have realized my mistake until I calmed down enough to recognize whatever pieces of you were left. If I hadn't had the collar on."

She stared at him. "But you protected me. I remember."

He hesitated. "Even as I was pushing you down, I was already grabbing for every bit of magic I had. I would've killed you by accident. I wasn't thinking straight."

"That's not what happened," she said firmly. "Let's not play the 'what if' game. I want to find Lyre and get the hell out of here."

Ash looked away but not before fear lanced his expression. She knew what he was thinking: chances were Lyre hadn't been as lucky as them when that explosion went off. Gritting her teeth, she got to her feet and stepped up to him. He blinked at her, his expression puzzled.

She forgot what she'd been planning to say. That boyishly questioning expression on his face was just like the badass draconian in her kitchen with a pink can of cream soda in his hand. It was so absurdly out of place that it was charming. She had to clench her hands to keep from dropping into his lap and kissing him until all her shaky, lingering fear was burned away.

She gave herself a mental slap. Get a grip. It was the survivor's high. She'd already vowed never to kiss him again. Ever.

"We will find Lyre and leave," she told him fiercely. "That is exactly what's going to happen, got it?"

He blinked again. His lips curved. "Yes, ma'am."

"Are you laughing at me?" she demanded.

"No, ma'am."

She narrowed her eyes to slits. His mouth twitched as he worked for a neutral expression. She wondered if she could make him laugh. She'd never heard him laugh.

Oh God. What was she thinking? It was survivor's syndrome. And possibly a bit of Damsel-in-Distress syndrome. So he'd saved her— again. That was no reason to start swooning. He'd just admitted to having almost killed her.

"Let's go," she said abruptly.

He finally got up and they started into the trees. The rain was lightening a little, but the sound of it on the leafy canopy above was loud enough to drown out all other noise until they got close enough to the Consulate to see orange light flickering through the dark tree trunks. This light wasn't from any electric bulb. They stopped at the edge of the trees, the front lawn of the Consulate stretching before them, and stared.

CHAPTER

-23-

HALF THE CONSULATE was a pile of broken, twisted rubble. The other half was on fire. Prefect cruisers and vans formed a barrier at the far edge of the lawn, their flashing lights adding to the chaos. Guns fired randomly from both sides. Flashes and booms from magic attacks burst into being and died just as fast as over fifty prefects, haemons, and daemons battled on the burning Consulate's front lawn.

Piper pressed both hands to her mouth. Ash shifted closer, his shoulder brushing hers. She could feel his tension. The sight before them was horrifying. Unmoving bodies were scattered across the lawn like discarded toys. The prefects hunkered behind their vehicles, firing indiscriminately with mundane and magical ammo. The daemon group was tucked into the rubble of the collapsed side of the Consulate, launching their own attacks as they sheltered amidst the bones of the house.

The haemons, she wasn't surprised to see, were caught in the middle, trapped in the lethal crossfire. Her heart pounded in her throat as she scanned the rain-obscured profiles for a familiar one. Had her mother escaped?

"We'll never find Lyre in this," she whispered. Her throat closed as she realized they would have to leave him. She wouldn't allow herself to consider the chances of him being alive to find. What if he was hurt? What if he needed them?

Ash glanced at her. "That's not what you said would happen."

She swallowed, not in the mood to be teased. "That was before—"

Fingers tickled her sides and ran down her hips. Lips brushed her ear.

"Hello gorgeous."

Piper spun around and met exhausted but still mischievous gold eyes.

"Lyre!" She threw her arms around him and crushed him in the tightest hug she could manage.

"Owww," he complained even as he wrapped his arms around her and squeezed back. He disentangled and stepped back to examine her. "You don't look too worse for wear, considering you were buried under half a house."

"We got out okay," she told him, examining him at the same time. His shirt was burned and his face bloodied, but he had no serious injuries. "How did you make it out?"

"I had to book it across the house to get away from some daemons, so I was at the other end when the bomb went off." A long pause, then he said in a whisper, "I thought you were both dead."

He flicked a glance at Ash then pulled Piper closer. She thought he wanted another hug—until his hand cupped her cheek. Then his lips were against hers, brief but urgent. The kiss was over almost as soon as it had begun, leaving her reeling as Lyre turned to Ash and gave him a friendly slap on the back.

"Glad to see you alive, man," he congratulated Ash. "I never would've found you if not for Zwi. She led me straight to you."

Piper quit staring at the spot where Lyre had been standing—and kissing her! Why did he keep choosing the worst times ever to kiss her?—and turned to Ash, surprised to see Zwi perched on his shoulder, frantically nuzzling his cheek.

"Did you know Zwi can turn big?" she blurted.

Ash didn't quite look at her as he nodded. He said nothing.

Lyre cleared his throat and flashed her a half-smile. "By the way, Piper. I like the mud-wrestling look. I think it would work better without clothes though."

"Lyre—" she began warningly.

"Quiet," Ash hissed. "Something is wrong."

"What?"

Ash stepped back to the edge of the trees. Piper faced the battlefield again. It was quiet. Still. No one was moving, daemons, haemons, and prefects alike crouched in readiness, watching, waiting.

"No," Ash whispered. "No fucking way."

Piper sank slowly into a crouch, caught in the spell of silence even as she wanted to demand answers. Everyone out on the lawn was staring toward the corner of the lawn farthest from Piper, Ash, and Lyre. What were they all looking at, waiting for?

The answer came too soon.

In unreal silence, a prefect cruiser flew into the air like a toy thrown by an angry child. It dropped into the middle of the lawn with a terrible metallic crash, skidded comically on its nose in the mud, then toppled over onto its roof. A second car followed, lights still flashing, before landing on its side and rolling into the ruins of the house.

Piper hardly noticed the trajectory of the second car. Her attention was locked on the sight revealed by the removal of the two vehicles. With its path now cleared, the most horrifying beast she'd ever seen lurched into the open.

Its body was the same size as the cars it had been hurling, but it seemed twice as large with all the tentacles. It looked like a massive, scaled, warty octopus with dull red skin patterned in random, ugly whorls. Those huge tentacles rippled bonelessly as the monster half crawled, half dragged itself onto the lawn. There it paused, apparently surveying the scene even though it had no discernible eyes.

No one moved. They all seemed too terrified to even breathe.

The beast's front tentacles whipped out with terrifying speed. It snatched two prefects around the middle, yanking them effortlessly into the air. The beast reared back, revealing a huge, fang-lined hole underneath its bulbous head. Before anyone could react, before its victims could do more than scream, the monster shoved the two humans into that wet hole. It tilted forward as it pulled the tentacles out of its mouth—without any people in their grasp.

Piper gagged. That monster had just *eaten* two prefects.

All at once the people on the lawn realized that holding perfectly still wouldn't save them. Pandemonium erupted. Guns went off, all aimed at the creature. Magic blasted, fireballs slamming into it. Half the fighters up and ran for it, bolting in every direction.

The beast bellowed, pulling all its tentacles in close. Its body deflated like a puffer fish, shrinking to a third its previous size. When the attacks continued, the beast reared, swelling back to its full size as it flung its tentacles in every direction. It bellowed again and flowed toward the nearest group of prefects.

Hearing its bellow chilled Piper's blood as déjà vu swept through her. She knew that sound. She remembered another sight of a red tentacle—wrapped around Ash's neck and dragging him back into the secret passageway at her house the night the Gaians had tried to steal the Sahar.

"The choronzon?" she choked. "*That's* the choronzon?" If she hadn't just seen it contract its body, she never would have believed it could fit inside the Consulate.

Ash nodded grimly, his face pale as he watched the monster slaughter a path through the prefects, heading toward the center of the lawn. Her mother had told her the Gaians had borrowed the choronzon from some allies. Piper had never imagined the idiots would still have the monster at their hideout.

She cast Ash a disbelieving look. "You *fought* that thing? *How?*"

Ash stared at the beast, jaw clenched tight, and didn't answer.

"It was being controlled," Lyre explained tersely. "Like a magic-dampening collar, only the choronzon was dampened *and* under someone's power. They were dictating its movements like a puppet. That made it weak and slow."

Just like Mona had said. Piper licked her lips. "It's not being controlled any more, is it?"

"No."

The monster bellowed again as it wrapped three tentacles around a car and rolled it out of the way. The four prefects crouched behind the vehicle ran for their lives. All the attacks on the monster were making it angrier. Through the haze of rain, Piper couldn't see if they were even injuring the choronzon. It plowed through the remaining prefects. Most of the haemons and daemons had already fled. The choronzon wasn't eating people anymore—it must have been full—but it kept on killing.

Choronzons came from the Underworld but they weren't daemons. What they were, really, was a kind of animal—terrible, murderous animals. They weren't daemons any more than a tiger was a human because it also lived on Earth.

"Well," Lyre said shakily, "I think it's become clear that we won't be searching for any evidence today. We should go."

Piper nodded numbly. She hoped Miysis had taken her uncle to safety. She'd have to figure out how to rescue him later.

The breeze kicked up, blowing icy rain into her back. She shivered, wrapping her arms around herself. She wished so badly she could go home. Instead, they would have to walk for hours to get back to their car, assuming the prefects hadn't towed it, and then drive for hours to confuse their trail before finding some new hole to hide in. She wanted to cry at the thought.

Rain whipped sideways as the wind gusted. Ash stiffened, looking over his shoulder. Across the lawn, the choronzon stopped in mid-attack. Its tentacles undulated like a person tapping their fingers in thought.

"That wasn't a natural wind," Ash whispered tersely. He turned into the fitful gusts, eyes narrowed to dark slits.

Piper watched the choronzon rear up, front tentacles waving as it opened its gaping maw as though tasting the air. A long-forgotten trivia fact about choronzons popped into her head. Her heart skipped in her chest. Choronzons hunted by scent and their strongest trigger was—

She whirled and grabbed Ash's arm, not daring to take her attention off the choronzon. The traitorous wind gusted again, blowing her wet hair into her face as it carried their scent straight to the choronzon.

"Ash," she gasped. "Ash, are you bleeding? Please tell me you're not bleeding!"

He stared at her in bewilderment then pulled up his shirt. A shallow, vertical scratch scored his abs below his ribcage.

"A rock when we were digging out of the hole ... Piper, what—"

"Get up," she yelled, yanking on his arm. He shot to his feet without question, surprising her until she realized he was staring beyond her, his face white. She glanced over her shoulder and saw exactly what she'd feared.

The choronzon was on the move, surging across the ground— straight toward them.

◦ ◦ ◦

They ran.

Piper could only make out the dark shadows of trees as they whipped past. She clung to Ash's hand, totally dependent on his guidance in the dark forest. Lyre pounded after them, audible every time his feet splashed through a puddle on the rain-soaked ground.

"What the hell is going on?" he panted furiously.

"Choronzons are blood hunters," Piper yelled. "Once they taste someone's blood, they'll hunt that person relentlessly until they kill him."

"So what?" he demanded.

"That choronzon got a taste of Ash back at my Consulate." Terror squeezed her. "And it's caught his scent. It's coming after him."

Lyre swore passionately. "What should we—"

"We run," Ash growled. "It's not that fast, not in these trees. We run and try to lose it. If we can't, then you two will run one way and I'll go the other way. Once it's off your trail, I'll escape where it can't follow."

For a second, Piper had no idea what he meant—then she realized. Without glamour, he had wings. He would fly. The choronzon couldn't catch him in the skies. Her fear dropped a notch. They would be okay. They could handle this.

They burst out of the trees into a small clearing. A stitch burned in her lungs but she ignored it. They had a lot more running to do before they escaped the—

Ash jerked backward and fell. She tripped over him before she could stop, crashing to the ground. Lyre skidded to a stop and turned back.

"Ash!" She crawled over as he groaned. Her stomach swooped sickeningly when she saw the arrow sticking out of his shoulder.

"What the hell?" Lyre gasped, kneeling on Ash's shoulder. "Where did that—"

"Get it out," Ash rasped. "Now!"

Lyre grabbed the shaft and ripped the arrow out, not taking the time to be careful. Ash arched with pain then slumped. He rolled onto his stomach and pushed up on his hands and knees.

"Ah, shit," he panted. He pressed one hand to his face. "Shiiiit."

"Ash?" Piper whispered.

He slowly shook his head, simultaneously listing to one side. Lyre grabbed him, steadying him. Ash sank back down.

"Shit," he said again. "Arrow was poisoned."

"Poisoned?"

"Poisoned," repeated another voice, rough like a chain smoker and high with glee. "And he never even saw it coming."

Piper looked up sharply. A woman stood a dozen feet away, a bow in her hands, arrow nocked and pointed at them. She was short and muscular with untamed hair and some sort of feathery cape falling down her back.

A flash of shadow above. Another woman dropped from the sky. As she landed, she folded huge, feathered bird wings against her back. Three more of the female daemons spiraled out of the sky and landed, all of them armed with bows. A total of twelve formed a half-circle of bristling arrows, all pointed their way.

Swallowing hard, Piper recognized them as harpies: Underworld daemons known for their mercenary habits and unfaltering loyalty to whoever paid them the most money.

Lyre made a sound of disgust. "Who sent you vultures to clean up? The same idiot who let that choronzon slip its leash?"

"*We* let the choronzon off its leash, dog," the first harpy said haughtily. "On purpose. What better way to flush out dear little Ash? Loose the choronzon and create a little wind to blow his scent around. We knew he was skulking around here somewhere, trying to salvage something from the mess he'd made." She sneered at Ash. "Not that anything you do now could save you."

Piper clutched Ash's shoulder as he pushed himself up. He swayed sideways until she propped him up.

"So ..." he slurred. "You're the ones who backed up the Gaians that night ... wouldn't've thought they'd have the cash to buy the likes of you."

"Oh, they weren't paying us. Our current employer merely loaned out the choronzon and us. As a favor, you know. We almost got you with our pet too."

"Who?" Ash demanded. "Who's paying you?"

The harpy smiled sweetly. "Why, the same one who's paying you, Ash."

Piper nearly choked. Ash was being paid to steal the Sahar? He was doing this all *for money*? Lyre had implied Ash was trying to save his own life!

"Not that anyone would pay you for this utter failure," the harpy went on with vicious delight. "Samael has decided he has no more use for his whipping dog. Didn't you realize he wanted you out of the picture after he sent Cottus to kill you?" She sighed dramatically. "But you just wouldn't die."

Piper struggled to breathe. Samael. Samael was the head of the Hades family, the family that originally stole the Sahar five hundred years ago and only reluctantly agreed to turn it over to the Ra family for it to be sealed away. It was exactly like a daemon warlord to agree to give up the Sahar while secretly hiring someone to steal it back.

And, apparently, Samael had hired Ash to do it.

No wonder Lyre said Ash would die because he didn't have the Sahar. To fail to fulfill a job for Samael was to sign your own death warrant.

"I'm hard to kill," Ash told the harpy, his voice still slurred. "What in the name of Acheron makes you think you can accomplish what Cottus couldn't?"

"You're already poisoned," the harpy taunted. "You—"

Ash flung a hand up. The air cracked like a snap of thunder. As one, the harpies were blasted off their feet. Half their bows splintered into pieces. Ash tried to straighten and almost flattened Lyre.

"Damn," he grunted. "Everything is spinning." He took a deep breath. "Help me up. The choronzon is getting close."

Piper and Lyre grabbed his arms and pulled him up. He leaned heavily into Lyre, throwing out one arm as though he were standing on a ship deck in high seas. Piper grabbed it, trying to steady him.

"You shouldn't be able to stand," the harpy leader shrieked, pushing herself to her feet. "How are you standing?"

Piper glanced sharply at Ash and remembered what he'd told her after the spider bit him back at the apartment. He was immune to most venoms and poisons. His body was already fighting it off. Relief swept through her.

The harpy spread her wings wide. Her shattered bow hung from one hand. "Fine. Die your way. It will be worse for you in the end."

The other harpies rose. All of them were grinning. Ash growled and lifted a hand, preparing to blast them again.

With the sound of shattering wood, the choronzon burst into the clearing behind them.

The harpies and the monster charged at the same time. Ash unleashed a blast of magic but lurched off balance. The magic only caught half the harpies, knocking them backward with impossible force. The other six screamed like angry birds.

Piper punched the first one to reach her, her fist breaking the woman's nose and throwing her head back. Her second punch hit the woman's exposed windpipe. The harpy staggered back, unable to breathe. Before Piper could find her next target, hands grabbed her. Claws dug into her flesh. She was wrenched upward.

She swung a foot up and kicked hard in a distinctly soft spot. A shriek of pain. The hands released her. She dropped, landing painfully on her knees.

272 | ANNETTE MARIE

In those few seconds of battle, the choronzon reached them.

Tentacles were suddenly everywhere. Harpies shrieked. Piper scrambled backward, pulling a knife from her boot. A tentacle whipped toward her. She raised her knife.

Someone grabbed her and yanked her backward. She thought it was Ash or Lyre—until she was yanked into the sky again. Another harpy slammed into them in the air, ripping her knife from her hand. A third harpy grabbed her other arm as they beat their wings, lifting her higher. She screamed and kicked furiously. They laughed, easily avoiding her flailing feet. As they shifted, she was awarded a glimpse of the ground, already thirty feet below.

The choronzon was a writhing mass of tentacles. There were four harpies sprawled unmoving in the grass and a fifth hung limply in the coils of a tentacle. The monster reared, its fanged mouth gaping as it bellowed its bloodlust.

On his knees before the beast was Ash. Even as she watched, he tried to rise and staggered, struggling with the debilitating effects of the poison. The choronzon lunged forward, tentacles lashing toward its long-desired prey.

Harpy wings appeared in front of her, blocking her vision.

From far below, a male voice cried out in agony.

Piper screamed a matching cry of denial. Harpies laughed as they swept her away into the dark sky, allowing her only one last glimpse of the choronzon through the rain as it reared high and bellowed its triumph to the uncaring night.

CHAPTER

- 24 -

"LET ME GO!" Piper yelled.

She didn't struggle against the harpy's grip. Judging by the distant flames of the burning Consulate, she was very, *very* high up. The other six harpies rose in slow spirals with lazy flaps of their bird-like wings. The fires of the ruined house were her only landmark. Everything else was darkness and icy rain.

"Where are you taking me?" Fear pounded through her. She couldn't see the choronzon anymore. She didn't know if Ash and Lyre were alive.

"Not far," the harpy holding her cackled. "Only a little higher, my dear."

Her blood chilled. "Higher *where*?"

"This should be fine." The harpy leveled out, beating her wings to hover gracelessly. With a sharp laugh, she let Piper go.

She screamed as she dropped. The harpy grabbed her arm again. Claws tore into her skin, bringing her up short. She screamed again as pain lanced her arm and shoulder. Another harpy grabbed her other arm and the two daemons stretched her between them, hanging her by her wrists over empty darkness.

The harpy leader maneuvered to hover in front of Piper. "Now, girl, I don't think I need to explain what will happen if you don't tell us what we want to know." She pointed downward and leered hideously. Harpy stereotypes were not exaggerated. The woman was *ugly.*

"Tell me," the daemon commanded, *"where is the Sahar Stone?"*

"I don't know!"

"You do know," the harpy snarled. *"You* had the fake Stone that fool Micah stole. You have the real one too, I know it."

"I don't have it!"

The leader slashed a look at the two harpies holding Piper. They let her slide a few inches in their grip. She swallowed a scream, squeezing her eyes shut against the terrifying darkness below her.

"I don't know," she cried. "I don't have it."

"Yes, you do! Tell me or we drop you to your death and search your shattered body instead."

"I don't have it!" Tears mixed with the rain. "Please. I don't have it."

The harpy made a sound of disgust. "If you don't have it, *who does*? Don't pretend you didn't take it."

"Ash," she gasped. "He stole it from me. He has it." Maybe they would take her back down and call off the choronzon before it was too late.

"He doesn't have it," the harpy sneered. "If he did, he would already be kneeling before Samael with the Stone and begging for leniency."

"He does! He stole it from me!"

"Liar," the harpy screeched. "You have it!"

"No, I don't!" Piper screamed. She wanted to cry from the lethal irony. The harpy was wrong about everything—*except* that Piper had the Sahar. "Ash has it," she tried again, her voice high with desperation. "Samael hired him, didn't he? Ash is keeping the Sahar for Samael."

"Hired him?" the harpy repeated with a cruel chuckle. "Perhaps I gave you the wrong impression. Samael doesn't *pay* little Ash. He,

how would you say it? Samael hurts Ash less if he stays obedient." The harpies all laughed.

"W-what?"

"Didn't he tell you?" the harpy taunted. "The noble Ashtaroth is nothing but Samael's whipping dog, his right-hand hitman. When Samael snaps his fingers, little Ash jumps to obey. Did you think he was helping you out of the goodness of his heart? He does nothing Samael doesn't command."

The harpies cackled, delighted by Piper's transparent horror.

"Now." The harpy hovered closer, getting in Piper's face. "Ash would only be following you around if you have the Stone or know where it is. One of the two. Tell me now or you die right here."

"I don't know!"

The harpy scowled. "Fine. I can see you are useless." She back-winged out of the way.

"No!" Piper screamed. "Don't drop me! Please don't!"

"We will," the harpy said, "unless you offer some real answers. No?" She gestured sharply to another hovering daemon. "Check her over. Tear off all her clothes if you have to but make sure beyond a doubt she isn't hiding the Stone on her." She smiled maliciously at Piper. "And if you are, my dear, we won't drop you. That would be painless compared to the death we'll give you if you've been lying."

The second harpy swooped in. She grabbed Piper's shirt, tearing open the front.

"Stop it!" she cried pointlessly. The Sahar in her pocket felt as cold and heavy as the touch of death itself. It would be moments, seconds, before they found it. She couldn't hide it, couldn't run away, couldn't even struggle without getting dropped. Terrified tears coursed down her cheeks as the harpy raked her claws over Piper's chest, checking for anything hidden. Micah, the mercenary bastard, had obviously revealed where he'd found the fake Stone.

"Hurry up," the harpy leader barked.

The other one growled. She grabbed at Piper's hip, tearing open the empty pocket on the right. She ripped the back pocket, tearing the side seam wide open. As she turned to the pockets on the left, Piper made a split second decision born purely out of spite.

If she was going to die, then she damn well wouldn't make it easy for them.

As the harpy's claws hooked her left pocket, Piper wrenched her left arm, tearing it out of the harpy's claws. She swung down, her doubled weight jerking the other harpy off balance. As they dropped, Piper jammed her hand into her pocket and closed her fist tightly around the Sahar.

The harpy leader screamed in triumph, diving at Piper. Knowing what was coming, knowing she would die, Piper pulled her arm out and cocked it back. She locked stares with the harpy leader in the instant before they collided. Time slowed as the final moment of her life stretched out, denying its imminent end.

Fist clenched around the Sahar, glare locked on her enemy's face, Piper summoned every last bit of strength she had, every searing flame of fury, every desperate, choking dredge of panic, and channeled it all into her fist as she let it fly right into the harpy bitch's face.

Her knuckles never touched the harpy.

Piper's thoughts splintered, doubled, twisted with alien power. The Sahar burned white-hot against her palm. White light burst from between her clenched fingers. Thunder split the air. The world rent all around her.

The harpy's skull burst apart like a shattered melon, spraying gore in every direction. The concussion blasted outward from Piper, a perfect half circle that expanded faster than sound. Harpy bodies exploded. Bloody feathers flew in every direction. Torn limbs and broken bodies arched through the air with eerie grace, caught on the pressure wave before they tumbled toward the distant, night-cloaked forest below.

The hand gripping Piper's other arm was torn away.

She plummeted. Something slammed into her. Claws sank into her arm. Suddenly she was dangling by the hand that still clutched the Sahar as one last harpy tore frantically at her fist. A cry of agony burst from her as talons ripped through her flesh. She clenched her fist as hard as she could, unable to reach the harpy holding her, unable to fight back. The air crackled as the harpy summoned magic.

Power tore into Piper's arm as the harpy's spell hit her. Excruciating, consuming agony slammed through her. Blackness swept over her vision. Her sight popped in on another wave of torture. She didn't realize she was falling until the dark silhouette of the harpy swooped away above her, clutching the Stone she'd blasted out of Piper's hand.

She dropped through black, empty space. The wind tore at her, howling in her ears. Her arm had gone numb. Her mind was numb. She was dead and her brain hadn't caught up with the fact. It would be over in a second or two.

Black oblivion sucked at her. She gave in to it, embracing the darkness as the invisible ground rushed up to claim her.

             c   c   c

Consciousness returned sluggishly. Pain came more swiftly. She groaned, then choked on a sob. God, her arm was a blazing inferno of agony. She could never have imagined so much pain. It was so terrible she didn't immediately realize she was being dragged.

Something above her grunted. She was gently set down. Whatever had a grip on the back of her shirt let go. She slumped in the mud, unable to find the strength to move. Whoever or whatever had been dragging her could do as they pleased. She didn't care.

She wondered briefly why she wasn't dead.

It wasn't right. If Ash and Lyre had died, she should die too. It was only fair. They were in this together. She felt a foggy, disjointed flash of regret that she'd never get to ask Ash all the questions burning in the back of her head. She wished she'd given him the Sahar. Then maybe he could have survived the choronzon. Or at the least, the harpy wouldn't have gotten it. Samael wouldn't have won.

Something snuffled her back, followed by a strange, low-pitched sound like a stuttering truck engine. Something warm nudged the side of her face. An animal whined.

Piper couldn't stand not knowing what was standing over her. Clenching her teeth, she rolled onto her back. Pain rocketed down her arm. Her vision went white with the intensity, blinding her. Then she realized it wasn't her vision. She was staring at a wall of white.

No … not a wall. Wings. White wings. Two gold spots appeared in front of her face—golden eyes with a stripe of black mane between them. The thing made another stuttering, chattering sound.

Piper blinked repeatedly. "Zwi?" she whispered.

The horse-sized dragon made a bass-deep trill that sounded disturbingly wrong. Zwi spread her enormous wings and flapped them once, then poked her muzzle gently into Piper's belly.

"You caught me?" she asked hoarsely.

Zwi bobbed her head. She trilled again and nudged at Piper. The message was clear: get up.

Piper shuddered. She couldn't. She had to. She had to know for sure. If Zwi was off rescuing Piper, chances were the dragonet no longer had a master to protect. She had to know for sure. With a deep breath, she carefully sat up. A cry escaped her as she pulled her wounded arm to her chest. She pointedly did not look at the damage. Holding it tightly in place, she awkwardly pushed to her feet with a few helpful nudges from Zwi. Her whole body hurt but mostly her arm. She couldn't feel her hand at all.

Zwi gave her a light push in the right direction then turned all her scales to black, practically disappearing. A hint of predawn glow had lightened the pitch-black night enough for Piper to make out the trail. She stumbled forward, numb inside. Dread slowly kindled in her gut. Tears trickled sporadically down her face.

She smelled the choronzon before she saw it. The trees began to thin. Zwi stuttered her strange, deep chittering before whining piteously. Piper swallowed a sob. She didn't want to see. She had to.

She shouldered a tree branch aside and stepped into the clearing.

The choronzon was sprawled in a mass of twisted tentacles. Yellow blood and foul gore splashed the grass and nearby trees like macabre graffiti. Its head was split open like a bomb had gone off in its skull. Massive wounds scored its body. It had fought hard before it died.

Nothing moved in the clearing. Nothing stirred.

She stared at the dead beast, trying to imagine what could have killed it. What even greater monster could have inflicted those terrible wounds on a creature known to be nearly invincible with its magic-resistant scales and impossible, crushing strength?

In the shadow of the dead beast, something moved.

A dark figure rose, a black wraith in the night. Wings as dark as midnight spread wide as he turned toward her. They slowly drew in again. He stepped forward.

Piper didn't move. She didn't even breathe as Ash came toward her.

For the first time, she looked on his true form.

Walk was too harmless a word for the way he moved. He drifted like a slinking shadow, each movement melting seamlessly into the next. It was so graceful, so sinister, that he had closed half the distance before she recognized the heavy limp with each step.

He stopped with ten long steps still between them. Silent, he waited—waited for her to pass judgment on him.

Her gaze raked over him, desperately searching for something familiar. Something human. Black, plate-like scales ran down his arms and covered the backs of his hands, leathery in texture, faintly glossy. They plated his fingers, each one ending in a deadly, curved claw. The scales were like living artwork, beautifully interlocking, mimicking the lines of his body, almost identical to a dragon hide. The dark armor spread over his shoulders, dipped down along his collarbones, and faded into dark lines that coiled over the upper half of his bare torso. She'd seen the same pattern drawn in shimmering red across his skin when she'd faced him in the Styx's fighting ring.

Scales edged his sides while leaving the muscled planes of his stomach and most of his chest bare. A handful of leather straps interrupted the expanse of his torso, baldrics for unseen weapon sheaths on his back. Behind him, a powerful, whip-like tail snaked in the grass, almost invisible in the darkness. His lower half was clad in dark pants of a heavy material. Straps crisscrossed his thighs, holding two empty sword sheaths in place. Below the calf, his legs lost their human-like composition. His black-scaled feet ended in three talons similar to Zwi's. He balanced on the balls of his feet with strong, steady readiness.

In his hand, he held a long, curved sword. Yellow gore smeared the double-edged blade.

Finally, she dared lift her gaze to his face.

Black scales edged his jaw and ran across the tops of his cheekbones. Dark, menacing designs dipped down his temples and coiled in the hollows of his cheeks. His hair, black in the darkness, was the only thing she recognized. Curved horns, sets of three on each side of his head, swept backward. She remembered tracing them in the darkness of the caved-in cellar.

The eyes that watched her were black as pitch, cold and unforgiving. There was no mercy in them.

The few similarities between this creature and the daemon she knew were meaningless. The being beneath the skin was as wholly different as his glamour. There was nothing of Ash in those icy midnight eyes. There was no familiar soul behind them, no heart, nothing.

She trembled, fought to breathe. For the first time, she truly understood what it meant when a daemon shaded. Shading was the mental release of glamour in the same way she now looked at the physical shedding of glamour. When daemons donned their physical glamour to look human, they bound themselves mentally to act human. Shading wasn't a shift from their normal behavior; it was a shift *back* to their true nature. As she stared at Ash's true form, she thought of all those times before when she'd seen his eyes go dark … *this* is what had been looking out at her.

He remained motionless, watching her with a cold expectancy. Believing she had died once already only made it harder to face death a second time—but delay was pointless.

"The Sahar is gone," she whispered into the choking silence. She pressed her injured arm tighter to her chest. "I—I tried. They—one of them … flew away with it."

He didn't react. Stared at her, silent, waiting.

"I'm sorry." She tried to take a deep breath but couldn't manage it. She wished he'd just kill her. The weight of his attention crushed her. She wanted to fall to her knees and beg for mercy. The aura of power around him was palpable. She could taste it in the air, the harsh tang of blood yearning to be spilled. The atmosphere was charged, electric with power waiting to be unleashed—enough power to tear gaping holes in one of the most feared monsters in the Underworld.

Behind her, Zwi shook her head and loosed a deep, somehow admonishing growl. Ash's gaze shifted toward the dragon. Released from his stare, Piper shook violently. She swallowed back a whimper. Desperately, she reminded herself that she'd faced his true self once before, even if she hadn't been able to see him. She remembered that he'd hugged her with that lethal strength, wrapped those black wings gently around her. He was the same as then. This was no different. It was—

His gaze slid back to her. Her heart jumped into her throat and her knees went weak. No, it was completely different.

Zwi slunk out from behind her. In a swirl of black magic, the dragon shrank back to her smaller form. With a shake of her head, she spread her wings and sprang into the air, gliding across the clearing to vanish into the trees. Piper wanted to scream at the dragonet to come back, not to leave her. Swallowing, she reluctantly brought her attention back to the dark creature before her.

Finally, he moved. He slid forward, closing the gap between them. When he was a step away, she squeezed her eyes shut, bracing for the killing blow.

A moment passed.

Careful, gentle fingers touched her chin and tilted her face up. She squeezed her eyes tighter.

"Piper." He exhaled slowly. "Piper, you need to try not to be afraid. I need your help."

His touch fell from her cheek then wrapped gently around her uninjured wrist. He pulled her arm up and pressed her hand to the horns on the side of his head. "You know me, Piper. Remember? You weren't this scared before. I need you to be strong this time too."

She shivered at his alien voice. Her shaking fingers touched the smooth, cool horns.

"Please, Piper," he whispered. "I can't use glamour because my wing is dislocated. I need your help to fix it." A silent pause. "I won't hurt you. I promise."

Breathing fast, she wrapped her hand around the top horn, squeezing until her fingers hurt. Fear bubbled in her, deep, visceral, and uncontrollable. Fear of the ultimate predator, of a powerful, alien creature far beyond her understanding.

From amidst the pieces of coherent thought and emotion left to her, a memory rose. Lyre's voice echoed in her head, hot with passion and frustration. *Some daemons you can't help but fear. You will always be afraid. It's human nature.*

She sucked in air, fighting for control. Lots of things were scary. Suck it up and deal with it. So what if Ash's true self was the most terrifying sight she'd ever seen, the most petrifying monster she'd ever faced? She could cope.

One last deep breath and she opened her eyes.

Black irises met hers. Terror sucked out the breath she'd just taken. She clenched her teeth and fought to remember his careful touch on her cheek. He wouldn't hurt her. He wouldn't. He'd promised.

"What do you need me to do?" she asked, her voice almost soundless.

His gaze searched hers for a second, then he stepped back, pulling her hand away from his head. He turned sideways and carefully unfurled one wing. The elbow joint wasn't right. Angling the wing toward her, he took her hand and placed it below the joint. She wrapped her fingers around hard muscle, surprised by the supple texture, like sun-warmed leather.

"Hold on as tight as you can," he told her. "Brace yourself."

With her injured arm tucked to her chest, she bent her knees, leaned back, and squeezed his wing as hard as she could.

He checked her stance, nodded, then braced himself. Inhaled. Held it. Then he jerked hard away from her, snapping the joint straight. The sickening pop of the bone slipping back into its socket was loud in the silence. He staggered, breathing hard. She let go and watched mutely as he gingerly folded both wings against his back.

His tail lashed from one side to the other as he recovered from the pain.

Her own pain was starting to overwhelm her. She pressed one shaking hand over her face. She felt sick with it all—the agony in her arm and the soul-deep terror of the daemon before her. She'd never known. She'd never realized what they truly were.

"Piper."

Her breath caught. Warily, she lowered her hand.

Ash stood in front of her. His eyes had lightened to a dull gray, his skin unmarked by pattern or scale—full glamour flawlessly hiding the monster underneath. His sword was gone, as were his wings and tail. Glamour was much more than illusion; it was a shifting of reality.

His shirt was torn and dirty from the cellar cave-in but without a single speck of choronzon blood. This clothing had been in a different plane of reality while he'd fought the choronzon, just as his strange black pants and weapons were no longer in this dimension. She could only imagine how daemons could bend physics to accommodate their whims.

"Ash." She exhaled sharply then swallowed hard. She understood now what Lyre had meant when he said she'd never look at a daemon the same again after seeing his true face. Her gut now knew what he was. At least she wasn't overwhelmed by fear anymore. As it faded, her head clearing, shame pricked at her. She'd been convinced he was going to kill her. How could she have lost faith in him so easily?

The memory of those merciless eyes, black with the night, flashed through her head. Yes, she knew how.

"Come on," he said tonelessly. "Lyre is back in the trees. His shoulder is broken but he should be fine. I'll wrap your arm."

Relief touched her. At least Lyre wasn't too badly hurt, though a broken shoulder was no small injury. Glancing at the choronzon, she wondered if it had been Lyre's cry of pain she'd heard as the harpies carried her away.

She tried to take a deep breath. "Okay," she agreed. Her voice came out hoarse and shaky.

Ash stepped away, putting a couple paces between them. "It won't be as bad in a few hours."

"What won't?" she asked with a frown.

He stared across the clearing. "The fear. It will fade … to a point. In a few hours."

Her feeling of shame grew. "I'll be fine, don't worry." She forced a smile. "Just don't ever show me that again and we'll be good."

He was already turning toward the other side of the clearing when she spoke. He paused. Slowly he looked over his shoulder. His face was a cool, distant mask as he appraised her. The weight of his judgment settled on her, almost palpable.

"Yes," he agreed, his voice empty of inflection. "You will not have to see me again."

He turned and walked away, leaving her to follow at her own pace and put whatever distance between them she wanted. She clutched her arm to her chest and stumbled after him.

He was alive. She was alive. Lyre was alive.

It was the only good thing about the entire night she could come up with. But at least they were alive.

CHAPTER
-25-

THEY DIDN'T EVEN make it back to Lyre before everything went wrong—again.

Two unfamiliar daemons stepped out of the trees before Ash reached them. He stopped. Piper came to a halt a few paces behind him, glancing over the newcomers. It seemed the group of daemons that had attacked the Gaians hadn't fled far during the choronzon's attack. These two looked a little worse for wear but were otherwise unremarkable: buzz cut, well-muscled army types. Their bearing was distinctly militaristic.

"We have the incubus," one of the two said without preamble.

Piper sucked in a sharp breath. She clutched her injured arm and wondered what the three daemons would do if she sat down where she was and refused to move until fate stopped bitch-slapping her at every turn.

Ash didn't immediately react. When he finally spoke, his voice was an icy, malevolent hiss.

"You do not want to get in my way right now."

Both daemons' stares darted toward the dead choronzon. The one who'd spoken spread his hands in a placating gesture. "If you want your friend, you'll have to come with us. If you want to walk away instead, we won't stop you."

Piper figured he really meant, "We *can't* stop you."

Ash grunted. "Lead us then."

The daemon nodded. He and his companion made an about-face. Ash followed. Piper trailed behind, stumbling every couple steps. Dawn tinged the horizon a pale pink but the forest was still dark. She realized with numb surprise that the rain had stopped. She wondered when. Everything was getting blurry at the edges. Her memory. The trees around her. Everything.

A strong arm wrapped around her waist. She blinked blurrily into Ash's face. Had she stopped walking? He'd come back for her. Another flicker of surprise penetrated her daze. She would have expected him to walk on, leaving the weak haemon girl behind.

"She's going into shock," an unfamiliar voice said. The military daemons had come back too. Huh.

"Look at her arm," the other said. "Her hand is—"

Ash made a sharp noise and the daemon fell silent. Ash tugged gently at her waist. She staggered back into motion, letting her head rest on his shoulder as he pulled her along. His arm was warm. Part of her wanted him to wrap his arms around her and hold her tight until everything bad went away. Another part of her didn't want him touching her ever again.

She absorbed nothing as they walked. Time passed meaninglessly. All the trees looked the same. Their daemon guides walked easily, strangely unconcerned. Ash guided Piper after them, taking a good portion of her weight off her weak legs. Numbness blanketed her thoughts. Only when she saw the smoldering remains of the Consulate did she realize where they were. Blinking slowly, she took in the scene.

At least a dozen prefects stood around, their hands resting on their holstered guns. New cruisers were parked behind the wreckage of the original ones. The prefects were waiting with ill-concealed impatience.

Nearly all the daemons from the earlier fight had made it through without injury. They too had that military bearing, soldiers awaiting command, as they eyed the prefects with distaste. Considering the battle they'd fought, they were in good shape—professionals even more so than the prefects.

Slumped in a line by the prefects were the surviving Gaians. They were bloody, dejected, and handcuffed. Piper's mother was not among them. She wasn't sure how she felt about that.

Sitting side by side at the feet of the daemon group were Lyre and —shock rippled through Piper's numb haze—Uncle Calder. They weren't bound or handcuffed but it was obvious they were supposed to stay put. Lyre was hunched in pain, gripping his shoulder with one hand, but he still smiled in relief when he saw Piper. Uncle Calder looked relieved too but his expression was grim.

"Well, well," a voice announced into the silence. "Why am I not surprised?"

Hatred flashed through Piper. She put the voice to a face a moment later as a familiar prefect stepped away from the main group and strode toward her. A handful of cronies followed in his wake. Piper gritted her teeth. Fury burned away her numbness, straightening her spine. It was the same sergeant who'd arrested her, refused to believe her story, and accused her of every crime the Gaians had committed or attempted to commit.

He was grinning in vindictive triumph. As he approached, his gaze raked over her. She tried feebly to hold the torn front of her shirt closed. He pulled his handcuffs off his belt. The two daemons who'd brought them tensed.

Ash was faster. He stepped forward to intercept the sergeant. The man's face blanched as he realized, far too late, what was coming. Ash's hand flashed out. He grabbed the sergeant by the throat and threw him backward. The man landed hard on his back, winded. Before he could gasp in a single breath, Ash's boot came down on the man's throat. He lifted his stare to the rest of the approaching prefects, freezing them in place.

Ash ground his boot slowly down. The sergeant's eyes bulged. He jammed both hands under Ash's foot, trying to relieve the pressure enough to breathe.

"I'm not in a conversational kind of mood right now," the draconian growled, "so I'll keep this simple. You are the first and the last prefect to ever arrest me. Try again and I'll kill you and your entire squad. Piss me off and I'll butcher your entire division. Mass slaughter would be a nice change of pace for me." He leaned down and bared his teeth at the sergeant's purple face. "I usually hunt much fouler prey than you."

He pulled his boot off the sergeant and stepped back. His cutting look sized up the downed sergeant and dismissed him as so far beneath respect as to be worthless. The draconian slid back to Piper's side and folded his arms impatiently.

The sergeant, coughing and gasping, stumbled to his feet. Outrage, mixed with fear he couldn't hide, twisted his face.

"If you—" he began in a croak.

Ash interrupted, his voice biting, colder than ice. "If you thought for even a second I would play nice a second time, you won't live long enough to regret your ignorance."

The man choked on the rest of his sentence. Tension thickened the air.

It shattered when Miysis, the daemon Piper had freed in the Consulate basement, walked out from between two cruisers. Three prefects trailed after him, looking anxious. The mysterious daemon smiled, his yellow-green eyes glittering as he came to stand beside her and Ash's daemon escorts. Both military daemons gave Miysis casual salutes.

"Now, sergeant," he said smoothly to the prefect, "you should honestly know not to antagonize a Taroth. They have terrible tempers."

The sergeant paled. His gaze darted from Miysis to Ash and back.

"What are you doing here?" Ash demanded. Piper's mouth fell open at the biting hostility suffusing his tone. "Go sharpen your claws on some other tree."

Miysis's eyes cooled to chips of green ice. "You could at least attempt to be civil, Ashtaroth. I am in a position to, at the least, save you from adding to your already brutal reputation by killing everyone here. Or do you enjoy being clothed in the blood of your victims?"

"There may be blood on my hands, Miysis, but there's far more on your conscience. Assuming you have one."

"And what would you know of consciences, Ashtaroth?" Miysis scorned.

"I—"

Piper put her hand on his arm and squeezed. Ash's mouth snapped shut as he turned a furious black glare on her. She barely managed not to cringe.

"Ash," she whispered, "I freed him from the Gaians' basement earlier tonight. He was a prisoner."

Ash slashed a derisive look at Miysis. "Him?" he snorted. "What game were you playing, cat?"

Miysis lifted his chin and tapped a finger to the collar still around his neck. "I misjudged. As did you the night the Sahar vanished, hmm?"

Ash receded into thoughtful silence, scrutinizing the collar. The two military daemons noticed the direction of Ash's calculating look and shifted protectively closer to Miysis. Miysis, however, ignored Ash as he shifted his attention to Piper. She shrank a little, no longer sure how to react to him.

"Piper," he said, his voice softening from the acerbic tones he'd used with Ash. "I'm glad you survived. I feared the worst when the house collapsed." He politely didn't check out her immodestly torn shirt.

"You got my uncle out. Thank you."

"Of course." His attention dropped to her injured arm, still pressed to her chest, and his brow creased.

The sergeant cleared his throat loudly. "Miysis, sir, we have business to address."

Piper blinked at the middle-aged sergeant addressing the much younger daemon as "sir."

"I know that," Miysis snapped. "Have patience, man. The girl is injured."

"The *girl* is the thief of your precious Stone. Ask her. Confirm it."

Piper went still at the sergeant's use of possessive. *Miysis's* Stone? Could it be ... ?

The daemon focused on Piper again. "Piperel, I am a truth-seer. I can recognize lies without fail. The prefects have agreed to accept my word in this matter. If you speak the truth, I will confirm it and you will be free from incrimination from this point onward."

"Why are they taking your word for it?"

His eyebrows rose. "Because the Sahar is far more my business than theirs."

She licked her lips. "You're a Ra, aren't you?"

Miysis smiled like a cat with a mouse under its paw.

Ash snorted. "He's their goddamn heir." He spat on the ground, disgust clear in his voice.

Piper took a deep breath, trying to calm the nerves twisting in her belly as her fears were confirmed. No wonder Ash hated Miysis. Miysis was heir to the most powerful Overworld family and the rightful owner of the Sahar. Ash was somehow tied to the Hades family, the most powerful Underworld family and repeated thieves of the Sahar. They were born to loathe each other.

Her brow furrowed as she looked at Miysis. "What *were* you doing in that basement then?"

"I was investigating the Gaians. I didn't expect them to have a choronzon to threaten me with, nor did I realize I was allowing them to put such a powerful collar around my neck when I declined to battle the choronzon." He sighed. "I will be laughed at for the next year."

"At *least*," Ash taunted.

"At any rate," Miysis said, ignoring Ash, "I've already questioned the Gaians and your uncle. The truth is clear: the Gaians committed all the crimes at the Griffiths Consulate *except* stealing the Sahar. They do not know where it is. They never had it. Your uncle does not know who stole the Sahar from the Consulate or who has it now."

Piper's heart clogged her throat. She struggled to keep her breathing even. Miysis had come so close to the truth; Piper had almost shown her uncle the Stone. Fear skittered up her spine as she realized Miysis was about to question her. If she lied, he would know.

If she admitted to having had the Sahar, to having hid it from everyone and run off with it—and then lost it—she didn't know what the consequences would be, but there would be punishment. At the least, if the general public knew she'd had the Sahar, they would always suspect she somehow knew where it was now. Daemons would continue to hunt her. She would *never* be free from fear of attack.

She faced the Ra daemon heir, knowing her future depended on the questions he would ask and the truth she had no choice but to give. The intent stares of everyone on the lawn burned her. She clutched her arm to her chest and tried not to look terrified. It all came down to this—to the questions of a truth-seer. It could be her saving grace or her final downfall.

Miysis's eyes slid from green to black. Power gathered around him, shocking in its strength because the active magic-depressor was still locked around his neck. No wonder Ash had laughed at the thought of Miysis being imprisoned by the Gaians. No wonder the Ra daemon had been so indifferent to his predicament. She was sure now he could have escaped any time he pleased but for some reason he hadn't. He'd waited, enduring humiliation for reasons of his own —for the real thief to appear, perhaps?

He shifted closer until Piper saw nothing but his black eyes, shadowed by his power. His hand lifted, fingers touching her chin. She bit her lip, remembering Ash's touch in that exact spot. Was Miysis equally as terrifying without glamour? Or were Overworld daemons different in their true natures?

"Piperel Griffiths," he intoned. His voice was as melodic as ever, even without inflection "Speak only truth in your answer." Silence pressed on her ears. His stare burned into her.

"Did you steal the Sahar Stone from the vault in the Griffiths Consulate?"

She blinked back tears as relief swamped her. She met Miysis's stare and answered in a clear, strong voice. "No, I did not."

Miysis nodded. Astonished disbelief stamped the sergeant's face.

"Do you possess the Sahar Stone?" the Ra daemon asked.

"No, I do not." Thank God. For the first time, losing the Stone didn't seem like a complete disaster.

Again, Miysis nodded his acceptance of her truth. "Do you know where the Sahar Stone is now?"

She licked her lips. She knew the harpy had taken it but she didn't know where. "No, I do not."

He hesitated. She waited, not daring to breathe. Finally, he nodded. "Truth," he declared. "All truth. The girl is innocent of all charges."

The sergeant stepped forward. "But—"

Miysis pivoted, the sudden movement embodying violence. He bared his teeth. "You doubt my ability, sergeant?" His voice was a deadly hiss. "You think she has deceived me? You think her simple answers somehow conceal lies?"

The sergeant backed away so fast he stumbled. "No, of course not. I—I mean—Forgive my presumption. I got carried away."

Miysis stared him down then turned back, this time to face Ash.

"Ashtaroth, speak only truth. Did you steal the Sahar Stone from the vault in the Griffiths Consulate?"

"No, I did not."

Piper clenched her hands into fists. Thank you, Miysis, she thought. Thank you for asking such specific questions. If he had asked only if Ash had stolen the Sahar, his answer would've been a lie. Ash *had* stolen the Sahar—just not from the vault.

"Do you possess the Sahar Stone?"

"No, I do not."

"Do you know where the Sahar Stone is now?"

"No, I do not."

"Truth," Miysis announced. He shot the sergeant a black-irised glare. "Anything else?"

"Ask him what he's doing here then."

Miysis focused again on Ash. "Why did you come here, Ashtaroth?"

Piper held her breath as Ash hesitated. He exhaled carefully.

"Piper came to rescue her father. I wanted to help her."

She closed her eyes, sagging in the release of tension. It didn't matter that her father had turned out to be Uncle Calder; Ash had spoken the truth and even made them look noble instead of suspicious. She would've opened her eyes again to see the sergeant's expression but it was so nice to have them closed.

"There you have it, sergeant." Miysis's voice had a weird hollow sound, too loud in her ears, like he was too close but far away at the same time. "They came on a rescue mission. They are innocent."

"You realize that leaves us with no leads at all?" was the angry reply.

"Then we have no leads. I would prefer to accept that truth than waste time and energy arresting innocents."

The air was buzzing in her ears. Everything seemed distant, unimportant, disconnected. Her arm throbbed in time to her heartbeat.

"Piper?" Ash whispered in her ear.

His strong arm wrapped around her waist, holding her up. She let herself lean into him. That felt so nice she gave up on standing entirely. He sucked in a breath when she went limp. He pulled her into his arms, tucking her injured forearm between their chests as he cradled her carefully.

"Miysis, where's your healer?" he demanded. His urgency didn't touch her.

Miysis's voice barked commands. The world was spinning but Ash's arms were steady and strong. Always strong. He was her only rock in the ocean of adversity that had flooded her life since the night of the attack on the Consulate. He was the only one who showed up again and again, his strength offered, nothing asked in return.

Shame choked her. Dredging up the determination from somewhere deep inside, she forced her eyes open. Her gaze found Ash's, his gray eyes pinched with worry.

"Ash ..."

"Shh. Don't worry. Miysis has a healer. You'll be fine."

She couldn't tell him she forgave him for his betrayal, his lies of omission. She couldn't tell him she understood why he'd done it or that she was sorry for holding it against him. She couldn't tell him he didn't terrify her now that she'd seen what he really was. But she had to tell him something.

"Ash, I ..."

He frowned and tilted his ear down, listening. She pressed her hand against the side of his head.

"Ash ... I like your horns. They're cool."

She smiled weakly at his baffled expression. Holding that image in her mind, she surrendered to unconsciousness.

CHAPTER
-26-

PIPER MUTTERED insults to no one as she dug the broom into the corner of the room. Glass was miserable to sweep. It either caught in the grooves between the planks of hardwood or it went rolling merrily across the floor. For the fourth time, she tried to sweep the glittering debris into a pile so she could scoop it into the garbage bin.

When she finally got the stubborn glass where it belonged, she leaned the broom against the wall and planted her hands on her hips, surveying the room. It wasn't the familiar space it should've been, considering it had been her bedroom less than a month ago. Now it was an empty square with chunks of drywall missing and a boarded-up window. All the furniture, broken beyond repair, had already been hauled out. Most of her belongings had gone with the rest of the garbage.

The Consulate had been abandoned for less than a week after the attack by the Gaians, but more than prefects had searched every inch of it. Countless, unknown daemons had pawed through her personal possessions, searching for clues about the Sahar's whereabouts. They had been neither careful nor respectful. Most of the Consulate had suffered the same treatment. The only silver lining was that, with so many daemons lurking about, no humans had attempted to loot the abandoned house. Not that it mattered much since almost everything had been damaged.

Bangs and thumps downstairs told her people were still hard at work trying to make the Consulate livable again. All the nearby Consulates had sent people to help. They were eager to have the Head Consulate back up and running so the Head Consul could make all those important, difficult decisions the other Consuls didn't want to deal with.

Somewhere downstairs, Uncle Calder was fielding endless phone calls. Her uncle didn't enjoy the mantle of authority and especially didn't like being chained to a desk. Unfortunately, he would be spending a great deal more time doing deskwork from now on. The daemon healer had done his best, but Calder's leg had been badly broken for days, not to mention the other abuse he'd suffered at the hands of the Gaians—and Mona. He would walk with a limp for the rest of his life. His participation in Piper's future martial training would be limited to the sidelines.

She lifted both hands, spread her fingers wide, and studied the backs. It amazed her to see her left hand whole and unbroken. White scars ran across the back like thin, twisting veins. They were ugly but the scars didn't impair movement or strength. She opened and closed her fingers just to prove it. She had other scars on both arms from the harpies' claws.

She'd been unconscious during her healing, but Calder told her afterward it had taken the combined skills of Miysis and two other daemons to repair her arm. She was glad she'd been unconscious, partly because it had saved her from the Ra daemon's truth-sensing magic. She knew he had more questions for her but he hadn't been able to wait around for her to wake after she'd been magically stitched back together.

So much made sense now that she knew Miysis was the Ra heir. She should have realized long before that the Ra family wouldn't sit back and wait for the Sahar to turn up. It sort of ticked her off that Miysis had figured out the Gaians were the culprits three days before she, Ash, and Lyre had. At least he'd never figured out the real truth.

He wouldn't be happy with Piper if he knew her real role—and who had the Sahar now.

That Miysis had let himself be captured by Gaians so as to infiltrate their headquarters was all fine and dandy for him, but it was his overprotective bodyguards/soldiers who had started the deadly fight. Piper didn't know how many had died that night. She hoped no one ever told her.

The Ras were still searching for the Sahar. There was no way for Piper to tell them their search was pointless without implicating herself. The Sahar would never be found. She was certain of it. Samael would not let it slip through his fingers again.

The mere thought of the head of the Hades family made fury burn through her. The two-faced bastard had never intended to go through with the agreement negotiated by the Consulates. Samael had publicly agreed to have the Sahar returned to the Ra family on the condition it was sealed away forever but he hadn't meant a word of it. He'd simply been biding his time until he could act.

His plan had been deviously simple: steal the Sahar back without anyone ever suspecting his hand in the theft. To the world, he would have magnanimously agreed to peace. When the Sahar vanished from the Consulate, he'd get all the private time with it he wanted because no one would know he had it. So Samael had sent Ash to perform the theft.

She remembered him standing alone at the edge of the Styx rooftop, rigid with tension as he tried to decide between two potentially deadly paths. Samael had wanted the Sahar without incrimination. Since Ash had been accused of the theft, Samael had also been incriminated. Without identifying the attackers at the Consulate, Ash hadn't had a hope of clearing his name—or Samael's.

But Ash hadn't had to stick with her and Lyre. Once he had the Sahar from Piper, she'd had no hold on him. No claim on his strength or protection. No reason for him to waste time and effort keeping her safe. But he'd stayed for no other reason than to help them, to try to save them along with his own skin. Maybe he felt he owed it to her after almost destroying her family by trying to swap the Sahar with a fake.

If Ash had abandoned them after that first day, she and Lyre would probably be dead. Some daemon or another would've caught up with them and killed them when they couldn't hand over the Sahar. She hadn't realized at the time that the lack of daemon attacks on them hadn't been for a lack of willing daemons. It had been because most daemons were too frightened of Ash to even try.

Some nights she wondered if she was looking for goodness in him that wasn't there. Other nights, she imagined a thousand ways to tell him thank you and none seemed good enough.

Her confliction over Ash, over whether she could forgive him or trust him, was with her constantly but it wasn't her only worry. Yes, she was no longer a felon on the run. Miysis had made sure to spread the word that Piperel Griffiths had not been involved in the theft. Life was on the verge of getting back to normal. But Piper didn't feel like *she* could go back to normal. Everything had changed.

Abandoning the cleaning, she stalked out of the room and down the stairs. She barely noticed the construction crew rebuilding the wall Ash had blown out while they were escaping the choronzon. There was only one person she wanted to see.

She flung the office door open without knocking. Her father looked up, his good eye narrowing. The other was hidden behind a crisp white bandage. She dropped into the chair in front of his desk and crossed her arms. Quinn gave her an impatient look as he pressed the phone against his ear. A muffled voice ranted from the speaker.

She stared back, not moving. Quinn had arrived home from the medical center hours ago. Every time she'd tried to talk to him, he'd shooed her away with dour warnings about all the work he had to catch up on. Well, she was done waiting. She was especially done being second priority for him—or fiftieth, or whatever the number actually was.

Realizing she wasn't budging, Quinn wrapped up the conversation quickly and smacked the phone back on the cradle.

"Piperel—" he began, his voice unrecognizably rough from the burns to his throat.

"We're talking *now*." She bit back a sarcastic comment about how maybe she was a teeny bit more important than soothing ruffled Consul feathers.

Quinn scowled—such a familiar expression. "What would you like to discuss?"

"Where to start? How about—why did you tell me Mom was *dead*?"

His shoulders tensed. He exhaled slowly, eventually meeting her glare with an impassive look. "Your mother is part of a violent group of vigilantes. At the time, it was the safest way to sever contact and protect you from her influence. You wouldn't understand the—"

"*Understand*? What does it matter? You *lied* to me that my mother died. When I was *nine*. Do you have any idea how—how traumatic that was?"

He met her fury with a cool lack of emotion. "What's done is done, Piperel. I did what was necessary to protect you."

Her hands trembled so badly she had to clench them into fists. Tears burned her eyes at the raw pain building behind her anger. "That's all you have to say?"

"It was not an easy decision, Piperel. Of course I didn't want to hurt you."

"Of course," she choked. She squeezed her eyes shut, trying to regain composure. She'd expected a shouting match, tearful apologies, guilty excuses for bad choices, but this? This indifferent wall of superiority? She couldn't fight that.

"The magic then. What about my magic?"

"Telling you the truth about your near death as a child would have served no purpose."

She took a deep breath, forcing down a scream of frustration. "What about reclaiming it then? Mom said—"

"A dangerous delusion I am very sorry she had the opportunity to share with you. She began obsessing about the idea even before she left. It's impossible."

"How do you know that?"

"Magic feeds on magic. Releasing one half of your power would quickly erode the seal on the other half. That's assuming anyone could successfully unseal one half without destroying the entire binding."

"But Mom said—"

"Your mother," he interrupted, his voice rising slightly, "is enchanted with the idea of you as a hybrid mascot. She wants you to join the Gaians and lead them in a rebellion to raze daemons off the face of the planet. She would risk your life without hesitation to see her dream become reality."

Piper sat limply, staring in disbelief.

Quinn's look was sharp. "Am I correct in assuming you are not interested in leading a racial genocide against daemons?"

She shook her head mutely.

"I have done everything I can to protect you from your mother, Piperel. What began as an unhealthy fascination with haemon rule grew into an obsession that drove her out of our lives. From what Consulate intelligence suggests, she is even more unbalanced now than ten years ago."

She hadn't seemed crazy to Piper. But then, she hadn't been quite right either.

"I hope you will trust my judgment, Piperel, and put everything your mother said out of your mind as the false hopes of obsession."

Her gaze dropped to her hands, twisted together in her lap. "How can I trust you," she said softly, her voice shaking, "when you've told me so many lies?"

A long, burning silence.

"I did what I did to protect you, Piperel."

With a deep breath, she raised her head again. "And the Sahar? Why did you give it to me that night?"

Quinn pulled some papers across the desk and straightened the pile. "I was being spied on, even in the Consulate. I gambled that the spies would never believe I was giving the Sahar to you. Away from me, it would be out from under their eyes."

She blinked rapidly, refusing to hunch under the pain of another wound. *Would never believe I was giving the Sahar to you.* Because she was so insignificant, Quinn had banked on the spies discounting her as a potential ally in protecting the Stone.

"It is unfortunate the Sahar was lost," he added.

That time she flinched, hearing all the unspoken accusations in the simple statement. She had failed to protect it. She had let the enemy get it. Not that Quinn knew who actually had the Sahar. She'd only told him about the harpies stealing it from her, not what they'd said about their master. But in his eyes, she had failed.

"Piper!"

She straightened out of her pained hunch as Calder shouted down the hall.

"Piper, he's here."

She stood jerkily and looked at her father. There wasn't a single word she wanted to say to him. She walked out.

"Piper!"

"Coming," she yelled to Calder. Excitement and anxiety cut through her emotional turmoil. The anxiety sharpened, dominating. Three weeks. It had been *three weeks*. Surely—

She rushed to the kitchen. The room had definitely seen better days. A huge chunk of granite had been broken off the island. Cupboard doors were missing, as was the pantry door. The only furniture left was the scorched but intact dining table and three of the original twelve chairs.

A familiar form was slumped wearily in one of those chairs.

"Lyre," Piper cried. She flew across the room and threw her arms around his neck.

It took him a moment to hug her back. He sighed into her hair. "Hey Piper. Sorry I took so long."

"You've been gone for a week and a half." She thumped down into a chair and studied his dirt-stained clothes and the circles under his eyes. Anxiety morphed into dread. He hadn't come with good news. She wasn't sure she could take any more heartache.

"Anything?" she whispered.

He pressed his lips together, staring at the table. Then he pushed his chair back a little and lifted a bundled blanket from his lap she hadn't noticed before. He gently scooped it against his chest then pushed aside the top layer.

A dark, reptilian nose poked out of the hole. The little dragonet sniffed halfheartedly at the air. With a forlorn mewling sound, she withdrew into the blanket bundle, hiding from the empty room.

"Zwi?" Piper choked out. "W-where … ?"

"I found her at the edge of Raven Valley. In the Underworld." Pain etched lines in his face. "I'm sorry, Piper. He went back to Samael."

She pressed both hands to her mouth, unable to breathe. No. No, he wouldn't have. Why would he do that?

Three weeks ago, at some point in the handful of hours between Piper losing consciousness and Miysis departing to continue his search for the Sahar, Ash had disappeared. No one had noticed him leave. He hadn't said a single goodbye. He'd just left, without warning or explanation.

When Piper first found out, she'd assumed Ash was steering clear of further truth-seeking questions from Miysis. Once the Ra daemon left, she'd been sure Ash would appear out of nowhere like he always did, quietly pleased to be reunited with them.

Days had passed. He hadn't come back.

Lyre, who'd stayed with Piper, had started asking around. No one knew where he was. No one had seen him. Lyre's daemon connections hadn't heard anything. Some suggested Ash had gone into hiding from Samael's assassins. Maybe he hadn't told them anything so Samael wouldn't bother them in his vengeful search.

After eight days of fruitless searching, Lyre had left for the Underworld. Maybe Ash had gone into hiding there. Lyre knew Ash well, had been reasonably confident he could track down the elusive draconian. Piper had sent him off with a cheerful wave, refusing to acknowledge the dark shadow of fear they both hid.

She'd never imagined Ash would do something as stupid, as suicidal, as going straight to the all-powerful daemon who wanted him dead.

"Why?" she choked. Tears threatened to spill over. "Why would he do that?"

Lyre stared at his lap as he absently caressed the bundle of blankets in which Zwi hid. "I don't know, Piper. Maybe he thought if he explained what happened, Samael would let it slide." His tone said he didn't believe it. "Piper … Ash always …" He swallowed hard. "Ash always goes back to Samael. He always does. I thought, this time, after Samael tried to kill him …" He pressed a hand against his face. "You don't know Ash like I do. Ash hates Samael's guts. But he goes back. He goes back to that bastard every time and I don't know why."

"But Samael hurts him," Piper whispered. "Remember what the harpies told me? That Samael hurts Ash? That that's why Ash obeys him? Why would he go back to that? Why wouldn't he run away or hide?"

"I don't know, Piper," Lyre said heavily. "Ash isn't a coward. He isn't a pushover by any stretch. If he went back, it's because he had to, not because he was afraid of the consequences of disobeying Samael. That Hades bastard has his chains wrapped around Ash but I can't for the life of me figure out what those chains are made of. Ash would never tell me. He won't talk about Samael at all."

"But—" She swallowed back the quaver in her voice and tried again. "But Samael wants Ash dead. What if—what if—"

"I don't know, Piper." Lyre blinked rapidly. His face twisted. "I couldn't get into the territory. They wouldn't let me. All I could find out was Ash definitely went back. No one knew what happened then, or if he … if he's still …" He pressed both hands to the quivering lump that was Zwi, unable to continue.

Piper pressed the heels of her hands to her temples, squeezing hard. "Is there anything we can do?" she choked. "Anything … ?"

"We can wait," Lyre whispered, "and hope he comes back. Either Samael will eventually send him out on another job or … or he won't."

Because Ash was dead. She finished Lyre's sentence in her head, the words burning like a betrayal, like a forsaking of hope.

"I've been thinking," Lyre said abruptly. Hate shone in his eyes, banishing grief. "About the choronzon. Remember what the harpies said? That Samael loaned the choronzon to the Gaians?"

She nodded slowly.

"Samael had to have known then, in advance, that the Gaians would try to steal the Sahar. Instead of stopping them, he lent them some of his lackeys, so if the Gaians managed to succeed, he was already in position to steal the Sahar from them in turn." He clenched his teeth. "That bastard was stacking the deck in his favor. If Ash failed, he already had a backup plan in place. From his perspective, Ash must have screwed up *both* his plans." He made a sound of disgust. "But what does it matter? The slimy bastard got the Sahar in the end. And we're the only ones who know it."

He lifted his gaze to hers. "Keep that in mind, Piper. We both need to be careful. Samael probably knows that we know. He could try to silence us."

She nodded her agreement as she struggled to control her fear. Lyre didn't know the half of it. He had no idea her true danger. Fighting to keep her expression blank, she drew in a shuddering breath and forced a smile. "Lyre, you must be exhausted. There are a couple bedrooms set up in the basement. Why don't you go lie down?"

He nodded, his hateful anger subsiding into a numb blankness. After a brief hesitation, he lifted Zwi's blanket bundle and set it in Piper's lap. He rose to his feet, lightly touched her cheek, then walked around her chair. A moment later, the door closed softly.

Zwi poked her nose out again, dully observing Lyre's absence. Piper lightly stroked the dragonet's silky mane. Zwi mewled brokenly.

"Is he alive, Zwi?" she whispered. She gathered the little creature against her chest and hugged her gently. "Please let him be alive."

If he was dead … if Samael had killed him … Piper couldn't stand the thought. Ash had fought so hard for them. He had saved her life over and over and gotten them all through that mess alive. If he'd died at Samael's hands, it was because Piper had failed him. She had let the Sahar be taken from her. If she'd managed to hold on to it, Ash could have fixed it so Samael would be satisfied. He would have let Ash live.

She'd failed him—in more ways than one.

But even after all that, she needed him. Needed his help and his advice. Desperately.

Lyre feared what Samael would do with the knowledge that Piper knew he had the Sahar. She feared far more what the Hades warlord would do if he knew what had happened when the harpies tried to take the Sahar from her.

She wasn't sure herself. She didn't understand what had happened. She only knew the results—and one scenario alone made sense.

She had used the power in the Sahar to kill the harpies.

Somehow, she had, without any magic of her own, tapped the power in the Sahar. She remembered the sudden duality of her thoughts like there was some other presence in her mind. She remembered the hot surge of power, the sudden flash of light coming from the Stone clutched in her fist.

The Sahar had killed the harpies. And Piper had wielded it.

The memory made her sick. The harpy's exploding skull. The spray of blood, the gore. Pieces of rent bodies falling through the air.

The harpy that had finally gotten the Sahar from her had witnessed that attack. When the harpy had carried the Sahar back to Samael, there was no reason to believe she hadn't also brought that tale of inexplicable power to Samael's ears.

Samael would want to kill Piper for knowing he had the Sahar. What would he do with the knowledge that Piper was the first confirmed person to have tapped its power since its original creator had wielded it to level an entire town five hundred years ago?

She had no idea how she'd done it or if she could do it again, not when neither Ash nor a thousand other daemons and haemons had managed to bend the Sahar to their will. But if Samael put the pieces together and realized how the magic-less haemon girl had killed a band of harpies in midair, the danger would be beyond comprehension.

Maybe Samael wouldn't care. Maybe he knew some obscure secret for wielding the Sahar.

She dared not hope.

A tear slipped down her cheek as she petted the abandoned, brokenhearted dragonet. Zwi made a soft trill before curling up and closing her eyes wearily. With a sigh, Piper cuddled the little creature closer. She would come up with some sort of plan. Lyre would help her. Maybe Miysis too, if he knew Samael had his Stone.

She lifted her chin, banishing despair. "Don't give up, Ash," she whispered. "I'm not giving up on you yet."

To be continued in
Book 2 of the Steel & Stone series:
BIND THE SOUL

Visit **www.annettemarie.ca** to learn more about the Steel & Stone series, discover more books by Annette Marie, and to sign up for her newsletter for new release alerts, exclusive giveaways, and more.

ACKNOWLEDGEMENTS

I would like to start with you, the reader. Thank you for reading! I hope you enjoyed it!

Thank you to Breanna for being my first reader, first sounding board, and first cheerleader. Your enthusiasm for my writing is priceless to me. I'm sorry about the cliffhangers. Really.

Thank you to Jillian for your keen editing eye, your ability to poke holes in all my faulty logic, and your refusal to let me get away with anything, ever. And I'm sorry about the eye thing. Really.

Thank you to my mother for getting me hooked on the written word and for supporting every decision I make. I learned how to work hard from you and I never would have made it this far without that.

Lastly, thank you to my fiancé for not being intimidated by my creative obsessions, for remembering everything I forget, for ensuring I never lose sight of the business side of writing, and, most importantly, for putting up with me every day. You're the best.

ABOUT THE AUTHOR

Annette Marie lives in Western Canada with her fiancé. Someday she'd like to get a cat. Maybe two.